A Dance of Ghosts

Kevin Brooks has written nine children's novels and has won several awards including the Canongate Prize for New Writing, Branford Boase Award, Kingston Youth Book Award, North East Book Award, Deutschen Jugendliteraturpreis Jury Prize, Buxtehude Bulle and the Golden Bookworm. *A Dance of Ghosts* is his first adult novel. He lives in North Yorkshire with his wife, Susan.

A Dance of Ghosts

Kevin Brooks

arrow books

Published by Arrow Books 2011

4 6 8 10 9 7 5

First published in Great Britain in 2011 by
Arrow Books
Random House, 20 Vauxhall Bridge Road,
London SW1V 2SA

www.random.co.uk

Addresses for companies within The Random House Group Limited can
be found at: www.randomhouse.co.uk/offices.htm

The Random House Group Limited Reg. No. 954009

A CIP catalogue record for this book
is available from the British Library

ISBN 9780099553816

The Random House Group Limited supports The Forest Stewardship Council®
(FSC®), the leading international forest-certification organisation. Our books
carrying the FSC label are printed on FSC®-certified paper. FSC is the only
forest-certification scheme supported by the leading environmental organisations,
including Greenpeace. Our paper procurement policy can be found at
www.randomhouse.co.uk/environment

Printed and bound by CPI Group (UK) Ltd, Croydon, CR0 4YY

For my mother, Marion Phyllis Brooks
18 September 1936 – 1 March 2010
∞
Sorry you never got to read it, Mum

I will dance
The dance of dying days
And sleeping life.

I will dance
In cold, dead leaves
A bending, whirling human flame.

I will dance
As the Horned God rides
Across the skies.

I will dance
To the music of His hounds
Running, baying in chorus.

I will dance
With the ghosts of those
Gone before.

I will dance
Between the sleep of life
And the dream of death.

I will dance
On Samhain's dusky eye,
I will dance.

Karen Bergquist Dezoma, 'An Autumn Chant'

A Dance of Ghosts

13 August 1993. Friday afternoon, 5.15. It's another sweltering hot day, and I'm driving home from work. The car radio is playing – 'Young At Heart'. I can feel the thin cloth of my cheap white shirt sticking to the stale sweat of my skin. My hands are moist on the steering wheel. The car windows are open and I can smell the stink of traffic and the heat of the baking streets. People are drinking outside pubs, getting ready for a hot night out. The sound of laughter and chinking glasses passes by in the stifling air.

I'm tired.

My head is aching.

But I'm going home now.

I'm happy.

I'm looking forward to the weekend. Two whole days with Stacy. No going to work, no getting up in the morning and putting on a cheap white shirt . . . just me and Stacy and a weekend of blue summer skies.

We can talk about the baby.

We can think some more about names.

We can slide away into our own perfect world and dream about what's to come.

At 5.30 I pull up outside our house, park the car, and turn off the engine. I pick up my jacket from the back seat, shut the windows, get out of the car, and lock it. I walk along the pavement and turn right, through the gate, and head up the garden path. Jingling my keys and humming quietly to myself, I skip up the front step and unlock the door.

I'm as happy as I'm ever going to be.

Inside the house, I drop my keys on the hall table and call out, 'Stacy! It's me . . . Stacy?'

There's no reply.

PART ONE

∞

WEDNESDAY 6 OCTOBER – FRIDAY 8 OCTOBER 2010

1

I was watching a man called Preston Elliot when I got the phone call that brought the ghosts back into my life. Elliot was nothing, just a cheapskate Essex Boy trying to make some easy money on the sly. He'd been involved in a minor accident at work which he claimed had resulted in a severe and ongoing back injury that supposedly prevented him from doing just about anything – walking, driving, working, sleeping. He was currently on long-term sick leave and had recently put in a compensation claim against his employers, an industrial cleaning business called StayBright. StayBright's insurance manager had hired an investigation company called Mercer Associates to look into the claim, and Mercer had subcontracted the case to me.

So there I was, sitting in my car on a cold and rainy October morning, trying to stay awake while I gathered evidence against a man called Preston Elliot. Like most of the work I do, it wasn't particularly demanding. I'd taken the case on Monday, started my initial surveillance on Tuesday, and this morning I'd got up early and followed Elliot from his low-rise council flat to a run-down terraced house in a scratty little side street on the south side of town. Two other men had been waiting for him in a white Transit van outside the house – a shortish ginger guy in a tartan jacket, and a lank-haired teenager with a pock-marked face – and for the last hour or so I'd been watching all three of them as they trudged in and out of the house, loading up a skip with pieces of old furniture and rusty radiators. I guessed they were gutting the place in preparation for some kind of renovation work – not that it made any difference to me what they were doing.

All I needed to know was that Preston Elliot was fit enough to drive, fit enough to walk, fit enough to spend all morning hefting tables and wardrobes and rolls of old carpet out of a house and into a skip.

I had plenty of video footage. I'd filmed him leaving his house that morning, walking without any obvious pain or discomfort. I'd filmed him getting into his car and driving across town. And right now I was filming him as he struggled through the rain carrying a stained old mattress on his back.

I checked my watch and clicked on my digital voice recorder. '10.47 a.m.,' I said into the the recorder. 'Subject continues to work at the house. Surveillance ends.' I turned off the voice recorder, clicked off the camcorder . . .

And that was when my mobile rang.

There was no sense of foreboding to the sound of the ringtone, nothing to suggest that this was a moment that might return to haunt me, or that in days to come I'd wonder what would have happened if I hadn't answered my phone that morning . . .

No . . . there was nothing like that at all.

My mobile just rang. And I just took it out of my pocket,

checked the caller ID, saw that it was Ada, my secretary, and answered it.

'Hey, Ada.'

'Where are you?' she said.

'Croke Street, down by the football ground. I'm just finishing up on the StayBright thing –'

'Are you coming back to the office?'

'Yeah.'

'How long will you be?'

'I don't know. Why?'

'You've got a client.'

'A client?'

'Yeah, you know . . . someone who pays you to work for them.'

'You're a funny woman, Ada.'

'I know. Anyway, she's here, in the office.'

'What does she want?'

'I don't know, she won't tell me anything. She wants to talk to you. Do you want her to come back later, or should I tell her to wait?'

'Yeah, ask her to wait. I won't be . . . hold on a minute.'

While I'd been talking to Ada, the ginger man in the tartan jacket had come out of the house, got into the Transit, and reversed it across the road. At first, I'd just assumed that he was driving off somewhere – maybe to get some cigarettes or something – but when he stopped in the middle of the street and turned off the engine, and when I saw Preston Elliot coming out of the house and start walking towards me with a ball-peen hammer in his hand, it was pretty obvious that I'd been spotted. And that Elliot was about to do something about it.

'John . . .?' I heard Ada saying. 'Are you still there?'

Elliot wasn't much to look at. A squitty little man, he had a small head, cropped hair and a pair of glasses that didn't seem to go with his face, and up until then I hadn't really considered him to be any kind of a threat. But now . . . well, now he had a ball-peen hammer in his hand, and he was heading straight for me, and the look in his eyes made me realise – far too late – that he was one of those runty little men who'll pick a fight at the drop of a hat just to prove that size doesn't matter.

'Shit,' I muttered, glancing quickly over my shoulder.

'John?' Ada said. 'John? What's going on?'

'I'll call you back in a minute,' I told her, ending the call.

My options, I realised, were fairly limited. I could stay where I was and try to bluff it out – pretending to be an estate agent was my usual cover in this kind of situation – or I could start the car and get the hell out of there as fast as I could.

I looked at Elliot again. He was about ten metres away from me now, and from the look on his face – a mixture of pent-up aggression and mindless resolve – I didn't think he'd go for the estate-agent bluff. But the road up ahead was blocked by the Transit van, and there were cars parked on either side of the street, making it far too narrow for a quick U-turn, so the only way out was by reversing all the way back along the street. And I was shit at reversing at the best of times.

'Ah, fuck it,' I said, sitting back in the seat and lighting a cigarette.

As Elliot drew level with the car, I was mentally setting the odds as to what he was going to do. Evens, he'd just stand there waving the hammer around, shouting and cursing at me from the pavement; 2-1, he'd try to yank the door open; and 3-1, he'd give the car a whack or two with the hammer, probably going for the bonnet or the door.

As it turned out, I was wrong on all counts.

He just walked up to the side of the car, stopped by the door and stared at me for a moment or two, and then – with an air of almost admirable nonchalance – he swung the hammer and smashed it into the side window. There was a loud *CRACK!* as the window shattered, showering my face with chunks of safety glass, and then all at once the car seemed to explode in a fury of noise and chaos. The wind came gusting in, blowing loose papers all over the place; the cold rain hissed in through the broken window, stinging the side of my face; and Preston Elliot's raging voice bellowed in my ear.

'*I KNOW WHAT YOU'RE FUCKING DOING, YOU NOSY FUCKING CUNT! WHAT DO YOU THINK I AM? YOU THINK I'M FUCKING STUPID? HERE, GIVE US THAT FUCKING THING...!*'

'That fucking thing' was my camcorder, and as he reached in and grabbed it off the ledge above the dashboard, I tried to snatch it back off him. But he was too quick and too strong for me, and before I could do anything else to stop him, he'd yanked the camera out of the car and thrown it down on the rain-sodden pavement. As I heard the expensive crack of shattering metal and plastic, my immediate thought was, 'Shit, there goes the best part of a grand.' But Elliot hadn't finished yet. And as he started pounding away at the camcorder with his hammer – *smack, smack, smack* – smashing it into a thousand little pieces, I felt something flash through me, some kind of unfamiliar passion . . .

I still don't know what it was.

I definitely wasn't angry. Or aggrieved. And I wasn't even that bothered about the camcorder. It was just a thing . . . a piece of equipment. It didn't *mean* anything to me. And besides, I knew I'd probably claim the cost of it back from StayBright's insurers anyway. But there was just something about the way Elliot was smashing it up that galled me . . . it *offended* me. The sheer stupidity of it, the pointlessness, the unnecessary level of violence . . .

Whatever it was, I found myself getting out of the car and approaching Elliot as he leaned down again and gave what was left of the camcorder another hefty thump with his hammer, and before I really knew what I was doing, I heard myself saying to him, 'Hey, come on, Preston . . . there's no need for that . . .'

He froze in mid-hammer swing, stayed perfectly still for a moment, then slowly turned to face me. His staring eyes reminded me, oddly, of the eyes of a porcelain donkey that my mother used to keep on the mantelpiece.

I gave Elliot my best placatory smile, holding up my hands to let him know that I wasn't a threat, and I was just about to say something else to try to calm him down, when all of a sudden he stepped towards me and said, 'I'll give *you* "there's no fucking need for that." ' And then he swung the hammer at me.

I moved quickly enough to avoid the worst of the impact, and thankfully Elliot had gone for me with the handle of the hammer instead of the business end, but it still caught me a glancing blow on the side of my face, and although it didn't really hurt that much, it was enough to send me staggering back against the car.

And that was enough for me. Holding the side of my face, I just stood there in the rain, leaning against the car, and watched in resigned silence as Elliot went back to the remains of the smashed-up camcorder and began stomping the broken pieces into the ground.

Over at the house, his two colleagues were watching him as well, both of them standing in the doorway, smoking cigarettes, neither of them showing much interest. I could see other spectators as well – residents watching from their windows, little kids on bikes pointing and laughing . . . an old man with an old dog, the old man disdainfully shaking his head – this kind of thing never happened on the street in *his* day – while the old dog impassively lifted its leg against the back wheel of a parked car. They were all just watching. No one wanted to get involved. It was just something to look at, that was all: a small-headed man angrily smashing a camcorder to pieces in the rain.

It was something to talk about later on.

Eventually, after about a minute or so, Elliot either ran out of energy or decided that he'd done enough damage, and after a final cursory kick at the shattered mess on the ground, he straightened up, took a couple of deep breaths, and turned to me.

'All right . . .' he said, breathing heavily. 'Now you can

fuck off. And if I ever catch you following me again, if I ever see your fucking face *anywhere*, it won't be bits of your camcorder in the gutter, it'll be bits of your fucking brain. D'you understand me?'

'Yeah,' I said. 'I understand.'

'You'd fucking better.'

I smiled at him.

I thought for a moment he was going to hit me again, but all he did was stare at me for a couple of seconds, the hammer swinging gently in his hands, then he spat on the ground, wiped his mouth, and began walking back to the house.

I watched him all the way.

I watched his colleagues grinning at him and patting him on the shoulder, I watched him light a cigarette, and then I watched them all get into the Transit van and drive off slowly down the street. I waited until they'd turned the corner at the end of the road, waited a little more, and only then did I fetch an empty carrier bag from the back of my car, get down on my knees, and start gathering up all the bits of smashed-up camcorder from the ground.

I found the memory card in a shallow brown puddle. It was soaking wet, of course, and there was a bit of hammer damage to the top left corner, but apart from that it didn't look too bad. There was a chance it might still work. And if it did, Preston Elliot was fucked.

And if it didn't . . .?

Well, I could always get more evidence against him. Or someone else could. Or maybe no one would, and he'd get away with conning some money out of his employers. But in the end . . . well, it didn't really matter, did it? It didn't *mean* anything.

Not to me, anyway.

Nothing means anything to me.

Not any more.

Back in the car, I put the carrier bag full of camcorder bits on the back seat, lit a cigarette, and checked myself out in the rear-view mirror. There was a small cut above my right eye where a bit of broken safety glass had nicked me, and the side of my face was marked with a raised red welt from the hammer handle. Blood was running from the cut, mingling with the sheen of rain on my face, and there were pale pink spots on my shirt collar. As I took a tissue from the glove compartment and started cleaning myself up, my mobile rang again. I gave my face another wipe, rested the cigarette in the ashtray, and put the call on speaker.

'Hi, Ada.'

'John?'

'Yeah, sorry about that, I got a bit –'

'What the hell's going on?' she interrupted. 'Are you all right?'

'Yeah, I'm fine. It was nothing –'

'It didn't *sound* like nothing.'

I picked up my cigarette and took a long drag. 'Really,' I said. 'Everything's fine. I'll tell you all about it when I get back.'

'Are you coming back now?'

'Yeah . . . is the client still there?'

'Yes.'

'OK. Tell her I'll be there in about fifteen minutes. And Ada?'

'What?'

'Be nice to her, all right? Talk to her. Make her a cup of tea or something . . . are you listening?'

'Yeah,' she drawled. 'I'm listening. Be nice, talk to her, cup of tea . . . anything else?'

'Try not to fart too much.'

She laughed.

I ended the call, dropped my cigarette out of the window, and drove off into the rain.

2

The town of Hey is pretty much the same as any other medium-sized town in the south-east of England. It's got a town centre, housing estates, supermarkets, a bypass, outlying villages, a river, a park, pubs, clubs, fights, drugs . . . it's got 200,000 people living 200,000 lives, and it's got no more goodness and no less shit than any other place I've ever been to.

It's Any Town, Anywhere.

It's Hey, Essex, England.

It's where I live.

It's where I come from.

My office is situated on the second floor of a three-storey building at the lower end of Wyre Street in the middle of the town centre. Wyre Street is a narrow pedestrianised lane that runs parallel to the High Street. It's mainly populated with small businesses, like mine, and independent shops that can't afford to be located in the High Street: hippy shops, comic-books shops, skateboard shops, candle shops . . . the kind of shops that don't make much money and never last more than a year or two.

It's OK.

It's a street.

It's where I work from.

It was getting on for midday by the time I got back to town. I left my car in the usual place – a council car park in the old market square – and walked up the steep stone steps that link the car park to Wyre Street. The streets were as quiet as you'd expect on a rainy Wednesday lunchtime, and most of the people I passed were too busy keeping themselves out of the rain to pay any attention to me, but I still got a few wary looks as I made my way back to the office. It was only to be expected. I'd been driving in the rain with no side window, so I was soaking wet and dishevelled. My face was still bleeding, the welt from the hammer blow had swollen up and was starting to turn blue, and I was carrying a manky old carrier bag filled with smashed-up bits of camcorder.

If I'd seen myself in the street, I probably would have been a bit wary too.

When I reached the office building, the front door was open and George Salvini was lounging against the porch wall smoking a cigarette. A middle-aged man, and always impeccably dressed, George runs an accountancy business from an office on the ground floor.

'Hello, John,' he said, grinning at my appearance. 'You're looking very gorgeous today.'

'Thanks, George,' I said, nodding at him as I went past into the corridor and started climbing the stairs.

The second floor of the building is all mine. It has a corridor with a cinnamon-coloured carpet, a toilet with a sink and hot water, and a window that looks out onto the alley at the back of the building. The door to the office has a pebbled glass panel lettered in faded black paint – *John Craine Investigations* – and I can still remember the childish kick of pride and excitement I used to get whenever I saw those three simple words: *John Craine Investigations.* But that's all it is now – a memory, as faded as the paintwork on the glass. And as I opened the door and went in that day, I didn't feel anything at all. No kick, no pride, no excitement. I was a private investigator. It was a job, that's all. It paid the bills.

I shut the door behind me and looked over at Ada. She was sitting at her desk across the room, almost hidden behind a wall of papers and box files and computer stuff – monitor, printer, scanner. Ada was over sixty now, but she still looked the same as she'd always looked: overweight, tired, dressed like a bag lady. Today she was wearing a scratty old cardigan over an XXL Nirvana T-shirt, and although I couldn't see her feet, I knew that she'd be wearing her foul-smelling old furry slippers.

I smiled at her.

'Jesus *Christ*, John!' she said, getting up from her desk. 'What the fuck happened to you?'

'It's all right,' I told her. 'Honestly, it looks a lot worse than it is . . .'

'I *knew* something had happened,' she said, coming over to me and peering closely at my face. 'I just knew it.' She took out a tissue, spat on it, and started dabbing at my wounds.

'Please, Ada,' I said, gently easing her away. 'It's OK . . . really.'

'Who did it?' she asked.

17

'Preston Elliot. You know, the StayBright insurance case?'

She frowned. 'I thought that was just routine surveillance.'

'Yeah, it was. It just got a bit out of hand, that's all.'

She stared at me. 'A bit out of hand?'

I held up the carrier bag and shook it. 'We need a new camcorder.'

'Shit,' she said. 'Do you know how much that cost?'

I took the damaged memory card from my pocket and passed it to her. 'Can you see if this still works?'

'I doubt if it will,' she said, taking it from me and studying it. 'But I'll give it a go.' She looked at me again. 'Are you sure you're all right? That lump on your face doesn't look too good.'

'Yeah, I'm fine,' I said, gazing round the office. It looked the same as ever: Ada's desk, a window, a couple of easy chairs against the wall, a fridge, filing cabinet, stationery cupboard. And over to the right, the connecting door to my private office.

'Is she in there?' I said to Ada.

'Who?'

'The client,' I sighed. 'The woman who's been waiting to see me. Remember? The one I asked you to be nice to?'

'Oh, right,' Ada said. 'Yeah, I thought she'd be more comfortable in there.'

'What's her name?'

Ada shook her head. 'She didn't say.'

'Did you ask her?'

'I'm not your receptionist.'

'Yes, you are.'

She frowned at me again. 'I thought we agreed that my job title was administration manager?'

'Yeah, and the administration manager's responsibilities include secretarial work and receptionist duties.'

She grinned. 'Really?'

'Yeah, really,' I said, smiling back at her. 'It's a good job we don't get many face-to-face clients, isn't it?'

She shrugged. 'Well, you're not exactly in the ideal state for face-to-face meetings yourself at the moment, if you don't mind me saying.'

'I'm a private investigator,' I said. 'I'm *supposed* to look rough and mean.'

She snorted. 'You don't look rough and mean. You just look as if you've been beaten up, that's all. There's nothing remotely rough or mean about that. In fact, if anything –'

'Yeah, all right,' I said, looking at my watch. 'Do you want to go and tell our nameless client that I'll be with her in a minute, please?'

'OK.'

'I'm just going to clean up a bit first. Would you mind making us some coffee?'

'Coffee?'

'Yeah.' I gave her a look. 'Is that all right?'

She shrugged. 'I suppose so.'

'And could you call the garage too? My side window got smashed. I need someone to come round and fix it. The car's in the car park.'

She raised her eyebrows. 'Anything else?'

I smiled at her again, glancing down at the furry slippers

19

on her feet. They were purple. And today she was wearing a matching purple crushed velvet miniskirt that was equally as old and threadbare as her slippers.

'Very nice,' I told her.

She smiled. 'You're too kind.'

'I know.'

I cleaned myself up as well as I could in the toilet along the corridor, then I towel-dried my hair, slicked it back with my fingers, and took a final look in the mirror. I wasn't exactly presentable, but I didn't look quite so much like a beaten-up wino in a cheap black suit any more.

The face in the mirror looked back at me for a moment, asking me why I was bothering with my appearance. *What's the point?* it said. *What do you care what you look like, or what anyone thinks of you? You don't really care if this woman in your office gives you a job or not, do you? So why are you even bothering?*

I didn't have an answer to that.

I sniffed, slicked back my hair again, and went back to the office.

She was sitting in the chair across from my desk, staring vacantly at a mobile phone in her lap. She had a thin and angular face, no make-up, and shortish silvery-grey hair. Her clothes were prim and cheap – a brown tweed coat over a pale blouse and a long shapeless skirt – and she wore the kind of glasses that teachers and librarians usually favour – unnecessarily large, with a coloured plastic frame. I guessed she was about forty-five.

'Sorry to keep you waiting,' I said as I came in and shut the door. 'I got held up with something.'

She looked across at me, flashing a quick nervous smile, and I saw her take in the state of my face, but she didn't say anything. She just tightened her smile for a moment, then leaned down and put the mobile away in her handbag.

I went over to my desk. 'I'm afraid my secretary didn't get your name.'

'It's Mrs Gerrish,' she said. 'Helen Gerrish.'

'John Craine,' I said, offering my hand. 'Pleased to meet you, Mrs Gerrish.'

She gave me that tight little smile again and shook my hand. Well, I say she *shook* my hand – it was actually no more than the briefest brush of her fingertips. It felt like the frightened touch of a very frail and very cold child.

As I sat down at my desk, I was trying to remember where I'd heard her name before. Gerrish . . . Gerrish . . . it definitely rang a bell, but for the moment it just wouldn't come to me.

'So, Mrs Gerrish,' I said. 'What can I do for you?'

She hesitated for a moment, looking down at her hands in her lap, and then – without looking up – she said, 'It's my daughter . . . Anna. She's missing.'

'Anna?'

She nodded.

And now I remembered the name. It had been on the front page of all the local newspapers about a month ago, and maybe in one or two of the nationals too. Anna Gerrish, a woman in her early twenties, had gone missing after leaving work one night. She'd simply put on her coat, walked out of the door, and no one had seen or heard from her since.

'Anna Gerrish . . .' I heard myself mutter.

'I expect you read about it,' Mrs Gerrish said.

'Yes . . . yes, I did.' I looked at her. 'How long has it been now?'

'Four weeks and two days.'

'Have the police made any progress?'

She let out a bitter little laugh. 'Progress? No, the police haven't made any *progress*. As far as I'm concerned, they haven't done anything at *all*.'

'I'm sure they're doing their best –'

'No, Mr Craine,' she said firmly. 'I don't believe they are.'

'Really? What makes you say that?'

She shrugged. 'They haven't found her, have they? They haven't found *any*thing. And they don't even seem to be trying. They haven't made a televised appeal or a reconstruction of her last known movements . . . they haven't done anything like that. And they keep telling me that this kind of thing happens all the time . . . that if someone over eighteen *wants* to disappear without telling anyone, there's very little they can do about it.'

'Well,' I said, trying to sound sympathetic. 'It *is* quite common for young people to simply –'

'No, Mr Craine. Not my Anna.' Mrs Gerrish's eyes were fixed firmly on mine now. 'She wouldn't do that to me. She just *wouldn't*. She's not that kind of girl.'

I didn't bother asking her what kind of girl she imagined *would* do that to her mother. Instead, I asked her what she thought might have happened to Anna.

She shook her head, and I could see her eyes beginning to moisten. 'I just . . . I really don't know. All I know is that if Anna *was* safe and well, she would have let me know.' She took a tissue from her handbag and wiped daintily at her eyes. 'She would have let me know, Mr Craine . . . believe me. I know my daughter. She wouldn't just . . . she wouldn't . . .'

There was a knock at the door then, and Ada came in carrying two cups of coffee on a tray. She came over and put the tray on the desk. The coffee was in proper cups and saucers, not the usual chipped old mugs, and Ada had also provided a bowl of sugar, teaspoons, a little jug of milk, and a plate of biscuits.

'Will there be anything else, Mr Craine?' she said, smiling obsequiously at me.

I looked at her, shaking my head. 'That's all, thanks, Ada.'

She gave me a little curtsey, then turned round and walked out, glancing over her shoulder and wiggling her fat arse in a sexy-secretary kind of way as she went.

I waited for her to close the door, then I turned back to Mrs Gerrish. She'd stopped crying now and had gone back to staring at her hands. They were in her lap again, obsessively twisting and tearing at the tissue.

'So, Mrs Gerrish,' I said. 'What is it you'd like me to do, exactly?'

She looked up at me, frowning almost disdainfully, as if I'd just asked her the most unnecessary question in the world. 'I want you to find my daughter, Mr Craine.'

'Why me?' I said.

'I beg your pardon?'

'Why did you choose me? There are plenty of other investigation agencies, bigger companies with more resources . . .'

'You were recommended,' she said.

'By whom?'

She looked slightly uncomfortable for a moment. 'Well, to be honest, Mr Craine . . . I did try some other agencies, but none of them were willing to help. The last one I went to, a company called Mercer Associates, they suggested that I contact you.' She smiled thinly. 'No offence meant, Mr Craine, but if *you're* not able to help me, I really don't know what else I can do.'

I nodded, smiling. 'No offence taken, Mrs Gerrish. None at all. Do you remember who you spoke to at Mercer?'

She shook her head. 'I can't remember her name . . . it was a young lady. She said they don't handle domestic cases, only corporate work . . . whatever that is.'

I nodded. 'And do you mind me asking why you came here in person without making an appointment first?'

'Does it matter?'

'No, no . . . of course not. I'm just curious, that's all. Most of my personal clients either contact me by telephone first or get in touch through my website.'

She looked down at her lap again, and when she spoke again I knew she was lying. 'Yes, well . . . I *was* going to call you, but I happened to be in town today getting some shopping, and when I passed your office . . .' She shrugged. 'Well, I just thought I'd call in.' She looked up at me. 'I didn't think you'd mind.'

I smiled. 'I don't.'

'So will you help me?'

I don't know why I didn't say no. I didn't *need* the work, for a start. And even if I did, the prospect of working for this strangely unappetising woman didn't exactly fill me with joy. There wasn't even anything particularly interesting about the case. It would probably involve a lot of fairly tedious work without much hope of success. And if, as Helen Gerrish had claimed, the police really hadn't made any progress, that either meant that there wasn't anything to find, or that they were fairly sure Anna had simply gone away of her own accord.

But, despite all that, I didn't say no.

And, even now, I still don't know why.

I just opened my mouth and found myself saying, 'If I do decide to help you, Mrs Gerrish, you'd have to understand that there's very little I can do that the police haven't already done. No matter what you think of them, I can assure you that the police have far greater resources for finding people than I have.'

'Yes, I understand that.'

'And, unlike the police, my services aren't free.'

'Money isn't a problem, Mr Craine. My husband and I have sufficient funds.'

'Does your husband feel the same way as you? About hiring a private investigator, I mean?'

'Yes, of *course*,' she said, just a little too forcefully. 'He's as desperate to find Anna as I am.'

Yeah? I thought. *So how come he's not here?*

'All right,' I said, removing a writing pad from the desk

drawer. 'Let me take a few basic details first, and then we'll see about getting a contract drawn up. Is that OK?'

She smiled, the first genuine smile I'd seen from her, and reached into her handbag. 'This is the most recent photograph I have of Anna,' she said, passing me a 6" x 4" colour print. 'It was taken about a year ago. You probably remember it from the newspaper reports.'

I thought it slightly odd that she just happened to have a photo of Anna in her handbag, even though she claimed that she was only in town to do some shopping . . . but I let that pass and concentrated on studying the photograph.

Helen was right, I did remember it from the newspaper reports. It was a posed picture, a head-and-shoulders shot, and it looked as if it'd been taken in a studio. Anna was trying to look sultry and mysterious – her head turned demurely over her shoulder, all pouting lips and come-to-bed eyes – and she seemed to be reclining on a red leather divan. There was nothing unprofessional or overly tacky about the photograph, it was simply that the intended effect just didn't work. Anna was trying too hard, for a start, and although she was reasonably attractive – almond eyes, long black hair, a nice face, pretty mouth – there was something about her, something indefinable, that robbed her of any allure.

She looked hollow to me.

Haunted.

Used up.

'She was a model,' Mrs Gerrish said proudly. 'Well . . . she was *hoping* to be a model. It's what she always dreamed of.'

I nodded. 'She didn't make her living from it, then?'

'No . . . it's a very hard business to break into. And, of course, you have to make certain sacrifices if you're really determined to make it.'

'What kind of sacrifices?'

'Modelling is the kind of work that requires you to be available all the time, just in case something suddenly turns up. So Anna was forever turning down excellent job opportunities because she didn't want to tie herself down.'

'I see . . . so where was she working when she disappeared?'

Mrs Gerrish hesitated. 'Well, it was only a temporary post, a part-time catering position . . .'

I looked at her, my pen hovering over the pad. 'I need the details, Mrs Gerrish.'

'The Wyvern,' she said quietly. 'It's a restaurant . . .'

I knew The Wyvern, and I knew that it wasn't a restaurant. It was a pub. And a shit-hole pub at that. The only menu you were likely to be offered at The Wyvern was a menu of Class A drugs.

'I don't know the address, I'm afraid,' Mrs Gerrish said. 'But it's –'

'It's all right,' I told her. 'I know where it is. Was Anna living at home?'

'No, she has her own little flat down near the docks. Do you want the address?'

'Please.'

She gave me the address and I wrote it down.

I said, 'Is it a rented flat?'

'Yes.'

27

'What's happening with it at the moment? Is Anna's stuff still there?'

Helen nodded. 'The rent was due last week . . . we've paid it up for another month.'

'Does Anna live on her own?'

'Yes.'

'She's not married?'

'No.'

'Boyfriend?'

'No . . .'

'Are you sure?'

'Anna would have told me if she had a boyfriend.'

'What about old boyfriends?'

'Well, yes, of course . . . she was always a very popular girl. I can't think of any names offhand at the moment . . .'

'Didn't the police ask you for their names?'

'Well, yes . . . but I told them I couldn't remember. I think they got them from somewhere else.'

Somewhere else? I thought. *What the fuck does that mean?*

'OK, Mrs Gerrish,' I said. 'I'll need Anna's phone numbers – landline and mobile, please.'

She gave me the numbers, I wrote them down.

'Have you got any other recent photos of Anna?' I asked. 'Anything a bit more . . . natural?'

'There's a few more at home, I think. They're not *very* recent –'

'OK, don't worry, we'll sort that out later. How about a key to her flat?'

'The police have Anna's keys, but I've got a spare at home.'

'Well, I'd like to take a look round her flat as soon as possible. Could you drop the key off later?'

She looked slightly pained. 'Well, it's a bit difficult . . . you see, I don't drive, and my husband has the car all day –'

'How about later on this evening?'

'He's working this evening.'

'All right,' I sighed. 'Where do you live, Mrs Gerrish?'

'Stangate Rise.'

I nodded. 'How about if I drive out later on and pick up the key myself? Would that be OK?'

She hesitated again. 'Well, yes . . . I suppose . . .'

I sighed to myself again. This was already beginning to feel like hard work.

'Would six o'clock be convenient?'

'Yes . . . six o'clock, that's fine.'

'Right. Perhaps it'd be best if we leave any more questions until then.'

'Yes . . . yes, of course. Would you like my address –?'

'My secretary will take all your details before you go. Just one more thing . . . do you know the name of the officer in charge of the police investigation?'

'Yes, it's Detective Chief Inspector Bishop.'

I paused, momentarily taken aback. 'Mick Bishop?'

'Yes. Do you know him?'

'My father . . .' I began to say, but I had to stop to clear my throat. 'My father knew DCI Bishop . . . they used to work together.'

'Your father's a policeman?'

'He used to be.'

'But not any more?'

'No.'

She looked at me, waiting for me to go on, but after I'd stared back at her for a while, letting her know that I didn't want to talk about it, she eventually got the message and reluctantly lowered her eyes.

'I usually charge by the hour,' I told her, clearing my throat again. 'But I think it's probably best in this case if we agree on a set rate for a limited period of time – say, three days – and then we'll both see how it's going and take it from there. How does that sound?'

'Yes, thank you, Mr Craine. That's perfectly acceptable.'

'And we'll need a retainer from you, if that's all right.'

'Of course. How much would you like?'

'My secretary will detail our rates for you. If you'd like to go through to the main office, she'll explain everything you need to know and draw up a contract.'

Mrs Gerrish got to her feet. 'Well, thank you again, Mr Craine. Really ... thank you very much.'

'You're welcome. I'll see you at six o'clock.'

She smiled her humourless smile again, turned round, and started walking out. I watched her go. She was one of those women who scuffle across the ground with small, quick steps, barely lifting their feet, as if they're somehow embarrassed about the process of walking.

I was just about to pick up the phone and call Ada to let her know what to put in the contract, when I heard the scuffling stop, and I looked up to see Mrs Gerrish peering back at me.

'Would you mind if I asked you a personal question, Mr Craine?'

'Not at all.' I smiled at her. 'I can't promise to answer it, though.'

She didn't return the smile. 'Have you always lived in Hey?'

I nodded. 'Most of my life. Why?'

'Well, it's just that . . . back in 1993, something terrible happened here. A young woman was murdered . . .'

I didn't say anything, I just stared at her.

This time she didn't look away. 'Her name was Craine . . . Stacy Craine . . .'

Inside the house, I drop my keys on the hall table and call out, 'Stacy! It's me . . . Stacy?'

There's no reply.

I look at my watch. It's 5.35.

'Stacy!' I call out again, going into the kitchen, then on into the sitting room. 'Where are you, Stace?'

I shouldn't be worried. She'll be upstairs taking a nap, that's all. It's a sweltering hot day, she's five months preg-nant . . . she's been feeling really tired recently. That's it. That's where she'll be. Upstairs, in bed.

Asleep.

No, I shouldn't be worried . . .

But I am.

Something doesn't feel right. Me, the air, the house . . . this moment. It's all wrong. There's a terrible coldness in my belly. A deadness in my mind. This, right now . . . this feels like a moment that I'm never going to forget.

And now I'm half-remembering something, something I'd seen but not registered when I'd entered the house just a

*minute ago, and with an awful sense of dread in my heart I go
back out into the hallway and stare intently at the hall table
. . . and my half-memory is right. The table is slightly askew
. . . not quite flush to the wall . . . as if someone has knocked
against it in passing and not put it back where it belongs. And
when I look down at the floor to the right of the table, I can
see what I didn't see before . . . the antelope's head. It's on the
floor. Our carved wooden antelope's head, six inches long,
that we bought at a junk shop for 50p . . . the carving that we
use as a paperweight for anything that needs posting . . .*

It's on the floor.

It shouldn't be on the floor.

*It belongs on the hall table. And if either of us ever knocks
it off, we always pick it up and put it back where it belongs.*

Always.

Without fail.

It's one of our stupid little things . . .

*And now I'm running up the stairs as fast as I can, and my
heart is pounding, and I'm shouting at the top of my voice,
'Stacy! Stacy! STACY!'*

'Mr Craine . . . ?'

I looked up.

Helen Gerrish was staring at me with a slightly puzzled
look on her face. 'Are you all right?'

'Yes . . . yes, I'm sorry. What were you saying?'

'Stacy Craine . . . I was just wondering, you know, as it's
quite an unusual name . . . if she was related to you in any
way.'

'She was my wife,' I said.

'Oh . . . oh, I'm *terribly* sorry. I hope you didn't mind me asking . . . it's just . . . well, I remember it, that's all. It was such an awful thing.'

'Yes, it was.'

'I'm sorry to bring it up. It must be . . . well, it must be very hard. I'm sorry.'

'That's all right.'

'Did the police ever find him? The man who did it, I mean. Did they catch him?'

'No . . .' I said quietly. 'No, the police never caught him.'

3

While Ada was sorting out the paperwork for Helen Gerrish in the main office, I opened up my laptop, logged on to the Internet, and Googled 'Anna Gerrish'. There weren't that many results: three entries from the *Hey Gazette*, one from the *Guardian*, and one from the *Daily Mail*. The first article in the *Hey Gazette* was dated Wednesday 8 September, two days after Anna was last seen. It was the lead story on the front page, accompanied by the same photograph that her mother had just given to me. The other two articles appeared on the following days – Thursday's was on page three, Friday's was relegated to page seven. After that, there was nothing. The stories in the *Guardian* and the *Daily Mail* were both no more than a paragraph or two, and neither of them added anything to the reports in the *Gazette*.

According to the report, Anna had been a barmaid at The Wyvern for about eighteen months. On the night of Monday 6 September she'd worked a late shift, finishing at one o'clock in the morning, and that was the last time anyone had seen her. No one knew where she'd gone after work, whether she was planning to meet someone, or go somewhere, or simply go home. And if she was planning to go home, no one seemed to know how she usually got back after a late shift, whether she walked, or took a taxi, or if anyone ever picked her up. No one, it seemed, knew very much about Anna at all. There were even conflicting reports as to what she'd been wearing when she left. Most of the staff at The Wyvern were fairly sure that she hadn't got changed out of the jeans and white vest she'd been wearing all night, she'd just thrown on a black leather coat and left. But a barmaid called Genna Raven was convinced that she'd seen Anna getting changed in the toilets. 'She was definitely wearing heels and a skirt when she left,' Genna was quoted as saying. 'And I think she might have put on a black top too.'

In terms of what actually happened that night, that was about all the newspaper reports had to offer. The rest of it was all padding: speculation, quotes from Mrs Gerrish and DCI Bishop, biographical information about Anna – where she'd gone to school, her modelling hopes, that kind of thing.

Reading between the lines, and judging by the way the newspapers had quickly lost interest in the story, I got the impression that apart from Helen Gerrish, who I guessed was the driving force behind getting the story printed in the first place, no one really believed that Anna had come to any harm.

And they were probably right.

But, unlike the media, I don't get paid to speculate.

So I went through the newspaper reports again, noting down any relevant information, and I put all that together with the photograph and the details that Helen Gerrish had given me, and I was just about to start making a few preliminary phone calls when I heard the outer office door open and close, followed by Helen Gerrish's tiny footsteps shuffling down the stairs, and a few moments later my door swung open and Ada came in.

'Phew,' she said, blowing out her cheeks and shaking her head. 'She's hard work, that one.'

'Yeah, I know. Any problems with the contract or anything?'

Ada shrugged. 'I don't think she even read it, to be honest. Just signed it and gave me the cheque.' Ada took a packet of cigarettes from her pocket and threw one over to me, and we both went over to the battered old settee beneath the window. I opened the window, and we sat down and lit our cigarettes.

Ada looked at me. 'You know Mick Bishop is the SIO on the Anna Gerrish case, don't you?'

'Yeah.'

'Are you going to be all right with that?'

'I don't see why not.'

She held my gaze for a moment or two, giving me her 'are you sure about that?' look, then she just nodded slowly and took a long drag on her cigarette. 'So,' she said, blowing out smoke. 'What's next?'

'I don't know . . . I'm going to look round Anna's flat this evening, and then I'll just take it from there, I suppose. Go and see Bishop, talk to Anna's work colleagues . . . see if anything turns up.'

'Do you think it will?'

I shrugged. 'Probably not.'

Ada tapped ash from her cigarette. 'If I had a mother like

Helen Gerrish, I think I'd have run away years ago.'

I smiled. 'Me too.'

She took another puff on her cigarette. 'Do you want me to call Bishop and set up a meeting?'

'Yeah, please. Tomorrow if possible.'

'OK. Anything else?'

'Did you get a chance to try that memory card yet?'

'Yeah, but I couldn't get anything from it. It might be worth asking Cal to have a look.'

I nodded. Callum Franks was Stacy's nephew. Over the years he'd often helped me out whenever I needed an extra pair of eyes or legs. He was a quick learner, and very reliable, and when it came to anything technical – computers, phones, recording equipment – Cal was in a league of his own. He could do virtually anything with a laptop . . . and when I say anything, I mean *any*thing. Legal or otherwise.

'OK,' I said, putting out my cigarette. 'Remind me to pick up the memory card before I go. I'll give it to Cal the next time I see him.'

Ada stood up. 'What are you going to do now?'

'I don't know. Did you get through to the garage about the car window?'

She nodded. 'They said they'd send someone out straight away.'

'Straight away garage time?'

'I'd imagine so.'

'What's that in real time?'

'Probably about two hours.'

'Yeah,' I said, stifling a yawn.

'Why don't you go home for a bit?' Ada said gently. 'Take a bath, change your clothes . . . get some rest. I don't mind staying on for the rest of the day.'

'Are you sure?'

She nodded. 'I'll call you a taxi.'

'You're an angel, Ada.'

'I know.' She looked at me, suddenly quite serious. 'Are you all right, John? I mean, you know . . . in yourself, generally. Are you OK?'

'Yeah . . . I'm fine.'

'Really?'

'Yeah.'

She looked at me for a long moment, seeking the truth in my eyes, and then – with a far from convincing nod of her head – she reached up and gently took hold of my chin, angling it to get a better look at the swelling on my face.

'You need to put some ice on that when you get home,' she said. 'Have you got any ice in that hovel of yours?'

'It's not a *hovel* –'

'Put a few ice cubes in a towel or a flannel, crush them up, and hold it against your face. It should help the swelling to go down. All right?'

'Yeah, thanks.'

She looked at me again, genuine concern showing in her eyes, then she said, 'I'll go and call you that taxi.'

My house – or my hovel, as Ada likes to call it – is in an old terraced street on the south side of town. It was originally a factory house, as were all the homes in Paxman Street, built over a century ago by the owners of the neighbouring engineering plant to accommodate the company's workers. For a hundred years or more, the mist and steam from the factory across the road has been breathed in by the bricks of the house, and on a hot day, or when a thunderstorm is coming, the walls give out a faint scent of oil. Sometimes, too, in the middle of the night, I think I can smell the tired skin of the factory hands who once lived here. I imagine them as short, dark, melancholy people, with sooted faces and small bitter eyes . . . and as I lie in bed, listening to their illusive whispers, I wonder if they're happier now, in their dreams of death, than they were in the toil of their lives.

It's not much, my house – upstairs, downstairs, two separate flats, a small back garden and an even smaller front yard – but it's mine, for what it's worth, and I feel safe and comfortable within the sanctuary of its stained old walls.

I live alone.

But I'm not alone.

When my mother died in 1997, she left me both the family home – the house where I was born and brought up – and the house in Paxman Street, which she'd bought with my father some years ago as a buy-to-let investment. At the time she died, there was only the one tenant in the house, a young woman called Bridget Moran, who lived in the upstairs flat, and as I'd already decided to sell the family home and use the money to set up my own investigation business, it just seemed sensible, and convenient, to move into the downstairs flat.

So that's what I did.

And I'm still here.

And so is Bridget Moran.

As the taxi dropped me off outside the house, Bridget was just coming out, and I was momentarily stunned to see that she'd had most of her chestnut-brown shoulder-length hair cut off and was now sporting a boyishly short peroxide-blonde crop. My sense of shock was only partly caused by how different – and how amazing – she looked with her new haircut. The main reason, the thing that just for a second had stopped my heart and turned me inside out, was that Stacy used to wear her hair in exactly the same style – short, blonde, spikily cute – and just for a moment, when I'd seen Bridget coming out of the house . . .

The moment soon passed.

Bridget was with her boyfriend, a vapid piece of meat called Dave. I'd never liked Dave. He had a confident smile, nice teeth, sideburns, an expensive suit and an equally expensive watch. He was the kind of man who keeps a golf umbrella in the back of his company car, the kind of man who wears shoes that squeak. I didn't know his surname, but I liked to think that it was Dave. 'Hi,' I could imagine him saying. 'Dave Dave, pleased to meet you. Yeah, right, absolutely . . .'

No, I didn't like Dave at all.

Not that it mattered . . .

'Hey, John,' Bridget said breezily as we met at the front gate. Then, 'Shit! What happened to your face?'

'Oh, nothing . . . just a stupid accident,' I muttered, trying not to stare too obviously at her hair. 'I fell over . . . down some steps.'

'You need to put some ice on that,' she said, looking closer.

'So I've been told.' I looked at her. 'I like what you've done to your hair.'

She smiled broadly, running her fingers through her hair. 'Really? You don't think it's too much, do you?'

'No . . . it really suits you.'

Dave Dave, who'd been gazing idly around the front yard as we talked, feigning indifference, suddenly butted in. 'Come on, Bridge,' he grunted, taking her by the arm. 'We'd better get going.'

'Yeah, OK.' She flashed a smile at me. 'See you later, John. And don't forget the ice.'

I smiled at her, nodding perfunctorily at Dave, and stepped aside to let them pass. I paused for a moment, wondering if I should turn round and wave goodbye . . . but after I'd thought about it for a while, I decided not to bother, and I just went on into the house instead.

Bridget's dog, Walter, was waiting in the hallway when I opened the front door. A big old greyhound, he was sitting at the foot of the stairs with a chewed rubber bone in his mouth. I reached down and scratched his head.

'Hey, Walter,' I said. 'How's it going?'

His tail thumped, his mouth fell open in a lazy dog smile, and the rubber bone dropped to the floor. I bent down, picked it up, and gave it back to him.

'There you go.'

He looked at me, took the bone in his mouth, and dropped it again. He was nearly fourteen now. His muzzle was slack and pale, and the brindley grey hair on his back was streaked with white. He was nearing the end of his life.

But, for Walter, that wasn't so bad. Getting old isn't the same for dogs as it is for us, because – unlike us – dogs don't know they're going to die.

I left him where he was and went into my flat.

The familiarity of my living space greeted me, as usual, with its dusty and settled silence. It's a place that's always felt lived in: a front room, spacious and high, with plain wooden furniture and solid old walls; heavy double doors leading through into the bedroom; and then a stepped stone archway that takes you down into a cramped little kitchen area at the back. A narrow door at the far end of the kitchen opens through to the bathroom, and twin glazed doors lead out into the brick-walled garden at the rear.

It's how it is, how it's meant to be, and that's how I like it.

And it holds no memories for me.

And I like that, too.

I went over to the old armchair beneath the high window in the front room, and I sat down and lit a cigarette. My eyes were stiff and heavy, and deep inside me I could feel a distant weight of tiredness that at some point, I knew, was going to creep up behind me and drape a blanket over my head – a cold, black, greasy old blanket. And when that happened, I wouldn't be capable of anything. I'd be in the black place, the place where I can't move, where I've never been able to move . . . the place where there *is* nothing else . . . nothing at all. And when I'm there, I've been there all my life, and I'll remain there for the rest of my life, draped in the darkness. I can't do anything. I don't want anything. What's the point? Fifty years from now, we'll all be dead anyway. We'll all be floating back to the stars or buried in the dark underground, caked in clay, riddled with worms and insects, centipedes, chafers, slugs . . . and nothing that happens now will mean a fucking thing.

That's how the black place makes me feel.

But I wasn't there yet.

I finished my cigarette, went into the kitchen and swallowed a handful of painkillers, then came back to the armchair and poured myself a glass of Scotch. I lit another cigarette, took a long slow drink, and breathed out slowly as the heat of the whisky soaked down into my gut and then rose up into my heart like a warm balloon.

I poured myself another, and then I just sat there, drinking and smoking in the rainy-grey light of the afternoon, until I fell asleep.

I woke up to the sound of my mobile ringing. The daylight was beginning to fade now, and as I fumbled the mobile out of my pocket and put it to my ear, a car rolled down the street outside and the dimness of the room was briefly illuminated by a slow sweep of headlights.

'Yeah?' I said into the phone.

'Hi, John,' a familiar voice replied. 'It's Imogen . . .'

Imogen Rand was a good friend of mine who'd once been more than just a good friend. Her father, Leon Mercer, was the owner and managing director of Mercer Associates.

'Hey, Immy,' I said. 'I was going to call you later –'

'Yeah, right. Of course you were.'

'No, really . . .'

43

'Are you all right, John?' she interrupted. 'You sound a bit –'

'Yeah, sorry. I just woke up.'

'Late night?'

'Well, kind of . . .'

'I can call back if you want.'

'No, it's all right.'

'Are you sure?'

'Yeah,' I said, glancing at the clock. It was 4.55. 'I needed to wake up anyway.'

'OK . . . well, it's just a quick call. Has a woman called Gerrish been in touch with you yet?'

'Yeah, I saw her this afternoon. She told me that you'd recommended me.'

'Well, you know it's not the kind of thing that we'd take on, and I thought you might find it interesting . . . are you going to do it?'

I lit a cigarette. 'I told her I'd give it three days.'

'Right, well . . .' she said hesitantly. 'The thing is, John, I saw Dad last night, and I mentioned it to him, and he told me that Mick Bishop is the SIO on the Anna Gerrish case. Of course, if I'd known that at the time, I wouldn't have put Helen Gerrish in touch with you, at least not without asking you first. Sorry, John, it just didn't occur to me to find out –'

'It's all right,' I assured her. 'It's not a problem. I knew about Bishop before I made up my mind anyway.'

'Really? So you're still going to do it?'

'Yeah, why not? History is history.'

'I suppose . . .'

'What did you think of her anyway?' I asked.

'Helen Gerrish?'

'Yeah.'

'Not much. I mean, yeah, I feel *sorry* for her and everything, but . . .'

I laughed.

'What?' she said. 'What's so funny?'

'You, feeling sorry for someone.'

'Hey,' she said, pretending to take offence. 'Just because I don't give a shit about people, that doesn't mean I'm not sympathetic.'

'Right, so you felt really sorry for her, *but* . . .?'

'Well, she was lying, for a start.'

'About what?'

'I don't know, but she was definitely lying about something. At least, she was when she talked to me.'

'Yeah, I got the same feeling too. What else didn't you like about her?'

'It's not a question of not *liking* her, John . . . well, actually, come to think of it, it is. I *really* didn't like her one bit. And I'm sure that if I met her husband, I wouldn't like him either.'

'What about Anna? Do you think you'd like her if you met her?'

'Probably not.'

'You're all heart, Imogen.'

'Fucking right, I am.'

We talked on for a little while longer about nothing much in particular – the StayBright/Preston Elliot case (which I told her was coming along nicely), her father's ailing health, and the possibility of her taking over as MD of Mercer Associates – and then I realised how late it was getting, and that I had to be at Helen Gerrish's at six, so we said our goodbyes, and I called for a taxi to take me back into town, and by the time the taxi arrived I'd taken a quick shower and changed my bloodied clothes, and was ready to face the world again.

4

Helen Gerrish lived with her husband in a small red-brick house on a modern commuter estate called Stangate Rise about two miles out of town. It was one of those estates with hundreds of houses that all look the same and dozens of streets that all look the same, so it's really easy to get lost. Which I did. And that was one of the reasons I didn't get there until just gone quarter to seven. Another reason was that the garage still hadn't been round to fix the broken window in my car, and the rain was still pouring down, so I'd had to spend twenty minutes or so patching up the window with a couple of old Sainsbury's carrier bags and about a mile of grey duct tape before I left. And one more reason for being late was that I'd had to stop on the way to answer a phone call from DCI Bishop.

It was strange to hear his voice again. The last time I'd seen him was eighteen years ago at my father's funeral, and although he'd only spoken to me briefly then – a very curt offer of condolences – I recognised his gruff Essex accent immediately.

'John Craine?' he'd said when I answered the phone.

'Yeah?'

'DCI Bishop. Your secretary called me this afternoon.'

'Yes, thanks for –'

'What's your interest in Anna Gerrish?'

'Didn't my secretary tell you?'

'I'm asking you.'

I sighed. 'I've been hired to look into her disappearance –'

'By who?'

'Whom.'

'What?'

'Nothing . . .'

'Who hired you?'

'I'm sorry, but I'd have to get my client's permission before –'

'What does your *client* want you to do?'

'Find Anna.'

'And how do you expect to do that?'

I lit a cigarette. 'Look, all I want is –'

'You're Jim Craine's son, aren't you?'

'Yes . . .'

'You probably don't remember me, but I used to work with your father –'

'Yeah, I remember you.'

He paused for a moment then, and although it was only a very slight hesitation, it was enough to give me an equally slight sense of satisfaction.

'So,' Bishop said, sniffing self-consciously. 'You're working this case then, are you?'

'Is that a problem?'

'Not as long as you keep me informed of what you're doing.'

I didn't say anything to that.

Bishop sniffed again. 'Are you working on it right now?'

I could have lied to him, I suppose. Or told him to fuck off. But I thought it best not to antagonise him unnecessarily. 'I'm just on my way round to Anna's flat,' I told him.

'What for?'

'Nothing in particular . . . I just thought I'd take a quick look round. Is that all right with you? I mean, it's not off limits or anything, is it?'

'No . . . but you won't find anything there. We've already looked.'

'I don't mind wasting my time.'

'Yeah, well . . . as long as you don't waste any of mine.'

'I'll do my best not to.'

'Good. So what about this meeting?'

'What meeting?'

'Your secretary said you wanted a meeting.'

'Oh, right, yeah –'

'What do you want from me?'

'Anything, really. Whatever you're willing to share with me about the Anna Gerrish case. Of course, I understand that you can't reveal any details of your investigation . . .'

I let my voice trail off, slightly surprised that Bishop hadn't interrupted already to tell me that he had neither the time nor the inclination to share *any*thing with me, and as the silence on the phone stretched out to a relatively eternal three or four seconds, I wondered what the hell was taking him so long. *You either meet me or you don't*, I thought. *You don't have to spend ages thinking about it.*

And then, quite suddenly, his voice came back on the line. '11.30 tomorrow morning,' he said brusquely. 'The

CID offices at Eastway. I've only got ten minutes to spare, so don't be late.'

And that was it. No goodbyes, no see you tomorrows, no nothing. He just said what he had to say, then hung up. I sat there for a while, smoking my cigarette and going over the conversation in my mind, trying to work out if it meant anything or not . . . but the only conclusion I came to was that my father hadn't been exaggerating when he'd told me, many years ago, that Mick Bishop was the most odious man he'd ever known.

I looked at my watch, saw that it was 6.30, and got going.

The streets of Stangate Rise were fairly quiet as I walked from my car to the Gerrishes' house, and I guessed that it was still too early for the commuters to be arriving back from London. They'd be here soon enough, though – driving home from the station in their £30,000 cars, tired and wet, stressed and bored, burdened with the knowledge that tomorrow morning they'd have to get up early, put on their suits, and start all over again.

And again.

And again.

And again.

Poor fuckers.

Or stupid fuckers.

It depends how you look at it, I suppose.

It was fully dark now, the estate glowing orange in the sodium gleam of the streetlights, and as I rang the bell of the Gerrishes' house I was vaguely aware of countless unseen TV screens strobing away behind the curtains of the houses all around me. There was something almost Christmassy about it, in a tacky kind of way.

Helen Gerrish seemed anxious when she opened the door, which was only to be expected. She was a nervous woman, caught up in a highly stressful situation. It would have been strange if she *hadn't* been anxious. But as she stood there in the doorway, smiling her tight little smile at me, I got the feeling that she wasn't just worried about Anna, she was worried about something else. Something that belonged to now. Right here, right now.

'Sorry I'm late again, Mrs Gerrish,' I said. 'I got a bit lost.'

She shook her head. 'No, no . . . that's fine, Mr Craine. No trouble at all.' She opened the door wider and stepped to one side. 'Please, come in.'

I followed her along a narrow little hallway into a box-like front room. It was very neat, very ordered, very suburban. Three-piece suite, widescreen TV, dull ornaments, blackwood coffee table, fake log fire. Over by the window, a man in a grey cardigan and green corduroy trousers was sitting in an armchair watching TV. He had a grim face, greying skin, and one of those wide upper lips that look as if they ought to have a moustache, but don't. He was older than his wife, in his mid-fifties at least, and his short black hair was greying at the edges.

'This is Graham, my husband,' Helen Gerrish said.

'Evening, Mr Gerrish,' I said. 'Good to meet you.'

He looked at me for a moment, nodded without smiling, then went back to watching the TV. I stared at him for a second or two, trying to see the man who his wife had assured me was 'as desperate to find Anna as I am', but either she'd been lying to me, or he was incredibly good at hiding his emotions. I turned back to Helen, remembering also that her husband was supposed to be working this evening, but I didn't say anything to her about that or his distinctly ill-mannered welcome. She looked embarrassed enough as it was.

'Here's Anna's keys,' she mumbled, passing me a key ring. 'The Yale one is for her flat, the other one's for the main door.'

'Thanks. Did you manage to find another photograph?'

'Oh, yes . . . I knew there was something else. I think there might be some in her room.' She looked over at her husband. 'Do you know if there are any photographs of Anna in her room, dear?'

He didn't answer, just carried on staring at the TV.

'Graham?' Helen said.

He looked up grudgingly. 'What?'

'Mr Craine needs another photograph of Anna. Are there any in her room?'

He shrugged. 'How should I know?'

'I just thought –'

'Why don't we both go and have a look?' I suggested.

She glanced at me, then looked back at her husband again. 'Is that all right with you, dear?'

'Is what all right?'

'If Mr Craine has a look in Anna's room.'

'What are you asking me for?'

As Helen stood there, obviously upset, her lips fluttering nervously in search of a reply, I saw the faintest hint of a sneer flash across her husband's face. It was an ugly little moment, a small horror from a small man in a small house, and just then I really didn't want to be in the same room as him any more.

'Is it this way?' I asked Helen, stepping towards the door.

'Uh, yes . . . yes,' she muttered, still quite shaken, but trying her best to hide it. 'Just up the stairs . . . uh . . . first door on the right.'

'After you,' I said.

Graham Gerrish was still staring blankly at the TV screen as we left the room and I followed his wife up the stairs.

'We haven't changed anything since Anna left home,' she told me. 'In her room, I mean. We've kept it just the way it was, you know . . . in case she wanted to stay over when she visited.'

'How old was she when she left?' I asked.

'Seventeen. She's a very independent-minded girl.'

'Did she visit very often?'

'This is it,' Mrs Gerrish said, ignoring my question as she opened a door, turned on the light, and ushered me inside.

When I stepped into that room, I really thought that she'd made a mistake and shown me into the wrong daughter's room, a daughter that she hadn't told me about . . . a daughter who was twelve years old. Because that's what it looked like – the bedroom of a twelve-year-old girl. Pink wallpaper, Mickey Mouse curtains, furniture that belonged in a doll's house. There was a little wooden chair with flowers painted on it, a minuscule dressing table, a single bed made up with crisp white sheets and embroidered blankets. There were frilly things all over the place, velvety cushions, brightly coloured ribbons. And there were teddy bears and stuffed animals everywhere – lined up on the bed, sitting on chairs, perched on top of a wardrobe. The only non-sugary-sweet thing in the room was a sleek black laptop on a table beside the bed.

'This is Anna's old room?' I said, trying to keep the disbelief from my voice.

'Yes . . . she liked to keep it neat.'

'And she slept in here until she was seventeen?'

'That's right,' Helen said, crossing the room towards a rack of plastic shelves standing against the wall. 'Yes, here they are . . . Anna's photographs.' She started looking through a collection of framed photographs positioned neatly on the shelves. All of the pictures were of Anna: Anna when she was a child, Anna when she was six or seven, Anna when she was twelve, thirteen, fourteen. I could hear Helen muttering to herself as she searched through the photos. 'I think we've got some recent ones here . . . I'm sure Graham framed some and brought them up . . .'

I wandered slowly towards her, looking around as I went, still unable to believe my eyes. 'Did she decorate the room herself?' I asked.

'Who, Anna? Goodness me, no. Graham would never have allowed that. He does all the DIY in this house. He's very good with his hands, is Graham.'

I bet he fucking is, I thought.

'I thought you said he was working this evening?' I said casually.

'Oh, yes . . . well, he thought he was, but there was some kind of mix up with the shifts or something.'

54

'Right . . . so what does he actually do, if you don't mind me asking?'

'He used to work for the Inland Revenue, but he was made redundant a few years ago. He has a security position now.'

'Security?'

'Yes, he works mostly in the big shopping precinct in town.'

I nodded. It wasn't hard to imagine Graham Gerrish patrolling the shopping mall, proudly wearing his security guard uniform . . . bullying children, ordering kids to get off their skateboards, telling people to put out their cigarettes . . .

'Is that Anna's laptop over there?' I asked Mrs Gerrish.

'No . . . that's Graham's. He keeps it in here because apparently it's the only place in the house where he can get a decent Internet connection.'

'Really?' I gazed round the room, looking for a router, but I couldn't see one anywhere. 'I would have thought with a wi-fi connection he'd have access all over the house.'

'I'm sorry . . . I don't know anything about computers . . . ah, here we are.' She turned from the shelves with a framed picture in her hand. 'I think this should do the job.' She passed me the picture with a satisfied smile. 'It was taken the year before last when Anna was on holiday.'

The photograph was mounted in a cheap white plastic frame. It showed Anna sitting on a wooden bench against an old stone wall, dressed in cut-off jeans and a bikini top. She was smiling dopily, and her eyes looked like tiny black marbles. There were grubby thumb marks around the edge of the frame.

'Very nice,' I said. 'Was this a holiday with friends? Work colleagues?'

Helen shook her head. 'Anna didn't say.'

'Do you know where she went?'

'I think it was Ibiza . . . or maybe Greece. Somewhere like that. Is it important? I could probably find out –'

'No, don't worry about it. It doesn't matter. Is it OK if I keep the picture for a while?'

'Yes, of course.'

'Thanks. Well, I'd better get going now, if that's all right.'

As Helen led me out and shut the door, I couldn't help feeling that I'd left part of myself behind in that strangely chilling room. I could sense the darkness, the silence. The dull black shine of the toy animals' eyes. I could feel the air, empty and still. And although it was too dark to see anything, I could still see those pictures of Anna. Her face, her eyes, her years, her life . . .

And, just for a moment, I thought I could hear her crying.

In the hallway at the bottom of the stairs, I surprised myself by turning to Helen and saying, 'You're more than welcome to come with me to Anna's flat . . . if you'd like to, that is.'

She hesitated for a moment, glancing instinctively at the door to the front room, as if she couldn't make any decision without asking her husband first. 'Well, yes . . .' she said, 'I think I *would* like to . . . I haven't been there since Anna disappeared. I'll just have to check with Graham –'

'Why don't you just go and get ready, get your coat and whatever else you need? I'll let Graham know that you're coming with me.'

'Well . . . he'd probably prefer it –'

'Go *on*,' I said, giving her a friendly nudge. 'Live dangerously for once.'

She smiled anxiously at me, still not sure about it, but I was blocking her way to the front room now, and she didn't want to offend me by pushing past, so in the end she didn't have a choice.

'I'll just be a moment, then,' she said, shuffling back up the stairs, where I assumed she kept her coat.

I waited until she'd gone, then I opened the door and went into the front room. The TV was still on, and Graham Gerrish was still slumped in his armchair in front of it, with the remote control still glued to his hand and his eyes still glued to the screen.

'Do you want to turn that off for a minute?' I said to him.

He looked at me with studied contempt. 'I'm sorry?'

'The TV . . . turn it off.'

'I don't see why –'

'I know what you do in your daughter's bedroom,' I said bluntly. 'I know that you sit up there watching porn on your laptop.'

I was half-expecting him to start ranting and raving at me then – how *dare* you, that's dis*gusting* . . . that kind of thing. But he didn't say anything at all, he just sat there, perfectly still, staring dumbly at me. And I knew then that I'd guessed right about the laptop.

'Look,' I sighed, 'I really don't care what you do, but I

57

imagine your wife wouldn't be too pleased if she knew what you get up to. So unless you want me to tell her, I suggest you turn off the TV and just listen to me for a minute, OK?'

He nodded, and turned off the TV.

'Right,' I said, sitting down. 'So tell me . . . what's the matter with you?'

He frowned. 'What do you mean?'

'Your daughter's missing, Mr Gerrish. Now I don't know if *you* love her or not, but your wife obviously does, and although this whole thing is totally fucking her up, she's still doing everything she possibly can to find Anna. But you . . .? All you seem to be doing is acting like a fucking arsehole and treating your wife like she's a piece of shit. *That's* what I mean.'

'I love Anna very much, Mr Craine,' he said matter of factly. 'I always have, and I always will. She means everything to me. She's my little girl.'

'So what's your problem? What have you got against me trying to find her? Is it the money?'

'Of course it's not the *money*,' he said, disgusted that I'd even consider such an idea.

'So what is it then?'

He closed his mouth tightly for a moment and made a strange little grinding motion with his teeth. Then, as if he'd finally made a decision to tell me the truth, he raised his eyes and looked at me. 'It's just . . . well, it's just . . .' He sighed. 'I don't want Helen getting her hopes up, that's all. I don't think it's good for her, you know . . . the way she is. It'll just make things all that much harder for her in the end.'

'Why do you think that?'

'Well, you see it all the time on the television, don't you? On the news. These girls . . . the ones who go missing . . . it always ends up badly, doesn't it?'

'On the news it does, yes,' I said. 'But that's only because if it ends up badly it *is* news. There are thousands who go missing who don't end up on the news, simply because nothing happens to them.'

He looked at me. 'So you think Anna might be all right?'

'I've really got no idea, Mr Gerrish. But what harm can it do for me to try and find out? Even if it does end up badly – and I'm not saying that it won't – Helen's not going to feel any worse just because her hopes have been raised, is she? And, in the meantime, she might just feel a little bit better.'

'Well,' Graham said thoughtfully, 'I suppose if you look at it like that –'

He broke off suddenly as Helen came into the room.

'Is everything all right?' she asked, instinctively aware of the change in her husband's demeanour.

'Everything's fine,' I said, standing up. 'We were just having a little chat.' I looked at her. 'Are you ready to go?'

She glanced at her husband. He tried smiling at her, but he obviously wasn't used to it, and all he really achieved was a strained look of constipated embarrassment.

'All right?' I said to Helen.

She nodded, frowning briefly to herself, and then we left.

5

Once we were out of the house and driving back towards town, Helen Gerrish gradually began to relax a little. And I soon realised that she was the kind of person who talks a lot when they're relaxed. In fact, as we approached the outskirts of Hey, passing through the superstore world of Sainsbury's, B & Q, Homebase, and Comet, I realised that she hadn't stopped talking for the last five minutes. And, of course, the only thing she wanted to talk about was Anna: Anna was this, Anna was that, Anna did this, Anna did that . . . it was as if she'd been waiting a long time to let it all out, and now that she'd started she just couldn't stop.

I was quite content to let her do all the talking. For one thing, it saved me the bother of having to say anything. And for another . . . well, I wasn't really listening to her anyway. I was too busy thinking about her husband instead. Graham Gerrish: a man whose seventeen-year-old daughter had slept in a room that belonged in the mind of a child abuser; a man who'd designed and decorated this room himself and used it now for viewing pornography; a man who professed to love his daughter, yet scorned his wife's efforts and desire to find her.

Yes, he was definitely a man worth thinking about.

It took another twenty minutes or so to get to Anna's

flat. It was in an area of town called Quayside, just south of the river. Quayside is the kind of place that's quiet during the day but comes to life at night, especially at the weekends. It used to be a working dock, but most of the old warehouses and boatyard buildings are now nightclubs – the Hippodrome, Tiffany's, the Quay Club. The surrounding streets are dotted with pubs, restaurants, and fast-food places, a lot of which have opened quite recently, and most of these newer establishments have a relatively safe reputation. But there are still one or two places around where the entertainment on offer is just as seedy as it was before all the bright young things arrived, and The Wyvern, the pub where Anna worked, was one of those places.

It was still raining as I pulled into the car park of a block of flats at the far end of Quayside, and as we got out of the car and crossed over to the flats, I could see the lights of the neighbouring nightclubs flickering brightly in the rain. It was still too early for the clubs to be open, but even now I could feel the promise of the night to come in the air: the noise, the heat, the dancing, the drinking . . . the fighting, the fucking . . . the promise of love and despair . . .

It was all there.

'. . . but, of course,' Helen Gerrish was saying, 'even though we were against her moving out in the first place, we still helped her out with the deposit.'

We'd reached the entrance to the flats now, and Helen, I guessed, was telling me about Anna's rent, or how she managed to afford it . . . or something like that.

I looked at her and smiled.

She opened the front door and I followed her up two

flights of steps to the second floor, then along a corridor to Anna's flat. As Helen put the key in the lock, I could tell that she was beginning to get anxious again. She'd stopped talking, and her face had become pinched and tense.

'Are you sure you want to do this?' I asked her. 'You can wait outside if you like. I won't be long.'

'No . . .' she said, pausing for just a moment. 'No, I'm all right, thank you.'

She opened the door and we went through into a darkened room. Helen turned on the lights, and I stood there and looked around. It was a fairly small place – sitting room, kitchen, bathroom, bedroom – but it wasn't excessively cramped. And while it wasn't spotlessly neat, it wasn't overly messy either. I could smell stale cigarette smoke, and there were several overflowing ashtrays dotted around the room. The second-hand furnishings had clearly come with the flat, and although the overall state of the place left a lot to be desired, I'd seen a lot worse in my time. All in all, it was just a typical low-rent living space, ideally suited for a young woman desperate to leave home.

As I started wandering around the sitting room, looking at this and that, Helen went over and sat down on a cheap settee.

'What are you looking for?' she asked me.

'Anything, really,' I said, scanning a row of shelves. 'Something that shouldn't be here, something that should be here but isn't . . .'

'The police have already searched here, you know.'

I nodded. 'When was that?'

'The day after I reported her missing. DCI Bishop told

me that they didn't find anything suspicious.'

'Do you know if he thinks she came back here that night?'

'He said it was impossible to tell. No one *saw* her coming back, but it would have been late . . . and, besides, the kind of people who live around here . . .'

I looked at her.

She shrugged. 'Well, they don't like to get involved, do they?'

I stood in the middle of the room and took a final look round, but I got the feeling that there was nothing here to tell me anything. It was a room that could have belonged to anyone, as bland and anonymous as a hotel room. No personal touches, no ornaments, no pictures, no books. It was just a place to watch TV.

I went into the kitchen, but there was nothing useful in there either. The fridge had been cleared out, the sink was empty. A small cupboard held a few cans of vegetables and a packet of crackers, and there was a drawer full of the usual kitchen stuff – cutlery, clingfilm, aluminium foil – but that was about it.

'Did the police clear out the fridge?' I asked Helen as I went back into the sitting room.

She shook her head. 'I'm sorry, I don't know.'

'Are you all right there?' I said.

She was perched on the edge of the settee, all hunched up, her hands held tightly together in her lap.

'Yes . . . yes, I'm all right, thank you. Just . . . well, you know . . . you can't help thinking about things, can you?'

'No,' I said. 'No, you can't . . .'

She looked at me for a moment, her eyes glazed and haunted.

I said, 'I'll just go and have a quick look in the bedroom and bathroom, and then we'll get going, OK?'

She nodded.

I went into Anna's bedroom and turned on the light. The smell of cigarette smoke was stronger in here, and the room was a lot messier than the sitting room – piles of clothes all over the place, the bed unmade, dirty cups and plates on the floor. I went over and took a closer look at the bed. I wasn't sure what I was looking for, but it didn't take me long to realise that – whatever it was – I wasn't going to find it in an unmade bed. It was impossible to tell when it had last been slept in, and even if there were any tell-tale signs that Anna had been sleeping with someone – which, as far I could tell, there weren't – that still wouldn't tell me anything.

I moved away from the bed and started searching through a chest of drawers that was set against the wall. It had six drawers; two smaller ones at the top, the rest full-size. The two at the top were underwear drawers, the next one down was T-shirts and tops, the one under that was jeans and trousers, and the next-to-last drawer contained skirts. It all seemed quite ordinary, the sort of clothing you'd expect a young woman without much money to own. Nothing too stylish or expensive, most of it quite practical and plain . . . the kind of clothes you'd buy at Primark or Tesco or TK Maxx.

In the bottom drawer though . . . well, the clothing in the bottom drawer wasn't quite so ordinary. It wasn't that it was any more fashionable or expensive than the rest of

Anna's clothes, it was just that it was totally different in style. These clothes could never be described as practical and plain; in fact, if anything, they were the opposite. Incredibly short skirts, fishnet stockings, studded leather belts. Tiny strips of material with zips on the front, which I guessed were some kind of top. Leather trousers, ripped denim jeans that were more rip than jean, a little white shirt and school tie . . .

It was possible, of course, that there was a perfectly innocent explanation for all this – maybe Anna had been doing some glamour modelling, or maybe this was the kind of stuff she wore on hen nights, or maybe she just liked dressing up a bit outrageously when she went out . . .

Or maybe it was just me? Maybe these clothes weren't outrageous at all, and I was just jumping to the conclusions of an out-of-touch, out-of-style, out-of-date forty-year-old man.

I was crouched down on the floor, staring into this drawer full of confusion, trying to work out what, if anything, it meant, when I heard a quiet shuffle in the doorway behind me, followed almost immediately by Helen Gerrish's frail little voice.

'Have you found anything yet?'

I quickly closed the drawer and stood up. 'No . . . no, nothing yet, I'm afraid . . .'

'Is there anything I can do to help you?'

Yeah, I thought, *don't ever creep up on me again.*

'I don't think so,' I said, glancing around the room. 'I'm just about done in here, anyway.' Which I wasn't, but I didn't want to keep poking around in Anna's things with her mother looking over my shoulder, and it didn't seem quite right to ask Helen to leave me alone either. So, noticing a few items of jewellery beside a little box on the bedside table, I said to Helen, 'Actually, you could have a quick look through Anna's jewellery for me while I check the bathroom . . . if you don't mind.'

'Her jewellery?'

'Over there,' I said, indicating the bedside table. 'Just see if there's anything missing . . .'

'But I don't know –'

'It's all right, just have a look. You might remember something.' I smiled at her. 'OK?'

'Well, if you think it might help.'

I watched her as she moved hesitantly over to the bedside table, sat down on the edge of the bed, and started picking reluctantly at the pieces of jewellery. She handled the necklaces and bracelets as if she could hardly bear to touch them, and the look on her face – a pained and sickened expression – was a look that verged on disgust. It was like watching someone retrieving their lost contact lenses from a steaming pile of dog shit.

I stood there watching her for a moment or two, briefly transfixed by her oddness, then – with a baffled shake of my head – I left the room and went into the bathroom.

There wasn't a lot to look at in there – toilet, bath, sink, cupboard. There was a toothbrush and toothpaste in a glass on the sink, and in a cupboard over the sink there were several more items which I would have expected Anna to take with her if she'd been planning to go away – Tampax, talcum powder, make-up remover, nail files . . . stuff like that. There was a fair amount of over-the-counter medication in there too – paracetamol, Gaviscon, Benylin, Night Nurse. In fact, the cupboard was so packed full that I doubted if anything had been removed from it. Which, again, suggested that maybe Anna hadn't just packed a suitcase and left.

The cupboard wasn't all that sturdy, and as I closed the door and pushed it shut I heard a load of stuff inside falling over. I thought about just leaving it, but that didn't seem right, so I carefully inched open the door again . . . and half a dozen bottles and tubs fell out, scattering pills and God-knows-what all over the floor.

'Shit,' I muttered.

Helen called out from the bedroom. 'Is everything all right in there?'

'Yeah,' I called back. 'I just dropped something, that's all. Nothing to worry about.'

It was quite a poky little bathroom, with not much room for manoeuvring, and as I kneeled down on the floor to start clearing up the mess, my foot bashed into the bath panel and knocked it loose.

'Fucking *hell*,' I whispered, turning round to inspect the damage.

Nothing was broken. The plastic panel had just come away, as if it hadn't been fixed on properly in the first place. And when I looked closer, pushing the loose panel back and peering into the space under the bath, I realised that the panel was *supposed* to be loose, because Anna had been using the space behind it as a hiding place. And what she'd been hiding in there, and what was still in there now, was heroin. Four wraps of heroin, a syringe, a box of needles, a packet of alcohol swabs, and a spoon.

And that changed things. It changed Anna's life and the world she inhabited. It made her more vulnerable, more desperate, more liable to risk. It made her more likely to associate with the kind of people who might want to hurt her. And if she *was* an addict, which was by no means definite, as it wasn't *impossible* that she just used the stuff now and then . . . but if she *was* an addict, she'd never have willingly gone away and left all her gear behind.

And that changed the way I was thinking.

The way I was thinking now was that although Helen Gerrish's reasons for worrying about her daughter were wrong, it was beginning to look like she was probably right to be worried.

When I went back into the bedroom, Helen was still perched on the edge of the bed, but she'd given up on the jewellery now and was just sitting there staring at nothing.

'Are you all right?' I asked quietly.

She turned slowly and looked at me. 'Yes . . . yes, I'm fine, thank you.'

'Any luck with the jewellery?'

She shook her head. 'No, I'm sorry . . . the only thing of Anna's that I'm familiar with is a necklace she wore all the time, and that's not here.'

'What kind of necklace? Can you describe it?'

'It's a silver half-moon on a silver chain . . . she's had it for years.' Helen looked thoughtful for a moment. 'You know, I don't even know where she got it from . . .'

'A silver half-moon?' I said.

Helen nodded. 'She should be wearing it in the photograph I gave you.'

I took the photo out of my pocket and saw that she was right. Sunlight was glinting from a small silver crescent on a necklace around Anna's neck.

'OK,' I said, 'well, that's something.'

'Are we finished here now?'

I nodded. 'If that's OK with you.'

'Yes,' she said quietly. 'Yes, I'd like to go home now.'

6

It was getting on for nine o'clock when we left the block of flats and walked back to my car. The rain was still falling, thin and cold in the night, and the streets of Quayside were beginning to stir with a few early clubbers and drinkers. As I opened the passenger door, and Helen got into the car, I could hear the shrieks and machine-gun heels of a gaggle of good-time girls making their way into the night. I wondered briefly what the next four or five hours would hold for them – love, sex, happiness . . . a drunken slap in the face?

I looked down at Helen. 'Would it be all right if I found a taxi to take you home?'

'A taxi? Yes . . . yes, of course . . .'

'It's just that The Wyvern's not far from here,' I explained. 'So I might as well pop in there while I'm down this way, you know . . . see if anyone knows anything.'

'Yes,' Helen repeated. 'Yes, of course.'

'Are you sure you don't mind?'

She shook her head.

I looked at her sitting there – forlorn and lost, old before her time – and I thought about changing my mind. But she wasn't paying me to look after her, was she? She wasn't paying me to comfort her soul. She was paying me to find her daughter.

70

And, besides, I needed to be on my own for a while.

I needed time to think.

And I really needed a drink.

There was a taxi rank just along from the nightclubs, and I managed to get Helen in the cab with the least unsavoury-looking driver. She didn't look all that happy as the taxi pulled away, and I couldn't help feeling a tiny pang of guilt, but it wasn't that hard to ignore it.

As I got back in my car and started heading down towards the old part of Quayside, trying to remember exactly where The Wyvern was, I noticed a silver-grey Renault about thirty metres behind me. It was too far back to see the driver, but I was pretty sure that I'd seen the same Renault parked in the street outside the block of flats.

It was probably nothing, but I made a note of the registration number anyway, and when I eventually found the street where The Wyvern was – a narrow little lane called Miller's Row – and I saw that the Renault was still behind me, I momentarily slowed down, as if I was turning into Miller's Row, then at the very last second I changed gear and kept going straight on. I didn't speed up at all, I just drove quite steadily away from Quayside, up into town, and then I took a series of right turns that gradually brought me back down to Quayside, and by the time I'd reached Miller's Row again, there was no sign of the Renault. I parked the car halfway along the street, turned off the engine, and waited.

Two cigarettes later, there was still no sign of the Renault.

I got out, locked the car, and headed up the street to The Wyvern.

When I was a teenager, The Wyvern was almost exclusively a bikers' pub. Unless you were a biker, or a drug dealer, or you wanted to get beaten up, you didn't go in there. Most of the clientele were members of a motorcycle gang called Satans Slaves (who, just like their more illustrious rivals, the Hells Angels, don't bother with apostrophes – a grammatical error that probably doesn't get pointed out to them all that often . . . at least, not to their faces anyway). There was always something going on at The Wyvern back then – fights, drug deals, stabbings, shootings – and over the years the pub has been raided countless times. It's been closed down, re-opened and refurbished under new management, closed down again, re-opened again . . . and gradually it's become a place that isn't quite so intimidating as it used to be. Most of the bikers have gone now – gone to wherever old bikers go – but there's still usually a few hanging around whenever you go in, a vestigial presence of scabbed leather, studs, patchouli oil, and spunk-stained jeans.

It's a reasonably spacious pub, and when I went in that night it was already fairly busy. Most of the clubbers drink in the newer pubs around Quayside, but some of the more adventurous are attracted by both the seedy atmosphere of The Wyvern and its plentiful supply of drugs, and I reckoned that about half of the people in there that night were regulars, and the other half were just looking to score. The regulars were a mixture of dealers and users, old punks and even older hippies, and an assortment of low-level criminals and out-and-out nasty bastards. I could see some of them checking me out as I crossed over to the bar, trying to work out who and what I was – potential customer, rival, threat, police – but dressed as I was in a plain black suit and dark shirt, and with my face still cut up and bruised from this morning, I was kind of hoping that I didn't look like anything much at all, just a slightly beaten up forty-year-old man in a slightly downtrodden plain black suit. The kind of man who's not even worth the bother of looking at.

There was a video jukebox at one end of the bar – currently playing something by Slipknot – and on the wall at the other end of the bar there was a widescreen TV showing an Ultimate Fighting bout. The customers were making a fair bit of noise too, so when I got to the bar and finally caught the attention of the barman – a psychobilly guy with greased black hair, lip rings, and a teardrop tattooed under his eye – I had to lean over the bar and shout to be heard.

'*Pint of Stella and a large Scotch!*'

'*What?*'

'*PINT OF STELLA AND A LARGE SCOTCH!*'

As he nodded his barman nod and set about getting my drinks, I turned round and casually scanned the room. I was still getting a few sly looks, but no one was paying me any serious attention. Everyone was just getting on with their business – drinking, laughing, talking, dealing . . .

'*That's £5.95, mate.*'

I turned back to the bar and gave Psycho Billy a £10 note. As he went over to the till to ring it up and get my change, I drank the Scotch in one go and washed it down with a mouthful of Stella.

'*There you go*,' Psycho Billy shouted, handing me my change.

I passed him my empty Scotch glass. '*Sorry*,' I yelled. '*Could you put another double in there?*'

He gave me a quick nasty look – *why the fuck didn't you ask for two in the first place?* – then took the glass, refilled it, and brought it back. This time, instead of handing me my change, he just dropped the coins on the bar.

'*Thanks*,' I shouted. '*Is Genna working tonight?*'

'*What?*'

Just then the Slipknot track finished and something a bit quieter came on.

'Genna Raven,' I repeated, not quite so loudly. 'Is she working tonight?'

Psycho Billy's face hardened. 'Who wants to know?'

'Me.'

'Yeah? And who are you?'

'John Craine.'

'What do you want with Genna?'

'Not much . . . just a quick chat.'

'Does she know you?'

'No.'

'Are you a reporter?'

'No.'

'Police?'

I sipped my beer. 'Do I look like police?'

'What do you want with Genna?'

'Look,' I sighed. 'Just tell her I'm here, will you? John

Craine. I'll be around for the next hour or so.'

And, with that, I left him standing there and walked away, looking for somewhere to sit.

About twenty minutes later, just after I'd been up to the bar for another Stella and Scotch, a dark-haired young woman wearing jeans and a white vest came out from a door behind the bar and started collecting empty glasses. I'd already been watching another barmaid for a while – who was also dressed in jeans and a white vest, which I guessed had to be The Wyvern's idea of a uniform, although it only seemed to apply to the female bar staff – but this first barmaid hadn't looked over at me once, so I didn't think she was Genna Raven. The second one though, the dark-haired girl, I was pretty sure that she was Genna, because she started glancing over at me as soon as she came through the door, so I assumed Psycho Billy had already had a word with her, telling her what I looked like and where I was sitting.

I kept my eye on her, waiting for her to look over at me again, and when she did, I just gave her a faint nod and what I hoped was a reassuring smile, and left it at that. If she wanted to talk to me, she knew where I was. And if she didn't . . .? Well, if she didn't, she didn't.

For the next fifteen minutes or so, I just sat there, with my head down, soaking up the heat of the noise, the heat of people, the heat of the whisky and beer . . . occasionally glancing up at the video jukebox or the TV screen, but not really seeing anything . . .

*

I never really see anything any more.

Only Stacy.

I don't *want* to keep thinking about her all the time.

I don't *want* to keep remembering that day . . .

But it never leaves me. It's always there . . . always. In my blood, my flesh, my bones, my heart . . .

It is me.

And now I'm running up the stairs as fast as I can, and my heart is pounding, and I'm shouting at the top of my voice, 'Stacy! STACY! STACY!'

There's still no reply.

At the top of the stairs, the bedroom door is closed . . . we never close the bedroom door . . . and now I can sense it, smell it . . . I can already feel it killing me. The whole world hums in my head as I open the door . . . and there she is – my essence, my love, my purity, my bride . . .

Ripped open on the bed.

Naked.

Butchered.

Bled white.

Dead.

'You wanted to see me?'

I looked up to see the dark-haired barmaid standing in front of me with a tray full of empty glasses in her hands.

'Genna Raven?' I said.

'Yeah . . .'

'I'm John Craine –'

'I know who you are. What do you want?'

76

Up close, she had a stunningly pretty face, and there was something about the almost-perfect symmetry of it that reminded me a little of Stacy. But whereas Stacy's complexion had been as perfect as her face, Genna's skin was terrible – scarred with pockmarks, peppered with blackheads and acne . . .

'I haven't got all fucking night,' Genna said. 'Are you going to tell me what you want or not?'

'Yeah, sorry,' I said, smiling at her. 'I wanted to talk to you about Anna Gerrish –'

'Nuh-uh,' she said firmly, shaking her head. 'No way.'

'Just a few questions, that's all.'

'Are you from the newspapers?'

I shook my head. 'I'm a private investigator.'

'Yeah, well . . . I'm already in enough shit for talking to the papers about Anna.'

'Why?'

She stared at me. 'You don't do that round here, do you? You don't talk to the press, you don't talk to the cops, no matter what. You just keep your fucking mouth shut.'

'So why did you talk to the press in the first place?'

She shrugged. 'I don't know . . . it just seemed . . .'

'Were you and Anna friends?'

'Fuck, no. Anna didn't have any friends . . .'

'So why –?'

'Look,' she said, glancing over her shoulder towards the bar. 'I can't talk now, OK? But I've got a cigarette break in fifteen minutes. I'll be in the smoking area out the back.'

Smoking area? I thought to myself as she turned away

and headed back to the bar. *There's a smoking area? Shit. Why don't they put up a fucking sign or something?*

I went up to the bar and got myself another beer, and after wandering around the pub for a while I eventually found the smoking area. It wasn't much, just a brick-walled yard at the back of the pub with a few plastic tables and chairs. The ashtrays on the tables were brimming with rainwater and cigarette ends, and one end of the yard backed on to the toilets, so the whole place stank of piss and sodden cigarettes and smoke. And it was still raining too. But I suppose if you're stupid enough to smoke in the first place, you're not going to be too concerned about standing outside in the cold and rain in a brick-walled yard that smells of shit . . .

There were only three other people out there: a straggly-haired man in a combat jacket, a younger man who looked like Mark Kermode on steroids, and a teenage girl with street-worn skin. They were all standing together at the far end of the yard, and I guessed from their body language and a few overheard words that the girl was trying to buy drugs from the two men, but that she didn't have enough money, so she was trying to persuade them to let her pay tomorrow . . . and the two men in turn were trying to persuade her that all she had to do was take a quick walk down the street with them to their car, and she could pay them in kind right now. Her answer to that was, 'You must be fucking *joking* . . . I'm not *that* desperate, you hairy cunt.' And the straggly-haired man said something else to her, which I couldn't quite hear, and she punched him playfully on the arm, and they all started laughing . . .

Strangely enough, it felt all right.

It *wasn't* all right, of course . . . there was nothing *all right* about it. But it was nowhere near as shitty as it could have been, and despite everything – the cold and the rain and the underlying ugliness of it all – I actually felt pretty good. It was a relatively quiet place to be. It wasn't too hot or too crowded. And even the rain was beginning to ease off a little, fading to a thin misty drizzle, and I found that if I stood against the wall at the side of the yard, I barely noticed it at all. And that's where I was, sipping my beer and smoking a second cigarette, when the teenage girl walked past me with a satisfied grin on her face and her hands stuffed deep into her coat pockets, followed a few moments later by the two men. The pumped-up Mark Kermode look-alike carried on past me, following the girl back into the bar, but the straggly-haired man stopped beside me.

'You need anything?' he said.

I shook my head. 'No, I'm all right, thanks.'

'You sure?' He smiled, showing a gap in his front teeth. 'I got Es, H, crack, weed . . . whatever you want.'

'Have you got anything that'll take me back in time?' I heard myself say.

He frowned. 'You what?'

'It's all right,' I said, smiling. 'I was just –'

His eyes went cold and he stepped towards me. 'Are you taking the fucking piss?'

I didn't move or say anything, I just stared at him, and for a weird little moment I wondered what he'd do if I spat in his face. How far would he go? Would he just hit me?

Beat me up? Break a few bones? Stab me? Shoot me? Kill me?

'What are you fucking smiling at?' I heard him say.

And then another voice. 'Fitch? For fuck's sake, leave him alone . . .' And I looked round to see Genna Raven standing there, smoking her much-needed cigarette. The tone of her voice and the look on her face was that of a weary headmistress having to deal with a harmless bully for the third time in a week.

'Hey, Genna,' Fitch said, suddenly all smiles again. 'You know this guy?'

'Why don't you go and get yourself a drink, Fitch?' she suggested.

'You buying?' he grinned.

She stared at him.

He turned to me, still grinning, and said, 'I'll see you later, OK?'

And then he went back into the bar.

'Sorry about that,' Genna said. 'But he wouldn't have done anything anyway. He's all mouth. Most of them are.'

I smiled at her.

She dropped her cigarette to the ground and lit another. 'So . . . you're a private investigator?'

I reached into my pocket and passed her one of my business cards. She glanced briefly at it, then slipped it in her back pocket.

'Who are you working for?' she asked.

'I'm afraid I can't tell you that,' I said. 'You know, client confidentiality –'

'It's Anna's mum, isn't it?'

I smiled, but said nothing.

Genna puffed on her cigarette. 'Well, it's either her mum or her dad, and that dirty old bastard's not going to want anyone poking around in his business, so it's got to be her mum.'

I lit a cigarette. 'Do you know Anna's father then?'

'Not personally, no. But I know his type.'

'What do you mean?'

She hesitated. 'I'm not sure if I should be telling you this . . .'

'You don't have to if you don't want to,' I assured her. 'It's entirely up to you what you tell me. But if you think it might help me to find Anna . . .'

She sighed. 'I don't even know if it's the truth or not. For all I know she was just making it up . . .'

'Making what up?'

'This stuff about her old man . . . how he used to fuck her and everything, you know . . .'

'He abused her?'

'Yeah . . . it went on for fucking years, according to Anna. Started when she was just a little kid, and the dirty fucker carried on doing it until she was . . . well, I don't know, until she left home, I suppose.'

I took a long drink of beer. 'When did Anna tell you about this?'

She shook her head. 'I don't know, quite a while ago. It was after work one night. It was someone's birthday and we all stayed on for a few drinks and stuff . . . Anna didn't usually join in with that kind of thing, but I think she was pretty out of it that night. I found her crying her eyes out in the toilets . . . this would have been about two or three in the morning, and when I asked her what was the matter, she started pouring her fucking heart out to me about her bastard fucking father. She told me everything . . . and I mean *every*thing. Poor bitch.' Genna pulled on her cigarette and blew out a long stream of smoke. 'It's no wonder she was so fucked up.'

'How do you mean?'

'Well, her whole life, you know . . . everything. She was a total fucking mess.'

'How long had she been using heroin?'

Genna looked at me. 'You know about that?'

I nodded.

'Not all that long,' Genna said. 'A few years, maybe.'

'How much did she use?'

Genna shrugged. 'She was always trying to quit, so sometimes she got it right down to hardly anything, but then she'd get back on it again and start using more.'

'Do you know where she got it from?'

'Could be anyone. It's not hard to buy stuff round here.'

'What about money? I imagine it'd be hard to maintain a habit on just a barmaid's wages.'

'Fucking right.'

'So where did Anna get the extra money from?'

Genna shrugged. 'No idea . . .'

'Did she earn anything from modelling?'

Genna just laughed.

'How about prostitution then?' I said.

She stopped laughing. 'I wouldn't know anything about that . . .'

'About what?'

She shrugged.

'Come on, Genna,' I said gently. 'I just need to know, that's all.'

She looked at me. 'Anna wasn't a whore, OK? I mean, she didn't do it all the time or anything. She just . . . well, she just needed the money sometimes. A lot of them do it, you know . . .'

'Addicts?'

'Yeah . . . it's the only way they can get enough cash.'

I nodded. 'Would Anna have worked through an escort agency or anything?'

'Christ, no. She'd just . . . well, sometimes she might pick up someone in here, but most of the time I think she just worked the streets.'

'Would she do that after work?'

'Yeah . . .'

'Do you think that's where she was going the night she disappeared?'

'Probably. I mean, we all knew, you know . . . she'd finish work, get herself all tarted up in the toilets, probably shoot up at the same time, then she'd put on her coat and fuck off.'

The door to the smoking area swung open then, and Psycho Billy leaned through and called out, 'Fuck's sake, Genna, how much longer are you going to be?'

'Yeah, all right,' she called back. 'I'm just coming.' As Billy went back inside, she dropped her cigarette on the ground and said to me, 'I've got to go.'

'Did you see anyone following Anna that night?' I asked her.

'No.'

'Did she have a boyfriend?'

'I don't think so.'

'Pimp?'

Genna shook her head. 'Anna didn't have anybody. She *knew* plenty of people – work colleagues, customers, dealers – and it wasn't as if she didn't get on with them, or that they didn't like her . . . I mean, she wasn't lonely or anti-social or anything. She was just . . . I don't know . . .'

'Solitary?' I suggested.

Genna nodded. 'Yeah . . . it was like she lived in her own little world, her own little bubble . . . do you know what I mean? You could *be* with her, talk to her, spend a night working with her, and it'd all seem fine . . . but then afterwards, later on, there'd just be this empty space in your head where your memories of her should be.' Genna looked at me. 'Does that make any sense?'

'Yeah,' I said slowly. 'Yeah, it does.'

She sniffed and sighed. 'Look, I really have to go –'

'All right,' I said. 'And thanks, you know . . . thanks for taking the time to talk to me. I really appreciate it.'

'OK,' she said hurriedly, turning to go.

'Did you tell any of this to the police?' I asked her.

She paused. 'No.'

'Why not?'

'They never asked me anything.'

'Right . . . well, thanks again, Genna. And if you think of anything else, my number's on the card I gave you – office and mobile. Call me any time.'

'Yeah . . .'

'And good luck with it,' I said.

'With what?'

'Staying clean.'

She looked at me for a moment, instinctively rubbing at the faded old needle tracks on her arm, and then, without another word, she turned round and left.

I didn't stay there much longer. Another quick drink and a cigarette while I mulled over what Genna had told me, and then I was on my way. The rain had stopped altogether now, and although the night was still cold, the air felt fresh and clear. As I headed back down the street, I could hear the heavy bass thump of music in the distance – *doomp-doomp, doomp-doomp, doomp-doomp, doomp-doomp* – and I guessed the nightclubs were beginning to come alive.

I looked at my watch. It was 10.45.

Later than I'd thought.

And now that I was out in the fresh air, I was also beginning to realise that I was a little bit drunker than I'd thought. I started thinking about a taxi then. I knew it was the sensible thing to do, but it would mean leaving my car here overnight, and that would mean having to come back and get it in the morning. But if I *didn't* get a taxi, if I drove home in this condition and got stopped by the police . . .

That's what I was thinking about, not really paying attention to anything else, when three things happened almost at once. The first thing was, I spotted the silver-grey Renault parked halfway down the street, and although there was undoubtedly a gap of about half a second or so between seeing it and *realising* that I'd seen it, I really don't think that half-second delay made any difference. The second thing was, as I paused to think about the Renault, a voice called out to me from the shadows of an alley on my left.

'Got a light, mate?'

And the third thing was, as I turned instinctively to the sound of the voice, a heavily-ringed fist hammered into the side of my head.

After that, it's all a bit vague. I half-remember staggering back against a brick wall, almost knocked out by the blow, and then I think someone hit me again, this time low in the belly, and as I doubled over in pain, someone else grabbed me by the arm and kind of half-swung, half-dragged me into the alley, and then I think I must have lost my balance and fallen over – or maybe they hit me again – because the next thing I knew, I was lying on the ground getting the shit kicked out of me.

It was too dark, and it happened too quickly, for me to get a look at them, and I didn't get to hear their voices either, because they never said a word. They just piled into me – kicking, punching, stomping . . . all in furious silence, and all I could do was lie there and take it. After a while my body didn't seem to belong to me any more. It was just a thing, a lump of meat, and whatever was happening to it was happening a long way away.

I don't know how long the beating lasted – probably no more than thirty seconds or so – and I have no recollection whatsoever of the kick to the head that finally knocked me out . . . all I know is that some time later I woke up in the alley, slumped against the wall, covered in blood and hurting like hell.

I was cold and wet.

It was raining again.

I checked all my pockets, but nothing was missing. Wallet, phone, keys, money . . . it was all still there. As I took a deep breath, sucking down the ice-cold air, I felt something bubbling in the back of my throat.

I coughed, bringing up blood.

It hurt.

I spat it out.

'Fuck,' I said.

Then I leaned over and threw up.

7

I drove home via the back roads, keeping to a steady 40 mph all the way, and somehow I managed to get back without crashing the car or getting stopped by the police. Lights were showing in the windows of Bridget's flat, and her boyfriend's car was parked outside the house. And when I went inside, I could hear the sound of soft music playing upstairs.

I let myself into my flat, went into the front room, and poured myself a glass of whisky. I drank half of it, topped it up, then lit a cigarette and went into the bathroom. When I looked at myself in the mirror, I was surprised to see that my face wasn't too badly mashed up. There was an ugly red swelling on the side of my head where the first punch had landed, a deep gash above my left eye, and a nasty-looking cut on the bridge of my nose. But apart from that, and a split bottom lip, it was nowhere near as bad as it could have been.

I drank more whisky and leaned in closer to the mirror, my attention drawn to a very faint indentation in the swollen red skin on the side of my face. When I looked even closer, I could just make out the outline of a ring-sized skull embedded in the broken skin. For some reason, I found myself smiling for a moment . . . but it didn't last long. Smiling hurt too much.

I turned to one side and cautiously examined the back of my head. It didn't feel so good – bruised, swollen, painful to the touch – and when I took my hand away it was thick with blood. The rest of my body felt pretty bad too – my belly, sides, shoulders, legs . . . everything ached like hell. I opened the cupboard over the sink, found some painkillers, and swallowed them down with a mouthful of whisky. Then I turned on the shower, running it as hot as it would get, and as the steam built up, misting the mirror and opening my pores, I got undressed and looked down at my beaten-up body. It was a mess – bruised all over, swollen and discoloured, the skin cut open and red-raw in places – but, again, there didn't seem to be any serious injuries.

I finished my cigarette, dropped it in the toilet, and got into the shower.

I stood there for a long time, ignoring the pain as the hot water rinsed all the blood and dirt from my skin, then I turned the shower to cold for as long as I could bear, which wasn't long, then I got out and carefully dried myself, put on my ratty old dressing gown, went back into the front room and sank down into the armchair beneath the high window.

Another glass of whisky, another cigarette . . .

I looked at the clock.

It was just gone midnight.

Rain-mottled street light filtered in through the window, lifting the darkness just enough to show me the shapes of things. Shelves, furniture, walls. Things. I glanced up at the clock again, watching the second hand sketch its slow, blind circle . . .

A moment in time – gone.

And another.

And another.

And another . . .

The seconds passed, taking too much away.

Taking nothing.

I was tired. Drunk. My head was throbbing. I wanted to close my eyes and not open them again until everything was all right. But I knew that nothing was ever going to be all right.

I didn't want to think about anything – Anna Gerrish, her mother, her father . . . Genna Raven, the silver-grey Renault, the faceless men who'd beaten me up. I didn't *want* to wonder who they were or why they'd attacked me. But what else did I have to do?

Just as I was starting to think about it though, muffled sex sounds began lumping down through the ceiling. Rhythmic creaks, *oomfs* and moans . . . the sounds of coupling bodies.

Bridget and Dave.

I turned on the television, cranked up the volume, and searched through the channels until I found something I didn't mind too much. It was an old film, a Western – either *Rio Bravo* or *El Dorado*. I can never remember which is which. This was the one with John Wayne, Dean Martin, and Ricky Nelson . . . not that it really mattered. I set the volume loud enough to cover the noise from upstairs, filled my glass with whisky, and drank myself to sleep.

8

At some point during the night I must have got up out of the armchair, turned off the television, and got into bed. I have no recollection of doing it, but when I woke up in the morning, the television wasn't turned on any more, and I was definitely in my bed, and – as far as I knew – no one else had been in my flat. So it must have been me.

It was still quite early, not quite seven o'clock, and the grey light of day was only just beginning to creep through the windows. The rain had stopped, but the air was damp and cold. A blustery autumn wind was rattling the glass in the kitchen window.

My body had stiffened up during the night, and it took me a while to get out of bed and start getting ready for the day, but after I'd been through the usual routine – bathroom, coffee, painkillers, cigarette, toast, eggs, coffee, cigarette, bathroom – well, I didn't actually feel any better, but I certainly didn't feel any worse.

For the next half-hour or so, I busied myself doing not very much, then at eight o'clock I called Ada at home.

'What?' she answered bluntly.

'And a very good morning to you, too,' I said.

'What's good about it? And why are you calling me so early?'

'I just wanted to let you know that I won't be coming in this morning, that's all. Is it OK if I leave everything to you?'

'You *always* leave everything to me.'

'Yeah, I know. I just meant –'

'I know what you meant, John,' she said gently. 'Of *course* it's all right. Where are you going to be if I need to get in touch?'

'I've got a meeting with Bishop at 11.30, and I want to try and see Cal before I go.'

'Bishop called you then?'

'Yeah.'

'He's a nasty fucker, isn't he?'

'Yep.'

I heard her lighting a cigarette. 'So how did it go last night? Did you find anything at Anna's flat?'

I gave Ada a brief rundown of what I'd found out about Anna – the heroin, the prostitution, the possibility that her father might have abused her – but I didn't mention anything about the Renault or the beating.

'So,' Ada said when I'd finished. 'What do you think it all means?'

'I don't know,' I admitted. 'Maybe it doesn't mean anything.'

'Apart from the fact that her life was a fucking mess.'

'Yeah, I suppose . . .'

'Why are you talking like that?'

'Like what?'

'All lispy and puffy.'

'Puffy?'

'You said *thuppothe*. It sounds like you've got a mouth full of cotton wool.'

I ran my tongue over my split lip. 'Uh, yeah . . . it's just a . . . it's nothing. Just a cut lip. I'll tell you about it later on.'

'Ooh,' she mocked. 'I can't wait.'

'Yeah . . . well, I'll probably get back to the office some time this afternoon, OK?'

'All right.'

At about half past eight, just as I was about to leave, I heard the sound of raised voices upstairs. Bridget and Dave, arguing. I couldn't make out most of the words, but I could hear the tone of the emotions: anger, frustration, placation, pleas – *You don't understand . . . I do . . . No, you don't . . .*

After a while, the argument subsided and a low sobbing began. Bridget, crying. A few minutes later, angry footsteps came thudding down the stairs, the front door opened, then slammed shut. Dave Dave, storming out.

I waited until I'd heard his car start up and pull away, with the inevitable screech of tyres, then I opened my door and went out into the hallway. I could still hear Bridget crying quietly, and just for a moment – a very brief moment – I found myself gazing up the stairs, wondering if maybe I should go up there and . . .

And what? I asked myself.

Comfort her?

Hold her?

Tell her she's better off without him?

I shook my head, locked my door, and left.

*

Cal Franks had at least four mobile phones, maybe more. There were his two 'regular' phones, which he used for straightforward, everyday calls. There was another which he'd fitted with some kind of signal booster, in case of poor reception. And then there was his 'special' phone, which – according to Cal – was totally anonymous, impossible to listen in to, and completely untraceable.

I didn't know what he used this special phone for, and I didn't want to know.

I'd already called him on one of his regular numbers before I left that morning to see if he was awake and available, and surprisingly – since he usually stayed up most of the night and only went to sleep when everyone else was getting up – he not only answered his phone and told me to come on over, he actually sounded relatively sane. Which, for Cal, was also quite surprising.

It was around nine o'clock when I pulled up outside his house. The rain was still holding off, and there was even a hint of autumn sunlight glowing palely behind the clouds. It was still pretty cold though, and the wind seemed to be picking up.

A wheelie bin had been blown over at the side of the road, and the bin bags inside had fallen out and split open on the pavement. Bits of rubbish had been picked up by the wind and were flapping around in the air – empty crisp packets, polythene bags, plastic food containers – like confetti at a wino's wedding.

As I got out of the car and locked it, I wondered why I was bothering. Not only did the car not have a side window, but it was a cheap old pile of shit anyway. I mean,

94

who the hell was going to steal a twelve-year-old Ford Fiesta that was held together with body filler and carrier bags?

I pulled up my coat collar and headed along the street towards Cal's house. It was a tall old place with black railings and steep concrete steps leading up to the door. The walls of the steps were cracked and topped with birdshit-encrusted slabs, and the front door was daubed with years of graffiti. The shiny black CCTV camera mounted on the wall over the door didn't seem to fit with the overall shabbiness of the place, but it was an incongruity that fitted Cal to a T.

Cal had lived here since he was seventeen, by which time he'd already been thrown out by his parents and excluded from every school he'd ever been to. It wasn't so much that he was a bad kid – although he could be kind of wild at times – nor did his alienation have anything to do with a lack of intelligence or understanding. If anything, Cal was just *too* smart for school. He got bored very easily, and when he got bored, he started looking for something exciting to do. And, for Cal, something exciting usually meant something illegal. Like credit-card fraud, or hacking, or phishing, or mobile phone scams . . .

He was very good at what he did.

He'd never been caught, never been arrested.

And he made a *lot* of money.

There were rumours that a few years after he'd moved into this house, which at the time had been a squat, he'd very quietly become the owner. I didn't know if that was true or not. And, if it was true, I didn't know if he'd bought it legally or not. But, again, I didn't care. I liked Cal. And Stacy had liked him too – she was the only member of her family who did – and that meant a lot to me. And it meant a lot to Cal too.

He was twenty-eight now, and he'd been helping me out with things since he was fourteen, and in all that time he'd never, ever, let me down. So, as far as I was concerned, Cal was all right.

I rang the doorbell and waited, pulling up my collar against the wind. The feeling of the house hadn't changed from its days as a squat – although I imagined that Cal now charged some kind of rent – and as I stood there on the doorstep, I could hear various kinds of music playing in different parts of the house: some rap stuff on the ground floor, a guitar band on the second floor, an operatic voice sailing out from an open window on the third floor. It sounded good.

The girl who opened the door was no more than four-and-a-half feet tall. She was dressed in a pale-blue vest with a tiger's head on the front, a very short threadbare skirt, black tights, and monkey boots. Plastic bangles rattled on her wrists, silver studs glimmered in her ear, and strings of coloured beads were wound around her neck, together with a knotted thong of black leather and a small plastic doll on a chain. The king-size cigarette hanging from her lip-glossed mouth was far too big for her.

'Yeah?' she said, looking at me with glassy eyes.

'I'm here to see Cal.'

She took the cigarette from her mouth and looked over my shoulder. 'Who are you?'

'John Craine. Cal's expecting me.'

She stared at me for a moment, then shrugged and opened the door. I stepped through into a corridor cluttered with bicycles, bin bags, and damp clothes drying on racks. A high staircase led upwards on the right, and at the far end of the corridor was a large communal kitchen. The house smelled of wet clothes, soup, and marijuana.

The girl took the cigarette from her mouth and scratched her arm. 'Cal's down the hall,' she said. 'The basement flat.'

'Yeah, thanks.'

She wandered off up the stairs, and I headed down the hallway. At the end, a narrow stairwell with steep spiral steps led down into the basement. More CCTV cameras were mounted on the wall, and I knew that Cal was probably watching me as I moved stiffly down the steps. My legs were really aching now, and my knees didn't seem to want to bend – a condition not especially conducive to walking down stairs – so it took me a while to reach the bottom. When I finally got there, the door to Cal's flat – a solid chunk of reinforced steel – was already open, and Cal was waiting for me in the doorway. He looked as good as he always looked: a handsomely wasted face, an uncombed mess of jet-black hair, rings in his ears, eyebrow studs, a touch of eyeliner. He was wearing a plain black T-shirt, skinny black jeans, and black leather boots with red laces.

'Shit, Uncle Johnny,' he said, grinning wildly at the state of my face. 'What the fuck have you been up to?'

By the time Cal had shown me inside and made me some coffee, and I'd sat down at one of his work desks and briefly told him what had happened to me outside The Wyvern, I'd already realised that he was wired out of his head on something. His eyes were huge, he was twitching like a lunatic and licking his lips all the time, and he couldn't keep still for more than a second.

'How long have you been up for?' I asked him as he passed me a mug of coffee.

'I don't know,' he shrugged. 'Day or two . . . I'm working on something . . .'

'What sort of something?'

He jerked his head, indicating a worktop across the room. It was strewn with all kinds of technical stuff: several laptops in various stages of disassembly, mobile phones, wires, cables, routers, tools . . . bits of equipment that I couldn't even put a name to. I looked back at Cal, waiting for him to tell me what it was he was working on, but he'd already turned away from me and was walking back across the room towards his cramped little kitchen area. I'd always wondered why the kitchen area was so poky when the rest of his flat was comparatively huge. It had originally been two basement flats, but Cal had converted it into one large living area, with a small bedroom and bathroom at the far end. It was a low-ceilinged room, painted white all over, and most of it was taken up with the tools of Cal's trade: computers, monitors, printers, scanners, work desks, phones, cameras, TVs, recording equipment. There was a small recreation area in one corner, with a black leather settee and a huge widescreen TV, but in all the time that Cal had lived here, I'd never seen him use it.

'So these guys who beat you up,' he said, taking a can of

Red Bull from the fridge. 'Are they connected with something you're working on?'

'Well, that's the thing –'

'You didn't see their faces?'

'I didn't see anything. I'm not even certain that there were two of them.'

He popped the Red Bull and drank it down in one go. 'They didn't rob you?'

'No.'

'Made any enemies recently?'

I thought about Fitch, the straggly-haired dealer from The Wyvern, but Genna had said that he was all mouth, and I got the feeling that she was probably right. And then there was Preston Elliot . . . but somehow I couldn't see him going to all the trouble of following me around and lying in wait for me in an alley. It just wasn't his style.

'There was a car –' I started to say.

'Have you got a cigarette?' he interrupted.

I took out my packet. 'Listen, Cal,' I said, passing him a cigarette and lighting one for myself. 'When I went to The Wyvern last night –'

'You know the landlord there's a meth addict, don't you?'

'Really?'

'Apparently they cook it up in the kitchen –'

'Cal,' I said firmly.

He grinned at me. 'What?'

'Will you just shut up and fucking *listen* to me for a minute?'

He didn't stop grinning. 'Yeah, no trouble . . . go ahead, I'm all ears.'

'Right,' I sighed.

'All ears and no mouth.'

I glared at him.

He made a zipping motion over his mouth.

I waited a moment, staring into his endearingly lunatic eyes, and then I spoke slowly and calmly. 'Last night . . . before I was attacked . . . I think someone was following me in a silver-grey Renault.'

Cal said nothing, just raised his eyebrows.

'I thought I'd lost them,' I went on. 'But just before the first guy hit me, I saw the Renault parked down the street. Now, that doesn't *necessarily* mean that I was beaten up by whoever was following me in the Renault, but I'd say it's a pretty good bet. Wouldn't you?'

Cal just looked at me, his mouth clamped shut.

'You can talk now,' I sighed.

He smiled. 'Did you get the number?'

'Yep.'

'Shit. Why didn't you just say so in the first place?'

'I would have if you hadn't kept –'

'Interrupting you?'

I looked at him. 'Have you got a pen?'

'Just give me the number,' he said, grabbing the nearest laptop.

I gave it to him, and watched as his fingers skipped across the keyboard, his eyes fixed manically on the screen.

'How long is this going to take?' I asked, glancing at my watch.

'That's odd,' he said, frowning at the screen. 'Are you sure you gave me the right number?'

'Yeah.'

He nodded. 'You couldn't have misread it, or maybe just remembered it wrong?'

'I don't think so. Why, what's the matter?'

He tapped a few more keys, then shook his head. 'It's a blocked number. The database won't give me any details.'

'What does that mean?'

He carried on staring at the screen for a few moments, then he took a thoughtful drag on his cigarette. 'It means,' he said, blowing out smoke, 'well . . . it *could* mean that you're in a lot of trouble.'

'Why?'

He looked at me. 'A blocked registration number usually means the vehicle's registered with the military, the police, or secret services.'

'Secret services?'

'Yeah, you know, MI6, MI5, GCHQ . . .' He smiled at me. 'You haven't been fucking around with spooks, have you?'

I shook my head. 'Not as far as I know.'

'If it's a police vehicle,' Cal went on, turning back to the screen, 'I can probably work out a way to access the details. But if it's military or intelligence . . . well, that's a bit more tricky. More risky too.' He looked back at me, and I could tell that he was intrigued now, desperate to know more about the case. But despite his tendency to jabber away all the time, especially when he was speeding, Cal would never just come out and ask me what I was working on. He'd always wait for me to tell him. And if – for whatever reason – I didn't want to discuss the case with him, he'd simply accept my decision without question.

'Do you remember that local girl who went missing about a month ago?' I said to him.

He thought about it for a moment, then nodded. 'Yeah . . . Anne Mellish or something? She was a model –'

'Anna Gerrish.'

'That's it.'

'And she wasn't a model. She was just . . .' I paused for a moment, annoyed with myself for thinking of Anna as *just* anything – just a barmaid, just a junky, just a part-time whore. She was just a person. 'Well, anyway,' I went on. 'Anna's mother has hired me to look into her disappearance. That's what I was doing at The Wyvern last night. Anna was a barmaid there.'

Cal nodded. 'And what about the Renault and the guys who beat you up? What's their connection?'

'I don't know.'

'What's the situation with the police? Are they still looking for her . . . have they got any leads or anything?'

'I'll find out in an hour or so,' I said, glancing at my watch. 'I've got a meeting at 11.30 with the DCI in charge of the case.' I looked at Cal. 'Do you know Mick Bishop?'

He scowled. 'Yeah . . . I know him. He's a cunt.'

'Yeah.'

Cal frowned. 'Didn't he have something to do with the charges against your dad?'

I nodded. 'You could say that.'

Cal looked at me, waiting for me to go on. When I didn't, he took the hint and changed the subject. 'Well, anyway, I'll see what more I can do with the registration number if you want . . . it might take a while, though.'

'Yeah, thanks, Cal.'

'And if there's anything else I can do . . .'

I shook my head. 'Not just yet . . . I want to try and find out if there's anything more to all this first.'

'Yeah, OK,' Cal said, unable to keep the disappointment from his voice.

'But I'll let you know as soon as I need you,' I told him. 'All right?'

The smile he gave me then wasn't the grin of a street-wise hustler, it was the smile of the child he used to be. The smile of Stacy's little nephew.

'You know I really like working with you, Nunc,' he said almost shyly.

'Don't call me Nunc,' I said, smiling at him.

'How about just Nuncle?' he grinned.

'How about I kick your arse?'

He laughed.

I looked at my watch. 'I'd better go,' I said. 'Oh, I nearly forgot . . .' I took the damaged memory card out of my pocket and passed it to him. 'Can you see if you can do anything with this?'

'What happened to it?' he said, examining the card.

'It got hit with a hammer.'

He looked at me, his eyebrows raised.

I shook my head. 'You don't want to know.'

He glanced back at the card again. 'I'll see what I can do.'

'Don't spend too much time on it, it's not that important.'

'Whatever you say.'

I stood up and took out my wallet. 'What do I owe you?'

'For what?'

'The registration number, the card . . .'

He waved me away. 'Don't worry about it.'

'You sure?'

'Yeah, just . . . well, just remember what I said, all right? I like working with you. I miss it when you don't come round.'

I looked at him, trying to think of something to say, something that would tell him how much he meant to me . . . but in the end I just kind of nodded, and he nodded back, and that was about it. I think we both would have liked to have held each other then . . . but, for whatever reason, it just didn't happen.

We didn't speak for a while as Cal showed me out of the flat, and I could tell that he was beginning to come down from whatever it was he'd been taking. But after he'd waited patiently for me to hobble up the stairs, and we were heading along the hallway towards the front door, he suddenly seemed to perk up again.

'What did you think of Barbarella?' he asked me, grinning once again.

'Barbarella?'

'Yeah, the girl who answered the door . . . her name's Barbarella Barboni.' He looked at me. 'She used to be an acrobat . . . well, she still is I suppose. The circus sacked her.'

'*What?*'

'She was with that circus that came to Hey in the

summer. You know the one I mean? She did all the acrobat stuff, you know . . . tumbling, juggling, that human pyramid thing. She was really good, apparently.'

'So why did she get sacked?' I asked, slightly bemused.

He shrugged. 'I don't know . . . she's never really talked about it.'

I looked at Cal. 'Has this actually got anything to do with anything?'

He shook his head. 'No, I was just telling you, that's all.' He grinned again. 'She's very bendy.'

'I bet she is.'

'She's also a very fine pickpocket. So, you know, if you ever need a pocket picking . . .'

'I'll bear it in mind.'

We were at the front door now.

Cal said, 'I'll let you know if I find out any more about the Renault, and I'll get back to you about the memory card as soon as I can.'

'Thanks.'

He opened the door.

I said, 'Get some sleep, Cal. All right? I'll see you later.'

He nodded, and I left him standing there in the doorway.

As I headed back to my car, I heard him call out, 'See you later, Nunc.'

I was still smiling as I got into the car.

9

My father didn't have a particularly happy life. He joined the police force when he was sixteen, and despite a lifelong struggle with often debilitating depression, he rose steadily through the ranks until he finally made Detective Inspector in 1989. It was during his time as a Detective Constable with Hey CID that my father first met and befriended Leon Mercer, who was then a DC too. Another officer based at Hey at this time, and already gaining something of a reputation, was PC Mick Bishop. Leon and my father continued working together throughout the late seventies and early eighties, and even when they were both promoted to Detective Sergeant and transferred to different divisions, they still remained close friends. Bishop, meanwhile, was also beginning to rise through the ranks. Although some years younger than Leon and my father, he was the first of the three to reach Detective Inspector. Leon made the grade about twelve months later, and my father was finally promoted two years after that, at the age of forty-four.

Three years later, he took his own life.

It's a complicated story, and even now I don't know all the details, but there's no question that it all began with allegations and counter-allegations of police corruption.

My father was a good policeman. He didn't possess any

outstanding attributes – no stunning intellect or insight, no instinctive flashes of detective genius . . . in fact, if truth be told, in terms of the skills he had, he was no more than average at best. But he was methodical, committed, determined . . . and, above all, he *believed* in what he did. He truly believed that, as a police officer, it was his duty to keep and preserve the peace and to uphold fundamental human rights with fairness, integrity, impartiality, and diligence.

And that, to me, made him a good policeman.

But it also meant that he was unable to keep his mouth shut when his colleagues *didn't* act with fairness and integrity, and that, in effect, was the root of his undoing. It wasn't that he was a high-minded idealist, or in any way naive about the realities of police work. Far from it. He knew, and to a certain extent accepted, that police officers are no different to anyone else. They're just people, human beings, with the same flaws, the same desires, the same weaknesses as the rest of us. So, inevitably, there will always be police officers who abuse their power and use it to their own advantage. My father knew that. He also knew, as most of his colleagues did, that throughout his career, Mick Bishop was one such officer. Bishop bent the rules, he broke the rules. He broke the law. He hurt people, humiliated people, corrupted people. He acted with neither fairness nor integrity.

But he got results.

And although my father was aware of Bishop's criminality, he was never actually in a position to prove it until January 1992, when he received a video in the post. The video, captured by a hidden CCTV camera and sent anonymously, showed Bishop and two other men torturing a drug dealer in the bedroom of a house in Chelmsford. The dealer was tied to a chair, and Bishop and the other two took turns beating him with baseball bats and burning him with cigarettes until eventually he told them what they wanted to know. The final shot showed Bishop leaving the house carrying five kilos of cocaine in a black leather holdall.

My father personally passed this video and the accompanying letter – which gave further details of the incident – to his immediate superior, DCI Frank Curtis.

Some days later, having heard nothing back from Curtis, he went to see him. To my father's utter disbelief, Curtis told him that there was no proof whatsoever that such an incident had ever occurred, that the video was a fake, that Bishop had been nowhere near Chelmsford at the alleged time and date, and that he had a cast-iron alibi to prove it. There was no trace of the supposed drug dealer, and the address given in the letter didn't exist. Curtis then went on to accuse my father of making false statements about a fellow officer in a deliberate attempt to ruin his career.

My father, understandably, was dumbfounded.

Even more so when he was suspended from duties pending a full investigation.

Three weeks later, while still on suspension, he was summoned to a meeting with the Detective Chief Superintendent and asked to explain the presence in his station locker of two kilos of cocaine and £25,000 in cash. He was also asked if he had any comment to make about an alleged relationship he was having with an eighteen-year-old girl called Serina Mayo, who'd recently been a key witness for the prosecution in the high-profile trial of a serial paedophile.

According to Leon Mercer – from whom I gathered almost all of this information – my father was advised by his union representative to say nothing about these allegations, and that's what he did. Even when further evidence was produced – including photographs – which proved beyond doubt that he had indeed been having an intimate relationship with Serina Mayo, my father still refused to make any comment.

Two days later, while my mother was visiting her sister for the day, he locked himself in his office at home, drank most of a full bottle of whisky, and shot himself in the head.

In a suicide note addressed to my mother, he categorically denied the allegations of corruption, insisting that the cocaine and cash had been planted in his locker, and that he suspected DI Bishop and possibly DCI Curtis of colluding in a plot to discredit him. But he didn't deny that he'd been having an affair with Serina Mayo.

'I'm so sorry, Alice,' he wrote to my mother. 'I don't know how it happened or why. It just happened. It was, quite literally, an act of madness.'

My mother, of course, was devastated.

Five years later, she died of breast cancer.

The corruption charges against my father, and his allegations against DI Bishop, were never investigated.

It was 11.10 when I left my car (unlocked) in a small public car park at the back of the police station at Eastway. I followed a paved pathway round to the front of the building where smooth stone steps led me up to the main entrance doors. A thin grey drizzle had begun to fall, and the yellowing sky was dark and low. I paused on the steps, lit a cigarette, and stood there for a while watching the mid-week traffic as it coiled back and forth along the Eastway approach. Headlights flashed dully in the rain, horns beeped, exhaust smoke hazed in the cold damp air. Just in front of the steps was a low-fenced quadrant of town grass, and beyond that a broad pavement with wooden benches and raised stone flower beds. In summer, the stretch of grass attracts school kids and lunching workers who sit around with ice creams and Cokes watching the Eastway traffic as if there's nowhere else they'd rather be. But now, on this cold October day, the only sign of life was a tramp in a cheap plastic raincoat foraging in bins, and two street youths and a wet dog sitting on a bench in the rain.

I finished my cigarette, headed up the steps, and went through the main doors into a pale and empty reception area of Plexiglas, tile, and pinboards. A uniformed desk sergeant took my name and told me to take a seat. I sat down on a red metal chair that was bolted to the floor, expecting a longish wait, but two minutes later a podgy-faced young man in a thin white shirt came through the security doors and introduced himself to me as DC Wade. As he escorted me back through the security doors and along a grey-carpeted corridor, I could hear muffled sounds coming from behind half-closed doors – the quiet tapping of keyboards, computer beeps, muted voices. It all sounded surprisingly dull, more like a social-security office than a police station.

We took the lift to the third floor, down another grey corridor, and then DC Wade showed me into a room.

'Take a seat, Mr Craine,' he said. 'The DCI will be with you in a minute.'

He went out and shut the door behind him, leaving me alone in the room. I'd never been in a police station interview room before, but I'd seen enough cop shows on TV to recognise one when I saw one: off-white walls, plain table, two hard chairs, a double-decked tape-machine on a shelf. I draped my coat over the back of one of the chairs and sat down.

It was 11.29.

Twenty minutes later, the door swung open and DCI Bishop breezed in, talking the busy-man's talk as he came. 'Sorry to keep you waiting, John, but something important came up. You don't mind if I call you John, do you?' His hurried words stopped when he saw my battered face, and for a moment he just stood there looking at me. Then, after blowing out his cheeks, he gave me what can only be described as a shit-eating grin. 'Christ,' he said, sitting down opposite me. 'I hope we've got it on record that you looked like that *before* you came in.'

I didn't say anything, I just looked at him. He hadn't changed all that much since the last time I'd seen him. Same wiry black hair, same hard-set mouth, same cold dark eyes. He had a quarter-inch scar on his clean-shaven jaw, and in the dull light of the room his skin looked hard and white. He was dressed in a dark-blue blazer with silver buttons, a pale-blue shirt, and a burgundy tie pinned with a thin gold chain.

'Can I get you a coffee or anything?' he asked me.

'No,' I said. 'I'm fine, thanks.'

He grinned again. 'Ice pack? Painkillers?'

'No, thanks.'

He nodded. 'OK, well . . . I think I already mentioned that I don't have all that much time to spare, so if it's all right with you . . .'

He paused for a moment as I glanced at my watch, and the corners of his mouth tightened slightly. I looked at him, waiting for him to go on. He said nothing for a moment, just carried on staring at me, and then, after a time, he eased his chair back from the desk, crossed his legs, and casually cocked his head to one side.

'You used to work for Leon Mercer, didn't you?' he said.

'Yeah.'

He nodded. 'I know Leon, he was a good officer. We worked some big cases together over the years . . . how's he doing now? I heard his health's not so good.'

'He's doing OK.'

'Semi-retired, I hear.'

I nodded.

Bishop nodded back. 'So when did you start working for Mercer Associates?'

'Sixteen years ago.'

'Right . . . so that would have been . . .?'

'About a year after my wife was killed.'

He nodded again, trying his best to look sympathetic, but he had neither the face nor the heart for it. Which was fine with me. I just wanted this charade to be over – him asking me questions that he already knew the answers to, me having to answer them because I wanted something from him . . .

It was all just a nasty little game.

'It must have been a really hard time for you,' Bishop said. 'First your father, then your wife . . .'

'Yeah,' I said, staring into his eyes. 'It totally fucked me up.'

'Well, of course . . . it would.' He sniffed and cleared his throat. 'So . . . you left Mercer in '97 and set up your own business – is that right?'

'Yeah.'

'Why?'

'No particular reason. My mother died, I came into some money . . . I could afford to set up on my own.' I shrugged. 'It was something to do . . .'

'Do you enjoy it?'

I looked at him. 'What?'

'Owning your own company . . . being a private investigator – do you enjoy it?'

'Does it matter?'

He looked at me for a while, his head cocked slightly to one side, as if he was thinking about something . . . then he took a breath, leaned back in his chair, and sighed. 'I checked the case file this morning to see if there's been any progress on the investigation into your wife's murder,' he said. 'We *are* still looking for him, you know. We haven't given up.'

I looked back at him, holding his gaze . . . saying nothing, showing nothing.

'We'll find him eventually,' he said, his eyes never leaving mine. 'It's just a matter of time.'

'Right . . .' I said vaguely, 'well, that's good to know. But it's not what I'm here about.'

Bishop didn't say anything for a few moments, he just carried on staring at me, his dark eyes unreadable . . . and then, with an unnecessary sniff and a curt nod of his head, he pulled his chair back to the table, glanced at his watch, and got down to business. 'Right,' he said briskly, 'Anna Gerrish. I take it you've been talking to her mother?'

'I can't –'

'Yeah, yeah,' he said impatiently. 'There's no need to give me all that client confidentiality shit again. Let's just assume, hypo-fucking-thetically, that you're working for Helen Gerrish, all right? You haven't told me anything, you haven't breached her trust. OK?'

I nodded.

'Good. So what do you want from me?'

'Well, I know you can't give me any details about the case –'

'What details do you want?'

I looked at him, slightly taken aback.

He shook his head. 'There *is* no fucking case, John. That's all the detail you need to know. All that's happened to Anna Gerrish is she's met some bloke who's promised her the world and they've fucked off together somewhere in his customised Golf GTI. Give it a couple of months and she'll probably come crawling back home.'

'Are you sure?'

'Yeah, I'm sure. It happens all the time.' He shrugged one shoulder. 'All right, so I might be wrong about the specifics – maybe she just fucked off on her own, or with a girlfriend, or maybe she met an older man with a nice sensible Volvo or something – but it's all the same thing. We get at least two or three of these so-called missing persons every week – my daughter's gone missing, my son's disappeared, my husband, my wife . . . none of them ever come to anything. The trouble is, people simply can't accept that someone they've known for years, perhaps even *loved* for years, can suddenly just decide that they've had enough.' Bishop looked at me. 'That's all there is to it, John. Believe me. Anna Gerrish is safe and well somewhere. And there's no evidence whatsoever to suggest otherwise.'

'What about the report in the *Hey Gazette*?'

'What about it?'

'Well, if you're saying that this kind of thing happens all the time, how come the paper picked up on Anna's disappearance?'

'Because her mother kept nagging them, that's why. And because Anna was reasonably attractive.' Bishop shrugged. 'The press don't give a shit if there's anything *in* a story or not . . . as long as it sells, that's all they care about. And pretty girls sell.'

'But if Anna's safe and well somewhere, why hasn't she contacted her mother?'

'Who knows? Maybe she hates her, maybe she *wants* her to suffer . . .' Bishop shrugged again. 'Whatever the reason, it's not our concern. Anna's a grown woman. She can do what she wants. If she doesn't want anyone to know where she is, that's entirely up to her.'

'You searched her flat?'

Bishop sighed. 'Yes, we searched her flat.' He was beginning to talk to me as if I was an annoying child.

I said, 'There didn't seem to be anything missing. I mean, I got the impression that she hadn't packed any clothes or toiletries or anything.'

'How can you tell if there's anything missing without knowing what was there in the first place? And, besides . . . well, you were in her flat, you must have seen the kind of stuff she had in there. She's not going to bother coming back for any of that shit if she's been whisked off her feet by some knight in shining armour, is she?' Bishop looked at me, a hint of smugness showing in his face, then he glanced at his watch. 'Right,' he said, 'well, if that's all –'

'You know she used heroin, don't you?' I said.

He froze for a moment. 'What?'

'Anna . . . she used heroin.'

'How do you know that?'

I half-smiled at him. 'I'm an investigator. I get paid to find things out. It's what I do.'

Bishop didn't react to my flippancy, he just stared at me for a second or two, his face quite still, and then he said, 'Have you told her parents?'

'No.'

He nodded. 'They don't need to know.'

'OK,' I agreed. 'But surely it means –'

'It doesn't *mean* anything. She used heroin . . . so fucking what? Do you really think we didn't already know that?'

I stared at him. 'You knew?'

'Fuck, yes.'

'And I suppose you know –'

'That she worked the streets? Yeah, we're perfectly aware of that too.'

I shook my head in disbelief. 'And you *still* think that nothing's happened to her?'

'All right, look,' he said impatiently. 'Here's how it is – Anna Gerrish *wasn't* the nice young girl that her mother thinks she was, she *wasn't* an aspiring model, she wasn't anything. She was just another junky who sold her cunt to get high. OK? That's the reality. Girls like that disappear all the time. They meet a new dealer, a new pimp . . . or maybe they find a punter who thinks he can rescue them from a life of depravity . . . fucking whatever, you know?' Bishop looked at me. 'If we tried to find every girl like Anna who ever disappeared, we'd never have time to do anything else.'

'So . . . are you telling me that you're *not* actively looking for her?'

'I'm *telling* you what's what,' he said, his voice getting harder now. 'I'm *telling* you that the Gerrishes don't need to know the truth about their lovely little daughter, because all that's going to do is make things even worse for them, and what's the point of that? And I'm *telling* you that, if I were you, I wouldn't bother wasting my time, *and* everybody's else's, looking for someone who doesn't want to be found. That's all I'm telling you, John. So why don't you just find yourself something else to do for the next few days, then tell the Gerrishes that you've done your best and send them a bill.' He leaned back in his chair and smiled coldly at me. 'How does that sound?'

'It sounds,' I said, 'like you're warning me off.'

117

Bishop laughed. 'If I was warning you off, you'd know about it.'

'Yeah? What would you do? Get someone to beat me up in an alley?'

The smile stayed on his face, but I could tell it was a strain, and after a few moments he gave up the pretence, sniffed hard, and looked at his watch again. 'Right,' he said, getting to his feet. 'Well, I think we're about done here, don't you?' As he came round to the front of the desk, I stood up to meet him, but he'd had enough of me now, and he didn't even look at me as he crossed over to the door. I stayed where I was for a few moments – buttoning my jacket, brushing imaginary dust from my trousers – just to annoy him, and then I slowly sauntered over to the door.

Before opening it and ushering me out, Bishop handed me a business card. 'My mobile and office numbers,' he said, his voice oddly neutral. 'Let me know if you find anything. All right?'

As I nodded and put the card in my pocket, he gave me a final look, and just for a moment – a very brief and unguarded moment – I saw in his eyes an intensity of pain and sorrow that burned right down to his core, and as he opened the door and ushered me out, and a waiting DC Wade started to escort me out of the building, I couldn't help wondering if what I'd just seen was the truth at the heart of Mick Bishop, or just a fleeting reflection of my own broken life.

10

As I followed DC Wade along the corridor back to the lift, I was half thinking about Mick Bishop – the things he'd said, the things he hadn't said – and at the same time I was half looking out for anyone with a skull ring on their finger. I still wasn't totally convinced that Bishop had anything to do with me getting beaten up, but his reaction when I'd hinted at it, together with the fact that he hadn't asked me how I'd received the injuries to my face, had given me a lot to think about. But, even so, I wasn't really expecting to see the hand that formed the fist that had smashed into my head last night . . .

And I didn't.

What I did see, though, as the lift door opened and I stepped aside to let some people out, was a face I hadn't seen for a long time. His name was Cliff Duffy. He'd been a DC when my father had died, and he was still a DC now. Our eyes met as he passed me by, but we didn't openly acknowledge one another.

I kept my eye on him as I followed DC Wade into the lift, watching which way he went, and just as the lift doors were closing, I reached out and held them open, said 'Hold on a minute' to Wade, and before he could stop me I walked quickly along the corridor and caught up with Cliff

Duffy just as he was entering a room. He stopped and turned round as I touched his arm, and as I made a show of shaking his hand and smiling broadly at him, I whispered under my breath, 'Blue Boar, half an hour . . . it's important, OK?'

He didn't answer me, just carried on shaking my hand, but the almost imperceptible nod of his head told me that he'd heard me. I gave him a parting pat on the arm and went back to the lift, where DC Wade was waiting impatiently for me.

'Sorry,' I told him. 'Cliff's an old friend of my father's . . .'

Wade said nothing, just pressed the button for the ground floor.

About ten years ago, Cliff Duffy had got in touch with me about a problem he was having with his eighteen-year-old son. The problem, Cliff had explained to me, was that he'd been working on a small-time fraud case that had unexpectedly developed into a much bigger operation which involved several high-profile politicians, including the MP for Hey West, Meredith Chase, who at the time was a member of the Shadow Cabinet. Cliff's role in the operation was relatively minor, but he'd been part of a surveillance team that had managed to obtain a number of photographs showing Meredith Chase in a series of intimate situations with a seventeen-year-old boy. Unfortunately for Cliff, he'd made the mistake of taking some of these photographs home with him one night, and even more unfortunately, it just happened to be the night when his estranged son, Richey, had let himself into his parents' home in the early hours of the morning, looking for anything he could steal and sell in order to fund his drug habit. This wasn't the first time Richey had made such a visit, and although Cliff and his wife were devastated every time it happened, they'd learned to simply swallow their despair, keep quiet about it, and accept it. And they would have been quite happy to do the same this time if it wasn't for the fact that Richey, it seemed, had stolen the surveillance photographs of Meredith Chase.

'So,' Cliff had said to me, 'you can see the situation I'm in. Once Richey realises who the man in the photographs is, the first thing he's going to think of is blackmail. Or he might just sell the pictures to the tabloids if the price is right. Either way, my career would be over.'

He didn't say it, but I think Cliff knew that if the worst came to the worst, it wouldn't only be his career that was over, but his marriage too. The shame and embarrassment of their son's criminal lifestyle coming to light would have been too much for Mrs Duffy to bear, and although I'd never met her, I got the impression that she blamed Cliff for all their son's problems.

The reason Cliff had brought his problem to me was that, firstly, he knew me fairly well having worked with, and respected, my father over the years, and he believed that he could rely on me to be discreet. And secondly, his son Richey was always on the move – living in squats here and there, staying with friends, sometimes sleeping rough – and Cliff simply didn't have time to go looking for him because he was still involved in the Meredith Chase investigation. Also, while Cliff didn't actually admit it, he'd never been particularly good at detective work, which was why he'd remained a DC for most of his career.

So, anyway, I told Cliff that I'd see what I could do, and within a couple of days I'd traced Richey to a squat in North London, and after making sure that he hadn't made any copies of the photographs, I simply stole them back and returned them to Cliff.

He was so incredibly relieved and grateful that not only did he give me a very generous cash bonus, he also promised me, hand on heart, that if he could ever do anything for me, anything at all, all I had to do was ask. And although I think he probably regretted this offer when I asked him, there and then, if he could find out what had happened to the gun that my father had used to shoot himself, and if possible return it to me, he didn't renege on his promise. It took him a while, and I'm still not exactly sure where he got it from, or how, but he did.

To this day, Cliff has never asked me why I wanted the gun. And I wouldn't have known how to answer him if he had.

It was close to two o'clock when Cliff finally showed up at the Blue Boar, and by then most of the lunchtime trade had finished and the pub was beginning to empty out. It was a smallish place in a quiet side street in the Dutch Quarter, an old part of town that's known for its steep cobbled lanes and narrow houses.

I was sitting at a table near the far end of the bar when Cliff came in. I raised my hand to let him know where I was, and watched him as he made his way over. He was a beaten-down man, a man who'd long since given up caring about anything. He had a mournful face, with a down-turned mouth and sagging cheeks, and he walked with a slouching air of resignation. He looked pretty much like what he was: a just-about-functional drunk.

I had a large Scotch waiting for him on the table, and as soon as he'd shaken my hand and sat down, he picked up the glass, took a drink, put the glass back down, then immediately picked it up again and took another drink, this time finishing it off.

'You want another?' I asked him.

He nodded. 'Might as well.'

I went up to the bar and ordered another large Teacher's for Cliff and half a Stella for myself, then I took the drinks back to the table.

'Thanks,' Cliff said, taking the glass from me. 'Cheers . . .'

I touched glasses with his and took a drink of lager. 'So,' I said. 'How's it going, Cliff?'

He shrugged. 'Same as . . . you know.'

'How's your wife?'

'She left me last year.'

'Oh, right . . . sorry. I didn't know.'

He shrugged again and took another drink.

I said, 'And what about Richey? How's he doing now?'

'Fuck knows . . . I haven't seen him for two years. He could be dead for all I know.'

I didn't know what to say to that, so I just sipped my lager and said nothing.

Cliff looked at me, a sad smile bringing a touch of light to his face. 'It's all right, John,' he said kindly. 'You don't have to go through all this small-talk shit with me . . . neither of us really need it, do we?'

'I suppose not.'

He nodded. 'OK, so let me get some more drinks in and then you can tell me what you want.'

'No, you're all right,' I said, taking his empty glass from him. 'I'll get them.'

He started to protest, but his heart wasn't in it, and I could tell that he didn't have enough pride left to care about pride any more.

It didn't take long to tell Cliff what I was working on. He was a good listener, and he didn't need everything explaining to him. And, of course, he already knew who Anna Gerrish was. But in terms of any inside knowledge, that was about as far as it went.

'Sorry, John,' he told me. 'But I didn't have anything to do with the case. In fact, I didn't even hear about it until the *Gazette* ran the story.'

'Did Mick Bishop take charge of the investigation straight away?'

Cliff thought about that for a moment, his drunk-steady eyes roaming blindly around the room, and then eventually he said, 'I don't know . . . I mean, I suppose so, but . . .'

'But what?'

He looked at me. 'Is that what this is about? Mick Bishop?'

'I just want to know why he took the case, that's all.'

'Why shouldn't he?'

'Come *on*, Cliff . . . you know what I mean. He's a DCI,

for Christ's sake. He's Mick fucking Bishop. What the hell is he doing taking charge of a shitty little missing-persons case?'

Cliff shrugged. 'Well, maybe he only took it on after the press got hold of it. You know what he's like . . .'

'No, you see, that's the thing, Cliff,' I said, staring intently at him. 'I *don't* really know what he's like.'

Cliff stared back at me for a moment, digesting what I'd just said, and then suddenly he became quite animated – holding up his hands, vigorously shaking his head. 'No . . . no way,' he said, as firmly as his drunkenness would allow. 'Absolutely not . . . I'm sorry, but I'm not getting into that.'

'Into what?'

'Mick Bishop. No fucking way . . .'

'Look,' I said softly, trying to calm him down. 'I'm not asking you to grass him up or anything. I don't want to know any details of what he's done in the past, or what he gets up to now . . . I just want to know what kind of man he is.'

'What kind of *man* he is?' Cliff said with a bitter snort of laughter. 'I'll tell you what kind of man he is – he's the kind of man who can fuck up my already fucked-up career just like that . . .' Cliff tried to click his fingers, but failed. 'He's the kind of man,' he went on undaunted, 'who, if he knew I was in here talking to you about him, wouldn't think twice about squashing me into the ground. *That's* the kind of fucking man he is.'

'Yeah,' I said. 'But he's not *going* to know, is he?'

Cliff shook his head. 'I've got eighteen months left, John. Eighteen months, and then I'm out on a thirty-year pension. And I've already got a cushy little security job lined up.' He looked at me. 'I'm not risking that . . . I just can't. I'm sorry . . .'

'OK,' I said, smiling at him. 'I understand . . .'

'You know that I would if I could –'

'It's all right, Cliff,' I assured him. 'Honestly, it's not a problem.'

He nodded at me, then busied himself draining his drink for a few moments, and before he had a chance to tell me that he had to get back to the station, I asked him if he'd like another quick one before he went. He made a show of glancing at his watch, but that's all it was, and I was already on my feet with his glass in my hand when he looked back at me and slurred, 'All right, go on then. Just one more.'

It took another couple of rounds before Cliff forgot his reticence and started opening up to me about Bishop, and after he'd rambled on about the old days for a while, I gently brought him back to the present.

'Can you think of anything about Anna Gerrish that Bishop might want to keep quiet?' I asked.

Cliff, quite drunk now, gave me a one-eyed frown. 'Keep what quiet?'

'The Anna Gerrish case,' I said slowly. 'Is there anything about it that Bishop might want to keep quiet? I mean, why would he *not* want her disappearance investigated?'

'Right . . . right, yeah . . . I see what you mean. You think he's trying to bury it?'

'Maybe . . .'

'Why would he do that?'

'I don't know . . . what do *you* think?'

Cliff took a drink and thought about it. After a while, he looked at me, his head wavering slightly, and said, 'It was the same with your father . . . with Bishop, I mean. It's always been the same with him.'

'In what way?'

'There's only two things that Bishop cares about – money, and looking after himself. That's why Jim . . . your father . . . well, as soon as he went after Bishop . . . he was as good as dead already.'

'Dead?' I said, too surprised to say anything else.

Cliff's eyes widened and he waved his hands around. 'No, no . . . no, sorry, I didn't mean that . . . not *literally* dead. Shit, I'm sorry, John . . . I just meant, you know, that Jim never had a chance of bringing Bishop down, he never had a fucking chance. Bishop's been doing it too long . . .'

'Doing what?'

'Making money . . . pay-offs, bribes, drugs . . . whatever. He's made a *lot* of money over the years, a *fuck* of a lot . . . although God knows what he spends it on. The bastard never goes anywhere, never takes a holiday . . . drives a fucking Honda . . . lives on his own in the same semi he's always lived in –'

'What about family, friends . . .?'

'He's got no family, as far as I know. No friends, no wife, no girlfriend . . . nothing. Whatever he does with his money though, he's fucking good at making it. Good at covering his tracks, good at sniffing out anyone or anything that might bring him down . . .' Cliff shook his head. 'Jim was never *bent*, for fuck's sake. He was the cleanest cop I've ever known. I mean, all right, the thing with the girl was pretty stupid, and there's plenty who'd say that *whatever* your colleagues get up to, you keep your mouth shut about it . . . but the rest of it, the idea that Jim was on the take . . .' Cliff looked up at me. 'Your father was framed, John. Bishop set him up.'

'Yeah, I know.'

Cliff didn't say anything to me for a few moments, he just sat there looking at me, doing his best to keep his head steady. His eyes were getting heavier by the second now, and for a moment or two I thought he was falling asleep, but just as his head started sinking down to his chest, a glass broke behind the bar. The sound elicited the usual momentary hush, followed by muted cheers and laughter, and when I looked back at Cliff, he was sitting bolt upright in his chair.

'Yeah, so anyway . . .' he said. 'This thing with what's-her-name . . . the missing girl . . .'

'Anna Gerrish.'

'Yeah, that's it . . .' He blinked slowly. 'What was I saying?'

'I'm not sure –'

'Oh, yeah . . . about Bishop. I mean, yeah, if you're right about him trying to bury the case, he's either doing it for money or to protect himself.'

'How can there be money in it?'

'Shit, John, I don't know . . . I'm just . . .' His voice trailed off as his head began dropping again and he wearily rubbed his eyes. 'I'm fucked,' he said. 'I've had it . . .' He looked at me. 'Sorry . . .'

Ten minutes later we were both in the back of a taxi – Cliff fast asleep, snoring drunkenly, while I just sat there gazing out of the window, almost too drunk to despise myself.

But not quite.

It didn't take long to get to Cliff's house. I asked the driver to wait while I helped Cliff inside and got him settled down on the settee in his sitting room. He didn't say very much as I loosened his tie and helped him off with his shoes – at least, he didn't say much that I understood – but then, just as I was going, I heard him call my name, and when I turned back to him, he said, 'Don't worry about it, all right? This . . . you know . . . all this, everything . . . don't worry about it . . . it's OK.' He smiled crookedly at me. 'Life's too shitty to worry about.'

I got the taxi driver to drop me back at my office. When I got there, George Salvini was taking another of his many cigarette breaks, leaning against the wall in another of his many expensive three-piece suits, and as I walked up to the door, and I saw him taking in my appearance, I wondered what he must think of me – half drunk, bruised and battered, dressed as ever in a dull black suit . . .

'Ada's just left,' George said to me, smiling.

'Sorry?'

'Your secretary, Ada, she left some minutes ago. She asked me, if I see you, to tell you that everything is up to date, there's a note for you on her desk.'

'Right . . .' I said. 'Thanks.'

He smiled again. 'You're very welcome.'
I left him to his cigarette and went up to my office.

Ada's hours of work are pretty much up to her. She basically works for as long as she needs to, and then she goes home. Some days that might mean being in the office from nine till five, or later, other days she doesn't even bother coming in at all. It suits her, and it's fine with me. And it's what we agreed on when I poached her from Mercer Associates shortly after setting up my own business.

Today, clearly, there hadn't been all that much to do.

There were some cheques for me to sign on my desk, a list reminding me of the phone calls I had to make, and – in the note that George had mentioned – a summary of the calls that Ada had taken that morning.

All of it could wait.

I went into my office, closed the blinds, and poured myself a drink. I looked at the clock on the wall. Tick, tock . . .

It was 15.45.

I sat down on the settee and closed my eyes.

Ripped open on the bed.
  Naked.
  Butchered.
  Bled white.
  Dead.
  I cradle Stacy's ruined body in my arms, howling and sobbing . . . holding her for ever, for ever, it's all I can do. I can't let go. I can't ever hold her enough . . .

I can't.

There's nothing left.

After a timeless time – a thousand years, a minute, a day – I wipe a smear of blood from her mouth, kiss her cold lips, and whisper goodbye. I have to let go now, Stacy. Just for a while. I have to call the police. I don't want to. I want to stay here with you, holding you in my arms . . . I don't want to let you go. But I know if I stay here, I'll stay here for ever, and if I stay here for ever I might as well be dead. And dead's no good to me now. Not yet. I have to attend to the business of death.

I opened my eyes, wiped the tears from my face, and took a long shuddering drink from the whisky bottle. A flood of wretchedness welled up inside me, a feeling so awesome and desperate that it defied all logic and reasoning. Stacy was dead . . . for ever. The child she was carrying, our child, was dead . . .

For ever.

The tears filled my eyes again as I went over to the wall safe, opened it up, and took out my father's pistol. I slipped off the safety catch, went back to the settee, and sat there for a while with the gun in my hand, wondering – as I'd wondered so many times before – where my father had got it from. Did he buy it? Was it police issue? Had he owned it for years, or had he got hold of it specifically to end his own life?

I slipped off the safety catch and wondered how it would feel to rest the barrel against my head and gently pull the trigger.

It wouldn't feel like anything, I told myself.
It wouldn't feel like anything at all.

Twenty minutes later, I reset the safety catch, put the pistol back in the wall safe, and lit a cigarette instead.

11

The office was dark and quiet when I woke up, the whole building hushed with the edgy silence of a time and place that isn't meant to be heard. I could hear the light spit of rain on the window, the unconcerned hum of a water pipe, a low groaning creak from somewhere downstairs . . .

There is no silence, not anywhere. If you listen hard enough, you can hear the sound of the machine beneath your skin.

I reached for my whisky glass and took a long, slow drink, savouring the sedate heat of the alcohol.

My head hurt.

My legs ached.

It was 8.55 p.m.

Time to get going.

I lit a cigarette and set about trying to remember where I'd left my car.

An hour or so later, after I'd walked back to the Blue Boar to pick up my car – stopping only at a cashpoint in town and for a couple of quick drinks in the pub – I was driving slowly along a street of terraced houses at the back of Hey Town's football ground. London Road looked much the same as any other residential street on the south side of town – parked cars, satellite dishes, pavements glistening dully in the street-lit rain – and during the day there was no way of telling that this street, together with a handful of others, was at the heart of Hey's red-light district. At night though, especially late at night, when the skinny young girls appear on the streets, and the men in cars come creeping around . . . well, it's not hard to guess what's going on then.

I hadn't seen any working girls yet, but I guessed that as the rain was still coming down quite heavily, I'd probably find most of them up by the railway bridge at the far end of London Road.

I drove on, constantly checking in the rear-view mirror for any sign of the Renault. I was keeping my eyes open for it all the time now, and although I hadn't seen it since getting beaten up, I wasn't going to take any chances.

Halfway along London Road, I caught sight of several girls hanging around in the arches next to the railway bridge up ahead, and a few more taking shelter in the tunnel itself. I checked in the mirror again, seeing nothing but rain and an empty street, and I slowed down and pulled in at the side of the road. I turned off the engine, lit a cigarette, and waited.

A number of cars went by me during the next few minutes. Most of them just drove past the girls and carried on under the bridge, but some of them momentarily slowed down – window-shopping, I guessed – and a few of them actually stopped. The one girl I saw getting into a car couldn't have been more than sixteen.

With a final look over my shoulder, and satisfied that

there wasn't a silver-grey Renault in sight, I got out of the car and headed for the bridge.

I'm not sure what kind of reaction I was expecting from the girls, but once they realised that I wasn't a punter or a cop, and that all I wanted was information about Anna – and that I was prepared to pay pretty well for it – most of them were friendly enough. The only trouble was, most of them, if not all of them, were addicts of some kind or other – heroin, crack, meth – and they were usually pretty out of it when they were working, which didn't make for the best witnesses in the world. Most of the girls knew who Anna was, even before I'd shown them the photograph. And they knew about her reported disappearance too. But that was about it. As one girl put it, 'She wasn't a regular. She'd come down every other night for a while, then we wouldn't see her at all for a couple weeks, then she'd start showing up again.'

When I asked this girl, whose name was Lizzie, what kind of person Anna was, she just shrugged and said, 'Fuck knows . . . I don't think she ever said a single word to me. She kept herself to herself, if you know what I mean.'

'Do you remember anything about the night she disappeared? It was 6 September, a Monday.'

Lizzie laughed. 'You must be fucking joking . . . I can't even remember what happened this morning.'

It was much the same story when I asked the other girls about Anna – she wasn't here all the time, she didn't mix with us when she was here . . . and, no, I don't remember the night she disappeared – and I'd almost given up hope of finding out anything useful when Lizzie came up to me and suggested I talk to a girl called Tasha.

'I don't know if she'll know any more than the rest of us,' Lizzie said. 'But I remember her talking to Anna a couple of times . . . so, you know . . .' She smiled at me. 'You got a cigarette?'

I took out an almost full packet, slipped a £20 note inside, and gave it to her.

'Where do I find this Tasha?' I said.

Lizzie nodded in the direction of the tunnel. 'Her on the left, the blonde.'

From a distance, Tasha looked like a perfectly ordinary – if slightly underdressed – fifteen-year-old girl, and I suppose that was the intention. But up close, she didn't look quite so young. She was heavily made-up – pink lipstick, black eyeliner – and her blonde hair was dyed, the roots showing through. She was wearing a faded denim jacket over a sheer black miniskirt and a low-cut top, with black stockings and knee-length high-heeled boots. Beneath the make-up, her once-pretty face was tired and gaunt. She was chewing gum and chain-smoking cigarettes.

She didn't say anything when I went up to her, she just looked at me – like she couldn't give a fuck – and took a hard drag on her cigarette. I told her who I was and what I was doing, and I asked her if she remembered Anna Gerrish.

'Yeah,' she said. 'I remember Anna.'

'Was she a friend of yours?'

'No.'

I nodded. 'Lizzie told me that you talked to her sometimes.'

'So?'

'What did you talk about?'

A car cruised past, a Vauxhall Astra, the driver checking out Tasha. Tasha stared back, her eyes a mixture of expectation and contempt, but the car didn't stop. She turned back to me. 'Why should I tell you anything?'

I shrugged. 'For money?'

'How much?'

'That depends on what you know.'

She snapped her gum. 'I already lost thirty quid from the guy in the Astra. He would have stopped if you weren't here.'

'Thirty quid?' I said, surprised it was so low.

'Twenty-five then,' said Tasha, misreading my reaction. 'Whatever . . . I can't spend all night talking to you, I've got a living to make.'

I took out my wallet and passed her three £10 notes. 'There's more,' I said as she took them from me, 'if you tell me what you remember about Anna.'

Tasha tucked the notes away in the top pocket of her denim jacket. 'We didn't talk about anything really,' she said. 'I mean, I don't even know why she spoke to me. She never talked to any of the others. She was kind of cold, you know . . . like she was always a million miles away.' I waited while Tasha dropped her cigarette to the ground and lit another. 'I only spoke to her twice, as far as I can remember,' she went on. 'The first time she told me all this crap about being a model, which I don't think even *she* believed, and the second time . . .' Tasha paused, trying to remember. 'I don't know . . . I think it *might* have been something about her old man, but this was about five or six weeks ago when there was a lot of really good gear around and I think we were both pretty wasted at the time . . .'

'Do you remember what she said about her father?'

Tasha shrugged. 'Just the usual shit, probably . . . you know, the same old Daddy-used-to-fuck-me story. I've heard it so many times now that I just kind of blank out whenever I hear it . . .' She looked at me. 'Have you lost something?'

I was patting my pockets, looking for my cigarettes, but then I remembered that I'd given them to Lizzie. 'You couldn't spare a cigarette, could you?' I said to Tasha.

She smiled as she offered me her packet. 'You're supposed to be paying *me*.'

It was a nice smile.

I lit up and said, 'Can you remember anything about the night Anna disappeared? It was about a month ago, a Monday –'

'Yeah,' Tasha said. 'I know what day it was.'

I looked at her, unable to keep the surprise from my eyes.

'What?' she said. 'You think I'm lying?'

'No, of course not. It's just . . . well, none of the other girls could remember that far back.'

'I'm not one of the other girls, am I?'

I nodded. 'Do you mind me asking why you remember that night in particular? I mean, no offence, but I'd imagine that one night down here is pretty much the same as any other night.'

'It was the guy in the car,' Tasha said. 'That's why I remember that night. This guy . . . I don't know, there was just something about him. At first I just thought he was one of those punters who *want* to pick up a girl, but when they get down here they can't go through with it, like they're too scared to actually *do* it, you know? So they just end up driving round looking at us, then they probably go home and have a wank. But *this* guy . . . well, he kept coming down, almost every night for about two weeks, and as far as I know he never actually stopped for any of us, he just drove around having a good look . . . but I didn't get the feeling that he was scared of anything. In fact, if anything, it was the opposite . . . there was something really fucking scary about *him*.'

'How do you mean?' I asked.

'Well, he just had that look, you know . . . like the whole world meant absolutely *nothing* to him. Do you know what I mean? He was one of those ice-cold fuckers who don't give a shit about anything or anyone.'

'And you saw him that night?'

'Yeah, he picked up Anna.'

'Are you *sure*?'

'Yeah,' Tasha nodded. 'Hundred per cent. I saw her getting in his car. I mean, it was the first time this guy had ever stopped . . . that's why I remember it.' She waved her cigarette hand towards the far end of the tunnel. 'Anna usually worked down there . . . there's a little lay-by just past the tunnel. I suppose she thought it was a handy place for the punters to stop. Anyway, that night, I saw this guy's car coming up London Road, and he did his usual thing –

slowing down and giving us all the eye – and then he just drove past, as usual. But then, when he got to the lay-by, I saw him pull in.'

'And Anna was there that night?'

'Yeah . . . she hadn't been there all that long, maybe half an hour or so . . .'

'What time was this?'

'Pretty late, about two-ish, something like that. Anna worked at The Wyvern . . . she didn't finish there until one.'

'Did you see her getting into the car?'

'Sort of . . .'

'What do you mean?'

'Look,' Tasha said, taking my arm and positioning me so that I was looking down towards the end of the tunnel. 'The lay-by's half hidden by the end of the bridge . . . see what I mean? If a car's parked close to the pavement, all you can see from here is the driver's side.'

I nodded. 'So if someone gets into the passenger seat, you can't actually see them doing it?'

'Right . . . but Anna was definitely there, and I saw this guy leaning across to open the passenger door, and when he drove off, there was definitely someone in the passenger seat.'

'But you couldn't say for certain that it was Anna?'

'No. But when I checked the lay-by a few minutes later, she wasn't there.'

She lit another cigarette, and offered one to me.

'Thanks,' I said, accepting a light from her too. 'This man . . . he drove off *away* from the bridge, not back this way?'

'Yeah, that's why I couldn't see who was in the passenger seat.'

I looked down the tunnel, trying to remember where the road led to. 'Have you told anyone else about this?' I asked Tasha. 'The police, newspapers . . .'

She shook her head. 'No one's asked me.'

'The police haven't talked to you at all?'

'Not to me, no. I don't know about the other girls . . .'

'Why would the police talk to the other girls but not you?'

'I don't know . . . I mean, they probably wouldn't. I was just saying, that's all.'

I nodded. 'Do you remember what kind of car it was?'

'Yeah, it was a Nissan Almera.'

I smiled at her. 'A Nissan Almera?'

She smiled back. 'I've got a five-year-old boy who's mad about cars.' She laughed quietly. 'Everywhere we go, he points them out and tells me what they are. *That's a BMW, Mummy. That one's a Zafira . . .*' She shook her head, her smile turning sad. 'So, anyway, yeah . . . I know my cars. It was a Nissan Almera.'

'Colour?'

'Green.'

'I don't suppose you got the registration number?'

She nodded. 'You got a pen?'

I managed to hide my surprise this time as I reached into my pocket and passed her a pen. She wrote the registration number on the back of her cigarette packet, then gave the packet to me. I shook it. It was at least half full.

'It's all right,' she said. 'You can keep them. I've got plenty more.'

'You sure?'

'Yeah.'

'Thanks.' I looked at her. 'Can you describe the man in the car?'

'He was oldish,' she said. 'Early fifties, maybe. Dark hair, pale skin. I couldn't see his eyes too well because he always wore those tinted glasses . . . you know the ones I mean? Not sunglasses, just ordinary glasses with tinted lenses.'

'Right.'

'But I *think* his eyes were dark.'

'What was he wearing?'

She shrugged. 'I don't know . . . just ordinary old-guy kind of clothes – a shirt, some kind of jacket . . . you know, the kind of stuff that's hard to remember?'

I smiled. 'Yeah, I know what you mean. Is there anything else you can tell me about him?'

She thought about it, then shook her head. 'No . . . I think that's pretty much it.'

'OK, well, thanks, Tasha. You've been really helpful.'

She shrugged again. 'Yeah, well . . .'

I took the remaining notes from my wallet – £65 – and gave them to her. 'Sorry,' I said, 'it's all I've got left.'

She didn't thank me or count the notes, she just put them in her pocket. 'What do you think happened to her?' she asked me.

'I don't know. I'll try and trace the car, see what I can find out . . .' I looked at her. 'Can I ask you something else?'

'You're all out of money now. What are you going to pay me with?'

I hesitated, not sure if she was joking or not.

But then she smiled and said, 'Yeah, go on, then. What do you want to know?'

'Well, it's just . . . I mean, I know you probably don't like the police that much, but how come you haven't told them what you've just told me? You know . . . the car, the registration number, what the guy looks like. You could have just made an anonymous phone call.'

Her smile had faded now. 'What good would it have done?' she said simply. 'If this guy's done something to Anna, it's already done. Catching him now's not going to help Anna, is it? So all that would have happened if I'd told the police was they'd have come down here every night scaring all the punters away, and that would have meant finding somewhere else to work for fuck knows how long, maybe even moving to another town. It's bad enough doing this as it is . . . none of us need any *more* shit to deal with. Do you know what I mean?'

'Yeah . . .'

She shook her head. 'I know what you're thinking –'

'I'm not thinking anything –'

'Yeah, you fucking are. You're thinking what a selfish cunt I am. I'm so fucking wrapped up in myself that I don't give a shit about all the other girls that this guy might pick up and do whatever he does to them . . . all I care about is me.' She glared at me. 'Well, you're fucking right. That *is* all I care about – getting enough money to get enough shit to get wasted enough to get me through another fucking day.'

'That's not what I was thinking,' I said quietly.

Neither of us said anything for a while, we just stood there in the shelter of the tunnel, smoking our cigarettes in awkward silence . . . until eventually I broke the impasse by taking out my wallet again and passing Tasha one of my business cards.

'If you remember anything else,' I told her. 'Just give me a ring. OK?'

She nodded. 'Will you let me know if you find out what happened?'

'Yeah, of course . . .'

I watched, slightly bemused, as she searched through her pockets. Then, with another heart-warming smile, she looked at me and said, 'I seem to have run out of business cards.'

I laughed.

She laughed too, a real eye-twinkling giggle, and just for a moment she didn't seem quite so tired and gaunt any more.

I said, 'How can I get in touch with you again? I mean, if I've got anything to tell you about Anna.'

She smiled sadly. 'I'm down here most nights. Just . . . you know . . .'

I nodded. 'I'll come and find you.'

'OK.'

'And thanks again.'

'Yeah,' she said softly, lowering her eyes. 'Now, fuck off, before I start liking you.'

I wanted to talk to some of the other girls again before I went back to my car, to see if they knew anything about the man in the Nissan Almera, but most of them seemed to have disappeared. The only one I could see was a tall red-headed girl, and she was having an argument with a big Asian guy, who she seemed to know well enough to keep slapping in the chest, and I thought it was probably best to leave them alone. So, with everything that Tasha had told me still buzzing around in my head, I made my way back to my car.

Almost as soon as I'd got in, I saw someone approaching the car from the passenger side. It was a young woman, and as she got closer I recognised her as one of the girls I'd spoken to earlier. She was a little older than the others – in her mid-twenties, I'd guess – and she was dressed in tight jeans, a bra-top, and a black leather coat.

As she came up to the car, smiling seductively, I wound down the window.

She leaned in, showing me what she had to offer, and said, 'Have you finished your *detecting* now?'

'Yeah, thanks.'

She ran her tongue over her lips. 'Can I offer you anything else before you go?'

I was just about to say, 'No, thanks,' when a siren suddenly wailed and the road lit up with a flashing blue light, and before I knew what was happening, the girl had run off, and two uniformed policemen were getting out of their patrol car and striding purposefully towards me.

12

The initial offence I was charged with was kerb crawling, but while they were taking down my details, one of the officers noticed the smell of alcohol on my breath, and I was subsequently breathalysed and arrested for drink-driving too. As I was being driven away in the back of the patrol car, I caught a glimpse of the girl in the black leather coat talking to one of the other girls. She obviously hadn't been arrested, and she didn't even seem bothered by the presence of the police, which pretty much convinced me that my arrest had been set up.

There was no doubt in my mind that Bishop was behind it, but as to why . . .? I wondered if he could have been the man in the Nissan. *An oldish guy,* Tasha had said. *Early fifties, dark hair, pale skin, dark eyes* . . . it *could* be Bishop, give or take a few years. And if Bishop *had* done something to Anna, or even if he was just one of her customers, it would explain why he didn't want me investigating her disappearance. But Tasha's description was pretty vague, and Mick Bishop was by no means the only dark-haired, pale-skinned, middle-aged man in the country. In fact, the description *could* be stretched to fit Graham Gerrish. Maybe he knew that Anna worked the streets at night, and maybe he'd just driven out there and picked her up with the fatherly intention of helping her sort her life out . . . but then something had gone wrong. They'd argued, had a fight . . .

Or maybe he'd picked up his 'little girl' for another reason altogether.

I sat back, closed my eyes, and thought about it.

When we arrived at the police station, I was taken to the custody suite and told I'd have to wait until the custody officer was free to see me. There was no one else in the room, and I hadn't seen anyone else being processed as I'd been led through the station, so I guessed that orders had been given to make my stay as long and uncomfortable as possible.

And I was right.

After about half an hour in the custody suite, during which I was told that I wasn't allowed to smoke, the arresting officer took me along to the custody officer who laboriously explained both the kerb-crawling charge and the drink-drive procedure to me. My personal details were taken and checked – another long wait – and all my belongings were confiscated, including my cigarettes, phone, and the photograph of Anna Gerrish. I was asked countless questions about my medical history – specifically if I'd had any problems with depression, drug addiction, alcoholism, etc. – all of which I refused to answer. I also refused the offer to contact a solicitor. Next I had to provide two more breath specimens, *and* a blood and urine sample – which I knew for a fact was totally unnecessary – and, of course, this meant more waiting around for the appropriate medical staff. After that, I had my photograph, fingerprints, and DNA taken, and then the custody officer explained to me that after conferring with the arresting officer, it was his belief that if I was released immediately I'd more than likely get straight back in a car and commit another offence, and that, in view of this, I was to be further detained at the station overnight.

It must have been getting on for midnight by then – I was only guessing, as they'd taken my watch away – and I was hoping that the worst of it was over. I was really tired now, and while I wasn't exactly looking forward to spending the rest of the night in a cell, at least it would give me a bit of peace and quiet for a few hours, time enough to think, and rest, and maybe even sleep.

I should have known better.

'I'm afraid we're a bit busy tonight, Mr Craine,' the custody officer informed me as he led me down to the cells. 'It's just been one of those days.' He smiled at me. 'I hope you don't mind sharing.'

And with that, he opened the cell door and ushered me inside.

As the door clanked shut behind me, locking automatically, I looked over at a giant-sized man who was sitting on the edge of one of two small beds – his legs splayed wide, his empty eyes fixed hungrily on me. He was, without doubt, one of the nastiest-looking individuals I'd ever seen. A massive man, well over six feet tall and almost as wide, he had long, lank, greasy hair, half an ear missing, yellowed skin, long dirty fingernails, and a lightning bolt tattooed on his neck. He was wearing a purple tracksuit, the top unzipped, revealing a hairless fat chest underneath, and he was smoking a king-size cigarette with the filter ripped off. He was so huge, so solid and heavy, that the metal-framed bed was bending under his weight.

He grinned at me, showing tobacco-stained teeth. 'Well, now,' he said. 'Aren't you a sweet-looking thing.'

My father didn't overburden me with advice when I was growing up, but one of the things he taught me, a lesson I've never forgotten, was that although violence should be avoided whenever possible, it's an integral part of human nature. And, as such, you have to know how to use it when necessary.

'There are only three things you have to know about fighting, Johnny,' he told me. 'You hit your opponent before they hit you; you hit them as hard as you can, preferably with something other than your fists; and you hit them wherever it'll do the most damage. And remember, you're not trying to humiliate your opponent, or show them how tough you are, you're simply trying to hurt them as much as you can and incapacitate them as quickly as possible.'

And that's what I had in mind as the big bastard heaved himself up from the bed, cupped his hand over his groin, and began lumbering across the cell towards me. I didn't want to wait for him to reach me, and I didn't want to give myself time to stop and think about what I was doing, and so – ignoring every cell in my body, all of which were screaming at me to get as far away from him as possible – I willed myself to move towards him. As I did so, I saw a brief flash of surprise in his eyes, and maybe just a moment's hesitation in his walk, and that's when I looked up at the ceiling. By the time he'd instinctively followed suit and lifted his head back to see what I was looking at, I was close enough to slam my fist into his unprotected throat. I put everything I had into the punch, throwing it so hard that my feet actually left the ground for a moment, and the big guy went down like a sack. As he lay there on the floor, clutching his throat and gasping for breath, I took a step back and launched a cannonball kick at his groin, and then – just for good measure – I gave him an equally hard kick in the head.

He just lay there then, not moving, not making a sound, a thin dribble of blood oozing from his half-open mouth, and for a moment or two, I thought I might have killed him. And as I knelt down beside him to check for a pulse, I could already hear a self-recriminating voice in my head saying, *Now you've done it, haven't you? Now you've really gone and fucked things up.* But after a few heart-stopping seconds of fumbling around, trying unsuccessfully to find a pulse, I finally felt the faint movement of blood beneath my finger.

He was alive.

Everything was OK.

Nothing to worry about.

I reached into his pockets and removed his cigarettes and a lighter, then I went over and sat down on the bed, lit a cigarette, and waited for him to wake up.

It didn't take long. Within a few minutes he started groaning and coughing, and pretty soon he'd opened his eyes, spat on the floor, and heaved himself up into a sitting position. He didn't look too good – his right eye was blackening where I'd kicked him, his throat was swollen and red, and his face had turned a sickly grey colour. He couldn't sit up straight because of the pain in his groin, and every time he took a breath it sounded like he was dying.

'You all right?' I asked him.

He coughed, spat again, and looked at me. 'Fuck you.'

I threw him his packet of cigarettes, half of which I'd already removed for myself. He took one out and put it in his mouth, and I threw him his lighter. He lit the cigarette and immediately started coughing again. I took one of his cigarettes from my pocket and held out my hand, waiting for him to throw the lighter back. He glared at me for a moment, then grudgingly lobbed it over.

'Just so you know,' I said to him, lighting the cigarette. 'If you come anywhere near me again, I'm going to kill you. All right?'

'Fuck you,' he said again, but there was nothing in his voice – no venom, no violence, no threat – and I knew he was just making a noise, an animal response. He was hurt, wounded. Physically and emotionally. And I didn't think I'd have any more problems with him. But even so, as I watched him crawl back across the floor to his bed, and painfully clamber onto it, I knew I wouldn't be sleeping that night.

13

After a long and sleepless night, I was finally released from the cell at nine o'clock the next morning. The custody officer who let me out wasn't the same one who'd locked me up, and I got the impression that – unlike his predecessor – this one wasn't in on the set-up.

'What's the matter with him?' he asked me, looking over as Big Bastard started coughing his guts up again. He'd been doing it most of the night – coughing, choking, spitting up gobs of God knows what. But apart from that – and the two occasions when I'd had to put up with him crawling out of bed for a long, loud, and foul-smelling piss – he hadn't been any trouble at all.

'I don't know what's the matter with him,' I said, glancing over at the still-coughing Big Bastard. 'I think he's got asthma or something.'

I was let off with a caution for the kerb-crawling offence and bailed to attend court for the drink-driving charge.

'Where's my car?' I asked the custody officer as he passed me a large manila envelope containing my belongings.

He shrugged. 'Where you left it, I suppose.'

'Any chance of a lift?'

He laughed.

As I emptied out the envelope and started putting all my stuff back in my pockets, the custody officer passed me a form.

'Make sure everything's there,' he said, 'then sign at the bottom.'

It was all there – phone, keys, photograph, lighter . . . everything except the packet of cigarettes that Tasha had given me.

I looked at the custody officer. 'There should be a packet of Marlboro.'

He checked the form. 'There's no cigarettes listed here.'

'Are you sure?'

He looked at the form again. 'Sorry, mate . . . there's a cigarette lighter down here, but no cigarettes.' He looked at me. 'Are you sure you didn't finish them?'

I shook my head. 'I had them when I got here last night, and I clearly remember the custody officer taking them off me.'

'Yeah,' he said, smiling, 'but you were pissed last night, weren't you? We all forget things that happened and remember things that *didn't* happen when we're pissed, don't we?'

I looked at him – a harmless, passionless man – and I knew that he didn't have anything to do with whatever was going on here. As far as he was concerned, it was simply a matter of a missing packet of cigarettes. To Mick Bishop though . . . well, I had to assume that at some point last night, after I'd been locked up, he'd gone through my belongings, looking for anything that might interest him, and he must have spotted the registration number of the

Nissan Almera that Tasha had jotted down on the back of the cigarette packet . . . and the number must have meant something to him. And that had to mean that there was a link between Bishop and the Nissan, which in turn had to mean there was a link between him and Anna Gerrish. It *had* to. Why else would Bishop take the gamble of keeping the cigarette packet, in the hope that I wouldn't remember the registration number without it, when he must have known that once I'd realised what he'd done, I'd realise why he'd done it.

'Are you all right, son?' the custody officer asked me.

'Uh, yeah . . .' I told him. 'Yeah, I'm fine.'

'If you want me to check about the cigarettes, I could probably get in touch with one of the officers who dealt with you –'

'No, that's all right, thanks. Don't worry about it.'

When I left the police station, the rain had stopped and a pale-purple October sky hung low over the morning streets. There was a strange light to the air, an unreal haze that seemed to both clarify and deaden everything at the same time. It reminded me of the feeling you get when you come out of the cinema into the late afternoon daylight and you're suddenly faced with the humdrum brilliance of the real world again. The sights, the smells, the sounds . . .

It was all too real.

It was Friday morning. I was dirty and tired, my breath stank, my skin itched, my head was aching. And I didn't even have any cigarettes.

I headed off towards town.

I was coming out of a newsagent's on Eastgate Hill, tearing the cellophane off a packet of Marlboro, when I heard someone calling out to me. 'John! Over here!' And when I looked up, I saw Mick Bishop leaning across the passenger seat of a blue Vectra stopped at the side of the road. He pushed open the door and waved at me to get in. I thought about it for a second, realised that I didn't have much choice, and went over and got in the car.

'All right?' Bishop said as I closed the door.

'Yeah . . .'

He smiled at me. 'I thought you might need a lift back to your car.'

'Thanks.'

'London Road?'

I nodded.

He looked at me for a moment, slyly amused, then he pulled out into the traffic and drove away.

'Do you mind if I smoke?' I asked him.

'Do you have to?'

'Yeah.'

'All right, but open the window.'

I cracked the window and lit a cigarette, sighing audibly as I breathed out the smoke.

'Rough night?' Bishop said.

I looked at him.

'I just heard about it,' he said, smiling again. 'You really should know better, John. I mean, how are you going to carry on working if you're disqualified for a year? It's not as if you can chase after the bad guys on a bus, is it?'

'You just heard?' I said.

He nodded. 'Twenty minutes ago . . . I always check through the custody log at the start of the day shift, just to see what's been happening, you know? So, there I am, looking through it this morning, and what do I see?' He glanced at me. 'John Craine, detained overnight on kerb-crawling and drink-driving charges.'

I'd already noticed that he was wearing the same clothes he'd been wearing yesterday – the dark-blue blazer, the pale-blue shirt, the burgundy tie pinned with a thin gold chain – and he didn't strike me as the kind of man who'd wear the same clothes two days running. And when I added that to the fact that he hadn't shaved since I last saw him either, I knew that he was lying. He hadn't just come into work. He'd been at the station all night.

'You look tired,' I said to him.

He sniffed. 'It's a tiring job.'

He didn't say anything else for a while, he just kept quiet and concentrated on manoeuvring his way through the town-centre traffic. It was a good opportunity for me to mull things over – what was Bishop up to? what did he want with me? what was I going to do next? – but I was simply too drained to find any answers. So, instead, I just smoked my cigarette and gazed out of the window, watching the world pass by – the boiling chatter of the High Street, early-morning shoppers scuttling around in insect lines . . . taxi drivers, office workers, old husbands and wives . . . people, humans . . . all going somewhere, following their desires . . . a faithful motion of blood, flesh, and bones . . .

The business of life.

*

The business of death. 23 August 1993. Monday morning, nine o'clock. Ten days after Stacy was killed. It's another sweltering hot day, and I'm sitting in an office at Eastway police station with Detective Inspector Mark Delaney. I'm hungover, sick, my sweated skin soured with the stink of stale alcohol. DI Delaney is updating me on the investigation into Stacy's murder.

'I'm afraid there's no easy way of doing this, John,' he says, leafing through some papers in a file. 'I can skip over the specifics if you'd prefer –'

'No,' I tell him. 'I need to know what happened.'

He looks up from the file. 'Are you sure?'

'Yes.'

He holds my gaze for a moment, genuine concern showing in his warm brown eyes, then he nods his head and looks down at the file again. 'All right. Well, as you know, the post-mortem was carried out last week, and we now have some further preliminary forensic results.' He pauses for a moment, taking a quiet steadying breath, then continues. 'The pathologist's report concludes that while the primary cause of death was manual strangulation, Stacy also suffered numerous stab wounds, several of which would have been fatal.'

'How many?'

Delaney looks up at me. 'I'm sorry?'

'How many stab wounds?'

He looks down again. 'Seventeen . . . all of them inflicted with the same weapon – a long, broad-bladed knife.'

'Have you found it yet?'

'Fingertip searches are still being –'

'Have you found it yet?'

He looks at me. 'No.'

'Did he rape her before stabbing her?'

'We believe the wounds were inflicted during the rape.'

'And then he strangled her?'

'Yes.'

'John?'

I rubbed my eyes and turned to Bishop. 'Sorry, what did you say?'

'Business or pleasure?'

'What?'

He sighed. 'London Road . . . last night. Were you down there for business or pleasure?'

'Just asking a few questions,' I said.

'About Anna Gerrish?'

'Yes.'

'Did you get any answers?'

'Not really.'

'What does that mean – *not really*? Either you got some answers or you didn't.'

I couldn't be bothered to say anything, so I just shrugged.

Bishop didn't like that. 'Do you remember me telling you to keep me *informed* about what you're doing?' he said, a snide edge to his voice.

'Yeah, I remember.'

'Well, which part of that don't you understand? It's not *that* fucking difficult –'

'I've been locked in a cell all night. How was I supposed to –?'

'That was *after* you talked to them,' he spat. 'I want to know what you're doing *before* you fucking do it, not afterwards.'

'I didn't *know* I was going to talk to them,' I protested. 'I just happened to be down here last night . . .' As I said it, I realised that we were on London Road now. 'I mean, I didn't come down here on purpose. I was just –'

'Passing through?' Bishop sneered.

I watched him as he slowed the car and pulled up at the side of the road, and I wondered what he'd say if I asked him why *he* hadn't been down here talking to the girls about Anna. *What are you trying to hide, Mick?* I imagined myself saying. *What do you know about Anna? What do you know that you don't want anyone else to know? What the fuck are you doing?*

'All right, listen,' he said sternly to me. 'From now on, you don't do *any*thing without telling me first, OK? I want to know who you're talking to, why you're talking to them, and what they tell you. Do you hear what I'm saying?'

I shook my head. 'You don't have the right –'

'Listen, *cunt*,' he hissed, leaning towards me and staring into my eyes. 'This is about me and you, that's all. Understand? Just me and you. And what you've got to understand is that I can do whatever the fuck I want.' He raised his hand and pointed his finger at me. 'And *you*,' he said, jabbing the rigid finger into my chest. 'You can't do fuck all about it.' He smiled coldly at me. 'You think last night was bad? Well, if you ever fuck me about again, I'll make sure you spend the rest of your fucking *life* locked up in a cell with the nastiest bunch of cunts you can imagine. They'll rip open your face and piss in the hole. They'll fuck you senseless, one after the other. And then they'll do it again, and again, and again. And in the end you'll be begging someone to cut your fucking throat.' He smiled again. 'Do you get the picture?'

'Yes,' I said. 'I get the picture.'

'Good.' He patted me on the shoulder. 'Now get the fuck out of my car.'

14

The girl who let me into Cal's house this time was tall and willowy, with waist-length red hair and eyes like a Roswell alien. She was wearing black lipstick and a long black cardigan, and as she led me down to Cal's basement flat, she didn't say a single word. Didn't even smile. She just waited for Cal to open the door, looked briefly at him, then floated off back up the stairs.

'Is she from the circus too?' I asked Cal as he showed me inside.

'No, she's from Birmingham.'

He was barefoot, dressed only in a T-shirt and boxer shorts, and I guessed he'd only just got out of bed.

'Do you want me to come back later?' I asked him.

'What for?' he said, lighting a cigarette.

I heard the cistern flushing then, and as I looked over towards the bathroom I saw the diminutive figure of Barbarella Barboni, the sacked acrobat, coming out. She was naked, but it didn't seem to bother her.

'Hey,' she said, raising a hand and smiling at me. She looked at Cal. 'Is there any coffee?'

Cal nodded. 'This is John, my uncle . . . you met him before, remember?'

She smiled at me again. 'Yeah.'

'Listen, Barb, we've got some stuff to do . . .'

'No problem,' she said breezily. 'Just let me get dressed and I'll leave you to it.'

Cal watched her as she went into his bedroom, then he turned to me. 'You want some coffee?'

'Please.'

He peered at me for a moment. 'You look like shit, John.'

'Thanks.'

'You want something to eat?'

I don't really like eating. To me, it's nothing more than a refuelling process, something you have to do to stay alive. And I particularly don't like eating when it has any kind of social connection. So my natural response when I'm asked if I want anything to eat is to say no. And I almost said no to Cal. But the mention of food made me realise that I hadn't eaten anything for a long time, and that I was, in fact, desperately hungry.

So I said, 'Yeah, something to eat would be good, thanks.'

'What do you want?'

'Got any eggs?'

'What kind of eggs?'

'Chicken?'

He smiled. 'How about eggs Benedict? I make a *very* mean eggs Benedict.'

I didn't even know what eggs Benedict was. And twenty minutes later, after Barbarella had left us alone, and I'd shared a big plateful of food with Cal, I still didn't know what it was. But it did the job. It filled a hole. And, with the help of three cups of coffee, it gave my energy levels a much-needed boost.

But it still wasn't enough.

'Listen, Cal,' I said. 'I really need your help with something –'

'You've got it.'

'No, just listen to me, OK? I'll explain everything in a minute, and I'll tell you what I want you to do, but first of all . . . well, the thing is, I'm totally fucked at the moment. I've been working this case non-stop, and I haven't slept for God knows how long, and I've got a feeling that today's going to be another long slog.' I looked at him. 'So, I was wondering . . . you know . . . well, I was just wondering if you've got anything that'll keep me going for a while.'

'Well, yeah . . .' Cal said hesitantly. 'But I thought . . . I mean, I thought you'd given up all that?'

'I just need something for today, that's all.'

'Well, OK . . . if you're sure . . .'

I didn't say anything, I just looked at him.

He gazed back at me for a while – and I could see the concern in his eyes – but then he just nodded his head, got up, and went into his bedroom. When he came back out, fully dressed now, he was carrying a brown plastic prescription bottle.

'They're black bombers,' he said, passing me the bottle. 'You don't often come across them these days, but there's this Portuguese guy I know . . . anyway, they're slow-release amphetamines. You only need to take one at a time.'

I looked at the bottle. It contained about half a dozen plain black capsules.

'Thanks, Cal,' I said, taking one out and swallowing it with a mouthful of coffee.

'Yeah, well . . .' he said guardedly. 'Just don't go crazy with them, all right? I mean, shit, if Stacy was here . . .'

'I know,' I said. 'She'd kill me.'

Cal smiled. 'And me.'

We looked at each other in silence for a while, and I knew that we were both feeling the same unfillable emptiness – the despair of knowing that Stacy wasn't here, and that she'd never be here again . . .

'All right,' I said to Cal, lighting a cigarette. 'Let's get on with it.'

After I'd told him everything I knew about the case, and everything that had happened to me in the last few days, Cal just sat there for a while, not saying anything, just quietly thinking things through. As for me, the amphetamine had kicked in now – with an uncharacteristically *un*edgy kind of rush – and my mind was beginning to buzz with all kinds of new ideas and fresh possibilities about everything: Anna Gerrish, Mick Bishop, the guy in the Nissan . . .

'So,' Cal said eventually, 'you *think* that Bishop went through your stuff when you were locked up, but you don't know for sure?'

'Well, no . . . not for sure. But –'

'Give me your phone.'

'What?'

'Your mobile, let me see it.'

I took out my phone and passed it over. He glanced at the connection sockets, then got up from the settee – we were sitting in the small recreation area in the corner of his flat – and he went over to one of his work desks and started searching through a tangle of cables.

'What time did you get to the police station?' he asked me.

'I'm not sure . . . about eleven, I think.'

He'd found the cable he was looking for, and I watched as he plugged one end into my phone and the other end into a hand-held device that looked a little bit like a credit-card reader. He connected the device to a laptop, hit some buttons on my phone, waited a while, then pressed some keys on the device and watched as a stream of data appeared on the laptop screen. He lit a cigarette and studied the screen for a while, scrolling up and down through the information, then he nodded to himself and turned back to me.

'Your phone was accessed at 02.17 this morning,' he said. 'I take it that couldn't have been you?'

'No, I was definitely locked up by then.'

'OK, well, whoever it was, they had a good look through your address book, your texts, your call logs . . . pretty much everything, really.' He came back over to the settee and gave me back the phone. 'It's clean, by the way. No bugs or tracking devices.'

'Thanks.'

He sat down. 'So, basically, if it *was* Bishop who went through your stuff, he's now got all the information on your phone – who you've been calling, who's called you, who's in your address book –'

'You're in my address book,' I said, suddenly realising. '*All* your numbers . . . *and* I called you recently –'

'Doesn't matter,' Cal said. 'He won't get anywhere if he tries to trace my numbers. But if there's anything else . . . you know, anyone in your address book, or anyone you've been in touch with . . . anything that Bishop could use . . .?'

'I don't think so . . . I mean, I'll have to check, but I don't think there's anything to worry about.'

'All right,' Cal said, lighting a cigarette. 'So let's assume that it was Bishop, and that he took the cigarette packet because it had the registration number of the Nissan that this girl told you about –'

'Tasha.'

'Right, Tasha.' He looked at me. 'Do you think Bishop knows it was her? He obviously knows that you were down there talking to the girls, but would he know which one gave you the number?'

'I don't know . . . probably. I didn't *see* anyone watching me when I was talking to her, but the cops who arrested me must have been hanging around somewhere nearby, so I wouldn't be surprised if they saw us together, and they would have told Bishop.' I looked at Cal. 'Do you think I should warn her? If Bishop's linked with this Nissan somehow, and he knows that Tasha's a possible witness . . .'

'You really think Bishop might do something to her?'

I thought about it, wondering if I was just being paranoid about Bishop, but then I remembered the story about him torturing the drug dealer in Chelmsford, and I recalled the look of venom in his eyes when he'd jabbed me in the chest a few hours earlier, and I knew that I wasn't being paranoid. Bishop was a violent man. If he wanted something badly enough, he wouldn't care what he had to do to get it.

'I'll go down there tonight and tell Tasha to be careful,' I said to Cal.

'Maybe I should do it,' he said. 'Bishop might have someone watching the girls, and if he finds out that you've been down there again . . .'

'Yeah, I suppose you're right.'

After I'd told him what Tasha looked like, and where he could find her, we got back to talking about the Nissan.

'She could be lying about it, you know,' Cal said. 'Just making it all up . . . you know what junkies are like.'

'Yeah, but why would Bishop keep the cigarette packet with the registration number on it if it didn't mean anything?'

Cal shook his head. 'I don't really understand why he kept it anyway.'

'Because he knew that I'd had a few drinks last night, and he was guessing that without the packet I wouldn't remember the number. And if I didn't remember the number, then I couldn't try to track it . . . shit.'

'What?'

'Well, if I *didn't* have the number, what would I do?'

'You'd go back to Tasha . . . fuck, yeah, I see what you mean. If Bishop thinks you don't have the number, he's going to try to get to Tasha before you do.'

'And she's probably got a record, so he'll know where she lives.'

'Fuck,' Cal said. 'We need to find her as soon as possible. Tonight might be too late.'

'I don't see how we can. She won't be on the streets now, and even if we could find some of the other girls, they're not going to tell us where she lives.'

'Do you know her surname?'

I shook my head. 'And Tasha's probably her street name anyway.'

'So we don't know her surname, or her real first name, and we don't know where she lives –'

'We need to look at this differently,' I said.

'What do you mean?'

'We can't get to Tasha before Bishop, can we?'

'No.'

'So we have to stop Bishop getting to Tasha.'

'Right. And how the fuck do we do that?'

'By letting Bishop know that I *have* got the registration number she gave me.'

'Have you?'

I rolled up my sleeve and showed him the number I'd written on my arm when I was in the back of the patrol car last night. 'It's something I learned from my drunk days,' I told Cal. 'You can't trust yourself not to forget anything, or not to lose anything, when you're drinking. So if you *really* need to remember something, write it down where it can't get lost.'

It was Cal's idea to check out the registration number first.

'It won't take long,' he told me. 'Once we've found out whatever we find out, we can decide how to let Bishop know.' He went over to his work desk and started tapping away on a laptop. 'I'm still working on that other registration number you gave me, by the way,' he said. 'The Renault.'

'Any luck?'

'Not yet. I've still got a few more things to try, but it's not looking too hopeful at the moment.'

'OK. Well, let me know if you find anything.'

While Cal set about entering the vehicle details I'd given him, I gave Ada a quick call at the office.

'I'm at Cal's,' I told her. 'He's helping me out with the Anna Gerrish case.'

'How's it going? Are you getting anywhere with it?'

'Well, kind of . . .'

'Kind of?'

'It's complicated. There's a chance that Bishop might have something to do with it. Personally, I mean.'

'Really?'

'Well, I haven't got any proof yet, but I'm pretty sure that he's got *some*thing to do with it. He's made it clear that he doesn't want me looking into it, and I'm fairly sure that he's having me followed.'

'Did he have anything to do with you getting beaten up the other night?'

'How do you know about that?'

'George Salvini. He said it looked like you'd been through a meat grinder –'

'It wasn't that bad, Ada.'

'You should have *told* me.'

'Yeah, I know. I'm sorry. I was going to –'

'Was it Bishop?'

'I don't know . . . I'm fairly sure that he wasn't one of the men who attacked me, but it's possible he was behind it.'

Ada sighed. 'Is there anything else you haven't told me?'

I thought about lying to her for a moment, but I knew

she'd find out about the drink-driving charge eventually, so I decided I might as well tell her. 'I was arrested last night –'

'Oh, John . . .'

'It's all right,' I told her. 'It was a set-up. I didn't actually *do* anything –'

'What was the charge?'

'Kerb crawling and drink-driving. But, like I said –'

'Kerb crawling?'

'It was a set-up, Ada –'

'And what about the drink-driving? Were you over the limit?'

'Well, yeah, but –'

'Shit, John. You could lose your fucking licence.'

'I know,' I said, looking over at Cal. He was clicking his fingers at me, drawing my attention to the laptop screen. 'I have to go, Ada,' I said. 'We'll talk about this later. But listen, if Bishop or anyone else from the police calls –'

'I don't know where you are.'

'Thanks. I might be in later, but if I'm not –'

'Just let me know what's happening, John. All right?'

'Yeah.'

'Promise?'

'Cross my heart . . .'

'And be careful, OK?'

'OK.'

I ended the call, lit a cigarette, and went over to Cal.

'I've got it,' he said, pointing at the laptop screen. 'The Nissan's registered to a Charles Raymond Kemper. Fifty-three years old, no points on his licence, a home address in Leicester.'

'Leicester?'

'Yeah. I've done a quick search through all the usual databases – phone listings, utilities, council tax, electoral roll – but I haven't found anything else so far.' He looked at me. 'Does the name mean anything to you?'

'Charles Raymond Kemper . . .?' I shook my head. 'Not as far as I know.'

'I'll do some more checking,' Cal said. 'See what I can find out.'

'All right, but leave it for now. There's something else I want you to do. And we need to let Bishop know about the registration number too.'

'Have you got his mobile number?'

'I think so,' I said, taking Bishop's business card from my pocket and studying it. 'Yeah, here it is. What do you think we should do? Just text him the number?'

Cal nodded. 'There's no point in letting him know we've got the name too. Do you want to send it anonymously?'

I thought about it, then shook my head. 'If he doesn't know who it came from, he might think Tasha sent it. You know, he might think she's trying to blackmail him. And then he'll definitely go after her.'

'Yeah, but if he knows that *you* sent it –'

'It doesn't matter, does it? He already knows that Tasha gave me the number, and he must have known there was a chance I'd remember it.'

'Yeah, all right,' Cal said. 'But instead of using your mobile, why don't we use one of my untraceable phones instead? Just text him the registration number, nothing else, and sign it with your initials.'

'What's the point? If he knows it's from me anyway –'

'He'll *think* it's from you,' Cal said, smiling. 'He'll be 99% certain that the text came from you, but he'll still try to trace it, just to make sure. And the trace will take him halfway round the world and back. And eventually, after three or four hours, his IT people will realise that the trace is going round and round in circles, and they're never going to get anywhere with it.'

'And what's that going to achieve?'

Cal smiled again. 'It'll keep him busy for a while, waste his time . . . give him something to think about.'

'And piss him off.'

'Yeah, that too.'

I smiled. 'OK, let's do it.'

After he'd sent the text, Cal said to me, 'All right, what next?'

'CCTV cameras,' I said. 'Can you hack into them?'

'What kind of CCTV?'

'Just the usual stuff, you know . . .'

'Town-centre cameras, that kind of thing?'

'Yeah.'

He nodded. 'No problem.'

'What about old footage?'

'How old?'

'A month or so.'

He looked at me. 'The night Anna disappeared?'

'Yeah. I know it's a long shot, but if we can find any footage of the Nissan around the time that Anna was picked up that night, it might give us an idea of where she was being taken. Do you think you can do that?'

Cal had to think about it for a while, but eventually he said, 'Well . . . I've never actually tried hacking into archived recordings, but it should be easy enough. All the public surveillance cameras in Hey are operated by the council, and they probably store the archived footage on hard disks in their system . . .' He grinned at me. 'The security on the council's computer system is notoriously pathetic. In fact, it's so ridiculously easy to get into that some hackers think it's an insult to their intelligence and they refuse to go anywhere near it on principle –'

'Right,' I said impatiently. 'So you can get into it?'

'Yeah.'

'And if I tell you as much as I know about Anna's whereabouts that night, do you think it's possible to track her?'

'It all depends on the location of the cameras,' he said, turning to his laptop. 'All right, let's see . . . the first thing we need is a site map of all the cameras . . .'

I must have sat beside Cal, watching him do his thing, for at least a couple of hours, maybe longer. It was an incredible experience. Most of what he was doing was way beyond my comprehension, but although I didn't really know *what* he was doing, it was impossible not to admire the skill and tenacity with which he was doing it – his fingers skipping gracefully over the keyboard while his eyes focused almost fanatically on the screen . . . it was entrancing, like watching a genius at work. Of course, the amphetamine was really buzzing through me now, and I'm sure that played some part in the sheer intensity of my enchantment, but still . . . it was a hell of a thing to witness.

We didn't speak very much for the first hour or so when Cal was actually getting into the system, and that was fine with me. I'd done enough talking over the last few days to last me a lifetime, and I was perfectly happy just sitting there quietly, smoking cigarettes and staring dumbly at the inner workings of cyberspace as they streamed up and down the screen.

Once Cal had accessed the system though, we needed to work together, and that's what we did for the next hour and a half. Cal asked me questions – what time did Anna leave The Wyvern? what route would she have taken to get to London Road? what time did she get there? what time did she get picked up by the Nissan? – and I did my best to answer them as accurately as possible. We didn't get all that far at first because London Road was right at the edge of the area covered by the council's CCTV cameras, but Cal quickly realised that both the railway bridge itself and the neighbouring mainline and branchline tracks were covered by a number of Network Rail CCTV cameras, and once he'd hacked into their archived footage – which didn't take him long – we finally had the coverage that might just be enough to show us something.

'Now all we've got to do is find her,' Cal said.

It took us a long time, at least another three hours, and it was a painstakingly tedious task which gave both of us throbbing headaches and aching eyes, but eventually we reached the stage where we'd managed to track Anna – through a series of blurred and stuttered images – from the bottom of Miller's Row all the way down to London Road. And now Cal had loaded the footage from a camera that was located about fifty metres south of the railway bridge, looking back at the lay-by, and we were both peering intently at the screen, our eyes fixed on the smallish grey blob of a figure that we knew to be Anna Gerrish. We'd seen her arrive at the lay-by at 01.31, and now – according to the read-out at the bottom of the screen – it was 01.47. So far, nothing had happened. Although the picture quality was poor, the view from the camera couldn't have been better. It showed the whole of the lay-by, the tunnel entrance/exit, and the road leading towards it from the bridge. There was very little traffic around at that time of night, and none of the cars we'd seen so far had stopped at the lay-by.

We just had to wait.

'What time did Tasha say she saw the Nissan?' Cal asked me, without taking his eyes off the screen.

'She thought it was around two-ish.'

Cal nodded.

I leaned closer to the screen as headlights appeared in the tunnel . . . but the car didn't stop. I watched it drive past the lay-by, approach the camera, and then disappear.

I said to Cal, 'Where does this road go anyway?'

'South from here?'

'Yeah.'

'London Road ends at the entrance to the tunnel. After that it becomes Great Hey Road. It follows the railway tracks for a while, maybe half a mile, then there's a right turn that takes you back into town, but if you stay on Great Hey Road and keep going . . . hold on, what's that?'

Another pair of headlights had appeared in the tunnel, this time moving quite slowly. We both leaned in closer to the screen again. The headlights were on full, the glare making it impossible to see what kind of car it was. But as it approached the end of the tunnel, it definitely seemed to be slowing down.

'This could be it,' Cal said quietly.

The car was coming out of the tunnel now, its left-side indicator flashing. It pulled in at the lay-by, and as I watched the grey blob that was Anna walking towards it, I felt an irrational urge to shout out to her – *Don't do it, Anna! Don't get in the car!* But of course, after leaning in through the passenger window and talking to the driver for ten seconds or so, she got in.

'Shit,' Cal whispered.

The headlights were still on full beam as the car pulled away, and at that distance there was no chance of identifying the driver. But now the car was coming towards us, getting closer all the time . . . and we both had our faces almost pressed to the screen . . . and just as the car was about to pass the camera and disappear from view, another car appeared, travelling in the opposite direction, and our driver had to dip his lights. And just for a second, we had a relatively clear picture of our car. But it was, literally, only for a second, and then the car was gone.

'Did you see him?' I asked Cal.

'No, it was too quick.'

'Shit.'

He grinned at me. 'It's not live . . .'

'What?'

'It's a recording, we can watch it as many times as we want.' He started tapping the keyboard. 'You didn't *really* think it was live, did you?'

I leaned back in the chair, rubbing my eyes, trying to bring myself back to reality. I knew exactly where I was and what I'd been doing for the last few hours, but I was feeling that slightly odd sensation – a kind of gradually dawning awareness – that can come to you at the end of a really engrossing film. And that, in turn, was making me feel really uncomfortable. Because what I'd just witnessed wasn't a film . . . it wasn't a drama, played out by actors. It was real. A real girl, getting into a real car with a real man . . . a man who was quite possibly about to kill her.

There was nothing *engrossing* about that.

'There,' said Cal. 'That's as clear as I can get it.'

I looked at the screen. He'd re-run the CCTV footage and frozen it just before the car disappeared from view. The static image was still fairly blurred and grainy, but it clearly showed a man in the driving seat, and a girl in the passenger seat, and when I half closed my eyes and squinted at the faces, it was just possible to see – or, at least, to imagine – that the man matched Tasha's description, and that the girl was Anna. But, of course, my imagination was probably swayed by the fact that I already knew it *was* Anna.

'What do you think?' Cal said.

'Is that the best you can do?'

'I could enlarge it, but all that'd do is make it even blurrier.'

'You can't get it any clearer?'

'No . . . I know someone in the States who could maybe

clean it up a bit. But he's really expensive, and he's got a really long waiting list. He probably couldn't do it for at least a couple of weeks, probably a month.'

I leaned forward and squinted at the images again. 'It *could* be Bishop . . .'

'It *could* be anyone.'

'What about the car?'

'Well, it's definitely a Nissan Almera –'

'Is it?'

'Yeah, but I can't make out the number plate.'

I leaned back, lit a cigarette, and looked at my watch. It was just gone four o'clock. Deep down inside me I could feel the faint stirrings of the black place again, and I knew that it wouldn't be too long before it dragged me down into its void. But it wasn't quite ready for me yet. And the black pills in my pocket would help to keep it at bay for a while.

'What time does it get dark?' I said to Cal.

He shrugged. 'I don't know. Six, half-past . . .? Why?'

'Great Hey Road . . .' I said, gazing at the frozen image on the laptop screen. 'It carries on down to the coast, doesn't it?'

'Yeah,' Cal said, frowning at me, not sure why I was asking. 'It takes you out past the Ranges, through all those little villages . . . and it ends up at Hale Island.'

I nodded, remembering now. I hadn't been to Hale Island for years, but when I was a kid we used to drive down there on Sunday afternoons for family strolls on the beach . . . my mother and father walking together, talking quietly to each other, while I went off on my own . . . scuffing along the strandline, kicking up junk, looking for jewels – tropical beans, cuttlefish bones, mermaid's purses . . .

I was happy then.

'John?'

I looked at Cal.

He said, 'Are you all right? You look a bit –'

'Can you see if you can find some more footage of the Nissan?' I said to him, getting to my feet. 'Try and see where this guy went with Anna?'

Cal nodded. 'I can *try* . . . there's a few more Network Rail cameras that might have picked him up, but that's before the turn-off back to town. *After* that . . . well, I'll have to check, but I don't think there's too many cameras along Great Hey Road.' He looked at me, frowning again. 'Where are you going?'

'I'm just going to take a drive out there, before it gets too dark.'

'Out where?'

I looked at the image on the screen again. 'I'll start at the lay-by, and then . . . I don't know. Just keep going, I suppose.' I looked back at Cal. 'I know it sounds stupid –'

'Yeah, it does. I mean, you're not going to *find* anything, are you?'

'I know. But I just need to *do* something, Cal. Even if it's pointless . . . I need to feel like I'm doing something.'

He looked at me for a while, chewing his lip . . . and just for a moment he reminded me *so* much of Stacy. It wasn't just the family resemblance – although Cal did have the same natural beauty as Stacy – but the way he was chewing his lip and looking at me . . . Stacy used to do exactly the same thing when she was worried about me, especially when she was worried about my state of mind.

'It's all right,' I said quietly to Cal. 'I'm all right.'

'Honestly?'

I smiled. 'Yeah.'

He nodded. 'OK.'

'So you'll keep working on the CCTV stuff?'

'Yeah.'

'And you'll let me know –'

'I'll call you whether I find anything or not.'

'And if you've got the time –'

'I'll see what I can find out about Charles Raymond Kemper.'

'Thanks, Cal.'

'Oh, and before you go . . .' he said, fumbling around through the clutter on his desk. 'Hold on . . . where the fuck is it? I know I put it somewhere . . . ah, there it is.' He got up, came over to me, and handed me a flash drive.

'What's this?' I said.

'The video footage that was on that damaged memory card you gave me . . . I've transferred it all to the flash drive.'

It took me a moment to realise what he was talking about, but then I remembered – the StayBright case, Preston Elliot and his ball-peen hammer . . .

It seemed like a long time ago.

'Was it all still there?' I asked Cal.

'Yep.'

'You're a genius,' I said, pocketing the flash drive.

He smiled. 'I know.'

*

Before I left, I went to the bathroom and swallowed another pill. I knew that I'd pay for it later – because the longer the black place is kept at bay, the blacker it is when it finally comes – but later was later. Right now, my only real concern was how Stacy would have felt about me taking the pills . . . and as I went over and looked in the bathroom mirror, and my fucked-up eyes stared back at me, I could hear the anger and exasperation in Stacy's voice as she told me not to be so *stupid* . . .

You don't need pills, John. You don't need to keep doing this to yourself.

'I'm sorry, Stace,' I muttered, pocketing the bottle of pills. 'I'm just . . .'

Just what?

'Nothing . . . I'm just sorry.'

15

The business of death . . .

'Did he rape her before stabbing her?'

'We believe the wounds were inflicted during the rape.'

'And then he strangled her?'

'Yes.'

'How did he get into the house?'

'There were no signs of forced entry, so at the moment we're assuming that Stacy let him in. Which either means that she knew him, or she was somehow tricked into letting him in.'

'Do you know what time it happened?'

DI Delaney looks through the papers in the file. 'The pathologist estimates the time of death at between 3.30 and 4.45. Stacy's watch, which was broken during the attack, was stopped at 4.17.' He looks at me. 'You were still at work, John. You couldn't have done anything.'

It's a pointless thing to say, but I don't hold it against him. I ask, 'Have you got any witnesses?'

He shakes his head. 'Not yet.'

'No one saw anything?'

'We've still got some follow-up interviews to do, and we've got appeals planned for the press and local TV. We're doing everything we possibly can, John.'

'What about forensics?'

'The crime-scene evidence is still being analysed. No fingerprints have been found, so we're assuming he wore gloves . . . and preliminary reports indicate the use of a condom during the rape, so we don't expect to find any –'

'A condom?'

Delaney sighs. 'It's not unusual, I'm afraid. Rapists, sexual predators, murderers . . . they all watch CSI these days – CSI, Waking the Dead, Silent Witness . . .' He shrugs. 'They all know about DNA . . . at least, they think they do.' He looks at me. 'I'm sorry if I only seem to have bad news for you, John . . . but there is one thing that's giving us hope.'

I don't say anything, I just wait.

'During the post-mortem,' he tells me, 'the pathologist found a small piece of scalp in your wife's stomach.'

'Scalp?'

He nods. 'We think – and I have to emphasise that forensic work is still being carried out, so at the moment we can't be sure – but we think that at some point during the assault, your wife must have fought back, biting her attacker on the head . . . and, incredibly, we think she must have actually bitten off a piece of his scalp . . .'

'And swallowed it?'

Delaney shakes his head in admiration. 'Whether or not she knew what she was doing, making sure that he wouldn't get away without leaving his DNA behind . . . well, I don't know. But either way, what she did . . . well, all I can say is that she must have been a remarkable woman.'

'Yes . . . yes, she was.' And I'm crying now. 'Will you get DNA from this piece of scalp?'

He nods. 'There's no reason why not. It's got everything the forensic team need – blood, skin . . . hair. We're expecting the results within the week. Of course, everything then depends on matching the DNA to a suspect. If we can match the DNA profile to a profile we already have on our database, we've got a result. But if not, if the man who killed Stacy has never been arrested before . . .'

'But he probably has.'

Delaney nods cautiously. 'Probably, yes. This doesn't look like the work of a first-time offender. But just because he's done it before, that doesn't necessarily mean he's been arrested before.'

'So . . . we just have to wait.'

'Yes, I'm afraid so. As I said, we should have the DNA results by the end of this week, and I promise I'll let you know as soon as I get them.'

'Thanks.'

'And, in the meantime, if anything else turns up . . .'

I nod my head, getting to my feet.

What else is there to say?

Nothing.

I just have to wait.

I'd told Ada that I didn't have any proof of Bishop's involvement in Anna's disappearance, but the simple truth was that I didn't have proof of anything at all. Despite everything Cal had done, hacking into the CCTV system and searching through hours of footage, all we'd really done was confirm what Tasha had told me, that Anna had been picked up by a man in a Nissan Almera. That was it.

That was all I knew. I had no idea who the man was, no idea of his intentions, no idea what he'd done with Anna.

For all I knew, Bishop had been right when he'd suggested that Anna had simply 'met some bloke who's promised her the world and they've fucked off together somewhere'. Maybe the man in the Nissan *was* just a punter intent on rescuing Anna from her life of depravity . . . or maybe he was nothing more than just another punter. Charles Raymond Kemper, a lonely businessman from Leicester, visiting Hey for a sales conference or a meeting with investors . . . he picks up Anna, takes her to a nice quiet spot somewhere, pays her to do what he wants, then drives back to town and drops her off somewhere.

Why not?

I didn't know.

But although I'm a stone-cold realist, and I have no belief whatsoever in anything even remotely supernatural, spiritual, or mystical . . . when I'd watched that blurred video footage of Anna Gerrish getting into the Nissan, I knew that I'd been watching a ghost.

Anna Gerrish was dead.

I had no doubt about that.

And I knew that I wasn't going to find her by simply driving around, following the possible route of what was possibly her last journey, but I also knew that she *could* be out there somewhere – buried in a shallow grave, left to rot in a lonely copse, or just discarded at the side of the road somewhere, thrown away like an unwanted toy – and if she *was* out there, she would have been out there for a whole month by now . . . and no one had made any effort to find her.

No one had gone looking for her.

No one had cared.

And I can't say for sure that I cared either. I cared about *some*thing, but whether it was the ghost of Anna Gerrish that was willing me on, or the haunting echoes of Stacy's death, or just the amphetamine-fuelled yearning of my own self-pity . . . I simply didn't know. I was just doing what I was doing – driving through the late-afternoon streets, looking for something, anything . . .

The daylight was beginning to fade as I passed along London Road, the pale purple skies edged with the dying redness of the sun. There was no sign of Tasha or any of the other girls. The streets were quiet and empty. I drove on. Through the tunnel, under the bridge . . . and then I slowed down and pulled in at the lay-by. It was just a lay-by: a dull grey crescent of gravelled concrete and weeds, an over-flowing litter bin, cigarette ends strewn on the ground . . . a small and desolate place. In a verge at the back of the lay-by, clumps of wild grass swayed stiffly in a roadside breeze. I could feel the emptiness in the air.

It was no place for anyone to spend the last half-hour of their life.

I pulled away and drove off.

The hedge-lined greyness of Great Hey Road led me out of town, past the turning back to Hey, out into a semi-rural world of ploughed fields, out-of-town pubs, and small housing estates with rundown mini-markets where kids in tracksuits hung around benches waiting for things to happen. The further I got from Hey though, the more rural the landscape became, and as the farmlands passed by in a blur of abandonment – ramshackle buildings, polythene greenhouses, wasteland nurseries selling cheap pots and poorly-made bird tables – I realised just how many places there were where a dead body could be left with little fear of it being found: ditches, woods, overgrown streams, hedgerows, old quarries, deserted farm buildings. And I knew, as I approached the Ranges – a large expanse of wooded moorland that was used by the Army for military exercises – I knew that if Anna was out *there* somewhere, it was quite possible that she'd never be found.

I was trying to think logically, telling myself that if her abductor was a local man, he might well know about the Ranges, but if he wasn't – if he *was* a man from Leicester called Charles Raymond Kemper – then he probably wouldn't know the area that well, and if he had a dead body in his car that he was desperate to get rid of, he'd most likely just pick the first suitable spot he came across . . . probably somewhere much closer to town.

Which was logical enough reasoning . . . at least, it would have been if I'd known for sure whether Anna's abductor was local or not. But I didn't.

I didn't even know if he existed.

I slowed the car and turned off into a deserted picnic area at the edge of the Ranges. It wasn't much of a place, just a concreted square with a wooden table in the middle, surrounded by acres of litter-strewn scrubland, and as I parked the Fiesta and turned off the engine, I wondered if it was worth getting out of the car for a quick look round. It was an ideal spot for getting rid of a body – remote, but easily accessible; out of sight of the road, but not suspiciously so;

and bordered on all sides by tangled hedgerows, drainage ditches, brambles, nettles, fallen trees . . .

As I lit a cigarette and gazed out over it all – wondering once again what the hell I was doing – my mobile rang. It was Cal, and he sounded quite excited.

'I think I've got something, John,' he said, the words spilling out rapidly. 'Where are you?'

'I'm at the Ranges . . . what do you mean you've got something?'

'You need to turn round and head back towards town. Have you got a map? There's a camera –'

'Hold on a second,' I said, trying to slow him down. 'Just tell me what you've got first.'

'OK, well . . . I've been doing what you asked me to do, looking for more footage of the Nissan, and I found a couple of CCTV cameras on Great Hey Road . . . there's one at the junction with the road back to town, and another about a mile further on at a railway crossing on the branchline . . . you know, one of those barrier crossings?'

'Yeah, I know the one you mean.'

'All right, so I worked out roughly how long it would have taken the guy to drive from the lay-by to the junction, and then on to the crossing, and I hacked into the stored footage at the times I estimated he'd be there . . . and guess what? I only fucking found him, didn't I?'

'Where? At the junction?'

'At the junction *and* the crossing.'

'And you're sure it's the same car?'

'Yeah, but –'

'The same driver?'

'It's the same guy –'

'What about Anna? Is she –?'

'Fuck's *sake*, John,' he said angrily. 'That's what I'm trying to *tell* you. Just listen to me, all right? Are you listening?'

'Yeah, sorry –'

'OK,' he sighed. 'Right, well . . . when the Nissan passes the junction, there's definitely someone in the passenger seat. The footage is still too blurred to tell if it's Anna Gerrish or not, but whoever it is, she's in the car when it passes the junction. But then . . . well, if he'd carried on at the same speed, he should have got to the railway crossing about a minute later, but he didn't. I double-checked the footage, going back a minute, then forward a minute, but there was still no sign of the Nissan. So then I fast-forwarded the tape –'

'Did you find him or not, Cal?' I said impatiently.

'He passed the crossing half an hour later.'

'What?'

'The Nissan passed the junction at 01.55, and it didn't get to the crossing until 02.26.'

'Shit.'

'Yeah, and the thing is, when it got to the crossing there was no one in the passenger seat.'

'Are you *sure*?'

'Fucking positive. I've watched it over and over again. I've paused the video as the car crosses the tracks . . . in fact, I'm looking at it on my laptop right now. It's definitely the same car, with the same guy in the driver's seat, and there's *definitely* no one in the passenger seat. No one in the back seats either. Unless they're hidden away somewhere, there's no one else in that car but the driver.'

'Shit,' I said again.

'Exactly.'

'So that must mean –'

'He's stopped off for half an hour somewhere between the junction and the crossing, and during that time he's got rid of Anna.'

'If it *is* Anna.'

'We *know* it's her, John.'

'Yeah . . .'

'And now we know where to find her. I mean, it's half a mile at the most between the junction and the crossing . . . there can't be that many places on that stretch of road where you can park a car without it being seen. You need to get going, John, before it gets too dark –'

'I'm on my way,' I said, starting the car and reversing across the picnic area. 'I'll call you when I get there. In the meantime, if you can get hold of a detailed map of the area –'

'I'm looking at it on Google Earth right now. I can try sending it to your mobile if you want.'

'Who the hell do you think I am?' I said, reversing into the picnic table. 'Jack fucking Bauer?'

By the time I got back to the railway crossing it was almost 5.30 and the daylight was nearly gone. It was that pre-dusk time of day when the light becomes hesitant, unsure what to do with itself, and the form of things is indistinct. There were no streetlights here, and as I pulled in at the side of the road on the south side of the crossing, the view up ahead seemed to lack definition – the grey ribbon of the road itself merging into a green-grey dullness of roadside ditches, low hedges, and barren trees.

I lit a cigarette and called Cal.

'Where are you?' he said.

'At the crossing. Are you still looking at the road on Google Earth?'

'Yeah, and I've found a few places that might be worth checking out. If we assume that he killed her *and* dumped her body somewhere between the junction and the crossing, then he would have had to find a place where he could park the car and do his stuff without being seen. Right?'

'Yeah.'

'OK, well, the road from the junction is pretty well lit for about half a mile, and the only places he could possibly pull off and park are in the fields on either side of the road, but the hedges are quite low around there, and he'd still be out in the open. But further on, heading towards the crossing, there's no lighting *and* there's a couple of places where he could get off the road and not be seen. Do you want me to direct you to them?'

'Yeah.'

'You're facing north, right?'

'Yeah.'

'OK, the nearest one to you is about four hundred yards away, on the left-hand side of the road. That's *your* left. All right?'

'Yeah,' I said, pulling away. 'What am I looking for?'

'There's a right-hand bend in the road, and just past that there's a little dirt track that leads down to a patch of wasteground that looks as if it's filled with piles of gravel or something . . . some kind of roadworks storage, I suppose. Are you there yet?'

'I'm just at the bend . . . hold on. Yeah, I can see the track . . . but there's a gate.'

'A gate? I can't see any gate.'

'Well, it's there,' I said, stopping beside a six-foot-high wire-mesh gate. 'And it's locked . . . it's got a big brass padlock on it.'

'Yeah . . .' Cal muttered. 'I can see it now. It's not very clear . . .'

'I don't think he'd bother with a locked gate, Cal. Even if he could get it open, it'd be too risky. He'd have to stop the car, get out, pick the lock, open the gate –'

'Yeah, OK. Well, leave it for now . . . you can always check it out later. The other place I found looks more promising anyway.'

'Where is it?' I said, pulling back onto the road again.

'Keep going for about another two hundred yards and you should see a lane on your right. I think it's some kind of access road. It heads down towards the railway tracks, and there's a few little buildings down there . . . railway buildings, probably. But there's all kinds of other shit down there too – piles of pallets, old girders, sleepers, rusted machinery –'

'Just a minute, Cal,' I said, slowing the car and peering over to my right.

'Are you there already?'

'No . . . I'm looking at something else.' I stopped the car. Although there was very little traffic, the road here was quite narrow, with nowhere safe to pull in, so I flicked on the hazard lights. 'Can you check something for me?' I said to Cal.

'What is it?'

'I'm about fifty yards north of the gate, and on the right-hand side of the road there's a kind of lay-by . . . but it's cut off from the road behind a strip of trees, so you can't actually see into it from the road. It's like one of those pull-off areas for lorry drivers . . . can you see it yet?'

'I'm still looking . . .'

'There's a slight bend in the road just past it, and the entrance on the north side – the town side – is blocked by two big piles of earth.'

'Yeah, I've got it now.'

'What do you think? It's got to be a pretty isolated spot, because if you're coming from town the first entrance is blocked, and the other entrance, which I suppose is the *exit* really, that's a really tight turn.'

'Yeah, and if you're coming the other way you'd have to cut across the road right after the bend, and you wouldn't want to do that.'

'Can you make out what's in there?'

'Well, like you said, it's not really a lay-by, it's just a lane . . . a pull-off area. I can't see any buildings or anything. It looks like there's a little stream running alongside it . . . maybe a ditch. It veers off to the right about halfway along and heads down a bank towards the railway tracks.'

'I'm going to take a look.'

'Are you sure?'

'Yeah, there's something about it . . . I don't know. It feels . . .' *Like a dead place*, I was going to say. *It feels like a dead place.* Which it did. It felt rotten, decaying, empty, soulless . . . but, for some reason, I didn't want to voice those feelings.

'Listen, Cal,' I said, glancing over my shoulder to check that the road was clear. 'I'm just going to put the phone down for a minute, OK? I've got to make a U-turn and . . . well, you know what my driving's like.'

'OK.'

I put the phone on the passenger seat and glanced over my shoulder again. The road behind me was clear, but I had to wait for a lorry to rumble past from the opposite direction. Once it had gone, I put the car into gear and swung a tight U-turn so I was heading back in the direction I'd just come from, and then almost immediately I slowed down again to make the 180-degree left turn into the lay-by. It was just a narrow track at first, curving round to the right, before gradually straightening out into a slightly broader stretch of gravelled concrete. The night was almost fully dark now, and as I drove slowly towards the widest part of the lay-by, the beam of my headlights lit up the gloom in front of me. The lay-by itself was just a flat slab of emptiness, a pot-holed lane with a bulge in the middle. There were a few scraps of litter around – an empty KFC box, some burger wrappers, carrier bags hanging in trees – but none of it looked fresh. This wasn't a well-used place. The surrounding trees and hedges seemed to lean in towards the lay-by, giving the whole place a tunnel-like sense of enclosure and isolation.

I parked the car and turned off the engine.

The silence was acute.

I sat there for a while, gazing around at the rapidly dimming surroundings, letting my eyes adjust to the darkness, and I tried to imagine what I'd be thinking if it was 2.30 in the morning and there was a dead body in my car. *Would you get rid of it here?* I asked myself. *Would you feel safe getting rid of it here? And, if so, where exactly would you dump it?*

I picked up my mobile.

'Cal?' I said.

'Is everything all right?'

'Yeah. I'm in the lay-by now. I'm just going to take a quick look round, OK?'

'Keep your phone on.'

'Yeah.'

I reached under the seat and pulled out a torch, checked it was working, turned it off again, then opened the door and stepped out. I'd already spotted the stream that Cal had mentioned – or, at least, I'd seen the top of a tree-lined clay bank that ran alongside the lay-by, stopping about halfway along, and I was pretty sure it was the bank of the stream that Cal had seen on Google Earth. As I crossed the lay-by, heading for the point where the bank dropped away, I could smell a growing sourness in the air – rotted leaves, waste, dead things. The stagnant odour of decay. There was a small gap between the end of the bank and a thick black tangle of hawthorn trees – just enough room for an adult man to squeeze through – and as I approached the gap, I turned on the torch. I'm not sure what I was expecting to see – footprints, maybe . . . a scrap of cloth caught on a branch – but, of course, there wasn't anything there. If anything *had* happened here, it had happened a month ago – time enough for the wind and rain to remove all traces of evidence.

I moved closer to the gap, raising the torch to see if I could make out what was on the other side. I saw darkness, an empty space, the tops of trees. I edged into the gap, turning sideways to avoid the worst of the thorns, and slowly eased my way through. My feet kept slipping on the rain-moistened clay and I had to grab hold of a thickish branch to steady myself. I cautiously inched forward, sweeping the torchlight over the ground in front of me. To my left, it was all trees – a dense thicket of hawthorn – while away to my right I could see the stream, a shallow run of muddy brown water oozing along a dirty clay ditch. To my immediate right, where the bank fell away, there was a surprisingly sudden drop of about eight to ten feet, at the bottom of which was a boggy black pool. The stream trickled down into the pool, before oozing away again into a sparse patch of littered woodland. The pool had clearly been used as a dump over the years, and as I shone my torch down into the darkness, I could see all kinds of discarded waste down there: great lumps of concrete, dried-up sacks of cement, rolls of rusted wire mesh, sheets of corrugated iron, an old metal trough, iron poles and rusted chains and . . .

'Shit,' I heard myself whisper.

There was a face down there.

The remains of a face.

There wasn't much left of it, and it was half covered by sodden strands of long black hair, but there was no doubt in my mind whose face it was.

Breathing slowly, I took the phone from my pocket and held it to my ear.

'Cal?' I said.

'What's happening, John?'

'I've found her.'

'*What?*'

'Anna Gerrish . . . I've found her.'

16

She was lying on her back in the shallows of the pool, completely naked, her body draped limply over a large sack of rubble. Her bone-white skin was streaked with grainy black mud and silt. One arm was twisted back under her body, and both her legs were bent at unnatural angles. I guessed she'd been thrown down the bank, or just dropped, probably when she was already dead, and the fall had broken her legs. There were dark gashes all over her body, possibly stab wounds, and a larger opening in the right side of her abdomen. I focused the torch beam on her neck, looking for the half-moon necklace that her mother had told me she always wore, but there was nothing there.

'John?' Cal said. 'Are you there?'

'Yeah . . .'

'Are you sure it's her?'

'As sure as I can be.'

'Where is she?'

I told him.

'And where are you?' he said.

'At the top of the bank, about ten feet above her.'

'Stay there,' he said firmly. 'Don't go anywhere near her, OK?'

'Yeah.'

'Are you going to call the police?'

'I have to.'

'Bishop?'

'No . . . I'll just call 999. Bishop's going to find out eventually, but I don't want to have to deal with him straight away.'

'All right, but we have to get our story straight first, before you call anyone –'

'What *story*?'

'Shit, John,' he said. 'Think about it . . . they're going to want to know how you found her, aren't they? And you can't tell them what we've been doing all day, all this shit with the CCTV cameras –'

'They won't care about that.'

'Maybe not, but if they start sniffing around me, which they would . . . well, I'd be fucked, John. Well and truly fucked.'

'All right,' I said. 'How about if I just tell them that I was following up on what Tasha told me? Bishop already knows that I talked to her, so if I just tell them what she told me about Anna getting picked up that night . . . all I'd have to say then was that I followed up on that information by driving around looking for places where her body might have been dumped . . . what do you think?'

'It's not very believable.'

'I know . . . but it's pretty much what actually happened, isn't it? Believable or not, it's not too far from the truth. The only thing I'd be keeping from them is how we narrowed down the search area.'

'Yeah, I suppose . . .' Cal said thoughtfully. 'Maybe you

should keep the Nissan out of it too? Bishop's going to be running the murder investigation, isn't he? And if he *has* got some kind of link with the Nissan . . . well, maybe it's just best to tell him as little as possible.'

'Yeah, but I texted him the registration number, remember? He already *knows* that I know about the Nissan. Although . . .'

'What?'

'Well, there's going to be a full-scale murder investigation, isn't there? And, yeah, Bishop's going to be in charge of it. But if he's got something to hide, he won't just have to hide it from me any more, he'll have to keep it from everyone else who's involved in the investigation.'

'Yeah, everyone who's not in his pocket.'

'They're not *all* bent, Cal.'

'You reckon?'

'Yeah, I do.'

'Shit . . .' he sighed. 'This is a right fucking mess.'

'Look,' I said. 'I'll call the police now, and when they get here I'll tell them as much of the truth as I can without mentioning you, OK?'

'And what about Bishop? What are you going to tell him?'

'I don't know . . . I'll see what happens.'

'That's it? You'll just "see what happens"?'

'Yeah.'

'It's not much of a plan, John.'

'Yeah, well,' I said, 'the best-laid schemes of mice and men . . .'

'What?'

'They gang aft agley.'

'*What?*'

'Nothing,' I muttered, looking down at Anna's pale body . . . naked, butchered, bled white . . .

Dead.

For ever . . .

'John?' Cal said. 'Are you all right?'

'Not really . . .'

'Do you want me to –?'

'Listen, Cal. I'll call you later, OK?'

'I can come out there if you want.'

'No . . . it's OK. I'll just . . . I'll call you later.'

The first police car turned up about fifteen minutes later – two uniformed constables in a patrol car – but even as I was showing them where the body was, more vehicles began to arrive, and within about an hour or so the once-gloomy isolation of the lay-by had been transformed into a brightly lit hive of activity. A crime-scene tent had been erected, floodlights blazed, there were uniformed officers all over the place, CID detectives, scenes-of-crime officers, a doctor, pathologist, photographer . . . all of them bustling around, doing what they had to do, which included asking me lots of questions. By the time Mick Bishop finally arrived, I must have told my story at least three or four times already. But as Bishop got out of his Vectra and immediately began taking control of the scene, I knew that it was going to be the story I told *him*, and how I told it, that really mattered.

I was sitting in the back of a car with a female officer called

DC Roberts when Bishop first arrived. Roberts was asking me some more questions – and also, I think, just keeping an eye on me – and as she carried on talking, I watched Mick Bishop striding around the lay-by, doing his thing – barking out orders, demanding answers, telling people where to go and what to do. He never once looked over at me. He spent very little time at the actual crime scene either. I saw him go through the gap between the end of the bank and the hawthorn trees, and in the bright white light of the floodlights I saw him gazing down at the pool below, but he didn't go any further. He just stared down at Anna's body for a while, asked a few questions, then turned round and came back.

And now, I could see, he was heading towards me.

He looked tired, his skin even paler than usual in the blaze of sterile white light, and there was a depth of cold determination to his eyes that I hadn't seen before. I didn't like the look of it at all. As he came round the back of the car, DC Roberts opened the door for him.

'We're going to need lifting equipment to get the body out,' he said to her. 'Sort it out, OK?'

'Sir,' she said, closing her notebook and getting out of the car.

Bishop waited for her to leave, then got in, sat down beside me, and closed the door.

'Why didn't you call me?' he said calmly.

'I called the police –'

'Why didn't you call *me*?'

'I didn't have your number.'

'I gave you my card.'

'Yeah, I lost it –'

'Bollocks.' He stared angrily at me. 'I told you, didn't I? I fucking *told* you not to do anything without telling me first.'

'I was just driving around –'

'Yeah, so I've heard. You were just driving around and you just happened to find her. Is that the best you can do?'

'It's the truth.'

'Like fuck it is.' He stared at me. 'How did you know, John? How did you know where she was?'

'I didn't –'

'Come on, John,' he said, smiling thinly. 'You can tell me. Look, there's no one else here, just you and me . . . whatever you say to me now, I can't use it. So come on, humour, how did you find her?'

'I looked.'

'That's it? You *looked*.'

'Yeah. It wasn't that difficult, really. I just asked a few questions and went where the answers took me. Anyone could have done it if they'd made the effort.'

'What are you trying to say?'

I shrugged. 'Nothing . . . I'm just answering your question.'

We looked at each other in silence for a few moments, Bishop tapping his ring finger on his knee, his mouth tight, his eyes focused . . . and I could imagine the hum of his brain, the busy grey flesh behind his eyes, trying to work things out – assessing the options, running things through, considering this, considering that . . .

I was so tired – and drained by the speed – that my own grey flesh was dancing like a brain-damaged boxer.

Eventually, Bishop sighed and said, 'You know what your trouble is, don't you?'

'I'm sure you're going to tell me.'

He smiled. 'You're just like your father. He was a fucking pain in the arse too. And look where it got him.'

About an hour later, I was driven away to Eastway police station where I spent another hour or so sitting around, waiting to have my fingerprints and DNA taken again, for elimination purposes. I was then escorted to an interview room for further questioning.

'DCI Bishop's still at the crime scene,' a uniformed PC told me. 'But he shouldn't be long. So if you'd just like to wait in here until he's available . . .'

'Can't someone else do it?' I said.

'Sorry . . . DCI's orders.'

He closed the door, and I sat down and waited.

I just have to wait. And wait . . .

And I wait.

Monday, Tuesday, Wednesday, Thursday . . . long days and eternal nights of oblivion, living for nothing, waiting for nothing . . . what is there to wait for? DI Delaney will call me soon about the DNA results from the piece of flesh retrieved from Stacy's stomach, and then I will either know or not know the identity of the man who raped and butchered the love of my life. But even if the killer is identified, even if he is arrested, charged, tried and convicted . . . what difference will it make?

What happened cannot be unhappened.

Stacy will always be dead.

And for ever is a long long time.

So why do I wait?

What am I waiting for?

It's Friday 27 August, about 10.30 at night, and I'm sitting in the front room, drinking whisky, trying to drink myself to sleep. This is where I sleep now. I haven't been in the bedroom since the day it happened. I can't go in there any more. I spend my nights sitting on the settee, staring at the television, drinking whisky – and taking whatever drugs I have – until I pass out. And then I wake up and start all over again.

Tonight, I'm purely drunk. I have a couple of grams of cocaine somewhere, but I don't want cocaine now. I don't want to be awake. I don't want to think about anything. I just want to drink and drink and stare at the pictures on the television screen until I can't see anything any more ...

And that's what I'm doing when I hear a faint sound from the hallway, a soft metallic clack. It sounds like the letterbox flapping shut, the familiar sound of post being delivered ... but it can't be. Not at this time of night. I almost ignore it, too drunk to care if I'm hearing things or not, but for some reason I find myself stumbling to my feet and shuffling out into the hallway ... and there, on the floor by the front door, is an envelope. A plain white envelope. I stare at it for a moment, then lean down and pick it up. My name is typed on the front – JOHN CRAINE – but nothing else. No address, no stamp.

I open the front door.

There's no one there.

I walk up the garden path, open the gate, and look up and down the street.

There's no one there.

I go back into the house, into the front room, and open the envelope. Inside is a single sheet of plain white writing paper. I take it out, unfold it, and read the typed message:

> The DNA retrieved from the hair and flesh sample in Stacy Craine's stomach is a 100% match with the DNA profile of ANTON VINER. Viner was convicted in 1977 for aggravated rape and sentenced to 15 years. He was released in 1985. He was arrested again for sexual assault in 1989, but the charges were dropped. Viner's current address is: 27 School Lane, Hey, Essex, HE15 9ES. This information will NOT be forwarded to DI Delaney until 09.00 tomorrow morning (Sat 28 August).

I read it again, and again . . . and again. There's no signature, no name, no indication who it's from. But it has to be from someone who either works in the crime lab or who has access to someone who works in the crime lab. I think about it . . . dredging through the sludge of my memory for anyone I know who could possibly fit the bill, and the only two names I come up with are Leon Mercer and Cliff Duffy . . .

Could either of them have sent it?

Does it matter?

I read the message again . . .

And again.

And, drunk as I am, I know what I have. I have an anonymous message giving me the name and address of the man who killed Stacy. A man called Anton Viner. A convicted rapist. I have his address . . . I know where he is. And in roughly ten hours' time, I know that he'll be arrested and taken into custody.

But until then . . .

Until then . . .

He's mine.

It was almost 10.30 when the door to the interview room opened and Mick Bishop came in. He was accompanied by a haggard-looking man in a shitty brown suit, who he didn't bother introducing. The two of them just sat down opposite me, and the man in the brown suit unwrapped two cassette tapes, loaded them into a tape-recorder, and turned it on.

'Right,' Bishop said wearily, his voice on automatic. 'This interview is being tape-recorded. My name is DCI Michael Bishop, Hey CID. Also present is . . .'

'DS Alan Coleman, Hey CID.'

'And . . .' Bishop looked at me. 'State your full name, please.'

'John Craine.'

'The date is 8 October 2010, 10.31pm. This interview is being conducted at Eastway police station in Hey . . .'

As he carried on going through the procedure, advising me of my rights, explaining this and explaining that, I very nearly fell asleep. It was too hot in there. Stuffy. The air felt used up, as if it had been breathed too many times. I wanted a cigarette. I wanted a drink. I wanted to go home and go to bed and close my eyes and forget about everything.

'Mr Craine?' Bishop said.

'What?'

'Do you understand what I've just told you?'

'Yes,' I said.

'Good. OK . . . let's get on with it.' He looked at me. 'At 18.37 this evening you called the police to report the discovery of a body in a lay-by on Great Hey Road. Is that correct?'

'Yes.'

'I'd like you to tell me what you were doing there.'

'I'm a private investigator. I was recently hired to look into the disappearance of a young woman called Anna Gerrish. After making some enquiries, I came to the conclusion that she'd been abducted from London Road in the early hours of the morning and that her abductor had driven off along Great Hey Road in the direction of Hale Island. So I followed that route, keeping my eyes open for places where a body might possibly be dumped, and the lay-by was just one of those places.'

Bishop just stared at me. 'Did you search anywhere else?'

'Not really . . .'

'Did you search anywhere else?' he repeated. 'Yes or no?'

'I stopped at a few other places, but I didn't actually get out of the car –'

'So,' he said. 'Let me get this straight – you were driving along Great Hey Road, looking for Ms Gerrish's body, and the first place you stopped at . . . or rather, the first place you stopped at and *got out of the car*, was the lay-by. Is that right?'

'Yes.'

'And how did you know exactly where to find the body?'

'I didn't . . . I just looked around –'

'You just looked around?'

'Yes.'

'And you found it?'

'That's right.'

He didn't say anything for a moment, just carried on looking at me, then he said, 'All right, let me ask you something else. How did you know that Anna Gerrish was dead?'

'I didn't –'

'But you went looking for her body anyway?'

'She was missing,' I said. 'No one had heard from her for a month. I thought there was a fairly good chance that she was dead.'

'But you didn't know for sure?'

'No.'

He paused again for a moment, slowly nodding his head, as if he was digesting what I'd just told him and carefully considering what to ask me next – but I knew it was all a show. He knew exactly what he was doing. And I was pretty sure that *I* knew exactly what he was doing too: *not* asking me anything about Tasha, or what she'd told me; *not* asking me anything about the Nissan, or the driver; *not* mentioning anything about the registration number I'd texted him. He didn't want any of *that* on tape.

He looked down, sniffed, then looked up at me again. 'Where were you on the night that Anna Gerrish disappeared, Mr Craine?'

'Where was I?'

He nodded. 'On the night of Monday 6 September, the early hours of Tuesday morning – where were you?'

I shook my head. 'I've no idea.'

'Think about it.'

I thought about it, then shook my head again. 'It was over a month ago, I can't remember. I was probably in bed –'

'Probably?'

'Yeah, probably.'

'But you can't remember?'

'No . . .' I looked at him. 'Can you remember where *you* were that night?'

He stared back at me. 'I was here, in this very room, from midnight until three in the morning. I was interviewing a witness about an alleged assault.'

I smiled at him. 'You've got a good memory.'

'You think this is *amusing*, Mr Craine? A young woman, stabbed to death . . . her body dumped in a lay-by . . . you think that's *funny*?'

There was no point answering that, so I didn't.

Bishop just looked at me for a few moments, then he turned to DS Coleman beside him and said, 'All right?'

Coleman nodded.

Bishop glanced at his watch. 'Interview terminated at 22.41.'

Coleman turned off the tape-recorder.

'Is that it?' I said.

Bishop nodded.

'What about –?'

'The interview's over,' he said, turning to DS Coleman. 'Give us a few minutes, will you, Alan?'

With another silent nod of his head, Coleman got to his feet, removed the two tapes from the recorder, and left the room.

Bishop waited for him to close the door, then he sat back in his chair, crossed his legs, and smiled at me. 'You look tired, John.'

'You too.'

He sniffed. 'All right, listen to me . . . this is over for you now, OK? You're going to go home, go to bed, get some sleep, and then tomorrow morning you're going to go back to your shitty little office and get back to doing your shitty little job. Do you understand me?'

I said nothing.

'This is now an official murder investigation,' he went on. 'If you get in touch with anyone – and I mean *any*one – who has *any*thing to do with this case, and that includes the Gerrishes, I'll have you arrested for obstruction, wasting police time, perverting the course of justice . . . whatever the fuck I can think of. Have you got that?'

I nodded. 'Do they know yet?'

'Who?'

'Mr and Mrs Gerrish . . . have you told them?'

He sighed. 'They've been informed that a woman's body has been found, that's all. We can't tell them anything else until the identity's been confirmed.'

'But you know it's her, don't you? You know it's Anna?'

'What did I just *tell* you?' he said, beginning to lose his temper. 'This has got *nothing* to do with you any more. This is a *police* investigation. You are *not* police, you are *not* involved in any way, shape, or fucking form.' He leaned forward and spoke slowly, looking me in the eye. 'Now ... do you understand?'

'Yes,' I said calmly. 'I understand.'

'You'd fucking better.'

I looked at him. 'Can I go now?'

He sniffed again, pausing for a moment just to make me wait, then he jerked his head at the door. 'Yeah, go on, fuck off.'

PART TWO

∞

FRIDAY 22 OCTOBER – SATURDAY 23 OCTOBER 2010

17

Two weeks later, on a cold and misty Friday morning, I was sitting on an old wooden bench in my backyard, drinking coffee and listening to Bridget Moran as she told me about a fat little boy and a mouse.

I'd been seeing quite a lot of Bridget over the last ten days or so, mainly because she'd finally split up with Dave and didn't like being on her own too much, and although I often heard her talking to her dog, Walter, I knew that she needed a bit of human company every now and again. Of course, I liked to think that there was a *little* bit more to it than that, but I didn't really mind if there wasn't. If all I was to Bridget was a convenient pair of human ears, and if all we ever did was share the occasional cup of coffee together . . . well, that was perfectly all right with me.

After my interview at the police station – and after three or four days of stultifying depression, when all I could do was lie in bed and wait for the black place to leave me – I'd done what Mick Bishop had told me to do: I'd gone back to my shitty little office and got back to doing my shitty little job. Apart from one phone call to Cal, I hadn't got in touch with anyone who had anything to do with the Anna Gerrish case, including Helen and Graham Gerrish. I hadn't even sent them a bill. I'd just got back to living my

215

life, doing my job . . . working insurance cases, tracing bad debts, tracking down the makers of pirate DVDs . . .

The Anna Gerrish case *was* over for me: I'd done what I'd been hired to do; I'd found her. It wasn't my job to find out who'd killed her. It wasn't my business to ask any more questions. Who was driving the Nissan that night? Who was Charles Raymond Kemper? Did Kemper kill Anna? Did Bishop kill Anna? If he didn't, what was he trying to hide? And if he did . . .?

No . . . it wasn't my business.

Right now, my business was investigating the alleged whiplash injuries suffered by a 48-year-old woman in a minor road-traffic accident. That's what I was being paid to do. And once Bridget had finished telling me about the fat little boy and the mouse, and after I'd had another cigarette, or maybe two, and perhaps another cup of coffee or two . . . that's exactly what I was going to do.

'You know the kind of fat kid I mean, don't you?' Bridget said.

She was dressed up warmly in a baggy old jumper and fleece-lined boots, her short blonde hair hidden beneath a red woollen hat, and she was sipping her coffee with both hands wrapped round the cup, like a small child drinking orange juice from a beaker.

'Sorry,' I said, smiling at her. 'I was miles away for a minute there. Who was this fat kid again?'

Just then, Walter wandered out through the back door. He paused on the step for a moment, sniffing the air, then he shook his head and lolloped across the yard. Bridget watched him with quiet affection as he found a bush, cocked his leg, scratted the ground, then went back in again.

'It's too cold for him,' she said.

'You should get him a coat.'

'He's got a coat.'

A veil of mist hung in the air, suffused with the sour tang of nettles. Small birds were flitting from wall to wall, and somewhere in the distance I could hear the unseasonal chimes of an ice-cream van.

I felt OK.

'Right,' Bridget said. 'Are you listening now?'

'I'm all ears.'

'OK, so . . . Wednesday morning, this fat kid came into the shop looking to buy a mouse . . .'

Bridget was the joint owner of a pet shop in town. It was only a small place, nothing fancy – no chinchillas or snakes or lizards, just fish, birds, mice, rabbits . . .

'. . . and I refused to sell him one.'

'You refused to sell him a mouse?'

'Yeah.'

'Why?'

She shrugged. 'I didn't like the look of him. He was one of those nasty fat kids with piggy little eyes, you know, the ones who always get what they want. If I'd sold him a mouse it would have been dead within a week. So I told him he couldn't have one.'

'What did he do?'

'The little shit went and got his dad. The two of them came back in the afternoon – fat kid, fat dad.' She smiled. 'Fat dad said that if I didn't sell his boy a mouse, he'd take me to court.'

217

'What did you do?'

'Told him to contact my lawyer.'

I lit a cigarette. 'There's probably a joke in there somewhere.'

'Probably.'

She raised the coffee cup to her mouth and gently blew at the steam.

I said, 'Why aren't you at the shop today anyway?'

She smiled. 'I'm skiving, the same as you.'

'I'm not *skiving* ... I'm just taking a break. I'll have to get back to it soon.'

'Yeah, well . . . it's my afternoon off. Sarah's in charge today.'

'Who's Sarah again?'

'My partner.'

'Oh yeah ... I remember you telling me about her.'

Bridget looked at me. 'Yeah, I did, didn't I?'

'What?'

'I told you about Sarah.'

'That's what I just said.'

'I know . . .'

She was still looking at me, and there seemed to be a question in her eyes. And I got the feeling that I was supposed to know what it was, but I didn't.

'What?' I asked her. 'What is it?'

She smiled. 'How long have we known each other, John?'

'I don't know ... about ten years?'

'Closer to thirteen, actually. Thirteen years. And in all that time ... well, I know we're not really *close* or anything, but we've talked to each other quite a lot, haven't we?'

'Yeah . . .'

'And I've told you quite a bit about myself – how I met Sarah, how we got the shop together, what I like doing, what I did when I was a kid . . . things like that. I mean, you *know* stuff about me, don't you?'

'Yeah . . .'

'But I still don't *really* know anything about you. I know that your mother used to own this house, and that your wife was killed . . . and I know what you do for a living, but that's about all.' She sipped from her coffee cup, looking at me over the rim. 'You don't mind, do you?'

'Mind what?'

She shrugged. 'Me . . . you know . . .'

'No,' I said. 'I don't mind.'

'Are you sure?'

'Yeah.'

She smiled. 'You can tell me to shut up if you want.'

I looked at her, my heart beating hard with an expectation that I wasn't sure I wanted. 'What do you want to know about me?' I asked her.

'Anything, really . . . whatever you want to tell me.'

'Like what?'

'Tell me about your wife.'

'Stacy?'

'Yeah . . . Stacy.' Bridget smiled. 'Tell me how you met her.'

It was the smile that did it, I think. Bridget's smile. If she'd been at all hesitant in asking me about Stacy, or if there'd been any trace of sadness or pity in her voice, I probably would have made an excuse and tried to change the subject. But the way she asked, as if the memory of Stacy was something to be celebrated, not mourned or avoided or tiptoed around . . . somehow that made all the difference. And as I began telling Bridget about the summer of 1990, I realised that this was the first time I'd talked to anyone but myself about Stacy since the day she was killed.

'I'd just finished my first year at university,' I told Bridget, 'and I'd come back home for the summer –'

'What were you studying?' she said.

'Philosophy.'

'Why?'

I looked at her. 'I don't know . . . I thought it'd be interesting, I suppose.'

'Was it?'

I shrugged. 'It was OK. I mean, to be honest, I didn't really know what I was doing back then. I didn't know what I wanted to be, what I wanted to do with my life . . . my father was hoping that I'd join the police force after I'd taken my degree –'

'The police?'

'Yeah, well, he was a police officer –'

'Really?'

I nodded. 'And so was *his* father . . . so, you know, it was kind of a family tradition.'

'So what does your dad think of you being a *private* detective?'

'He's dead now.'

'Oh . . . I'm sorry.'

I nodded again. 'Well, anyway . . . it was the summer of

1990, a Friday night, and I was having a drink in the Double Locks . . . you know the place I mean?'

'Yeah, down by the river . . . it's a nice pub.'

'Yeah, so I was just sitting there, a little bit drunk –'

'Were you on your own?'

'Yeah.'

'Why? I mean, didn't you have any friends or a girlfriend or anything?'

I shrugged. 'I didn't have a girlfriend at the time, no. I had friends . . . I mean, I *knew* people. I just . . . I don't know. I just liked being on my own, that's all.'

Bridget smiled. 'Fair enough. So you were on your own, a little bit drunk, and you were having a drink . . . then what?'

'I saw Stacy. She was with a group of people who I found out later were teachers from the school where she'd just started working . . . I suppose it must have been a teachers' Friday night out or something –'

'Or an end-of-term celebration?'

'Yeah . . . something like that. There were about a dozen of them – men and women, young and old – and they all seemed to be having a pretty good time. Stacy was at the bar with an older man when I first saw her. He was in his late twenties, early thirties, and I thought he was *with* her, you know . . .? The way he was standing really close to her, touching her arm, her shoulder, whispering in her ear . . . I thought they were a couple. But I still couldn't take my eyes off Stacy.'

'What did she look like?'

'Stunning . . . I mean, just really, really beautiful. Not in a fancy, glamorous kind of way, she was just . . . I don't know. There was just something about her. Her eyes, her face . . . everything. She was the most wonderful thing I'd ever seen.'

'Describe her.'

'What?'

'I want to know what she *looked* like. You know, was she tall, short, blonde . . .?'

'Blonde, yeah. Short blonde hair, blue eyes, pale skin . . . she wasn't tall.' I looked at Bridget. 'About your height . . .'

My voice trailed off and I lowered my eyes as I realised that my description of Stacy could easily have been a description of Bridget, and for some reason I found that oddly embarrassing.

'So did you make a move?' Bridget said, smiling. 'Or did you spend all night just looking at her?'

'Make a move?'

She laughed. 'You know what I mean.'

'Actually,' I said, 'if it wasn't for Stacy, I probably *would* have spent all night just looking at her.'

'So *she* made the first move?'

'Yeah . . . I'd been watching her for about half an hour or so, when I suddenly realised that she was staring right back at me from the bar. So I immediately looked away, you know . . . I probably started fiddling with my cigarettes or a beer mat or something in a vain attempt to make out that I hadn't been staring at her at all. But then the next thing I knew, I heard someone say, "Would you like to buy me a drink?" And when I looked up, there she was, standing right in front of me with an irresistible smile on her face.'

'And what did you say?'

'I said, "I'm sorry?"'

'Very cool.'

'I know. She didn't seem to mind though, she just kind of cocked her head and looked at me and said it again, "Would you like to buy me a drink?" And this time I said, "Yeah, yeah, I'd love to buy you a drink." And then I stood up and started going through my pockets, looking for some money, but all I had on me was a pound . . . one measly pound coin.'

Bridget laughed.

'So then Stacy said to me, "Would you like to borrow some money?" And that was pretty much it.'

'That was it?'

'Well, it turned out that she wasn't with the man at the bar after all, he was just a teacher at her school who'd been chasing after her ever since she'd first started working there . . . she didn't even like him.'

'But she liked you.'

'Well, we spent the rest of that night together, and the whole of that weekend, and after that we were together just about all the time. It was . . . I don't know. It was like I just didn't want or need anything else any more . . . all I wanted was to be with Stace, *all* the time. That's all that mattered.'

'You loved her.'

'Yeah . . . yeah, I did. I never even thought about going back to university, I just forgot all about it and moved in with Stace, and while she carried on teaching, I just took on any old jobs that were going, just to bring in some extra money. I worked on a building site, I was a postman, I worked in a call centre . . . I even had a job at the crematorium for a while.'

'Very nice,' Bridget said, raising her eyebrows.

'Yeah, well . . . I didn't care what I did. As long as I was with Stacy –'

'That's all that mattered.'

I smiled. 'Yeah.'

'So then what?' Bridget said. 'You got married . . .?'

'Yeah, then about eighteen months later we found out that Stacy was pregnant –'

I stopped at the sound of the doorbell ringing. As Walter started barking upstairs, I looked at Bridget. 'Are you expecting anyone?'

'It could be Melanie,' she said. 'A friend of mine. She said she might come over.' Bridget looked at me, and I felt her hand on my knee. 'I can tell her to go if you want.'

'No,' I said. 'It's all right . . . I'd better get back to work anyway.'

'Are you sure?'

'Yeah . . .'

'Maybe we can talk some more later on tonight?'

'Yeah, that'd be good.'

The doorbell sounded again.

Bridget smiled, getting to her feet. 'I'd better let her in. See you later, OK?'

I nodded, watching as she went back into the house and started yelling at Walter to be quiet. I lit a cigarette and sat there in the misty haze, trying to work out how I felt. I was slightly confused with myself for feeling OK about talking to Bridget about Stacy, but I *did* feel OK about it, and I guessed that was all right. I was only talking to her, after all. It wasn't as if I was *betraying* anything, was it? We were only *talking* . . .

'Yeah, I know, Stace,' I muttered. 'That's what they all say, isn't it? We were only fucking talking . . .'

It's all right, it's fine. I like her.

'John?' I heard Bridget say.

I looked up and saw her standing at the back door.

'There's a man here to see you,' she said. 'He says his name's Bishop.'

18

When I went inside the house, Bishop was standing outside my door, doing his best to ignore Walter, who was sitting at the foot of the stairs snarling quietly at him.

'I hope you don't mind, John,' Bishop said to me, glancing at Bridget as she followed me along the hallway. 'But I let myself in. It's a bit cold out there.'

Walter barked at him.

He glared at Bridget. 'Is that yours?'

'Sorry,' she said, taking Walter by the collar and leading him up the stairs. 'Come on, Wally, let's go.' She glanced over her shoulder at me, silently asking me if everything was OK.

I nodded at her. She nodded back and carried on up the stairs.

Bishop watched them go, waited until they'd gone, then turned back to me with the hint of a smirk on his face. 'I'm not interrupting anything, am I?'

'What do you want?' I said.

The smirk disappeared. 'I need to talk to you, John. And I'd rather not do it in the hallway, if that's all right with you.'

I opened the door and showed him inside, and without so much as a word he made his way into the front room and positioned himself at the window, standing with his hands in his pockets, peering out at the street. I followed him in, sat down on the settee, and lit a cigarette. He didn't say anything for a while, he just stood there with his back to me, which I guessed was intended to make me feel anxious or offended or insignificant or something . . . but I didn't care *what* it made me feel. I just smoked my cigarette and waited for him to say something.

Eventually, with a casual stretch of his neck and a better-get-on-with-it sigh, he reluctantly gave in to the silence.

'So,' he said, turning from the window. 'Who's the girl?'

'Bridget Moran,' I told him. 'She's my tenant.'

'You own this place then?'

I nodded.

He looked at me for a moment, knowingly nodding his head, then he adjusted his tie and wandered over to a ramshackle shelf that spans the width of an alcove next to the double doors. The shelf is dotted with all kinds of bits and pieces: glass jars, a painted wooden spoon, a framed photograph of Stacy, a mouth organ, a clockwork crab, a stuffed bird, a candlestick . . . Bishop picked up the clock-work crab, wiped it free of dust, and turned it over to examine the workings. The clockwork shell looked wrong in his hands, like a child's bauble in the hands of a giant. He poked at the crab's feet, pronging a broken claw with his thumb, then he put the toy back on the shelf and looked disdainfully around my room.

'Is she your only tenant?' he said idly.

'Sorry?'

'Miss Moran . . . is she your only tenant?'

'Yes.'

He grinned at me. 'What's the rent like?'

I didn't say anything, I just looked at him.

'Anyway,' he said, sniffing again. 'The reason I'm here . . . well, it's about the Anna Gerrish case.' He paused for a moment, put his hands in his pockets, and looked at me. 'You know the body's been identified, don't you?'

I nodded. 'It was in the papers last week.'

'DNA results confirmed it was Anna. The forensic team are still working on evidence from the site, but because of the length of time the body had been out there, and the fact that it was half-submerged for most of the time, it's been difficult to come up with any definitive conclusions. We know that she was stabbed to death, and we're almost certain that she was killed at the lay-by, or very close by, but we can't tell if she was sexually assaulted or not, and so far we haven't been able to ascertain an accurate time of death. And it's very unlikely that we will. But we're working on the theory that she was killed on the night she disappeared.'

I nodded again, keeping my eyes on Bishop, my head full of questions I wanted to ask but couldn't: *have you seen the CCTV footage? have you identified the car or the driver? have you talked to Genna Raven or Tasha? do you know how much I know? do you know that I know that you've got something to do with it?*

'Why are you telling me all this?' I said, putting out my cigarette and lighting another. 'You told me yourself, it's nothing to do with me any more. It's a police investigation. I'm not police. I'm not involved in any way, shape, or fucking form –'

228

'I know what I told you,' Bishop said coldly. 'But things change, John. Things *have* changed.'

'What kind of things?'

He paused for a second before answering, briefly looking away from me, and I wondered if this was the moment that I'd been half-expecting for the last two weeks – the moment when Bishop made his play and tried to implicate *me* in the death of Anna Gerrish. I hoped that it wasn't, but I'd had plenty of time to prepare myself for it, so I wasn't all that worried. I felt that I was ready.

I couldn't have been more wrong.

Bishop took a breath and spoke calmly. 'A number of human hairs were retrieved from under Anna's fingernails,' he said. 'And some of these hairs still had the roots attached, which means that the forensic team were able to extract DNA samples from the cells. Of course, we can't say for *sure* that the hairs came from Anna's killer . . .' He shrugged lightly. 'But it's fairly damning evidence.'

'Have you matched the DNA?' I said, my mouth suddenly dry.

Bishop nodded. 'Forensics confirmed it this morning.' He looked at me. 'The DNA profile of the hairs found under Anna Gerrish's fingernails is a one-in-a-billion match with the DNA profile of Anton Viner.'

'*Viner?*' I whispered.

'It's been checked and double-checked.'

'That's *impossible*.'

He's mine . . .

At approximately 01.45, at the heart of a shabby grey

council estate on the east side of town, I pull up at the far end of School Lane, park the car and turn off the engine. The street is empty. I shut the window, get out of the car, and lock it. Somewhere nearby, perhaps at the other end of the street, a party is going on. I can hear music, bass beats thumping. Shouts and laughter cracking the night. I walk along the pavement, swaying slightly, counting the house numbers until I get to 27. It's the same as all the other houses in the street: breezeblock grey, semi-detached, with curtained windows and a neglected patch of front garden. A warm wind drifts in the night as I stand at the front gate gazing up at the lightless windows, thinking of nothing . . .

There's nothing to think.

My father's pistol weighs heavily in my pocket as I open the gate and walk up the path. Apart from the distant sound of revelry, there's no sign of life anywhere – no twitching curtains, no barking dogs – just the empty night and the empty street and the empty purpose in my soul. I step up to the front door and ring the bell.

I'm as fucked as I'm ever going to be.

Nothing happens for a while, but I'm too intoxicated and too determined to wonder if Viner isn't home. He's here. He was always going to be here. I know it more than I've ever known anything. I ring the bell again, and this time, almost immediately, a light comes on upstairs. I put my hand in my pocket and take out a pair of gloves. As the upstairs window opens above me, I pull on the gloves, remove the pistol from my pocket, and move closer to the door.

'Who is it?' a voice calls down. 'Hello? Who's there?'

He can't see me. There's a narrow porchway roof above

the door, just wide enough to keep me out of sight. I ring the doorbell again.

'Fuck's sake,' the voice from above says. 'Hey . . . I'm up here . . . HEY! Who the fuck –?'

I press the doorbell again, and this time I keep it held down. The voice at the window curses and snarls for a little while longer, then eventually I hear the window slam shut and I know he's coming down.

I release the bell.

Through mottled glass at either side of the door, I see the landing light come on. I hear the muffled thump of angry footsteps coming down the stairs, and then the hallway light comes on. The patterned glass distorts the shape of the figure approaching the door, and for a moment I'm seeing a monster, a dark beast with an oversized head, but then the misformed monster yanks open the door, and all I'm looking at is a man. He's middle-aged, with long lank hair, a flabby face, sallow skin. His eyes are small. He's wearing a stained blue T-shirt and nylon track pants. A single strip of grubby white bandage is inexpertly tied round his head.

'What the fuck –?' he starts to say, his animal eyes glaring violently at me.

I raise the pistol and point it at his head.

His eyes widen.

I step closer, placing the barrel of the pistol between his eyes. 'If you say another word,' I tell him, 'I'll kill you. Nod your head if you understand.'

Trembling now, he nods his head.

'Move back inside,' I tell him.

He steps back into the hallway, his eyes fixed fearfully on

the gun. I walk him inside and close the front door behind me.

'Turn round,' I tell him.

'Whu —?' he starts to say.

I flick my wrist, rapping the pistol barrel against his skull. It's not a hard blow, but it's hard enough to hurt him.

'Turn round,' I repeat.

He turns round.

I put the gun to the back of his head.

'What's your name?' I say. 'If you lie to me, I'll pull the trigger.'

'Viner . . .' he mutters. 'Anton Viner.'

'Is there anyone else in the house?'

'No.'

Keeping the gun pressed to his head, I reach up and tug at the bandage on his head. It comes off easily. On the left side of his head, about three inches above his ear, there's a freshly scabbed wound. It's ragged and raw, the blood-brown crust edged with the pink of new flesh . . . and there's no doubt that it was caused by a bite. I can see toothmarks, the shape of a mouth . . . the shape of Stacy's mouth.

My head goes black for a moment . . . and I'm nothing. A speck of nothing floating in a void. My legs buckle . . . I'm falling, floating, drowning . . .

No.

I open my eyes, steady myself.

I wipe a tear from my eye.

And when I speak, my voice doesn't belong to me. It's the voice of a man with no life, no emotion. A voice of death.

'Sit down,' it says.

Viner hesitates for a moment, then clumsily lowers himself to the floor. I stand above him, looking down . . . down . . . down . . .

'Listen to me, Anton Viner,' the dead voice says. 'And don't make a fucking sound until I tell you to speak. Nod your head if you understand.'

He nods.

I wipe another tear from my face and carry on. 'Two weeks ago, a young woman was raped and murdered in the bedroom of her own home. One week ago, an anonymous businessman offered a £50,000 reward for information leading to the killer's arrest. And that's why I'm here, Anton Viner. Because I believe that you're the killer, and I want that £50,000.' I pause for a moment, hating myself for doing this, but knowing that I have to do it to completely satisfy myself. 'The only problem is . . .' I continue, 'I'm not supposed to do it like this. I'm not supposed to force my way into your house and point a gun at your head, and if the police were to find out, I'd be in a shitload of trouble. Especially if it turned out that you weren't the murderer after all. That would cause me all kinds of problems. So, you see, what I need from you is proof that you did kill her. Because then I can just take you in and collect my money, and no one has to know that I forced my way in and pointed a gun at your head. And even if you tell the police that's what I did, they're not going to give a fuck. But if you're not the killer, if you can't prove to me that you killed her . . . well, as I said, that would leave me with the problem of knowing what to do with you. And I'm afraid, if that was the case, my only answer would be to shoot you in the head. Now, do you understand what I've just told you? Speak.'

'Yeah . . . yes . . .' he mumbles. 'Yes.'

'Good. So, have I got the right man, or do I have to kill you?' I lean down and hold the pistol to the top of his head. 'You've got three seconds to answer me. One . . . two . . .'

'Yes!' he sobs, his shoulders heaving. 'Fuck don't . . . please don't kill me . . . yes, fuck, yes . . . it was me, I did her –'

I push the gun barrel into his skull. 'I don't believe you.'

'Please! It's true . . . I can prove it –'

'How?'

'Clothes . . . her clothes, I've still got them . . .'

'Where?'

'Upstairs . . .'

'Get up,' I say, kicking him viciously in the small of his back.

He clambers awkwardly to his feet. 'Please don't –'

'Shut up. Just show me the clothes.'

I follow him up the stairs and watch as he opens an airing cupboard on the landing. As he leans inside, I don't take my eyes off him for a second, keeping the gun on him all the time, just in case he's up to something . . . but he's too far gone to even think of trying anything. Sobbing, shaking, gasping for breath . . . he fumbles around inside the cupboard and pulls out a carrier bag, and I know before I look what I'm going to see.

'There,' he says, opening the bag and showing me what's inside. 'See . . . they're hers.'

Of course they're hers . . . they're Stacy's clothes. All scrunched up and browned with blood. They're the clothes she wore that day – a pale-pink vest, a white blouse, jeans, her underwear. Ripped, torn, bloodied . . . savaged.

A rage wells up inside me now, and I'm jamming the pistol into Viner's head, pushing him down to the floor, and there's some kind of animal noise coming out of me, a noise that wants for blood and bone and pain and despair, and all I want to do is kill him right now . . .

Right now . . .

My arm tenses, my finger moves on the trigger . . .

And I stop.

Not now.

I kick him in the ribs . . . once, twice . . . again . . . kicking so hard that his ribs crack audibly and his body jerks across the floor. He moans.

'Get up,' I tell him.

'I can't –'

I kick him again. He struggles to his knees, moaning and sobbing and holding his chest, and I'm just about to kick him again when he grits his teeth and straightens up and finally gets to his feet.

'Put the carrier bag back where you got it from,' I tell him.

He does what he's told.

I walk him at gunpoint down the stairs.

I walk him out of the house and down the street – not caring any more if there's anyone around – and when we get to my car I give him my gloves and tell him to put them on. He puts them on. I tell him to get in the driving seat. He gets in. I get in the passenger seat and tell him to drive.

'Where to?' he says.

'Just start the car and drive.'

Twenty minutes later we're driving through the outskirts of a quiet suburb called Hey's Weir, three miles east of town. It's a sterile terrain of anonymous low buildings, industrial wasteland, and – somewhat incongruously – an 18-hole golf course. Beyond the golf course lie the rolling lawns and well-tended gardens of the crematorium.

'Pull in over there,' I tell Viner as we approach a darkened pub. 'There's a car park at the back.'

'Why?' he says. 'What are we doing –?'

'I need a piss.'

I don't think he believes me, but as long as he pulls into the car park, I really don't care. And he does, of course. What else is he going to do? He slows down, turns off the road into the car park, and rolls to a halt.

'Get out,' I tell him.

'But I thought –'

'Get out.'

He hesitates for a moment, then gets out of the car. I get out too. The night is dark, no stars, no moon. It's three o'clock in the morning. I point the gun at Viner's head and walk him across to the edge of the car park.

'Stop,' I tell him.

He stops.

I look around at the empty night – no traffic, no people, no nothing. There's nothing here, just me and the man who killed my wife and baby. And both of us are less than nothing.

I put the gun to Viner's head and pull the trigger.

*

'Why?' Bishop said.

'What . . .?'

'Why is it impossible?'

I looked at him. 'Anton Viner . . .? You're telling me that Anton *Viner* killed Anna Gerrish?'

'No,' Bishop said. 'I'm telling you that Anton Viner's hairs were found under her fingernails. Why do you find that so hard to believe?'

'Because . . .' I began, struggling to clear the chaos from my mind. 'Because . . . well, I don't know, it's just . . .'

'He's a killer, John. A rapist. He's not going to *stop* doing it. They never do.'

'I know . . . but why would he come back here?'

'Who says he ever went away? Just because we never found him, that doesn't necessarily mean that he wasn't here . . . and even if he wasn't, even if he did leave Hey after he killed your wife . . . well, that was seventeen years ago. What's to stop him coming back now? This is his home, John. This is his territory. He *knows* Hey. He probably feels safe here. Safe enough to start killing again.'

I looked at Bishop. 'Are you *sure* it's Viner's DNA?'

'Positive.'

I kept on looking at him for a while, trying to read his eyes, trying to see what was inside his head . . . then I got up from the settee, went through into the bedroom, and started fussing around with the bed. I needed time to think, to understand . . . I just needed to do something. Bishop followed me as far as the double doors, stopping to lean against the doorway and watch me as I lifted the duvet, straightened it out, and threw it across the bed.

'There's a televised press conference planned for two o'clock this afternoon,' he said. 'We'll be naming Viner as the main suspect in the murder of Anna Gerrish, and obviously that's going to have repercussions. Which is why I'm here, really.'

'Repercussions?' I said, flapping the duvet again, trying to clear the fuggy cloud of body odour and stale sweat from the air.

He nodded. 'There's no point in trying to avoid the possible link between Anna's murder and that of your wife, because the media are going to make the connection anyway. Two murders with the same suspect is more than enough for them to label Viner a serial killer, and no matter how much we try to play it down, we're not going to be able to stop it. And I'm afraid that means that they're going to start looking into your wife's murder again, rehashing all the old stories, because – to them – she'll no longer be *just* a murder victim, she'll be the victim of a serial killer. And that alone would be sufficient for the media to come after you, John. But unfortunately . . . well, we're not going to be able to hide the fact that it was you who found Anna's body, and when the media get hold of *that* . . .'

'Shit,' I muttered.

Bishop nodded again. 'So you can see why I wanted to warn you.'

I looked at him. 'Can't you cancel the press conference? I mean, what's the point of it anyway?'

He shook his head. 'It's out of my hands, John.'

'I thought you were the SIO on this case.'

'I'm in overall charge of the operational side of the

238

investigation, yes. But it's become a lot more than just a murder investigation now, and that means there's a lot more people involved. PR people, team co-ordinators, media strategists . . . it's simply not possible for me to control everything.'

'But you're still in control of the actual investigation?'

'Yes.'

I stared at him. 'And how's it going?'

He stared back. 'Reasonably well.'

'Any idea where Viner might be?'

'We're working on it.'

'Any leads, witnesses . . .?'

Bishop said nothing, just carried on staring at me, his eyes perfectly still.

'What about CCTV footage from the night Anna disappeared?' I said. 'Any luck with that?'

He blinked once. 'We're working on it.'

19

In the summer of 1991, I worked for a few months as a handyman at the crematorium in Hey's Weir. Most of my time was spent cutting grass, burning old wreaths, digging flower beds . . . I basically did whatever I was told to do. I didn't mind. It was pleasantly thoughtless work, physically but not mentally tiring, and I was on my own most of the time. And, besides – as I'd explained to Bridget – as long as I knew that I'd be with Stacy at the end of the day, I didn't care what I was doing.

Occasionally, when the crematorium was busier than usual, I'd be asked to help out in the furnace room. I didn't get involved with the actual cremation procedures – I was mostly just moving coffins around or sieving the ashes – but it was while I was working in the furnace room that I met a man known as Dougie the Burner. Dougie was an intriguing man. In his late twenties or early thirties, he had an unruly mop of tousled black hair, twinkling dark eyes, permanently grubby skin, and an equally permanent lop-sided grin. He was slightly hunchbacked and he walked with a limp. And he always wore the same shabby old blue overalls. He smoked pipe tobacco in hand-rolled cigarettes, and for his lunch he'd eat a whole raw onion.

Although there was plenty about him that always

unnerved me a little – not least his resemblance to a hunch-backed Fred West – there was a lot about Dougie that I liked. I liked the way he never got angry about anything, never worried about anything, never took anything seriously. He just seemed to hobble his way through life, carelessly enjoying whatever came his way – burning bodies, sieving ashes, eating onions . . . he was perfectly content with his lot.

On a warm Friday night in July that year, just as the sun was starting to go down, I suddenly realised that I'd left my jacket at the crematorium earlier in the day. My wallet was in my jacket pocket, and Stacy and me were setting off early the next morning for a weekend away in Wales, and for some reason that I can't remember I decided that, rather than picking up my jacket in the morning, I'd go back and get it that night.

So I grabbed my work keys, got in the car, and drove out to the crematorium. It must have been around ten o'clock when I got there, and at first the whole place seemed as quiet and deserted as I'd expected. But as I got out of the car and headed across the car park towards the door at the side of the main building that led into the staff room where I'd left my jacket, I gradually became aware of a familiar low rumbling sound – the muffled roar of the furnace. I'd always assumed that the furnace was shut down at night, so I was a little surprised to hear it working, but I didn't really give it much thought. I just assumed that my assumptions were wrong. And as I approached the side door, and noticed that Dougie's car was parked at the back of the building, and that next to it was a dark-blue van I'd never seen before, I still didn't think anything of it. I just supposed Dougie must be working late, maybe checking the furnace or something, and that the van probably belonged to a friend of his who was helping him out . . .

I unlocked the side door and went inside. The staff room was dark, the lights turned off, but the adjoining door to the furnace room was open, and through the doorway I could see a flickering glow of bright orange flamelight. I could see Dougie too – standing beside the furnace, wiping his hands on a rag, looking over at me. He wasn't grinning. And then two men stepped into view from across the room. One of them was middle-aged, stout, with cropped white hair; the other one was a younger man with a dark complexion, possibly Turkish or Greek.

As the younger man reached into his pocket, Dougie stepped forward and took hold of his arm.

'It's all right,' I heard him say. 'I know him.' Dougie turned to me. 'Hey, John,' he said, grinning now. 'What are you doing here?'

What are you *doing here?* I thought.

'I left my jacket behind,' I said, staring at something I'd just noticed on the floor behind Dougie. 'I was just . . .'

Still grinning, Dougie glanced over his shoulder at the object that had caught my attention, then turned back to me. 'I hope you can keep a secret, John.'

The object on the floor was a roll of carpet. At least, that was my first impression. I was shortly to find out that it was actually just a *piece* of carpet, and that rolled up inside that piece of carpet was a corpse. The body, according to Dougie, belonged to a young gypsy man who'd been beaten up and shot to death by the father and uncles of an eight-year-old girl who'd been assaulted and raped by the dead man. The two men with Dougie weren't gypsies themselves, they were just fixers, hired intermediaries, people who 'got things done'.

Dougie seemed remarkably unconcerned as he explained all this to me. Grinning his care-free grin, he just rolled a big fat cigarette and told me all about it.

'It's just a little sideline for me, John,' he said casually. 'A bit of overtime, if you like. It's all quite simple really.' He lit his cigarette. 'When someone needs to get rid of something on the quiet, they get in touch with me, and I tell them when to bring it round. They bring it round, it goes in the burner . . . and that's it.'

'When you say "get rid of something",' I said, looking over at the rolled-up carpet, 'you mean . . . bodies?'

Dougie grinned. 'Bodies, yeah. Dead people. I mean, I burn them all day anyway, the only difference with these extra ones is they don't get a service, and I don't have to bother sieving them into urns.' His grin broadened. 'Plus, I get paid a lot more for these.'

'Really?'

He nodded. 'The going rate's a grand a time.'

I looked at him, suddenly wondering if the only reason he was being so open about this was that he wasn't planning on me being around much longer to tell anyone. I glanced over at the roaring furnace, then back at Dougie.

He laughed, realising what I was thinking. 'It's all right, John, there's nothing to worry about. As long as you keep your mouth shut . . .' His grin lost a little of its warmth. 'Is that going to be a problem?'

'No,' I said. 'No problem.'

'Good. Of course, if you *did* happen to let anything slip . . .' He turned round, casually flicked his cigarette into the burner, watched as it was instantaneously vaporised, then turned back to me. 'But that's not going to happen, is it?'

I shook my head.

'OK,' he grinned. 'Well, if you don't mind, I'd better get on. I don't want to delay these two gentlemen any longer.'

'Yeah . . .' I muttered. 'I'll just get my jacket.'

'Before you go,' Dougie said, reaching into his pocket and passing me a business card. 'If ever *you* need to get rid of anything . . .'

'Thanks,' I said, looking at the card.

All it had on it was his name, *DOUGIE*, and a phone number. I put the card in my pocket, retrieved my jacket, and left.

A few months later, I handed in my resignation at the crematorium and took up a better-paid job in a call centre. But I kept my promise to Dougie, I didn't say a word to anyone about his unofficial cremation business – I didn't even tell Stacy – and for some reason that I'll never quite understand, I also kept his business card. I never imagined that a time would come when I'd actually have a need for Dougie's services, and even now I still find it hard to believe that I really did call him before I executed Anton Viner.

But I did.

I called him before I left that night.

He didn't want to know any details, just what time I

wanted to bring the 'package' round. And when I told him that it had to be later on that night, probably in the early hours of the morning, he just said, 'All right, but it's going to cost you extra.'

And that was that.

I killed Viner in the pub car park. I wrapped his bloodied head in a bin-liner and dumped his body in the boot of my car. I drove to the crematorium, where Dougie was already waiting for me, and together we lugged Viner's body out of the car, into the furnace room, and finally into the furnace.

And that really *was* that.

I'd killed Anton Viner.

I'd shot him in the head and incinerated his body.

I'd erased his life from this world.

But now, seventeen years later, I'd just been informed by DCI Bishop that Anton Viner's DNA had been found on the body of Anna Gerrish.

Ghosts upon ghosts upon ghosts . . .

20

After Bishop left, I just sat in my chair beneath the window for an hour or so, smoking cigarettes and trying to work out what the hell was going on. It wasn't easy, thinking about Anton Viner and what I'd done to him all those years ago . . . it was something that I usually kept buried deep in the dark places inside my head, the places where I didn't want to go. It wasn't that I had any conscious guilt about what I'd done, I didn't regret it or feel any remorse. Nor did I have any good feelings about it either. There was no satisfaction, no sense of atonement or vengeance or closure . . . whatever that is. I didn't *consciously* feel anything about Viner's death at all.

But I *had* killed him.

I'd taken a human life.

And that leaves a hole in your soul. The hole fills, in time, but the new-grown flesh is never quite the same – it's scarred, wrong, tainted . . . it has something missing.

It takes something away from you.

So I didn't *want* to go back there, back to the dark place deep down inside me, but I knew that I had to think about Viner again now. I had to ask myself if there was any possibility, any chance at all, that the man I'd killed *wasn't* Anton Viner.

And that meant taking myself back to that night, back to

that shabby grey council house, back to the moment when I was standing over that lank-haired middle-aged man, looking down at the scabbed bite mark on his head . . . ragged and raw, the blood-brown crust edged with the pink of new flesh . . . seeing the toothmarks, the shape of a mouth . . . the shape of Stacy's mouth. And I had to take myself back to her clothing too, all scrunched up in a carrier bag, browned with blood . . . her pale-pink vest, her white blouse, her jeans, her underwear . . . ripped, torn, bloodied . . . savaged . . .

And I had to ask myself how drunk I was that night, how drug-crazed and lost and out of my mind . . .

Could I have imagined these things?

The bite mark, the clothes, the *proof* that Viner had killed Stacy.

Was it possible that I'd *not* seen these things?

'No,' I muttered. 'No.'

I'd seen them.

There were a lot more things I had to ask myself – could Viner have got Stacy's clothes from someone else, or could they have been planted in his house? could the anonymous message I'd received have been a set-up, a string of lies to frame Anton Viner and goad me into killing him? and, if so, who could have sent it? and why? and was it possible that the man I'd killed had only admitted to Stacy's murder because I hadn't given him an alternative . . . ?

And while I knew that none of these things were impossible, I also knew that the chance of *all* of them being true was virtually infinitesimal.

Anton Viner had killed Stacy.

The man I'd killed was Anton Viner.

I went into the kitchen, fetched a bottle of whisky and a glass, and took them back into the front room. I hadn't had a drink in two weeks, and as I sat down in the armchair and opened the bottle, I hesitated for a moment . . . thinking about it, almost changing my mind . . . but I didn't. I half-filled the glass, took a long shuddering drink, and lit a cigarette.

The only person who knew what I'd done to Anton Viner was Dougie the Burner, and even *he* didn't know for sure. He knew that I'd killed someone, or at least that I'd been involved in the killing of someone, and he knew that we'd cremated the body, and I assumed he knew – from the TV and newspaper reports at the time – that a man called Anton Viner was the main suspect in the investigation into the rape and murder of Stacy Craine, so it wouldn't be hard for him to work out whose body it was that we'd burned. But that was the point – *we'd* burned it. Dougie had burned it, just like he'd burned countless others. And he was never going to admit to that, was he?

Just as whoever had sent me the anonymous message about Viner wasn't going to admit to anything either. Not that they actually *knew* anything – although, again, once they'd found out that Viner had disappeared, they must have guessed straight away what had happened to him – but whoever it was, and for whatever reason they'd sent me the message, I was pretty sure they'd want to keep quiet about it. And even if they didn't, they didn't have any *proof* that I'd done anything.

And although the police had questioned me at the time about Viner's disappearance, they'd never seriously suspected me. There was a witness, a young man walking home from the nearby party that night, who'd thought he remembered seeing two men getting into a car, one of whom could *possibly* have been Anton Viner . . . but this young man had been drinking and smoking dope all night, and he couldn't be absolutely sure about anything . . . and so nothing had ever come of it.

I drained my glass, poured myself another, and lit another cigarette.

I couldn't think of any reason why anyone would suddenly want to link me with Viner.

And now that I'd had a couple of stiff drinks, I wasn't even sure why I was thinking about it anyway. Everything seemed too *circular*, too mixed up, too complicated to think about – Stacy, Viner . . . Viner, me . . . Anna, Stacy, me, Viner, Anna, me . . .

And Bishop.

'Shit,' I muttered. 'Fuck it.'

I picked up the phone and called the office.

Ada answered, 'John Craine Investigations,' sounding as grumpy as ever.

'It's me,' I said. 'Listen, something's come up . . .'

I told her everything that Bishop had told me about Anna Gerrish and Anton Viner, and then I went on to explain that the police were going to announce all this in a televised press conference at two o'clock.

'Which means,' I said, glancing at the clock, 'that in about half an hour's time, the media are going to start looking for me.'

'Where are you now?' Ada asked.

'At home.'

'Are you still working that insurance case?'

'I was this morning, yeah, but I think it's best if I leave it for now. Could you call Mercer and let them know?'

'Yeah, OK. But what are you going to do? The media are bound to find out where you live, so if you don't *want* to talk to them –'

'I'll see how I feel. I might stay here, I might not. They'll probably try the office first though, so the easiest thing for you to do is unplug the phone, lock up the office, and go home. If anyone from the media gets in touch with you, don't say anything. And if I need to speak to you, I'll use your mobile. OK?'

'Yeah . . . how long do you think this is going to last, John?'

'I don't know. Hopefully it'll all be over by the start of next week and we can get back to normality again. But let's just see how it goes over the weekend, all right?'

Ada sighed. 'I don't understand any of this, John. If Viner's a serial killer, what's he been doing for the last seventeen years? And why's he suddenly come back here and started killing again?'

'I don't know . . .'

'It doesn't make sense.'

'I know.'

'And it's not fair either . . . for you, I mean.'

'Nothing's *fair*, Ada,' I said. 'It's just the way it is.'

I poured myself another drink, turned on the television, and tuned in to Sky News. Adverts were showing. I muted the TV and went to the bathroom. When I came back, just as I was sitting down again, there was a knock at the door.

'John?' I heard Bridget saying. 'Are you there?'

I got up, went over to the door, and opened it. She'd put on a coat and was holding Walter's lead in her hand. Walter was sitting beside her.

'I'm just taking him out for a walk,' she said. 'I wondered if you wanted to come with us . . .'

'I can't at the moment –'

'That's all right,' Bridget said quickly. 'I just thought I'd ask –'

'Can you come in for a minute?' I said.

She looked at me for a second or two, then nodded. 'I'll just put Walter back –'

'No, he's all right,' I said, stepping back to let them both in.

'Are you sure?'

'Yeah, of course.'

As I showed Bridget into the front room, Walter padded across the floor, making a beeline for the settee.

'No, Walter –' Bridget started to say.

'It's all right,' I told her. 'I don't mind.'

Walter clambered onto the settee, sighed, and sank down comfortably with his head on his feet. Bridget went over and sat down beside him.

'Are you all right?' she asked me, glancing at the whisky bottle as she took off her coat and hat.

'Yeah . . .' I said, checking the TV as I sat down in the armchair. The weather was on. I looked back at Bridget. 'Sorry . . . I'm waiting for something . . . on the news. It might affect you.'

She frowned. 'What are you talking about, John?'

'Sorry,' I said, smiling at her. 'I'm not being very clear, am I?'

'Not really, no.'

'OK, what it is . . . the man who was here earlier, Mick Bishop, he's a police officer. And the reason –'

'There he is,' Bridget said suddenly, pointing at the TV. 'That's him, isn't it?'

On the screen, Bishop and two other men were shuffling their way onto a small wooden stage where a table and three chairs had been set up. There were microphones on the table. A jug of water, three glasses. On a hastily erected screen behind the table it said: *Essex Police: Working for OUR Community*.

'What's going on?' Bridget said.

'Sorry,' I told her, turning up the volume. 'I need to listen to this.'

The three men had sat down and the one in the middle was just beginning to speak. He introduced himself first, Chief Constable Stewart Wright, then he presented the man on his left, Detective Chief Superintendent Gerald James, and finally he introduced Detective Chief Inspector Bishop, described as being the officer in charge of the day-to-day investigation. DCS James then took over, stating simply that Anna Gerrish had been reported missing on 6 September and that her body had been discovered in a lay-by on Great Hey Road on Friday 8 October.

'At this stage in our enquiries,' DCS James explained, 'the cause of death is believed to be multiple stab wounds.'

I could sense Bridget glancing over at me now and then as

the press conference went on, but I didn't look back at her. I just kept my eyes on the screen and listened as James announced that following forensic analysis of crime-scene evidence, a comprehensive link had been established between the murder of Anna Gerrish and the murder of Stacy Craine in 1993.

'As some of you may remember,' James continued, 'the prime suspect in Stacy Craine's murder was Anton Viner, a convicted rapist who went missing shortly after the crime was committed. Despite an ongoing and exhaustive search by both national and international authorities, Anton Viner has still not been found.' James looked up from his notes and stared directly into the camera. 'However, we now have very strong evidence linking Anton Viner with the death of Ms Gerrish, and we're making a fresh appeal to anyone with any knowledge of this man's whereabouts to contact us immediately.'

As James held up an A4-sized mugshot of Viner and explained that photographs and further information would be made available to the media after the conference, I kept my eyes on Bishop. He wasn't looking at the photo that James was holding up, nor was he looking around at the audience, or into the camera . . . in fact, he didn't seem to be looking at anything at all. He was just sitting there, stone-faced, staring blindly straight ahead.

But then, as DCS James announced that DCI Bishop would be happy to answer any questions, Bishop suddenly came to life – raising his head slightly, looking around, taking control . . . a picture of calm efficiency.

The questions came thick and fast.

Are you treating Viner as a serial killer?

Has he killed more than twice?

Was Anna Gerrish sexually assaulted?

Is it true that she worked as a prostitute?

Bishop answered most of the questions quite briefly, refusing to comment on anything that might jeopardise the investigation in any way, which basically meant just about everything. However, when someone asked him how Anna's body had been discovered, he suddenly became a lot more talkative.

'Her body was found by a private investigator who'd been hired by Mr and Mrs Gerrish to investigate Anna's disappearance. While we'd prefer not to release any further details at the moment, we realise that if we don't, we may well be adding to the media pressure on Anna's family.' He paused for a second, glancing into the camera, and I felt that he was looking directly at me. 'So,' he continued, 'in view of this, we'd like to announce at this point that the private investigator who found Anna's body was John Craine.'

There was an audible silence from the audience for a moment, then cameras started flashing, an excited murmur filled the room, and everyone started shouting out questions.

'Is that the same John Craine who was married to Stacy Craine?'

'Yes,' Bishop said calmly. 'Mr Craine was Stacy's husband.'

'Did Anna know Stacy?'

'Not as far as we know.'

'What's John Craine's connection with Anna?'

'There is no connection. As I've already said, Mr Craine

is a private investigator. He was investigating Anna's disappearance –'

'How did he find her? What did he know that the police didn't?'

'I'm afraid I can't answer that at this –'

'Have you questioned him?'

'Mr Craine has been questioned, yes.'

'Is he a suspect?'

'We have no reason to believe that Mr Craine's discovery of Anna Gerrish's body is anything more than a coincidence.'

'But you have questioned him?'

'I've already answered that question.'

'Does Craine know Viner?'

'Not as far as we know.'

'How did he know –?'

'That's it for now, ladies and gentlemen, thank you,' Chief Constable Wright broke in suddenly. 'Press packs are available on your way out, and we will be updating you if and when any more information comes to light.'

More questions rang out as the three men got to their feet and shuffled off the stage – mostly questions about me – but the press conference was over now, the microphones turned off, and Sky News was returning to the studio presenters. As they started telling us what we'd just seen and heard, I turned off the television, took a long drink, and lit a cigarette.

'Well . . .' Bridget murmured, looking over at me.

I smiled at her. 'Confusing, isn't it?'

She nodded. 'A bit.'

I picked up the whisky bottle. 'Would you like a drink?'

'No, thanks.'

I poured whisky into my glass. 'Anna Gerrish's mother wasn't happy with the way the police investigation was going. She thought they weren't doing enough to look for her daughter. So a couple of weeks ago she hired me to see what I could find out.' I shrugged. 'It wasn't too difficult. I poked around a bit, asked a few questions, and after a while . . . well, like I said, it wasn't that difficult.'

Bridget looked at me, waiting for me to go on.

I drank some more. 'I can't tell you exactly how I found Anna's body, but it didn't have anything to do with Viner or Stacy. I didn't even *know* about Viner's connection with this until a few hours ago. That's what Bishop came here to tell me about.'

Bridget nodded. 'You don't have to justify anything to me, John.'

'Yeah, I know . . . it's just . . . well, the way Bishop explained it, you could easily have assumed –'

'No,' she said quietly. 'I didn't assume anything. I still don't really *understand* any of it –'

'Neither do I.'

She nodded again. 'Was he right about it just being a coincidence?'

'I don't know . . .' I sipped my drink. 'I really don't know.'

We were both silent for a while then – Bridget just sitting there, idly preening Walter's grey head, while I just sat there, drinking and smoking . . . not really thinking about anything any more, just letting things be, letting the alcohol sink down inside me and soak up all the stuff that didn't make sense . . .

'It must have been terrible for you,' Bridget said after a while.

'What?'

'Finding the body.'

'Which one?'

She hesitated, taken aback for a moment, not sure what I meant, but then she suddenly realised. 'Oh, shit . . . of course, your wife . . . God, I'm so *sorry*, I didn't mean –'

'No, it's my fault,' I said. 'I shouldn't have said it like that . . . sorry.' I shook my head. 'I'm such a fucking idiot sometimes . . .'

Bridget smiled. 'Just sometimes?'

'Most of the time, actually,' I said, returning her smile.

We carried on smiling at each other for a few moments, then Bridget looked away and carried on stroking Walter's head as she gazed casually around the room. As I sat there, half-watching her, I realised that the whisky was really getting to me now, weighing me down with its vaporous gravity, and I could almost hear a faint voice of sobriety castigating me for being so stupid, for drinking so much when I hadn't eaten anything for God knows how long, for being so weak when I needed to be strong . . .

But the voice was too far away to have much effect.

And I was already too drunk to care anyway.

'Is that Stacy?' I heard Bridget say.

Just for a second, I thought that she meant the distant voice in my head – *is that Stacy reproaching you for drinking too much?* – but then I looked over and saw that she was studying the framed photograph of Stacy on the shelf.

'Yeah . . .' I said, gazing at the picture as Bridget got up and went over to the shelf for a closer look. The photo was a head-and-shoulders shot of Stacy, taken on the day we'd got married. It wasn't much of a wedding – a register office service, with no guests, no fuss, no reception . . . just a couple of friends as witnesses and a few drinks in the Double Locks afterwards – but it was a day I'll never forget. Just the two of us, alone together in our own perfect world . . .

'She's beautiful,' Bridget said.

I nodded, unable to speak. In the photograph, Stacy was laughing, her eyes beaming, her face alight with joy . . . and just for a moment I was back there again, I was *there* . . . on our wedding day, sitting in the sun-dappled beer garden of the Double Locks, taking her picture. I'd just made a daisy crown for her, and when I'd placed it on her head it had looked so pure and wonderful – *she'd* looked so pure and wonderful – that I'd just *had* to take a photograph . . .

'How old was she then?' Bridget asked.

'Twenty-four,' I said. 'She was three years older than me.'

'She looks very happy.'

'Yeah . . .'

Bridget looked at me. 'I don't suppose it helps, does it?'

'What?'

She shrugged. 'Knowing that you loved each other . . . the memories . . . all the good things. I don't expect they give you much comfort.'

'Not really . . . in fact, sometimes I wonder if it might have been better if we *hadn't* loved each other so much. Well, better for me, anyway.'

Bridget shook her head. 'You don't mean that.'

'No . . . no, I don't.' I lit a cigarette. 'It's just . . . well, you know . . .'

She shook her head again. 'I can't even *begin* to imagine how you must have felt. It must have been unbearable.'

I sipped my drink.

'How do you do it, John?' Bridget asked quietly. 'How do you keep going when something like that happens?'

'I don't know . . .' I shrugged. 'I suppose you either keep going or you don't . . . I nearly didn't.'

'Really?'

I nodded. 'I pretty much fucked myself up for about a year after Stacy was killed. I just . . . I just couldn't live with it. I was drunk all the time . . .' I looked at the whisky in my glass, then glanced up at Bridget, half-smiling. 'I mean, I know I still drink too much now, but back then I'd start first thing in the morning and just keep going until I passed out. And I wasn't just drinking either. I was doing all kinds of shit – coke, speed, grass, downers . . . anything. I even started snorting heroin for a while. I didn't care what I did. As long as it took me away from myself . . . as long as it took me away from the reality of Stacy's death, that's all I cared about.' I drank some more. 'I was looking for oblivion.'

'What made you stop?' Bridget said.

'I don't know, really . . . I probably *wouldn't* have stopped if it hadn't been for a friend of my father's, a man called Leon Mercer. Leon had kept in touch with me after my father's death, and we'd got to know each other quite well . . . which was kind of weird, actually, because I'd gone out with his daughter for a while when I was about seventeen, eighteen, so he'd been my girlfriend's father, and boys are always frightened of their girlfriends' fathers, aren't they?'

'Yeah, I know what you mean,' Bridget said, smiling. 'My dad used to scare the shit out of any boyfriends I brought home.'

I nodded, taking another drink of whisky. 'Anyway, Leon kind of kept an eye on me after my father died, and then when Stacy was killed and I started drinking and everything . . . well, my life was a complete mess. I lost my job, I lost most of my decency, I lost whatever sense of purpose I might once have had . . . I lost just about everything. But Leon still kept in touch, kept ringing me up and coming round to see me, and I was probably really fucking horrible to him, just like I was really fucking horrible to everyone else, but Leon didn't give up. He didn't try to *change* me or anything, he just kept *being* there for me, looking out for me . . . caring for me.'

'He sounds like a good man.'

'Yeah, he is . . .' I said thoughtfully. 'He really is. When he came to me one day and offered me a job with his private investigation business, I was so fucked up I could barely walk, let alone work. And Leon *knew* that. And he also knew that I didn't know anything about investigation work, and that I'd probably turn down his offer anyway – which I did at first – but, despite all that, he still made the offer. And after I'd turned it down, he just told me to think about it, and that if I changed my mind, the offer would still be there . . . and a couple of weeks later, after I'd cleaned myself up a bit, I *did* change my mind . . . and that was it, really. Leon took me on, took me under his wing, started teaching me everything he knew about the business, and I gradually started living some kind of life again.'

Bridget nodded. 'And you stopped looking for oblivion?'

'Most of the time, yeah.'

She glanced at the drink in my hand.

I shrugged. 'I still feel the need for some shadows now and then.'

She smiled sadly.

I ran my fingers through my hair, feeling the numbness of my scalp, imagining the skull beneath the skin . . . that eyeless shell, cold and white . . . that lifeless lump of bone that guards our life yet forever signifies death . . .

Walter groaned, stretching his legs, and as Bridget patted his flank, he let out a tiny fart. Bridget smiled – the smile of an embarrassed child – and I couldn't help smiling too as Walter turned and craned his neck, giving his backside a slightly bemused sniff.

'Charming, isn't he?' Bridget said.

'Yep,' I said. 'He's a classy guy, all right.'

She laughed.

I drank some more.

The telephone rang.

I leaned down, picked it up off the floor, dropped it, and picked it up again. 'Hello?'

'Is that Mr Craine?' a female voice said.

'Who's this?'

'John Craine?'

'Who are you?'

'My name's Eileen Banner, I'm from the *Sun*. I was wondering if –'

'Shit,' I muttered, putting the phone down and disconnecting it.

'Is something the matter?' Bridget asked.

'That was a reporter from the *Sun*,' I told her, pulling my mobile from my pocket as it started to ring. The screen read *UNKNOWN SENDER*. I cut off the call and turned off the phone. 'This is what I meant earlier on,' I said to Bridget. 'You know . . . about this affecting you.'

'Sorry,' she said. 'I don't understand.'

'The press, TV people . . . now that Bishop's thrown them a bone they're all going to be after me like dogs. I can keep the phones turned off, and I can keep away from my office, but sooner or later they're going to start coming round here. And if I don't talk to them, which I won't, they'll just go looking for someone else . . . you, for example.'

'Me?' Bridget frowned. 'But I don't know anything –'

'You don't have to *know* anything. The media don't give a shit about *knowing* anything. All they ever want is something to talk about, something to write about . . . it doesn't matter what it is.' I looked at Bridget. 'If they come round here, and you open the door, they're going to link you with me whatever you say, or don't say . . . and the next thing you know you'll be "the mysterious blonde now

living with the husband of the serial killer's first victim",
and everyone's going to want to know all about you.'

Bridget just shrugged. 'So I won't open the door.'

I looked at her, struggling to focus now, and I wondered
if I should warn her about the possibility of the media
picking up on her resemblance to Stacy. And as I thought
about that, I suddenly realised that not only was she
roughly the same height and shape as Stacy, with the same
short blonde hair and blue eyes, but she was also about the
same age that Stacy would have been . . .

'Are you OK, John?' she said to me.

'What?'

'You don't look so good . . .'

'Uh, yeah . . .' I mumbled. 'I think I'm a bit . . .'

'Drunk?'

I smiled. 'Yeah . . . sorry. I didn't mean to . . . I was just . . .'

'Looking for shadows?'

'Probably, yeah . . . something like that. But look –'

'It's all right,' she said, getting to her feet and coming
over to me. 'I won't answer the door to anyone I don't
know, I won't talk to anyone, and I'll try not to let anyone
take any pictures of me. But I'm not going to move out or
anything, OK?'

'Yeah, no . . . I didn't mean that –'

'Whatever happens, I'll deal with it.'

'Keep your curtains closed.'

'Stop worrying, I've got it all in hand.' She was leaning
over me now, helping me out of the chair. 'You need to go
to bed.'

'Yeah, sorry . . .'

'And stop saying sorry.'

'Sorry,' I grinned.

'Come on, up you get.'

I don't really remember the rest of it. I have a vague recollection of being slightly embarrassed as Bridget took me into the bedroom and helped me into bed, but I'm not quite sure what I was embarrassed about. I assume that part of it was simply that I felt so stupid about being so drunk, but I've got a feeling that there was more to it than just that. There was the touch of Bridget's hand on my arm as she helped me into the bedroom, and then the dimly dawning realisation that I was in my bedroom with Bridget, and that she was putting me to bed ... and that I didn't know what was going to happen next. What did she want to happen? What did I want? What did she expect? Something? Anything? Nothing?

It was an embarrassing train of thought.

But nothing happened.

Almost nothing.

I remember her whispering, 'Go to sleep ... I'll see you later.'

And then I felt her lips on mine – a brief but gentle kiss.

And it moved me. It made me want to be with her, to hold her, to have her hold me. And with the touch of her lips still sweet on mine, I reached out for her ...

But she'd already gone.

21

It was dark when I woke up, and it took me a minute or two to work out where I was, what day it was, what time it was ... why I was lying in bed, fully dressed, with an aching head and a bone-dry mouth and a familiarly sour taste in the back of my throat ... and then I remembered.

'Shit,' I groaned, looking at the clock beside the bed.

The LED display read 19:32.

'Fuck.'

I got out of bed, went to the bathroom, then into the kitchen for a glass of water and four paracetamols. I lit a cigarette and went into the front room. The lights were off, the curtains closed (did I do that?). I reached out for the light switch ... and paused. I was beginning to remember everything now, and as I stumbled through the dimness over to the window, I could hear myself slurring drunkenly to Bridget about the press and the TV people – *now that Bishop's thrown them a bone they're all going to be after me like dogs*, I'd told her. *I can keep the phones turned off, and I can keep away from my office, but sooner or later they're going to start coming round here ...*

I stood to the side of the window, pulled back the edge of the curtain, and glanced outside. Across the street, a handful of reporters and a TV crew were hanging around by a streetlight at the far end of the factory wall. I watched them for a while, then closed the curtain and stepped back from the window.

'Shit.'

I remained motionless for a minute, digesting what I'd just seen, then I inched open the curtain again and took another quick look. I got the impression that they'd been there for some time, which either meant that they were waiting for me to come out, or that they didn't know I was in and they were waiting for me to come home. And from the way some of them kept glancing up and down the street, I guessed it was the latter. They'd probably arrived a few hours ago, and they'd probably rung the bell and been hammering on the door, and in my drunken stupor I simply hadn't heard anything. And with the curtains closed, and no one answering, they must have assumed that I was out.

I wondered where Bridget was . . .

And what she thought of all this.

And me.

What did she think of me?

And did I care?

I went out into the hallway and stood at the bottom of the stairs, gazing up into the darkness. No lights, no sounds . . .

'Bridget?' I called out.

No reply.

'Bridget?' A little louder this time.

Still no reply. And no barking either. Which either meant that she was out somewhere with Walter, or that they were both up there pretending to be out. Either way, there was no point in me going up.

I went back into my flat, put on my shoes and coat, then went out into the backyard. It was a cold night, the air damp and sullen under a starless black sky, and as I headed down the pathway towards the back wall, I realised it must have been raining quite heavily while I was asleep. Bushes were dripping in the darkness, the path was scattered with the debris of a hard downpour – washed-up soil, slugs, worms, bits of stick – and the sodden earth was alive with the sound of tiny wet things clicking and popping.

At the end of the path, I clambered up onto an old metal bin, hoisted myself over the wall, and dropped down into my neighbour's backyard. It was a yard that had evolved over the years into a flagstone shanty town of broken sheds and greenhouses all cobbled together with discarded wooden doors and acres of corrugated plastic sheeting. The sheds, I knew, were packed with crates and rusty tools and scraps of wood rescued from skips, and the greenhouses were piled high with empty seed trays and plant pots.

There was no one around. It was *EastEnders* time – or *Coronation Street* or *Emmerdale* – and the deaf old man who lived here would be stuck in front of his TV, just like everyone else, engrossed in a world of twisted love and daily disasters . . .

I made my way round the back of the house to a bin-cluttered alley that led me out into the street that runs parallel to mine. It looked almost identical to my street – the same terraced houses, the same frontyards, the same cracked pavements lined with too many parked cars . . . the only thing missing was a handful of reporters and a TV crew.

I lit a cigarette and headed for the nearest taxi rank.

*

Leon Mercer lived with his wife, Claudia, in a grey-walled four-storey house in a secluded avenue at the edge of town. It was a pleasant area, the gardens well-tended and the broad pavements planted with lime trees, and as I got out of the taxi and headed up a block-paved driveway towards Leon's house, I remembered the first time I'd ever been here. It was about a month or so after I'd started going out with Imogen. I was seventeen years old then, anxiously visiting my girlfriend's home for the first time, scared to death that I'd do something wrong, or say something stupid, or that her parents just wouldn't like me. And I remember feeling quite intimidated by the size and relative splendour of the house. I didn't know much about Leon Mercer then, but I knew that he was a police officer, like my father, and I was pretty sure that they were both the same rank, and so I couldn't understand why we lived in a modest semi-detached house in a very average street while the Mercers had a four-storey detached place in one of the wealthiest parts of town. I found out later that the house actually belonged to Claudia Mercer, a gift from her father, who'd made a pile of money from a string of retail sports shops . . .

I'd reached the front door now – a huge oak thing, set in an old stone porchway. I rang the bell and waited. A cold rain had begun to fall, and in the bright-white glare of security lights blazing from houses along the avenue, I could see the twist of yellowed leaves fluttering in the wind. There was a hint – perhaps imagined – of bonfire smoke and fireworks in the air, and as I stood there in the autumn night, the distant memories of childhood Guy Fawkes' nights drifted into my mind. Black horizons arced with rocket lights and starburst blooms . . . jumping jacks, roman candles, catherine wheels . . . a roaring bonfire, snapping and popping and crackling, the glowing red embers drifting up into the night . . .

'John!' a surprised voice said, bringing me back to the here and now, and I turned round to see Imogen standing at the open door.

'Hey, Immy,' I said.

She gave me an enthusiastic hug, kissing me on both cheeks, then led me inside and closed the door.

'God, John,' she said, taking me by the arm. 'I just saw the press conference about Anna Gerrish on the news . . . Why didn't you tell me you'd found her?'

I shrugged. 'Well, it's kind of complicated –'

'I tried ringing you, but I couldn't get through.'

'Yeah, sorry. The press started calling me so I turned all the phones off.'

'Are you OK?' she asked, gently squeezing my arm. 'I mean, this must be really hard for you . . .'

'I'm fine –'

'Christ,' she said, shaking her head. 'Anton fucking Viner . . . I still can't believe it.' She looked at me. 'Is Bishop keeping you up to speed on everything?'

I shrugged. 'He's told me what he thinks I need to know.'

'Yeah,' she muttered, shaking her head again. 'I bet he has, the piece of shit.'

I looked up then as I heard Claudia Mercer coming down the stairs.

'Hello, John,' she said, smiling. 'How are you, dear?'

'Not bad, thanks, Mrs M.'

'I've told Leon that you're here. He's in his study.'

'Thanks.'

'Would you like some tea or coffee?'

'No, thanks –'

'Something to eat?'

I shook my head.

She smiled again. 'Well, let me know if you change your mind.' And with that she wandered off down the hallway.

'She's never that nice to me, you know,' Imogen said, smiling.

'I heard that,' her mother called back.

Imogen looked at me. 'Don't spend too long with Dad, OK? He tries to hide it, but he gets tired really easily these days.'

I nodded. 'I just want a quick chat with him.'

'Will I see you later?'

I smiled. 'You can give me a lift home, if you want.'

'It's a date.'

Leon's study was a small but cosy room at the far end of the landing on the third floor. It was fairly cramped, filled to the brim with too much furniture and too many bookshelves and all kinds of clutter all over the place – files, papers, magazines, newspapers. He had a desk against one wall, a writing table against another wall; a plush leather armchair in one corner, a cushioned wicker chair in another. There were cupboards and filing cabinets, framed photographs and certificates on the wall, a small flat-screen

TV on a black glass table, with stacks of DVDs piled up next to it. Half a dozen lead-crystal decanters were lined up on a narrow mantelpiece above the blackened grate of a small open fire, and the black of night was showing through a small square window in the far wall. Leon was sitting at his desk when I went in, a laptop open in front of him. 'John,' he said warmly, closing the laptop and getting to his feet. 'Come on in, sit down . . .'

I went over and shook his hand, then sat down in the armchair.

As Leon lowered himself back into his chair and removed the reading glasses he was wearing, it was hard to keep the shock from my face. He was so much frailer than the last time I'd seen him, and that had only been two or three months ago. He'd looked like the same old Leon I'd always known then – big, strong, solid, bright-eyed. But now . . . well, he'd lost a lot of weight, for a start. But not in a good way. His yellowing skin hung loosely from his frame, giving his face a gaunt and haggard look, and the weight of it seemed to drag him down. His shoulders were stooped, his head bowed down. His eyes had dulled, too. And every movement he made was stiff and slow and obviously painful.

'I know,' he said, giving me a stoical smile. 'I'm a fucking sight, aren't I?'

'You don't look great,' I admitted, unable to lie to him. 'What is it – cancer?'

He nodded. 'Pancreatic.'

'Do you want to talk about it?'

'No,' he said, reaching for a brandy glass on his desk. He

took a sip and swallowed slowly. 'It tastes better than morphine,' he explained.

I nodded.

'Help yourself,' he said, glancing up at the decanters.

'I'm all right, thanks,' I told him.

'Sure?'

I nodded again.

He gazed into his glass for a moment, gently swirling the brandy, then he leaned forward and carefully put it down on the desk. 'So,' he said, looking over at me. 'How's it all going, John?'

I smiled. It was the same question he always asked me, and it always meant the same – are you drinking? not drinking? are you keeping away from the drugs?

'I'm doing OK,' I told him.

'Yeah?'

'A few lapses now and then.'

He nodded. 'I can smell it on your breath.'

I looked at him. 'I'm doing OK.'

He held my gaze for a few moments, looking for the truth, and all I could do was look back at him, not really knowing what my truth was . . . but, whatever it was, I was happy to let him see it. And if he'd wanted to say anything about it, that would have been perfectly fine with me too. But he didn't. He just took another small sip of brandy, coughed quietly, and slowly leaned back in his chair.

'I saw Bishop on the news,' he said.

'That's why I'm here.'

'I know. Tell me all about it.'

*

272

I told him everything then – from the moment Helen Gerrish had come into my office, to Bishop's unexpected visit earlier that day . . . I told Leon everything. He listened in silence, his head bowed down, his eyes closed, not saying a word until I'd finished. And even then, when he slowly looked up at me and opened his eyes, he still didn't say anything for a while. He just looked at me, deep in thought, digesting everything I'd told him . . . then he picked up his brandy glass, took another measured sip, licked his lips, put the glass down, and finally – after delicately clearing his throat – he let out a long sigh and began to talk.

'Why didn't you come to me earlier about this?' he said.

I shrugged. 'I didn't have any evidence . . . there was no proof –'

'You don't have any evidence now. All you've got is a dead girl, Viner's DNA, and a bellyful of bad feelings about Bishop.'

'I *know* Viner didn't kill Anna,' I said slowly, looking Leon in the eyes. 'It's simply not possible.'

Leon didn't say anything for a moment, he just held my gaze, and as he sat there looking at me, I tried to let him see the unspoken question inside my head. *Was it you, Leon? Did you send me that message about Viner all those years ago? Do you know what I did to him?*

'What we *really* need to know,' he said quietly, neither answering nor not answering my unspoken question, 'is why Bishop is lying to you. That's the key to it all.' He opened his laptop and started tapping keys. 'The trouble is, Bishop's nowhere near as one-dimensional as he likes

273

people to think. Believe me, I've known him a long time, and it's taken me years and years to realise that, in his own twisted way, he's a very complicated man.' Leon looked over the lid of his laptop at me. 'You probably don't think he's particularly intelligent, do you?'

'It depends what you mean by intelligent,' I said. 'I doubt if he'd be a stunning success on *University Challenge* –'

'Exactly,' Leon said, smiling. 'But for the last thirty-odd years he *has* been a stunning success as both a serving police officer and a highly efficient criminal, and that takes some doing.'

'You think he's a criminal?'

'I *know* he is.' Leon glanced at the laptop screen, then back at me. 'Corruption is a crime, John. It's not just a breach of trust, a bending of the rules, an abuse of power . . . it's a crime. A corrupt police officer is a criminal, it's as simple as that. And Bishop . . . well, come over here and look at this, see for yourself.'

As I got up and went over to his desk, Leon angled the laptop so we could both see the screen. At first, I couldn't quite make out what I was seeing, but when I looked closer I realised it was a stilled image from a poor-quality video. The resolution was terrible, the definition non-existent, and the colour was more grey-and-grey than black-and-white. But despite all that, I could still just about make out the four figures on the screen: a man tied to a chair, another two men standing behind him, one of them with a baseball bat in his hand, and Bishop . . .

I looked at Leon. 'Is this what I think it is?'

He nodded. 'It's a copy of the CCTV video that your

father gave to DCI Curtis, the one that shows Bishop and the others torturing the man in the chair.'

'Shit,' I said quietly, looking back at the screen.

'You don't need to see all of it,' Leon said. 'And I'm sure you know what happens anyway, but I just wanted to let you see what Bishop is capable of . . . are you ready?'

I nodded.

Leon tapped the keyboard and the video started up. Bishop was standing in front of the man in the chair, and as the video began, I saw him leaning down and yelling violently in the man's face. There was no sound, so the yelling was silent, but there was no mistaking the fury in his voice. The man in the chair was screwing his eyes shut and stretching his head back in a vain attempt to get away from Bishop, but Bishop just kept on screaming at him. And then, suddenly, he stopped. And with no hesitation at all, he drew back his arm and punched the man viciously in the face. The blow was so hard that the man – still tied to the chair – tumbled sideways to the floor. The two other men immediately picked him up again, and while they were doing that, I saw Bishop lighting a cigarette. He took a few hard puffs on it, said something to the man, now upright in his chair again, and as the man began shaking his head in wild-eyed fear, Bishop calmly stepped forward and speared the burning cigarette into his right eye.

'Jesus Christ,' I whispered as Leon stopped the video.

'And that was only the beginning of it,' he said, pressing more keys.

'He's a fucking madman.'

'No,' Leon said. 'That's the thing, I don't think he is . . . I think he just does whatever he has to do to get what he wants . . . whatever that may be. But I don't think he *enjoys* it. He just does it.'

'Do you think he's capable of killing someone?'

'Everyone's *capable* of killing someone,' Leon said, and for a fleeting moment I thought I saw a knowing look in his eye. 'But if you're asking me whether Bishop could have killed Anna Gerrish . . .?' He paused for a few seconds, thinking about it. 'Well, yes . . . I'm sure that he could. If he had what he thought was a good enough reason to kill her, he'd do it just like that.' Leon snapped his fingers. 'But I can't see him killing just for the thrill of it . . . and even if he did, he would have made absolutely sure that no one found out.' Leon turned his attention back to the laptop screen for a moment, fiddled with the touchpad, then looked up at me. 'The men who beat you up outside The Wyvern . . . you said you didn't get a look at them?'

I shook my head. 'It all happened too quickly.'

'But you mentioned that the man who hit you first had rings on his fingers.'

'Yeah . . .' I said, my mind suddenly flashing back to that night – leaving The Wyvern, walking down Miller's Row in the cold night air, the distant *doomp-doomp, doomp-doomp* from the nightclubs, the drunkenness whirling in my head . . . and then a voice calling out to me from the shadows of an alley, *Got a light, mate?*, and almost immediately the heavily-ringed fist hammering into the side of my head . . .

'Yeah,' I told Leon. 'He had rings on his fingers. One of them had a skull on it.'

Leon angled the laptop towards me. 'Is that him?'

The figure on the screen was a close-up still from the video. It was the man with the baseball bat, and Leon had frozen the picture just as he was raising the bat, so not only could I see the man's hard-bitten face, but also his hands. The picture was blurred and grainy, and it was hard to make out any details . . . but when I leaned in closer to the screen and squinted at the big silver ring on the man's right index finger, I knew that I was looking at a skull.

'His face doesn't mean anything to me,' I told Leon. 'But I'm pretty sure that's him. Who is he?'

'His name's Les Gillard, he's been working for Bishop for years.' Leon nodded at the screen. 'When that happened he was just a PC, only been on the job a few years.'

'And now?'

'It's hard to tell. He moved up through the ranks pretty quickly, and for the last ten years or so he's been making a name for himself in various Special Ops forces – SO12, SO13, 15 . . . you know, the kind of units who like to keep themselves to themselves. But whatever Gillard is now, I know that Bishop's still got some kind of hold on him.' Leon closed the laptop and looked at me. 'That's how it works with Bishop. He gets something on you, something he can use against you . . . and once he's got it, you're his for life, whether you like it or not. You'd be amazed at how many people he's got in his pocket – police officers, criminals, politicians, businessmen . . . he's a very powerful, and very dangerous, man.'

I nodded. 'So do you think it's possible . . .' I paused as Leon suddenly closed his eyes, gritted his teeth, and groaned. 'What's the matter?' I said, quickly getting to my feet as he doubled over, holding his abdomen. 'Leon? *Leon!*' As I moved round the desk towards him, he painfully straightened up and opened his eyes.

'It's all right,' he said, breathing hard. 'Honestly, I'm all right . . .'

'You don't look all right –'

'It was just . . .' He looked at me. 'Please, John . . . sit down. It's OK, really. It happens sometimes, that's all . . .' As he reached for the brandy glass and took a drink, I moved back round the desk. He looked up at me again. 'Will you *please* sit down, John?'

I sat.

'Thank you,' he said.

'Maybe I'd better go,' I suggested.

'In a minute . . . there's a few more things I want to go over with you first.'

'I can come back –'

'This name you got from the registration of the Nissan . . . Kemper, was it?'

'Charles Raymond Kemper.'

'Have you got any further with that?'

I shook my head. 'I'm seeing Cal again tomorrow, but so far he hasn't come up with anything.'

'OK . . . and you haven't found anything at all that links Bishop with the Nissan or Anna Gerrish?'

'No.'

He looked at me, his mind seeming to wander for a moment. Then his eyes regained their focus and he said, 'Do you need any help with the drink-driving charge?'

I smiled. 'My solicitor got it thrown out last week. Procedural errors.'

'Good.'

'You're tired, Leon,' I said, getting to my feet again. 'You need to rest.'

He nodded. 'I know, I know . . . but before you go, John . . .'

'What?'

'Leave Bishop to me for now, OK? I've still got a lot of close contacts in the job. I'll make some enquiries, see what I can find out, and I'll get back to you as soon as possible. But in the meantime . . . well, just don't go fucking around with him, that's all.'

'OK.'

He smiled at me, a sad and weary smile that seemed to take an awful lot out of him. 'And listen,' he muttered. 'Listen . . .'

His eyes were closing even as he spoke to me.

I turned quietly and started to leave. But just as I got to the door, I heard him speak to me again.

'You see this picture, John?' he said.

I turned round and saw him looking up at a framed photograph on the wall. It was a picture of Leon and my father, taken shortly before Dad died. They were together at a barbecue somewhere – red-faced in the sun, drinks in their hands, both of them smiling broadly at the camera.

'If ever you have any questions, John,' Leon said, 'and I'm not here to answer them . . . just remember that picture.'

I looked at him. 'What do you mean?'

He smiled again. 'You're a detective ... you'll work it out when the time comes.'

I shook my head. 'I don't understand –'

'You know, John,' he said vaguely. 'There's something I've been meaning to ask you for a long time ... something I've been thinking about ...'

'Leon,' I said. 'I really think you should get some rest now –'

'You see, what I can't understand, what I've never been able to figure out ...' He looked at me, his entire body quite still. 'When your father killed himself in his room ... why did he lock the door?'

'What?'

'It doesn't make sense, does it? If you're going to kill yourself, why make a point of locking the door first? What purpose does it serve?'

'I don't know . . .' I said, confused. 'I've never really thought about it . . .'

He smiled distantly. 'Perhaps you should.'

'Are you trying to say –?'

'I'm sorry, John,' he muttered, his eyes beginning to close again. 'Would you mind asking Claudia to come up here? I think ... I think I'm ...' He sighed hard. 'God, I'm so fucking tired.'

22

'How long has he got?' I asked Imogen.

'I wish I knew,' she sighed. 'But you know what Dad's like, he refuses to talk about it.' We were in her car – a ridiculously expensive black Mercedes – and she was driving me home. 'He has his good days and bad days,' she went on. 'Sometimes he's OK, other times . . . well, you saw what he was like tonight.'

I nodded. 'Is he at home all the time now?'

'Just about. He struggles into the office every now and then, and he still insists that I keep him up to date with everything that's going on with the business, but he spends most of his time in his study now.'

'What does he do up there?'

'I'm not sure . . . he's got a few things he's been working on for years – old cases, I think. He's forever emailing people, speaking to old colleagues . . .' She sighed again. 'He just can't seem to give it up.'

'Yeah, well,' I said. 'Maybe that's not such a bad thing . . . at least it's better than just lying around feeling sorry for yourself.'

'I suppose so . . .'

I glanced at her, realising how much she'd changed over the years. She didn't *look* all that different to the seventeen-year-old girl I'd once thought I loved – the same shiny black hair, the same graceful features, the same overall air of almost aristocratic elegance. But she'd grown up now. She was a married woman. She ran a business. She was confident, capable . . . she could deal with the world.

'What?' she said, smiling as she noticed me looking at her. 'What's the matter?'

'Nothing . . . I was just . . .'

'What? Just looking at me?'

'Sorry . . .'

She laughed. 'I'm not complaining.'

I gazed out of the window for a while, not saying anything. We were driving through the town centre now, and the night was alive with drinkers and clubbers – groups of girls, groups of men . . . short skirts, drunk eyes, T-shirts, no coats . . .

'So,' I said to Imogen. 'How's Martin?'

Martin was her husband, Martin Rand. A financier of some sort, he worked in the City, commuting to London every day. Apart from the fact that he was sickeningly energetic, and grotesquely good-looking, and unbelievably rich, I didn't really know very much about him.

'Haven't you heard?' Imogen said.

'Heard what?'

'We split up.'

'Really?'

She nodded. 'A couple of months ago . . . I thought you knew.'

'No . . .'

'That's why I'm living at home at the moment.'

'Oh, right . . . I thought you were just visiting.'

She looked at me. 'Are you *sure* I didn't tell you? I could have sworn . . .'

'I would have remembered if you'd told me,' I said. 'So what happened . . . ? Or don't you want to talk about it?'

'No,' she said lightly. 'It's no big deal. It was just . . . well, lots of things really. We just grew apart, I suppose.' She hesitated for a moment. 'And, you know . . . Martin had always wanted us to have kids . . .'

'And you didn't?'

She glanced at me. 'I wanted a family, yeah . . . but I wanted to carry on working too.' She shook her head. 'I didn't want to stay at home all day, changing nappies and cleaning up sick, while Martin carried on living his life, swanning around all over the world.'

I nodded, not sure what to say.

Imogen smiled at me. 'You never liked Martin, did you?'

'I never really knew him that well.'

'Yeah, but you still didn't *like* him.'

I looked at her. She was smiling at me.

I said, 'Are you doing all right?'

'Yeah,' she said, nodding. 'Yeah, I really am.'

'Good.'

'How about you? I mean, apart from all this stuff that's going on at the moment. How are you doing?'

'Well, you know . . .'

'The business OK?'

'Yeah, fine.'

'What about the rest of it?'

'The rest of what?'

'Your life . . .'

'I don't know,' I muttered, inexplicably embarrassed for a moment. 'I get up in the morning, you know . . . go to work, come home, do stuff . . .'

'What kind of stuff?'

I shrugged. 'Just stuff . . . the same kind of stuff that everyone else does. Read, watch television, eat, sleep . . .'

'Are you seeing anyone?'

'No.'

'Do you want to?'

I sighed.

Imogen looked at me. 'Sorry . . . I didn't mean to –'

'It's all right.'

'I'm just . . . I worry about you, John, that's all.'

'You don't need to.'

'I know,' she said, grinning. 'But I enjoy it.'

I smiled at her, and for a moment I was reminded of how close we used to be, and how different things used to be. Back then . . . it was a ghostless time – the spring before the summer, when the leaves that were falling now had yet to even form.

I looked out of the car window and saw that we were nearing the turn-off to my street. 'You'd better drop me off here,' I said to Imogen.

'Why?' she said, still smiling. 'Don't you want to be seen with me?'

'There were reporters waiting outside my house when I left,' I explained. 'And a TV crew too. If they see you with me . . . well, you know how it works.'

She glanced at her watch. 'But it's 10.30, John –'

'Oh, yeah, I forgot . . . they all go to bed at ten o'clock, don't they?'

She nodded, pulling in at the turning to my street and parking expertly at the side of the road. The engine of the Mercedes purred quietly, and for a second or two we just sat there in the warmth of the car, sharing an intimate silence. 'I've got a hat and scarf in the back of the car,' Imogen said after a while. 'It's not the most subtle disguise in the world, but if you *wanted* to invite me in for a drink, I could leave the car here . . .'

I looked at her, not sure what to think or say . . . and my uncertainty clearly showed in my face, because after a few moments Imogen smiled sadly and said, 'Some other time, maybe?'

'Yeah, I'm sorry . . . it's just –'

'I understand, John. Really, it's OK.' Her smile brightened, and she leaned across and kissed me. 'And you never know,' she added, brushing my cheek with her hand. 'A mysterious woman in a hat and scarf might just turn up one night, looking for some company . . .'

'I'll look out for her.'

'You do that.'

I couldn't see any reporters or TV people as I walked down the street towards my house, and I wondered briefly if perhaps they *had* all gone home and gone to bed early, but then – just as I was approaching my house – the door of a parked car opened and a sharp-eyed young woman clutching a digital voice recorder jumped out.

'Mr Craine?' she called out to me. 'Could I have a quick word about –'

'No,' I said firmly.

She took no notice, scuttling up to me, then scrambling along beside me, sticking the recorder into my face. 'How did you feel when you heard the news about Anton Viner, Mr Craine?'

'Wonderful,' I said. 'It really made my day.'

She was taken aback for a second, long enough for me to get to the house and get my key in the door.

'How did you find Anna's body, John?' she said. 'How did you know where it was?'

I didn't say anything, just opened the door.

'Did you *know* Anna, John?'

I went inside and shut the door, but before I'd got halfway along the corridor, the doorbell rang. I turned round and walked back along the hallway, reached up to the bell, and yanked out the wires. Then I just stood there for a while, in the silent darkness, waiting to see if she knocked on the door . . . and I was really hoping that she didn't, because I didn't *want* to do anything stupid, but I had a feeling that I might.

But she didn't.

I waited a couple of minutes, then a few minutes more – and while I waited I was listening hard for any sign of life from upstairs . . . but there was nothing. No sounds, no faint vibrations, no sense of any presence at all. And as I moved quietly back down the hallway and unlocked the door to my flat, I wondered where Bridget had gone. Was she out with friends somewhere? Dancing, drinking . . .

enjoying the night? Or maybe she'd decided to give Dave another chance. Maybe she was with him right now . . . in a fancy restaurant, a pub, a club, at his place . . . in bed together . . .

I didn't put the lights on when I went inside. I moved through the familiar darkness into the front room, sat down in the armchair, and lit a cigarette. The curtains were all still closed. The house was silent. I poured myself a tumbler of whisky, raised it to my lips, and drank deeply.

23

Around 8.30 the next morning I was smoking my second cigarette of the day with my third cup of coffee when I heard a commotion outside – hurried footsteps, raised voices, the sound of a dog barking. I got up and looked out through a gap in the curtains and saw Bridget and Walter struggling their way across the road, pursued by a gaggle of reporters and TV people. Bridget was saying nothing, keeping her head bowed down and her eyes fixed firmly to the ground, and Walter was just barking chaotically at everything. As they reached the front door, I went out into the hallway and met them coming in.

'Shit,' said Bridget, slamming the door on the reporters. 'They don't give up, do they?'

'Are you OK?' I asked her.

'Yeah, I'm fine,' she said, smiling at me. 'How about you?'

'Yeah,' I nodded. 'I'm all right. Look, I'm really sorry about all this –'

'Don't worry about it,' she said, shaking her head and waving away my apology. 'It's not your fault, is it?'

'Maybe not,' I shrugged. 'But I'm sorry anyway.'

'Me too,' she said, touching my arm. 'About last night, I mean . . .'

I looked at her, not sure what she meant.

'I meant to leave you a note,' she explained. 'To let you know where I'd gone . . . but I forgot. Sorry.'

'That's OK.'

'I went to see Sarah,' she said. 'We had some pet-shop business to sort out, you know . . . tax and stuff. And then we had a few glasses of wine, and I didn't want to drive home drunk . . . especially with all these reporters around –'

'It's OK,' I said. 'You don't have to explain anything to me.'

She smiled. 'I'm just telling you, that's all.'

'Well . . . thanks.'

'You're welcome.'

We looked at each other for a moment then – Bridget still smiling at me – and I realised that her coat was damp and her hair was glistening darkly with a light sheen of rain . . . and I remembered how Stacy's blonde hair used to darken in the rain, taking on the colour of rain-goldened straw . . .

'I'd better get a move on,' Bridget said.

I looked at her. 'Where are you going?'

'Work,' she said, glancing at her watch. 'Saturday's the busiest day of the week.' She grinned at me. 'Lots of fat kids wanting to buy mouses.'

I nodded, smiling. 'Are you going right now?'

'Yeah, I just need to get a couple of things from upstairs.'

'I was just on my way into town, so if you want a lift . . .?'

'Sure?'

'Yeah.'

'OK,' she said, heading for the stairs. 'I won't be a minute.'

*

There were even more reporters waiting outside when we left the house, and as we headed across the street towards my car they swarmed all around us like maniacs – shoving microphones in our faces, shouting out questions, blocking our way, taking photographs. Walter started up with his chaotic barking again, while me and Bridget just kept our mouths shut and concentrated on walking in a straight line. I was doing my best to stay calm, to not let the pushing and jostling bother me . . . and I was doing a pretty good job of it until, just as we reached my car, a particularly annoying photographer rammed his camera so close to my face, trying to get a shot of me and Bridget together, that I just couldn't help lashing out at him. As he shoved against me again, almost knocking me off my feet, I swung round and cracked my elbow into his camera, smashing it viciously into his face. He grunted in pain, stepping back and dropping the camera, and while he stood there clutching his bloodied nose, I leaned down, picked up his camera, and threw it over the factory wall. There was a momentary silence before I heard the satisfying sound of the camera splashing into the cooling pond beyond the wall, and then everything started up again – the scuffling, the jostling, the questioning, the digital whirr of cameras – and as we got into my car, I could just make out the bleating voice of the photographer I'd hit whining away in the background – *you brode my vucking node, you bartard . . . I'll vucking do you for dis . . . I'll vucking ab you . . .*

'Sorry about that,' I said to Bridget, making sure that Walter was safely in the back and locking the car doors. 'I didn't mean to hurt the guy –'

'Fuck him,' she said, fastening her seat belt. 'He deserved it.'

'You ready?' I asked her, starting the car.

She smiled. 'Let's go.'

About five minutes later, as we approached the north end of the High Street, Bridget glanced over her shoulder and said, 'I think we're being followed.'

'Yeah, I know.'

'Are they reporters?'

'In the BMW, yeah. There's a TV crew in the Range Rover behind them.'

Bridget looked at me. 'Aren't you going to try losing them?'

I shook my head. 'There's no point.'

'Why not?'

'I'm a shitty driver,' I said. 'And this is a shitty car. And, besides, they know where I'm going anyway.'

'Yeah, but they don't know where *I'm* going, do they? I don't want them following me to the shop, John.'

'I'll drop you off at the NatWest in the High Street,' I said, pulling up at the lights. 'You can cut through the bank and go out the back way into Wyre Street. It's only about five minutes from there to your shop.' I glanced in the rear-view mirror and saw that the BMW and the Range Rover were about three or four cars behind us. The lights were still red.

'But what if they follow me into the bank?' Bridget said.

'They won't.'

Before she could say anything else, I slammed the Fiesta

into gear, put my foot down and shot through the red lights. Horns blared as I swung the Fiesta to the right, narrowly missing an oncoming bus, and sped down the High Street for about fifty yards before screeching to a halt outside the bank.

'Go on,' I told Bridget, glancing quickly in the rear-view mirror. 'You're all right, they're still stuck at the lights.'

'Will you call me later?' she said, undoing her seat belt and opening the door.

'Yeah, if I can. Now get going.'

She jumped out, got Walter out of the back, and as they hurried off together into the bank, I drove off steadily down the High Street. Within twenty seconds or so, the BMW and the Range Rover were behind me again, only this time they were keeping a lot closer.

They were still right behind me when I drove round the market square and turned left at a *No Entry* sign into Wyre Street. It was strictly pedestrianised here – no cars, no parking – and I got a lot of nasty looks and angry shouts as I drove slowly up the street, crawling through the crowds of Saturday shoppers, which wasn't all that pleasant . . . but it was a lot better than having to park somewhere and walk to the office with a pack of reporters dogging my every step.

I parked the Fiesta on the pavement outside the office. I knew that it'd be gone within the hour, clamped and towed away, and I'd have to pay God-knows-how-much to get it back, probably more than it was worth . . . but I didn't really care. It was only a car. And it was about time I got a new one anyway.

A reporter and a cameraman were waiting at the door to the office, and when they saw me coming they immediately started hustling towards me – the reporter fiddling with his earpiece, the cameraman adjusting something on his camera . . .

'Sky News, Mr Craine,' the reporter called out as he approached me, somehow making the statement sound like a question. *Sky News, Mr Craine?* I didn't look at him, didn't say anything, just kept on going towards the office door.

'We're live on Sky News, Mr Craine,' I heard him saying. 'Could you tell us how you feel about your wife being the victim of a serial killer?'

I stopped and looked at him. His face was vaguely familiar from countless TV news reports, but I couldn't put a name to it. He was holding a microphone towards me, his head tilted slightly to one side and his mouth turned down, showing me how serious and sympathetic he was.

'This is live?' I said quietly.

'Yes, Mr Craine. You're live on Sky News.'

I smiled at him. 'Why don't you fuck off, you annoying cunt?'

And as he stepped back, momentarily stunned, I walked past him, unlocked the office door, and went inside.

I don't often go into the office at the weekend, but on the odd occasion that I do, George Salvini is always there, quietly getting on with some work in his office. He's usually on his own, but when I knocked on his door that morning and he let me in, he was with a neatly groomed

293

young man called Fabian who worked part-time for him. Fabian was perched on the edge of a desk, staring at a small TV on a table in the corner.

'Sorry about all this, George,' I said, glancing at the TV. It was tuned to Sky News, and the studio presenter was in the middle of apologising for the inappropriate language that had just been heard during an interview with John Craine.

'Not at all, John,' George beamed at me. 'It's all rather exciting, really. We were just watching your interview outside.'

'Yeah, good one,' Fabian added, grinning at me.

'Would you like some coffee?' George asked.

'No, thanks. I'm not stopping . . . I just wanted to use your back door, if that's OK?'

'Of course, of course . . .'

'There's no one out there, is there? No reporters?'

George looked at Fabian. 'Would you mind?'

Fabian nodded, smiling intimately at George, then he padded across the office towards a door in the far wall.

'He's a good boy,' George said, watching him go through the door.

I smiled.

George turned back to me. 'You look tired.'

'I am.'

He patted my shoulder. 'If there's anything I can do to help, just let me know. OK?'

'Thanks, I will.'

We both looked over as Fabian came back in.

'It's clear,' he said. 'No one's out there.'

'Thanks,' I told him, heading for the door.

'Mind how you go, John,' George called out.

'Yeah, you too,' I called back.

The door led me out into a carpeted corridor, at the far end of which was a cluttered storage area with a barred window and a fire door. I went over to the door, pushed down on the bar, gave it a shove, and stepped out into a narrow alley at the back of the building. The alley was enclosed behind a high brick wall crowned with shards of broken glass. Piles of retail debris were stacked against the wall: flattened cardboard boxes, bin bags, pallets, rolls of plastic sheeting. A sparse rain was falling, and I could hear the drops *tocking* loudly on clamp-shaped blocks of polystyrene. Someone had taken the trouble to paint *ALWAYS ON MY MIND* on the wall, and beneath that, *FUCK YOUR NOB*.

I pulled up my collar and headed off into the rain.

24

When I got to Cal's place, the first thing I learned was that the photographer whose nose I'd broken had reported me to the police and that I was now wanted for questioning on suspicion of assault and criminal damage.

'It was on Sky News just a minute ago,' Cal told me. 'And I heard it on the police scanner too.' He smiled at me. 'I think they might want to talk to you about calling someone a cunt on live TV as well.'

'Is there a law against that?'

'Fuck knows. Do you want some coffee?'

While Cal made coffee, I went over and sat down on the settee, lit a cigarette, and stared at the mute TV. A picture of me was being shown, with a *BREAKING NEWS* banner scrolling underneath that said *HUSBAND OF SERIAL KILLER VICTIM IN INTERVIEW OUTRAGE ACCUSED OF "ASSAULT" BY DAILY EXPRESS PHOTOGRAPHER*. After a few moments, my picture was replaced by a photo of Stacy, and then a blurred mugshot of Anton Viner appeared on the screen . . .

I picked up the remote and turned off the TV.

'So what's going on, John?' said Cal, sitting down next to me and passing me a cup of coffee. 'All this stuff about Anton Viner . . . is it true?'

I looked at him. 'Do you trust me?'

'Yeah, of course.'

'So if I were to tell you that I knew, without doubt, that Anton Viner *didn't* kill Anna Gerrish, but that I couldn't tell you how or why I knew . . . could you accept that?'

He hesitated for a moment, thinking about it, then simply nodded. 'Viner didn't kill Anna?'

'No.'

'And you know that for a fact?'

'Yes.'

'OK,' he said. 'That's good enough for me.' He smiled. 'So does that mean we're back on the case?'

I looked at him. 'I've got a funny feeling that you've never been off it.'

Although I'd told Cal two weeks ago to leave the case alone, I'd known all along that he wouldn't – he simply wasn't capable of it. I knew he'd just have to keep digging, keep poking around, keep lifting up stones to see what was under them . . . and I was right, that *was* what he'd been doing.

'The Charles Raymond Kemper that we're looking for doesn't exist,' he told me. 'I've run him through my automated search program and I've manually been through every possible database, using every possible combination of names and initials, and I haven't come up with anything that makes sense. The address in Leicester doesn't exist. There's no birth certificate for anyone called Kemper that matches the date of birth in the DVLA's records.' Cal looked at me. 'There's simply no trace of our Charlie Kemper anywhere.'

'So it's a fake driving licence?'

'Yeah, but there's more to it than that. Fake ID's not difficult, and driving licences are a piece of piss, but even with the really good fakes I can usually get behind the false information and find little traces of the real stuff, but with this one . . .' He shrugged. 'There's just nothing there. Nothing at all.'

'OK, so it's a false name and a false address . . . but the guy in the Nissan was real, wasn't he?'

'Well, yeah . . .'

'We saw him on CCTV.'

Cal gave me a look. 'It's gone now.'

'What's gone?'

'The stored CCTV footage, the stuff we found on the council's computer system. It's been wiped.'

'When?'

'About ten days ago.'

'Shit.'

'It's not really a problem . . . I've still got copies, and unless someone really knows what they're doing, it's almost impossible to completely delete anything.'

'Who could have wiped the footage?'

Cal shrugged. 'Anyone with access to the system.'

'Bishop?'

'I don't see why not.'

'All right,' I sighed, lighting another cigarette. 'What else have you got?'

He'd checked out Graham Gerrish pretty thoroughly, he told me, hacking into his laptop and confirming his fondness for very young girls, so it seemed very likely that he *had* abused Anna when she was living at home, but Cal hadn't found anything to suggest that Gerrish had been the man in the Nissan.

'I don't think he killed his daughter,' Cal said.

'No, he just fucked her.'

Cal looked at me.

I said, 'Did you manage to find Tasha?'

He shook his head. 'She's gone . . . I went down to London Road a couple of times last week, but there was no sign of her anywhere. One of the other girls told me that she'd just packed up all her stuff one day and left.'

'Did she say where she'd gone?'

'To her mother's in Chelmsford. It's where she goes when she's trying to get clean, apparently. I called someone I know in Chelmsford and got them to check out her mother's address.' Cal looked at me. 'Tasha's definitely there.'

I nodded, wondering if Tasha had decided to leave town of her own accord or if someone had persuaded her to go. 'What about Bishop?' I asked Cal. 'Have you done any checking on him?'

'Not yet . . . I've set up an automated search, and it's all ready to go, but I didn't want to do anything until I'd heard from you.' He lit a cigarette. 'I'm pretty sure that my software's safe, but Bishop's not stupid, he's probably got all kinds of alarm systems in place, and if he *was* to find out that someone was digging around in his life . . .' Cal looked at me. 'But, like I said, the search is all ready to go.'

'So you just have to press a button or something?'

'Yeah, basically . . .' Cal smiled. 'It's my own software program – all you have to do is put in a name and as many details as you've got, and the software does the rest. If there's something to find – no matter how insignificant – it'll find it. And it'll do it about a thousand times quicker than I ever could.' He smiled again. 'If it wasn't *quite* so illegal, I could market it for a fortune.'

'Right,' I said. 'But I imagine that you still make a little bit of money out of it, don't you?'

'I can't complain,' he grinned.

'How long will it take once it's started?'

He shrugged. 'It varies, depending on how much information is out there . . . could be a couple of hours, could be a couple of days.'

'Best start it now then.'

'Are you sure?'

'Yeah . . . everything about all this comes back to Bishop. Anna Gerrish, Viner, me . . . everything. I want to know why. I want to know everything there is to know about him. I want to know what the fucker's hiding.'

Cal got up, went over to his work desk and pressed a key on one of his laptops. He watched the screen for a few moments, then he took an iPhone from his pocket and rapidly thumbed its screen, and then, finally, he turned back to me. 'OK, that's it,' he said, putting the iPhone back in his pocket. 'If the program finds anything, it'll send it to my iPhone. So . . . what do you want to do now?'

I looked at him. 'Do you fancy a drive down to Eastway?'

I didn't particularly want to go to the police station, but I didn't want to spend the rest of the day trying to avoid getting arrested for assault and criminal damage either. And, besides, I knew that I'd have to deal with the charge sooner or later, and the later I left it, the worse it'd probably be.

Cal wasn't all that keen on visiting the police station either, but once I'd assured him that he didn't have to come in with me, that all he had to do was drop me off and pick me up again later, he was happy enough.

'It's not that I don't want to be *seen* with you or anything, John,' he told me as we drove away from his house in one of his several Mondeos. This one, like all the others, was totally anonymous from the outside – just another bog-standard black Mondeo – but on the inside, and under the bonnet, it was as well equipped, if not better, than a car worth twenty times as much. 'I mean,' Cal continued, 'you know I'd do *any*thing to help you . . .'

'Yeah, I know.'

'It's just that . . . well, me and the police . . .'

'It's all right, Cal,' I said. 'You don't have to keep explaining –'

'I think I'm allergic to them.'

'You're allergic to the police?'

'Yeah . . . whenever I'm anywhere near them, my heart speeds up and I start sweating like a pig.'

'That's probably just the drugs.'

He looked at me. 'You know that if I could wait for you in the car park, I would.'

'Yes,' I said patiently. 'I know you would.'

'But they're always looking out of their fucking windows down there, aren't they? Fucking cops . . . nothing better to do. And they've got all that ANPR shit now . . . automatic number-plate recognition. Not that they'd get anything from my plate –'

'Cal?' I said.

'What?'

'Just shut up and drive, will you?'

As he muttered a few more paranoid curses and carried on driving, and I wound down the window and lit a cigarette, my phone rang. I'd turned it back on that morning, hoping that any reporters would have given up trying it by now, and so far I hadn't had any unwanted calls. But I was still double-checking the caller display before answering every call, and when I looked at the screen now I saw the name LEON.

I hit the answer key. 'Hello, Leon.'

'John,' he said. 'Is it safe to talk?'

'Yeah, I'm with Cal.'

'All right, listen, I've been asking around about Mick Bishop and the Gerrish case, and there's definitely *some*thing going on, but no one seems to know what it is. Whatever Bishop's up to, he's playing it very close to his chest. But as far as I can tell . . . and you have to understand that a lot of this is guesswork, John. I really don't have enough information to *confirm* anything . . . but it would *appear* that the only evidence that links Viner to Anna Gerrish is one small sample of DNA, and I wouldn't put too much faith in that.'

'Why not?'

'The pathologist, Gerald McKee . . . have you heard of him?'

'No.'

'He's the pathologist that Bishop always uses when he wants things done his way.'

'You mean he's a bent pathologist?'

'Not really,' Leon sighed. 'He's just a sad old man with a few personal problems, the kind of problems that Bishop knows how to exploit. I doubt very much if McKee actually *lies* about anything for Bishop, but he's perfectly willing to conveniently overlook things or stretch the truth a little if it's in his best interests to do so.'

'But McKee wouldn't be involved in the DNA testing himself, would he?'

'Not as such, no. The testing's done at a contracted forensic laboratory, and I don't think even Bishop has got his hooks in there. But even so . . . well, I wouldn't trust any evidence that's passed through the hands of Bishop and McKee.'

'And there's nothing else at all that links Viner with Anna Gerrish?'

'Not as far as I know. I haven't been able to get a copy of the autopsy report, and no one that I've spoken to has actually seen it, but the prevailing opinion seems to be that there are very few similarities between Anna's murder and Stacy's.' Leon hesitated for a moment. 'Are you OK talking about this, John?'

'Yeah, go on.'

'Well, the knife wounds don't match, for a start. Anna was stabbed with a different kind of knife than the one used on Stacy. Also, Anna *wasn't* strangled . . . and she wasn't raped either.'

I took a breath, steadying myself. 'So, if it wasn't for the DNA, there'd be no reason to suspect Viner?'

'None at all.'

I paused for a moment, trying to piece things together – Bishop, Viner . . . Anna, me . . . Viner, Stacy . . . Viner, me – but I still didn't get it. I could just about see how I could *make* everything fit together, but only in the way that you can make all the pieces of a jigsaw puzzle fit together if you keep hitting them hard enough with a hammer.

'We're nearly there, John,' Cal said.

I nodded, wiping condensation from the car window and gazing out at Saturday morning shoppers scuttling along the pavement, their heads bowed down to the wind, their cold hands stuffed in their coat pockets. We were on North Street, just the other side of the Eastway roundabout.

'John,' I heard Leon saying. 'Are you still there?'

'Yeah . . . sorry, Leon,' I said. 'I was just thinking . . .'

'Listen, John, I have to go now –'

'Yeah, me too.'

'I'll let you know if I find out anything else.'

'Thanks, Leon.'

'No problem.'

As I ended the call and put the mobile back in my pocket, Cal said to me, 'Is it OK if I drop you off here?'

'Yeah, fine,' I replied.

He pulled in at the side of the road about fifty yards from the police station. 'Just call me when you've finished,' he said. 'And I'll come and pick you up.'

'OK.'

'Use the number I've just called you from.'

'What?'

He held up his iPhone. 'I just called you, so this number will be in your call log. It's a new one. Just dial the number, let it ring twice, then hang up. I'll know it's you. All right?'

I smiled at him. 'Yeah . . .'

'What's so funny?'

I shook my head. 'Nothing . . .'

'You think I'm being paranoid?'

I shrugged. 'There's nothing wrong with being paranoid.'

'Fucking right,' he said.

As I got out of the car and watched Cal drive away, I thought I saw a silver-grey Renault approaching the Eastway roundabout from North Street, but when I wiped the rain from my face and looked again, trying to catch a glimpse of the registration number, it had already turned left, heading away from me towards town, and all I saw was a rain-blurred flash of silver-grey disappearing behind a bus. I couldn't even be sure that it *was* a Renault, let alone *the* Renault.

'Who's being paranoid now?' I muttered to myself as I turned round and headed for the police station.

When I informed the reception officer who I was and what I was doing there, he just stared at me for a moment or two, his mouth half open, and I could almost hear the cogs whirring dimly inside his head as he digested the information, registered it, processed it, and finally came up with an answer.

'Just a minute,' he told me, reaching for a phone.

Ten minutes later I was sitting in Bishop's office, looking around at his bare white walls, his bare black desk, his bare beige carpet . . . it was one of the emptiest rooms I'd ever been in. Apart from Bishop himself, sitting across from me at his desk, there was nothing of him in that room at all. No photographs, no mementoes, no certificates . . . nothing. In fact, the only way of telling that it was Bishop's office was the sign on the door saying *DCI M Bishop*.

'Do you want coffee or anything?' he asked me.

'No, thanks.'

He sniffed. 'Anyway, it's all sorted out. There's nothing to worry about.'

'Sorry?'

'The assault charge, the photographer . . . I've had a word with him. He's withdrawn his complaint and he's not pressing charges.'

'Oh . . . OK, so that's it?'

'That's it.'

I almost said *Thanks*, but I just couldn't do it. I couldn't thank this man, not in a million years. And, besides, I doubted very much that he'd done whatever he'd done for my benefit anyway.

'Did you watch the press conference?' he asked me.

'Yeah.'

'What do you think?'

'About what?'

'Have you still got doubts about Viner?'

I shrugged. 'What can I say?'

'You could answer my question.'

'Why are you asking *me* about it? I don't know anything,

do I? You're the one with all the answers.'

He smiled. 'That's not how you felt yesterday.'

'Yeah, well –'

'You said it was impossible, didn't you? When I told you that Viner's DNA had been found on Anna Gerrish, you said that was impossible.'

'So?'

'So how come you've changed your mind?'

'I haven't changed my mind –'

'You still think it's impossible?'

'Look,' I said, trying to stay calm. 'You turn up out of the blue, and you tell me that the man who raped and killed my wife is suspected of killing not just another woman, but the woman I was hired to find, the woman whose body I *did* find . . . I mean, Christ . . . how do you *expect* me to react?'

Bishop studied me for a moment, his eyes fixed on mine, and then – with a self-satisfied nod – he said, 'All right, that's fair enough.' And then he tried to give me the kind of smile that says, *OK, the formalities are over, let's get the platitudes done and then we can say goodbye*, but it just didn't work on him. His smiles were all the same: cold, tight, empty of emotion and meaning.

'So,' he said casually. 'What are your plans now? Back to work, I suppose?'

'Probably not. It's not that easy investigating privately when you've got a pack of reporters following you around all the time. They kind of get in the way.'

'Right,' he nodded, feigning interest. 'Of course . . . it must be very difficult.'

'Yeah, it is.'

'Maybe it'd be a good time to take a break? Get away from it all somewhere.'

'You think so?'

He gave me a cold look. 'I'm only trying to fucking help.'

'Yeah . . .' I said, getting to my feet. 'Well, I'll think it over. Do you need me to let you know if I'm planning on leaving town?'

'Not particularly.'

I couldn't think of anything else to say then, so I just turned round and started to leave.

'John?' I heard him say.

I stopped. 'What?'

'Haven't you forgotten something?'

I turned to face him. 'I don't think so.'

'There's nothing you want to ask me about?'

'Like what?'

'Viner, maybe?'

'What about him?'

'Don't you want to know if we've found him yet?'

Shit, I thought.

'Have you?' I said.

'No, not yet.' He stared at me. 'You'll be the first to know, though . . . when we do. I'll see to it personally.'

DC Wade was waiting for me outside Bishop's office, and as I followed him along the corridor towards the lift I was trying to work out if Bishop knew anything about what I'd done to Viner, or if he was just guessing, or just fishing . . . or just fucking me around. There was no doubt I'd made a mistake in not asking him about Viner, but it was hard to see how Bishop could deduce anything definite from that alone. Unless, of course, he already suspected something . . . but then, if he had any inkling at all that I'd killed Viner, why the hell would he put Viner in the frame for the murder of Anna Gerrish? If, indeed, that's what he'd done . . . and I was only guessing at that.

As we approached the lift doors, I took out my mobile and dialled Cal's new number. I let it ring a couple of times, and I was just putting the phone back in my pocket when Cliff Duffy appeared from a doorway on my right.

'Hello, John,' he said, coming straight up to me and offering his hand. 'Good to see you again. How's everything going?'

He was looking directly into my eyes as I shook his hand, which was slightly unusual for Cliff, but then I felt something in his hand – possibly a piece of paper – and I realised that he was passing me a message.

'All right?' he asked, still shaking my hand.

'Yeah,' I said, nodding to let him know that I'd got it.

He turned to DC Wade and said, 'Is the DCI in his office?'

And as Wade answered him, 'Yes, but he's busy,' I took the opportunity to let go of Cliff's hand and slip the message into my pocket.

I didn't look at the message until I was safely in Cal's car and we were driving away from Eastway, heading back towards town.

'What's that?' Cal asked as I unfolded the sheet of notepaper.

'I don't know yet,' I said, lighting a cigarette and starting to read:

John. Overheard B making private call to someone called Ray 10.00 this morning. Your name mentioned. B angry with R about something, couldn't hear what. B arranged to meet R 19.00 tonight at Turks Head, off Roman Road.
Good luck.
C.

'What are you doing tonight?' I said to Cal.

'Why?' he asked, glancing at the notepaper in my hand. 'What is it?'

I smiled at him. 'Charles Raymond Kemper . . . I think we might have found him.'

25

Before dropping me off in town, Cal checked his iPhone to see if the search on Mick Bishop had come up with anything yet. It took him a while – scrolling up and down, reading this, reading that . . . and occasionally looking up to make sure that he was still on the road – but eventually he shook his head and said, 'Nope, nothing of any interest yet.'

'What's it given you so far?' I asked out of curiosity.

He shrugged. 'Not much. I've got his landline number, and I know what kind of car he drives, and when he passed his test, and where he lives, and how old he is . . .' Cal looked at me. 'It might take a while to get to the good stuff.'

'If there is any.'

'Yeah, well . . . we should know by the end of the day.'

I glanced out of the window. 'You can drop me here, Cal.'

'Sure?'

I nodded. 'How long do you think it'll take us to get out to The Turk's Head?'

'Not long,' he said, pulling up at the side of the road. 'Twenty minutes, maybe.'

'All right, so if we leave your place at six, we should get there by half-past at the latest. That'll give us plenty of time to check things out before Bishop meets this guy called Ray.'

'How are we going to play it when they get there?'

'I don't know yet.' I smiled at him. 'Don't worry, I'm sure we'll work something out.'

He nodded. 'OK, so you'll be at my place by six?'

'Yeah.'

'Where are you going to be until then?'

'Around.'

'Around where?'

'Just around.' I opened the car door. 'Let me know if the search comes up with anything, OK?'

'Yeah, but –'

'See you later, Cal.'

Bridget's pet shop is situated halfway down Market Street in a pedestrianised area on the west side of the shopping precinct. It's a small brick-built place, flanked by a confectionery shop that's always empty and an old-fashioned hardware store with a dusty window display of upright vacuum cleaners, pressure cookers, light bulbs, and dead wasps.

The rain was beginning to ease off as I made my way down Market Street, and in the distance I could see patches of clear blue sky breaking through the purple-grey blanket of cloud. It was unusually quiet for a Saturday lunchtime. The streets were busy, but not so busy that I couldn't keep walking in a straight line, and it wasn't long before I found myself standing outside Bridget's shop, smoking a cigarette, wondering what the hell I was doing there.

Why was my heart beating so hard?

Why was my blood racing?

And why did I have a tiny black planet spinning around inside my chest, whipping out threads of adrenalin?

I smoked my cigarette and stared at the ground.

I didn't know why.

I didn't know what I was doing there.

I put out my cigarette and began walking back the way I'd come . . . but after three or four steps I stopped, turned round, and went back.

I couldn't help it.

It didn't matter why.

When I entered the shop, Bridget was at the counter wrapping up bags of greeny-brown pellets for a plump old woman in a threadbare fur coat. The old woman had a huge purse in her hand and a wheeled shopping trolley at her feet, and she seemed to be buying up half the contents of the shop – rabbit food, drinking bottles, bowls, polythene bags full of hay and straw. Bridget was cutting off price tags with a small lock-knife and jotting down prices on the back of a paper bag, but when the bell over the door sounded, she stopped what she was doing and looked over the woman's shoulder at me and smiled . . . and just for a second I was sixteen years old again – stupid and pure, a blue-eyed animal, wanting and needing only this moment . . .

I closed the door.

As Bridget slipped her lock-knife into her back pocket and turned her attention back to the plump old woman, I wandered around the shop looking at things. One wall was packed with pet food and pet accessories, while the other side was reserved for the animals. There were racks of birdcages full of budgies and canaries, there were mice and hamsters in glass tanks, scurrying around in their toilet rolls and sawdust, and on the right-hand side of the shop the entire wall was lined with four tiers of fish tanks. The tanks bubbled and hummed, giving off a wonderful smell of pond water, and as I stood there watching the fish, breathing in the smell of the living water, I remembered the rivers and streams of my childhood – the jam jars full of bullheads, the newts, the frogspawn . . .

'Wanna buy a fish, mister?'

I turned at the sound of the voice to find Bridget standing behind me, wiping pet-food dust from her hands. The plump old woman had gone and the shop was empty.

'I'm just looking, thanks,' I said, smiling.

Bridget put her hands in her pockets and smiled back at me. Dressed simply in a jade-green jumper and jeans, she looked quite wonderful.

'How's it going?' I asked her.

'Not bad.'

'Are you on your own?'

She nodded. 'Sarah doesn't work Saturdays, and it's been so quiet today that I told Melanie to go home.'

'Who's Melanie?'

'She works here part-time. You know, weekends, school holidays . . .'

'Right . . . so what do you do about lunch?'

'Sandwiches, usually. Why?' She grinned. 'Are you offering to buy me dinner?'

'Well, yeah, if you want . . .'

'Why don't we just stay here?' she suggested. 'I've got enough sandwiches for two.'

'I'm not really all that hungry, to tell you the truth.'

'Neither am I,' she said quietly, stepping closer to me. 'But why don't you stay here for a while anyway? I can close the shop for an hour or two.' She reached up and gently ran her fingertip down the side of my face. 'We don't have to do anything if you don't want to,' she whispered. 'We can just talk.'

I nodded. I didn't want to talk.

Bridget smiled at me for a moment, then she cupped my face in her hands and kissed me lightly on the lips, before turning round and crossing over to the door. As she put the CLOSED sign up and locked the door, I said, 'Where's Walter?'

'Upstairs.'

'What's upstairs?'

'I'll show you,' she said, taking my hand and leading me through a doorway at the back of the shop.

The doorway took us into a small room that seemed to double as a kitchen and a storeroom. There was a sink, a water heater, a kettle and cups on a counter, and everywhere I looked there were stacks of cardboard boxes piled high against the walls.

'This way,' Bridget said.

I followed her up a narrow wooden staircase that brought us out onto an equally narrow landing where, halfway along, Walter lay curled up in a cushion-strewn dog basket.

'Hey, Walter,' I said.

He looked up at me and thumped his tail a couple of times, but he didn't make any effort to move. And given how warm and comfortable he looked, I thought that was fair enough.

'What is this place?' I asked Bridget, looking around. 'Does anyone live here?'

'Not at the moment. Sarah stayed here for a while after she left her husband, but she's moved back in with him now.'

'Why did she leave him?'

'He used to hit her. Still does, probably.'

'So why's she gone back to him?'

'God knows. She says she loves him . . .' She shook her head, dismissing it from her mind. 'Anyway,' she said, opening a door, 'this is the sitting room.'

I followed her through the door into a cramped but cosy-looking room. There was a small gas fire in front of a small settee, an armchair, a half-moon dining table, rugs and cushions on the floor, and at the far end of the room, a small bay window looked out onto the street below. The whole room seemed to have an air of timelessness to it.

'Very nice,' I said.

'Would you like to see the bedroom?'

I nodded, not trusting myself to speak.

She led me across the room to an adjoining door, opened it up, and ushered me into the bedroom. It was about the same size as the sitting room, and it had the same haunting sense of timelessness to it, but there was something else about this room, something else altogether. I didn't quite understand it, but as the pale autumn light filtered in through the curtains, illuminating the whiteness of an old-fashioned bed beneath the window, I felt as if I was in another country.

'Are you OK with this?' Bridget asked softly, closing the door.

'Yeah . . .' I said. 'Are you?'

She didn't say anything, she just took me by the hand and led me over to the bed.

She was pale and beautiful and she smelled of straw.

Afterwards, lying together in the waning light, we both retreated into our own quiet thoughts for a while. It was a good silence, a silence of breaths and comfort, and I felt no need to break it. Although the street was only a dozen or so feet below, the room seemed muted and still. There was no traffic noise, no footsteps, no human sounds at all – just a faint, indefinable whisper, like the hush of a coming wind.

I listened to a clock ticking, not caring what time it was.

My head was empty.

Thoughtless . . .

I was close to happiness.

After a while, Bridget nudged me with her foot. 'I'll have to get back to the shop soon.'

'Why?' I said, smiling at her.

'Because if Sarah finds out that I closed up, she'll kill me.'

'How's she going to find out?'

'You don't know Sarah . . .'

I rolled over and reached down for my jacket, patting the pockets until I found my cigarettes. 'Do you mind?' I asked Bridget, taking one out.

She shook her head. 'There's a bottle of whisky somewhere. Sarah's always liked a drop of good malt . . . I think it's in the cupboard over there. Just help yourself if you want.'

'I'm all right, thanks,' I said, lighting the cigarette.

'Sure?'

'Yeah.'

She smiled again.

I looked at her. 'I haven't done that for a long time.'

'What – refused a drink?'

'No, I meant –'

'I know what you meant, John,' she said, laughing gently. 'And I kind of guessed you hadn't.' She half sat up, looked me in the eye for a moment, then she lowered herself down, resting her head on my chest. When she spoke, I could feel the whisper of her words on my skin. 'I never thought this would happen.'

'Neither did I.'

'But it did.'

'Yes.'

'Are you glad?'

'Very.

'Good.'

I felt her hand moving down my body.

We slept for a while, half-slumbering together in the late afternoon stillness, and for the first time in years I didn't feel the need to be somewhere else. I didn't feel the need to *be* anything at all – someone else, something else, anything but me . . .

For now, I was perfectly content with who and what and where I was.

For now.

But the clock was still ticking, and I knew that nothing lasts for ever.

It was around 4.30 when Bridget sat up in bed, endearingly covering her breasts with the duvet, and nudged me with her elbow.

'I really have to get up now,' she said. 'If I don't cash up and get the money to the bank, Sarah really will kill me.'

I sat up and lit a cigarette. 'I'd better get going too.'

She looked at me, not saying anything, but I could see the question in her eyes.

'I have to meet someone,' I explained. 'My nephew-in-law.'

She smiled. 'Nephew-in-law?'

'He's called Cal. He works with me sometimes.'

'Oh, right . . . so you're working tonight?'

'Kind of.'

'Sorry,' she said. 'I'm just being nosy. You don't have to tell me –'

'No, it's all right,' I assured her. 'I don't mind you asking . . . it's just . . . well, it's not really work, as such. It's just something I need to sort out.'

'Is it to do with that man?'

'What man?'

'That policeman . . . what's his name? The one who came round to our house.'

'Bishop?'

'Yeah, him.'

'What makes you think it's about Bishop?'

'I don't know,' she shrugged. 'I just got a feeling about him, that's all. When he came to the house, and when I saw him on TV . . .' She shivered. 'I don't know . . . he just didn't seem *right*, if that makes any sense.'

'It makes a lot of sense.'

'Yeah, well . . . just be careful, OK?'

I smiled. 'OK.'

She kissed me, ruffled my hair, then got out of bed and started to get dressed. I lay there and watched her. In the dusky light, her hair was edged with a dust-pale shine and her skin was creamy white. There was a faint scar low on her belly and a small bruise just below her left breast. Her shoulders were broader than I'd imagined, spanning the ridge of her back with a delicate strength that mirrored the curve of her hips, and her backside was full, like a pale sun on a winter's morning. It was a body that deserved to be naked. And as she slipped into her underwear, then pulled on her jumper and climbed into her jeans, I wondered if I'd ever see it again.

'Have you seen my socks?' she said.

'Try under the bed.'

She found her socks and pulled them on, then went over and examined herself in a mirror on the wall. She ran her fingers through her hair, then leaned in close and plucked something from her lip with a hooked little finger.

'What time are you meeting your nephew-in-law?' she asked.

'Six o'clock.'

She came over and sat on the edge of the bed and bent down to put on her shoes. 'Are you going to be busy all night?'

'I don't know. It depends . . .'

'Sorry,' she smiled. 'I'm being pushy again.'

'No, it's all right. It's just that I really don't know how long I'm going to be . . . why don't I ring you later on?'

'Yeah, that'd be nice.' Still bent over, she tied her shoelaces in a double knot, brushed at the toes of her shoes, then lightly stamped her feet. Finally, she sat back up and looked at me. 'If it's not too late,' she said, almost shyly, 'maybe we could go out somewhere?'

'I'd like that.'

'Good.'

I smiled at her.

'Anyway,' she said, 'I thought you were getting up?'

'I am.'

'Go on, then.'

'I thought you had to go downstairs to cash up?'

She shook her head. 'You watched *me* getting dressed, now it's my turn to watch you.'

I stared at her, stupidly embarrassed, not sure what to say.

She smiled. 'It's all right, I'm only joking. I'll let you get dressed in peace.'

She glanced over her shoulder at me as she left the room, and the look on her face – a carefree smile of intimate amusement – sent a tingle through my heart.

It was quiet in the pet shop downstairs. The daylight was fading outside, shops were closed or closing, shoppers were on their way home. It was that time of day when the town gets a chance to rest before the bedlam of the night begins. In the shop, Bridget was cashing up, birds were fluttering softly in their cages, and the fish tanks were bubbling quietly in the evening light. I stood by the door, breathing in the musty smell of straw and grain, the rubbery tang of dog toys, the fresh leather scent of collars and leads . . .

I didn't want to leave.

I wanted to stay here.

I didn't want to be anywhere else.

'You'll ring me later then?' Bridget said.

'Yeah . . . I don't know what time it'll be –'

'It doesn't matter,' she smiled. 'Just call me when you can.'

I looked at her for a moment, remembering the scent of her skin, the touch of her lips, the breath of her whispered words . . .

'Go on,' she said softly. 'I'll see you later.'

I unlocked the door and stepped out into the twilight.

26

There were no reporters waiting outside my office when I got there, and my illegally parked Fiesta was gone. The building looked dark and empty, and as I let myself in and started climbing the stairs, I could feel the silence all around me. It was everywhere – in the air, the dust, the empty offices, the worn old wood of the banister . . . a sleeping silence.

My keys rattled far too loudly as I unlocked the office door and went inside. I didn't turn on the light. I moved quietly through the darkness, opened the door to my private office, and made my way over to my desk. I poured myself a large drink from the bottle in the drawer, then went over to the settee beneath the window. The blinds were open, the dark glass of the window glazed with the faint glow of streetlights, and as I sat down on the settee and lit a cigarette, a shadow of my stupid smoking head fell across the floor.

Stupid . . .

The blue-eyed animal.

Stupid and pure.

I wasn't pure. I was faithless and stupid and weak.

'I'm sorry, Stace,' I muttered. 'I'm *really* sorry . . .'

It's OK.

'No, it's not.'

You can't be sad all the time, John. Not for ever. It'll kill you. You have to be happy sometimes.

'I can't –'

Yes, you can. You were happy with Bridget just now, weren't you?

'Please don't –'

She's nice.

'Yeah, but she's not *you*.'

It's all right, John. Really, it's all right. Don't cry any more.

I sniffed hard, wiping snot and tears from my face.

I'm in your heart, John . . . always. No matter what.

'I know.'

I love you.

I thought I might just sit there in the silent darkness and sink down into a drunken nowhere for the rest of the night, but after five minutes or so of not drinking, not thinking, just staring thoughtlessly at nothing, something made me put down the untouched whisky glass and get up off the settee.

It was almost six o'clock.

I looked over at the wall safe, imagining the 9mm pistol inside, and just for a moment I thought of my father. I thought of him alone in his room, putting the gun to his head . . . and I remembered Leon's question: *If you're going to kill yourself, why make a point of locking the door first? What purpose does it serve?* And I wondered if there *was* a meaningful answer, or if – like almost everything else in this life – it was just one of those things, as purposeless as life itself.

I guessed I'd never know.

Cal was waiting for me outside his house when the taxi dropped me off. Dressed in a long black overcoat and a battered old trilby, and with his tousled hair sticking out wildly from beneath the hat, he looked like some kind of mutant Sam Spade.

'You're late,' he said.

'Yeah, sorry –'

'It's quarter-past six already.'

'I know –'

'And why don't you answer your fucking mobile? I've been trying to call you for hours.'

I pulled out my phone and checked it. 'Sorry,' I said, switching it on. 'I must have turned it off by mistake.'

'Fuck's sake, John . . .'

'What were you trying to call me about?'

He glanced at his watch. 'I'll tell you in the car.'

It was fully dark as we left Cal's house and headed north out of town. The Turk's Head, the pub where Bishop was supposedly meeting the man called Ray, was about two miles west of Stangate Rise, the estate where the Gerrishes lived. It was a large, family-friendly pub, with a restaurant and a beer garden and a children's play area, and although it was a fair way from town, it was usually pretty busy.

Traffic was sparse at this time of night – too late for going home, too early for going out – and Cal was making the most of the open roads, gunning the Mondeo along at well over 60 mph. His hands were tight on the steering wheel, his eyes were alight, and he was talking as fast as he was driving.

'Listen, what I was trying to tell you about, the search . . . it came up with something about Bishop, something really weird . . . well, it might not be anything, and it might not be really weird, but the thing is, it found this archive some-one's set up on a private site, like a local newspaper thing, a local history site or something –'

'Hold on,' I said.

'What?'

'First of all, I can't understand a word you're saying. And second of all, you're driving too fast.'

'We're late –'

'It doesn't matter. Just slow down.'

'But if we don't get there –'

'If you carry on driving like this, we won't get there at all.'

He nodded, licking his lips, and eased off the accelerator.

'OK,' I said calmly. 'How much speed have you taken?'

'Not much. I was just –'

'You need to get on top of it, Cal. Right now. OK? If you can't control yourself, we're not going anywhere.'

'I can control myself.'

'Yeah, well, do it then.' I looked at him. 'I don't want to hear another word from you until you've got your head sorted out. All right?'

He nodded.

I lit a cigarette and gazed out of the window. The moon was full, hanging low and pale in the sky, its cold light greying the night. We'd left the town behind now and were driving steadily along an unlit dual carriageway through a dying landscape of small villages and farmland. Ash trees lined the roadside, their branches almost bare, and beyond them lay the remains of an old forest. There wasn't much left of the forest now, and most of it was scarred with litter-filled ditches and the mindless rut of motorcycle tracks, but it was still just possible to imagine the primitive heart of the forest as it once must have been. Colourless in the cold of night, a tableau of dark earth and grasses and shallow black waters melting in the starless sky. Bones, scraps of beasts, like bleached jewels of winter scattered on the slopes of black hills. It would have been a desolate place, proud and savage and out of time . . .

I flipped my cigarette out of the window and turned back to Cal. 'All right?' I said.

He nodded. 'Yeah . . .'

'Are we OK?'

He grinned at me. 'Yeah, we're OK.'

'Good. So what was it you were trying to tell me?'

'Bishop's got a brother,' he said. 'And guess what his name is.'

Raymond Bishop, Cal explained, was a year younger than Mick. The two brothers had lived with their parents, Stanley and Gale, on a council estate in Ilford until the night of 18 March 1965, when – according to a report in the local newspaper – their house had caught fire and burned to the ground. Both parents had died in the fire, but Raymond and Mick had survived.

'Mick was eleven at the time,' Cal told me. 'And Raymond was ten. A follow-up report in the same newspaper three days later stated that the fire was caused by faulty wiring.'

'Did it say anything about how the two boys managed to survive?'

Cal shook his head. 'All it said was that they'd both been released from hospital and taken to a children's home in Brentwood, a place called Pin Hall.'

I looked at Cal. 'And . . .?'

He sighed. 'Pin Hall was destroyed in a fire in 1969. Nine people died, seventeen were badly injured. All the files, all the records . . . everything was lost in the fire.'

'Shit.'

'Yeah.'

'Faulty wiring again?'

'That's what it was put down to at the time, but a few years ago there was a cold-case investigation into allegations of abuse at Pin Hall, and they're fairly sure now that the fire was started deliberately.'

I lit another cigarette. 'So what happened to Raymond and Mick after the fire?'

'Well, the search program found plenty of stuff about Mick Bishop's history – when he joined the police, when he got promoted, various cases he's been involved in . . . that kind of thing. And if you read between the lines, it's pretty obvious that he's not the cleanest cop in the world . . . but there's no solid proof of anything. No big purchases, no second homes, no vices, no extravagances . . . I mean, his personal life is virtually non-existent. He doesn't seem to *do* anything.'

'What about Raymond?' I said. 'What happened to him?'

Cal shrugged. 'After the fire at Pin Hall . . . there's nothing.'

'Nothing?'

'Nothing at all . . . no trace of Raymond Bishop anywhere. It's as if he just disappeared off the face of the earth.'

'Maybe he died in the fire?'

Cal shook his head. 'His name would have come up at the inquest, and the search would have found his death certificate.'

'But it didn't?'

'No.'

'So he's still alive?'

'Not necessarily . . .'

'But you think he is?'

'Maybe . . .'

'Do you think he's Charles Raymond Kemper?'

'He could be . . .'

I looked out through the windscreen and saw that we were halfway along Roman Road now. Up ahead, just off to our left, I could see the black-timbered outline of The Turk's Head silhouetted against the clouded moon. I looked at the clock on the dashboard. It was almost seven o'clock.

'What do you think, John?' Cal asked me.

'I don't know,' I said. 'Let's go and find out, shall we?'

The car park was at the back of the pub, adjacent to the beer garden. There were floodlights at the back of the building that illuminated most of the garden, but the car park itself was unlit.

'Where do you want me to park?' Cal asked.

'Just drive round for a bit first,' I told him. 'I want to see if the Nissan's here.'

We circled the car park once, twice, and there was no sign of the Nissan, but as we approached the rear of the pub again, Cal slowed down and nodded his head towards a red Honda Prelude.

'That's Bishop's car,' he said. 'The Prelude.'

'Are you sure?'

He nodded. 'It was one of the first things that came up on the search.'

'OK,' I said. 'So Bishop's here . . .'

'Do you want me to park now?'

I nodded. 'Reverse into that space over there.'

As Cal backed the car into a parking space that wasn't too close to the pub, but gave us a reasonably good view of both the back door and the beer garden, I kept my eyes fixed on a broad window at the back of the building that looked through into the main bar. It was busy inside – families dining, drinkers drinking, fruit machines beeping and winking . . . it wasn't quite Saturday night yet, but it was getting there. There was a smoking area just outside the back door, a covered patio area with a few wooden tables and benches, and beyond that lay the beer garden and the children's play area. It was too cold and dark for any kids to be out playing, but the garden wasn't completely deserted. A young couple were sitting together on a bench, braving the cold for the sake of a few moments' privacy, and a handful of teenagers were messing about by the swings, drinking from bottles of beer and passing round a joint.

'What now?' Cal said.

I lit a cigarette. 'We wait.'

'For how long?'

'As long as it takes. If they're in there, they'll have to come out eventually.'

'Then what?'

'We see who Bishop's with, and we follow him.'

'What if Bishop comes out alone?'

'What do you mean?'

'What if Bishop's in there with Ray, and when they've finished talking about whatever they're talking about, Bishop decides to leave, but Ray wants to stay for a few more drinks. So Bishop leaves him there, and he comes out on his own –'

'And we've got no way of knowing what Ray looks like.'

'Exactly.'

I smiled at Cal. 'So what do *you* think we should do, Sherlock?'

He grinned. 'One of us needs to go inside. And it can't be you, because Bishop knows you . . . so, by process of elimination –'

'Look,' I said suddenly, staring over at the back door. 'That's him.'

As Cal gazed intently through the windscreen, Bishop and another man came out of the pub, turned right, and walked down to the far end of the smoking area. They seemed to be arguing about something as they went, with

Bishop doing most of the talking. The man he was arguing with was about the same size and height as Bishop, perhaps a little heavier. He had close-cropped dark hair, pale skin, a thin-lipped mouth . . .

'Shit,' I whispered. 'That's got to be his brother, hasn't it? That's *got* to be Ray Bishop.'

'No doubt about it,' Cal said. 'What do you think they're arguing about?'

'I don't know . . . but, whatever it is, I don't think Ray gives a shit.'

Ray was lighting a cigarette now, and as his lighter flared, momentarily illuminating his features, I could see quite clearly the look on his face as his brother continued berating him. It was a look of almost vacuous disdain; empty, mocking, unknowing, uncaring.

But then, as I carried on watching them, and I saw Mick throwing up his hands in despair, as if he'd finally had enough of his brother, Ray suddenly confounded my impressions of him by stepping forward and giving Mick what looked like a genuinely heartfelt hug. And although Mick held off for a moment, it *was* only for a moment, and then he was returning his brother's embrace, holding him tightly, patting his back, whispering words in his ear . . .

'Very touching,' Cal murmured.

'Do you think that's him?' I said, staring at Ray. 'I mean, do you think he's the one we saw in the Nissan . . . the one who picked up Anna?'

Cal thought about it, keeping his eyes fixed on Ray. 'It *could* be him, yeah . . . but I wouldn't swear to it.'

I nodded, watching as the two brothers finally let go of each other and resumed talking. Bishop was still far from happy, but he seemed a lot calmer now. After a moment or two, I saw him gesture towards his car. Ray said something, then nodded, and they both started walking towards the car park.

'They're leaving,' Cal said, reaching for the ignition.

'Just a second,' I told him. 'Don't start the car yet.'

I watched as they approached the Honda Prelude. Bishop unlocked it, Ray got in the passenger side, and after a quick look round the car park, Bishop got in and started the car.

'Now?' Cal asked, his hand poised on the ignition.

I shook my head. 'I'll tell you when.'

I waited until the Prelude had backed out of the parking space and was heading for the car-park exit, and then I told Cal to get going.

'Just keep it nice and steady,' I said, as he pulled away. 'And don't get too close.'

Cal did a surprisingly good job of following the Prelude – in fact, he probably did a lot better job than I would have done – and after about half an hour, when the Honda slowed, indicated left, and pulled in at the side of a residential road just out of town, I was pretty sure we hadn't been spotted.

'Keep going,' I told Cal. 'And keep your eyes straight ahead.'

As we drove past the parked Prelude, I turned my head away so that even if Bishop did happen to look at us, he wouldn't see my face.

'Pull in over there,' I said a few moments later. 'Don't indicate.'

Cal did as I told him, parking between two other cars at the side of the road about thirty yards further on from the Prelude. I wound down the window and adjusted the side mirror just in time to see Ray getting out of the car, turning up his coat collar, then leaning back in to say something to his brother. He smiled, reached in and patted Mick's shoulder, then stood back and watched as the Prelude pulled away and drove off. As it passed us by, I again turned my head away. When I turned back, I saw Ray opening a gate and heading up the front path of a small, semi-detached house. He paused at the front door, looked around, then unlocked it and went inside. After a few moments, lights came on downstairs.

'Now what?' Cal asked me.

I lit a cigarette. 'This is Long Road, isn't it?'

'Yeah.'

'Can you see the house number?'

Cal adjusted the rear-view mirror and gazed over at the house. 'One seven four, I think . . . yeah, one seven four.'

'Is your iPhone connected to all those databases you use?'

He smiled, reaching into his pocket and pulling out his phone. 'Just give me a few minutes.'

As he began doing whatever it was he was doing – thumbing and scrolling, jumping from screen to screen – I glanced admiringly at the battered old trilby hat on his head. He wore it well – tipped to one side, at just the right angle – and while it could easily have looked quite lame on somebody else, it looked just perfect on Cal.

'Nice hat,' I said.

'It's my detecting hat,' he grinned, without looking up from his iPhone.

I smiled. 'Thanks for all your help with this, Cal.'

He shrugged. 'No problem.'

'And I'm sorry if I was a bit pissy with you earlier on.'

'Pissy?' he said, smiling at me.

'Yeah, you know, when I was telling you to sort yourself out –'

'Forget it,' he said. 'You were right, anyway. I *was* a bit over-excited.'

'Yeah, well, I'm sorry –'

'Shit,' he sighed, shaking his head as he looked down at the iPhone screen.

'What is it?'

'Another dead end.' He studied the screen for a moment. '174 Long Road is one of a number of properties owned by a man called Syed Naveed. He rents them out through a letting agency called HRL Ltd, and their records show that 174 Long Road is currently leased to a tenant by the name of Joel R Pickton. But the references they've got are fake. Fake driving licence, fake passport, fake letter from Mr Pickton's fake previous landlord.'

'Do the records say how long the lease is for?'

Cal looked at the iPhone screen. 'Twelve months, paid in advance. He moved in at the end of July this year.'

I shook my head. 'Where the fuck does he get all this fake ID from?'

'I don't know,' Cal said. 'But it won't be cheap. Whoever he uses –'

'Hold on,' I said, my attention suddenly drawn to the house. 'The lights have just gone off.'

While I carried on watching the house in the side mirror, Cal turned in his seat and looked out through the rear windscreen. After about half a minute, the front door opened and Ray Bishop came out. He paused on the doorstep, looking up and down the street, then he shut the door behind him, went down the path, out the gate, and headed across the road towards a white Toyota Yaris.

'Do we follow him?' Cal said.

I watched Ray Bishop get into the Yaris.

'John?' Cal said.

I looked at him. 'Are you OK following him on your own?'

'Why? Where are you going?'

'I'm going to take a quick look round his house.'

Cal frowned. 'I'm not sure that's a good idea, John. What if he comes back? I mean, this guy might be a –'

'Ring me,' I said, opening the car door as the Yaris started up. 'Just keep him in sight, wherever he goes, and as soon as you think he's coming back, ring me and let me know. All right?'

Cal hesitated.

The Yaris was pulling away now.

I looked at Cal. He still wasn't happy, but as the headlights of the Yaris approached us from behind, he reluctantly nodded his head and reached for the ignition. 'All right,' he said, starting the car. 'But as soon as I ring you –'

'I'll be out like a shot,' I assured him.

I waited for the Yaris to pass us, gave it a few seconds, then got out of the car and slapped the roof. As Cal pulled away and drove off after the Yaris, I checked that my mobile was switched on, waited another minute – just to be on the safe side – then headed for the house.

27

I learned how to pick locks from a semi-retired investigator who used to work part-time for Leon Mercer. It wasn't actually a very useful skill to have in the world of corporate investigation and insurance fraud, which was lucky for me because I was never very good at it anyway. I wasn't totally useless, but I knew that I probably wouldn't be able to open the Yale lock on Ray Bishop's front door, so I went through a rusty old gate at the side of the house and headed round the back instead. There was no back garden as such, just a high-walled concrete yard cluttered with bins and bin bags, carrier bags, bits of scrap metal, car doors, seats, hubcaps, broken deckchairs . . . all kinds of shit. The wall surrounding the yard was high enough to screen me from the neighbours' downstairs windows, but I paused for a moment and looked around anyway, making sure that no one was watching me from any upstairs windows, then I went over to a glass-panelled door at the rear of the house and examined the lock. It was an old-fashioned mortice lock, loose and rattly, and I was fairly sure I could open it. I looked around all the crap on the ground, searching for something I could use to pick the lock, and almost immediately I spotted a carrier bag full of broken old tools. I went over and picked out a small handle-less screwdriver, and within a couple of minutes I had the door open and was stepping through into a small kitchen at the back of the house.

I shut the door behind me, took out a penlight, and looked around. The kitchen was very small and very cramped, neither overly clean nor excessively dirty. There was a stained porcelain sink with a warped wooden draining board, old cupboards, a rust-flecked boiler, a formica-topped table scattered with empty KFC boxes. I paused for a moment, listening to the silence, then I moved down a narrow hallway and went into the front room. The curtains were drawn, the lights off. As I swept the penlight around, I saw a room that didn't belong to anyone. It was a room that had been furnished from Argos: bland pictures on the walls, a thin carpet, a cheap two-seater settee and matching cheap armchair. The dining table and shelves were flat-packed white plastic wood, and the ornaments were straight from the ornaments page of the catalogue: lamp, vase, clock, a porcelain figurine of a doe-eyed child. A cut-price music system was stacked against the wall and a widescreen television loomed large on the floor.

There was nothing of Ray Bishop in here.

It was no more than the simulation of a room.

I left the room and headed upstairs.

Halfway up, a samurai sword was hanging from a cord on the stairway wall. At first, I thought it was just another ornament from the Argos catalogue, but when I paused on the stairs and looked closer, I realised that it was all too real. The blade – 24 inches of slightly curved, razor-sharp steel – even showed some signs of use. It was nicked here and there, the cracked edges beginning to rust, and several parts of the blade were discoloured with dark-brown stains. I stood there for a few seconds, gazing at the sword, trying to ignore the simmering fear in my guts . . . then I went on up the stairs.

There was a small landing, a bathroom, an empty box room, and a surprisingly large main bedroom. And when I opened the bedroom door and stepped inside, I knew straight away that this was where Ray Bishop *lived*. Up here . . . this was his home. I didn't even need to see it, I could sense it, feel it – a brutal vitality that sapped the air from my lungs.

I closed the door behind me and shone the penlight around. The walls were black, the paint seemingly applied with no care at all. It looked as if someone had simply rushed round the room, slapping on paint until the walls were more black than white. The only window, facing the street, was covered with a single heavy black curtain. There was no bed, just a blanket on the floor. The blanket was surrounded by a mess of scattered objects: syringes, phials, tissues, a spoon, a carton of milk, crackers, soda bread, yoghurt, cheese, nuts . . .

'Christ,' I whispered, stepping cautiously around the mess and sweeping the penlight around the room again.

The entire place was lined with wall-to-wall shelves stacked with all manner of extraordinary things: ropes and wires and chains, small wooden boxes, metal boxes, plastic boxes, cardboard boxes, baskets, tins, box files, piles of papers, pornographic magazines, newspapers, books, photographs, DVDs, knives, belts, axes, straps, tubes, packets of pills, small glass bottles . . .

It was like a nightmare haberdashery.

As I moved round the room looking at these things, my heart was beating hard, sucking the air from my throat, and I could feel the race of adrenalin imploring me to get out – *go, right now, get out of here, get OUT!*

But I couldn't leave yet.

I had to keep looking.

I didn't know what I was looking for . . . I was just looking.

It wasn't pleasant. The pornographic DVDs and magazines were sick with dull-eyed people doing fucking awful things . . . unnatural things, things that had nothing to do with sex, just violence. In the corner of the room, there was a small desk tented with a khaki blanket, and beneath the blanket was a computer screen, scanner, and printer. The monitor surround was painted black. I couldn't bear to go anywhere near it. I scanned the shelves again, looking at tongs, clips, dolls, masks, protein powder, clubs, execution stills, a leather-bound black bible . . . and right in the middle of all this madness, I came across a black-and-white photograph in a cheap cardboard frame. As far as I could tell, it was the only framed photograph in the whole room. It showed two teenage boys standing in front of a large grey house. They were both dark-haired, both pale-skinned, both unsmiling, both dressed in blue V-neck jumpers. I picked up the photograph and looked closer. In a granite block over the door of the house, I could just make out the words *PIN HALL*. I looked at the two boys again, quite certain now that I was looking at Mick and Ray Bishop. Mick was slightly taller than Ray, and although he was only a year older than his brother – about fifteen at the time of the picture, I guessed – it was clear that he was the dominant one. Standing just in front of his brother, his body tensed, staring hard at the camera . . . it was almost as if he was guarding him from the unseen eyes of the future, the eyes on the other side of the camera, the eyes of people like me.

As I turned my attention to the image of Ray in the photograph, I realised that the look on his fourteen-year-old face was almost identical to the expression I'd seen earlier that evening, when Mick had been scolding him about something outside the pub. The disdain, the emptiness, the lack of emotion . . .

It was unnerving.

I put the photograph back on the shelf and carried on looking. There were lots of books: Spinoza, Voltaire, Unamuno, *Genius*, *Skinned*, *Leviathan*, *How We Die*, *The Fabric of Reality*, *Killing for Company*, *Varieties of Religious Experience*, *The Character of Physical Law*, *Infinity and the Mind*, *Three Steps to Hell*. There were strange little ornaments: painted skulls, tiny skeletons, disturbing sculptures. There were things in jars: dead insects, pickled mice, embryos, divining bones . . . all kinds of untouchable and unknowable things. They held a silence and a sense of aged stillness that reminded me of exhibits in a small-town museum . . . but this was a museum that no one was meant to visit, a museum of a twisted mind. These exhibits were not meant to be seen.

After what seemed like an hour or so, but was probably closer to twenty minutes, I came across a small wooden chest hidden away at the back of a wardrobe. At first, I didn't understand why I felt drawn to it, why it felt different to all the other objects in the room . . . but after crouching down in front of the wardrobe and thinking about it for a while, I slowly realised that – unlike everything else – the wooden chest wasn't on display.

It was hidden away.

Out of sight.

I paused for a moment, wondering what that could mean . . . then I reached in, lifted out the chest, and opened it up.

It was filled with what, at first sight, seemed like nothing much at all, just a haphazard collection of random objects . . . bits of nothing: a shoe, a hair band, a broken watch, a pink cardigan, some rings, bracelets, a purse . . .

And a necklace . . .

A silver half-moon on a silver chain.

Anna Gerrish's necklace.

I don't know how long I sat there, crouched on the floor of that sickening room, staring into that box of gruesome souvenirs . . . and that's what they were, I realised. Souvenirs. This man – Ray Bishop, Charles Raymond Kemper, Joel R Pickton . . . whatever he wanted to call himself – this man had killed Anna Gerrish. He'd picked her up in his car, overpowered her, stabbed her, killed her, he'd discarded her body at the side of the road . . . and he'd taken her necklace. As a souvenir. To remind him of what he'd done.

As I looked down into the box, I *wanted* to be wrong. I

didn't *want* to believe that all those bits of nothing weren't bits of nothing at all, that they were bits of people, girls, women . . . all of whom were probably dead.

Killed.

Murdered.

'Fuck,' I heard myself say.

There were so *many* of them . . .

Did Mick Bishop know? I wondered. Did he *know* that his brother was a serial killer? Or was he only aware that Ray had killed Anna Gerrish? I took a pen from my pocket and cautiously lifted the silver necklace from the box. It was proof, I knew that. Proof that Ray Bishop had killed Anna Gerrish. But what could I do with it? Who could I trust with it?

I was still asking myself these questions when I heard a car pulling up outside.

I froze for a moment and listened hard. I heard the engine stop . . . then nothing for a few seconds . . . and then the sound of a car door opening and someone getting out. I knew it couldn't be Ray Bishop, because Cal would have called to warn me if he was coming back, but still . . .

I had to make sure.

Dropping the necklace into my pocket, I quickly got to my feet, went over to the window and pulled back the edge of the heavy black curtain. For a second or two, I tried to convince myself that the car parked outside the house wasn't a white Toyota Yaris, and that the man heading up the path below *wasn't* Ray Bishop . . . but I knew I was only wasting my time.

'Shit,' I said, as I heard him putting his key in the door.

The first thought that raced through my head was – what the hell was Cal *doing*, letting Ray Bishop come back without letting me know? But as I heard the front door opening, I quickly realised that there were more pressing things to think about. Ray Bishop was downstairs. Ray Bishop killed people. And any moment now, he'd be coming up here.

I heard the front door closing.

I wondered, briefly, if there was any chance at all that I could reason with him. I imagined him downstairs, standing in the hallway, perfectly still, sensing the presence of a stranger in his house.

No, he wasn't a man to be reasoned with.

I heard a cautious footstep on the stairs.

He killed people.

Another step, more confident now . . .

I pulled back the heavy black curtain and yanked at the window, trying to open it. But it wouldn't move. The frame was painted shut. I paused for a moment, listening again. He was coming up the stairs now, moving quite slowly, but I knew that I only had seconds to get out. I rushed over to one of the shelves, grabbed a bone-handled sheath knife, and hurried back to the window. Tearing away the curtain, I started hacking at the frame, trying to slice through the age-old paint, but it was too thick, too hard . . . it was like trying to cut through superglue.

'Fuck it,' I hissed, starting to panic now.

I could hear Bishop on the landing outside.

I dropped the knife, looked around, and saw a heavy glass jar on a shelf to my right. It was a gallon jar, filled to the brim with some kind of creamy-grey ash, and I was just stepping over to the shelf and picking it up when the bedroom door swung open and there was Ray Bishop, standing in the doorway, brandishing the samurai sword in his hand.

He was smiling.

I barely even looked at him. I just went over to the window, heaved the jar through the glass, and with the deafening crash still resounding round the room, I quickly scrambled out through the broken pane. As I heard Ray Bishop lunging after me, I let myself drop from the window, keeping hold of the sill, and at the same time I swung my body to the left, reaching out with my feet for a drainpipe that I vaguely remembered seeing and desperately hoped was there. But my feet felt nothing. No drainpipe, no foothold, just a sheer brick wall. And I had no time at all now. Ray Bishop was at the window, his head poking out, the sword in his hand, his eyes staring coldly into mine.

'Hello, John,' he said, still smiling.

I met his gaze for only a moment, then I closed my eyes, braced myself, and let go of the windowsill.

I don't remember falling. All I can remember is letting go of the sill, and then – almost immediately – a shuddering impact as I hit the ground. A sharp pain shot up my right leg, and as I rolled over and got to my knees, sucking in air, the pain rose up into my stomach, making me feel nauseous and faint. I was shivering, shaking, sweating in the cold night air . . . I wanted to lie back down in the dirt, curl up into a ball, and cry.

But the face at the window had gone now.

Bishop was on his way down.

I had to keep moving.

I forced myself to get up, forced myself to take a step . . . and the pain ripped through me again. But my leg held. It hurt like hell, but it wasn't going to kill me. The only thing that was going to kill me was the man who, right now, was opening the front door and coming after me with a samurai sword in his hand.

I took a breath, braced myself again, and started running. Down the path, out the gate, along the road . . .

I didn't look back to see if Bishop was coming after me. I didn't have to – I could hear him. He was running, not with any great speed or energy, but then I wasn't moving all that fast myself. I kept going, not knowing where I was going, just going. Across the road, round a corner into another street, and then – before Bishop turned the corner – I skipped clumsily over a low hedge into the front garden of a bungalow and ducked round the back of the house and into the back garden. As I stopped for a moment to catch my breath and rest my leg, I heard Bishop's footsteps entering the street. I kept still, trying not to breathe too loudly, and listened. The footsteps stopped for a moment – and I imagined Bishop standing still, gazing down the street, wondering where I'd gone . . . and then I heard him start running again. Along the pavement, towards the bungalow, his footsteps getting louder all the time . . . and then, at last, I heard them pass by and disappear down the street. I carried on listening for a while, just in case he decided to double back, but after a minute or two I was pretty sure that he'd gone.

There was no telling when he might come back though.

I looked around to see where I was. In the low light of the moon I could see that it was a fairly large garden, mostly laid out to lawn, with decorative wooden fences on either side. The lawn was split in two by a concrete path that led all the way down to another wooden fence at the far end of the garden, and in the middle of this fence was a gate. I had no idea what was on the other side of the gate, but it was a gate – it had to lead somewhere. And somewhere was all I needed.

I set off down the path – half running, half hobbling – trying not to make any noise, still listening out all the time for any sign of Ray Bishop . . . but I didn't hear anything. I didn't allow myself to wonder where he was now, or what he was doing, I just kept my eyes on the path and concentrated on getting to the gate. By the time I got there, and discovered to my relief that it wasn't locked, my leg was hurting badly and I desperately wanted to stop for a moment . . . just for a moment or two, to rest, to catch my breath, to think about things . . . but I knew that I couldn't.

This was no time for thinking.

I just had to keep going.

I opened the gate and stepped through into a narrow dirt track. There were fenced gardens on either side of the track, and although I couldn't see much further than ten yards or so in each direction, I guessed that if I followed the track to the right it would bring me back out on to Long Road, and if I went the other way . . .

I didn't know where I'd end up if I went the other way. All I knew was that I didn't want to go back to Long Road.

I went the other way.

About fifteen minutes later, after winding my way through a maze of back lanes and pathways, I finally emerged into an unknown side street that led me down to a busy roundabout at the north end of town, next to the old railway station. Long Road, I guessed, was about a mile away to the east, and so – I hoped – was Ray Bishop.

I made my way over to a bus stop, sat down on a bench, and lit a cigarette.

I looked at my watch.

It was nine o'clock.

The night was cold, my leg was numb . . .

I pulled out my mobile and called Cal.

There was no answer, no voicemail message, no nothing. The phone just rang. I tried another of his numbers, and then another, but the result was the same – no reply. And when I called his 'special' number, the one for the mobile that was totally anonymous and completely untraceable, and again got no answer, that's when I really started to worry. Cal *always* answered his mobile, wherever he was and whatever he was doing. And if you couldn't get him on one of his numbers, he was *always* available on another.

Always.

Without fail.

Unable to think of anything else, I started calling all the numbers again. I wasn't really expecting anything to happen, so when the second number I called was answered almost immediately, and an unfamiliar female voice said 'Hello?', I just assumed that I'd made a mistake and misdialled.

'Sorry,' I said. 'I think I've got the wrong number.'

'Don't hang up,' the voice said quickly. 'My name's Lisa Webster, I'm a paramedic, I need to know who the owner of this phone is.'

'What?'

'I'm a paramedic,' she repeated, speaking more calmly now. 'I need to know the name of the person you're calling.'

'What's going on?' I said, still confused. 'Has something happened to Cal? Is he all right?'

'Who's Cal?'

'Cal Franks –'

'Is he a young man, in his late twenties?'

'Yes, what's *happened* –?'

'Does Cal drive a black Mondeo?'

'Yes –'

'And could you tell me who you are, please?'

'John Craine –'

'John *Craine*?'

'Yeah, I'm Cal's uncle . . .' I took a breath. 'Could you *please* tell me what's happened to him?'

'Where are you, John?'

'Why do you want to –?'

'Are you in Hey?'

'Yes –'

'All right, listen. A man in his late twenties was attacked earlier this evening. He's been brought into Hey General Hospital, but as yet we haven't been able to confirm his identity. There was nothing in his pockets to tell us who he is, but this is his phone – one of three he was carrying – and

350

he was found beside a black Ford Mondeo, so it's very possible that he's your nephew.'

'He was *attacked*?'

'Yes, I'm sorry, it looks as if he was quite badly beaten. We managed to stabilise his condition in the ambulance on the way to the hospital, and he's undergoing emergency surgery right now, but I'm afraid that's all I can tell you at the moment. If you could come in to Hey General to confirm his identity –'

'Was he wearing a hat?'

'A hat was found nearby, yes.'

'A trilby?'

'Yes.'

'I'll be there as soon as I can.'

I called four taxi companies before realising that I was never going to get one at short notice on a Saturday night, and I was just about to call Imogen to see if she'd give me a lift to the hospital, when my mind suddenly flashed back to the moment I was hanging from Ray Bishop's windowsill, and he'd looked down at me, his eyes staring coldly, and said, 'Hello, John.'

He knew who I was.

And if he knew *who* I was – and I was guessing that his brother must have told him – then he probably knew where I lived. And even if he didn't, it wouldn't be too hard for him to find out . . .

I called Bridget's mobile.

'Hey, John,' she answered. 'I was just thinking about you.'

'Where are you?' I said.

'At home . . . why? Are you all right? You sound a bit –'

'Listen, Bridget, this is really important. I want you to get out of the house as quickly as possible. I don't have time to explain, but please . . . just trust me. You *have* to get out of the house right now. OK?'

She only hesitated for a moment. 'OK . . . if you say so. Where shall I go?'

'I'm at the old railway station, near the roundabout. Do you know where I mean?'

'Yeah . . .'

'Pick me up as soon as you can. I'll explain everything then.'

'All right . . .'

'And ring me as soon as you're out of the house and in your car. OK?'

'Yeah.'

'Go . . . *now.*'

She called me two minutes later.

'Are you in your car?' I said.

'Yeah.'

'Did you see anyone on your way out?'

'No . . .'

'Are you OK?'

'Not really. I mean, this is pretty fucking scary, John.'

'Yeah, sorry . . . but everything should be all right now. Just get going, don't stop for anyone, and when you get to the roundabout, drive round it two or three times before you stop to pick me up. All right?'

'Just drive round the roundabout?'

'Yeah . . . I'll be waiting for you.'

I moved from the bus stop and positioned myself at the south side of the roundabout, making sure that Bridget would see me when she arrived, and after about five minutes or so I saw a white Escort van with *HEY PETS* written on the side coming towards me. Bridget waved as she went past, and I nodded back, but I was more concerned with watching the road behind her. I was looking out for familiar cars – a silver-grey Renault, a green Nissan Almera, a white Toyota Yaris, Mick Bishop's Honda Prelude – or familiar faces in unfamiliar cars, or cars that were just acting strangely . . . following Bridget around the roundabout, slowing down without any reason, stopping suddenly – but by the time Bridget had passed by me again, making her second circuit of the roundabout, I hadn't seen anything untoward.

The next time she came round, I held up my hand and caught her eye, and she slowed down and pulled in beside me. As she leaned across and opened the passenger door, I saw that Walter was in the back of the van, sitting upright in a wicker basket. I quickly got in and closed the door, and Bridget immediately pulled away again.

'Where are we going?' she said.

'The hospital.'

She looked at me. 'What's going on, John?'

As we drove across town to the hospital, I told Bridget everything. She didn't interrupt me as I talked, she just drove the car, keeping her eyes on the road, and listened. There was a lot to tell, a lot of explaining to do, and by the time I'd finished we were almost at the hospital.

'Is Cal going to be all right?' Bridget asked.

'I don't know . . . the paramedic couldn't tell me very much, just that he'd been badly beaten.'

'Who do you think did it?'

'Some of Mick Bishop's people, probably. He must have had someone following us. Or maybe it was Ray Bishop . . . I don't know.'

'And you really think that Ray Bishop's going to come after you?'

I nodded. 'I know what he's done, what he does. I know what he *is*. And he must know that I'm not going to keep quiet about it. Which means that if he doesn't do something about me, or get someone to do it for him, he's fucked. So, yeah, I'm pretty sure he's coming after me.'

'And you can't call the police?'

'I can't *trust* the police. Mick Bishop owns too many of them. Whoever I call, even if it's just the emergency number, there's a good chance it'll get back to Bishop . . . and if he finds me, he'll kill me. Simple as that.'

'Do you really think he'd go that far?'

'What else can he do? I know that his brother's a serial killer, and I know that he's covered up for him on at least one occasion. The only way Mick Bishop can save his skin is by making sure that I don't talk.'

'So what are you going to do?'

'I don't know . . .'

We were approaching the hospital now, and as Bridget

slowed for the turning, I studied an information sign at the side of the road that gave the whereabouts of all the various departments and wards.

'Do you know where they're keeping him?' Bridget asked.

I shook my head. 'A & E, I suppose. I'd better ask at reception.'

She drove straight on, heading for the main hospital building, and we found a space in a car park close to the entrance.

'It's probably best if you stay in the car,' I told her.

She looked at me. 'Why?'

'There's a chance that Bishop might have someone waiting for me in the hospital, or he might even be in there himself. If you come in with me, they'll get both of us. But if you stay here . . .' I looked at her. 'No one else knows about this, Bridget. Just you and me . . .'

She nodded. 'What do you want me to do if you don't come back?'

'Give me an hour,' I said, jotting down a phone number on a scrap of paper. 'If I'm not back by then, call this number.' I passed her the piece of paper. 'Ask for Leon Mercer, but if he's not there, you can talk to his daughter, Imogen. They're both old friends of mine, and I'd trust them with my life. Just tell either of them exactly what's happened, and they'll know what to do.'

She nodded again. 'Why don't you just call them yourself, right now?'

'The more people I involve, the more people I put at risk.'

'You involved *me*.'

'I know, I'm sorry . . . but I had no choice.'

'You could have lied to me.'

'Yeah . . .'

'But you didn't.'

'No.'

She smiled at me, nodded her head, then leaned across and kissed me. 'Be careful, John.'

I looked at her for a moment, more haunted than ever now by the memories of Stacy that she brought to my heart . . .

'Keep the doors locked,' I told her. 'And call me if you need me.'

I got out of the car and went looking for Cal.

28

Lisa Webster, the paramedic I'd talked to on the phone, was a sturdy, dark-haired woman in her mid-forties. She met me at the main reception desk, and as I followed her along a maze of hospital corridors, she told me what she knew.

'We were called out at just gone eight o'clock this evening after an anonymous 999 call. The location we were given turned out to be a small industrial estate down by the river, and when we got there we found your nephew – if it *is* your nephew – lying in the road next to his car. There was no one else around, no other vehicles, so we still don't know exactly what happened. But he'd clearly been attacked, possibly by more than one person, and he was in a pretty bad state – unconscious, multiple fractures, bleeding heavily . . .' She looked at me. 'Whoever did it, they really went to work on him.'

'Is he going to be OK?'

'Well, he's out of surgery now, and he's conscious . . . but that's about all I can tell you, I'm afraid. I'm just a paramedic. Once we've brought a patient in, we don't really have any further involvement.'

'So how come you're still here?' I asked her.

'Well . . .' she said, looking slightly embarrassed. 'I just like to follow things through, you know? *I* spoke to you earlier on the phone, *I* asked you to come in . . . I didn't want to just leave it at that.'

'Right,' I said, looking at her, waiting for her to go on.

'And . . . well, I knew your wife.'

I stopped. 'You knew Stacy?'

She nodded. 'When you told me your name on the phone earlier on, I wondered if you were *that* John Craine . . . and now that I've seen you . . . well, I recognise you from the pictures on the news.'

'How did you know Stacy?'

'She was my daughter's teacher. I didn't really know her that well, but I met her a few times at school, and Megan – that's my daughter – she was always talking about Mrs Craine, telling me how nice she was . . .' Lisa looked at me. 'Meg was going through some really bad times back then, and Stacy helped her a lot. She was a good teacher, a good person. So, anyway, I just . . . I don't know . . . I just wanted to let you know, I suppose. I never really got the chance to thank Stacy properly . . .'

I nodded. 'How's your daughter now?'

'She's wonderful.' Lisa smiled. 'She has her own daughter now . . . Bethany. Beth's just started school herself . . .' Lisa looked at me. 'Sorry, I'm rambling.'

I smiled. 'That's OK.'

She glanced down the corridor, then turned back to me. 'Your nephew – if it *is* your nephew – is in the ICU ward. I can take you in to see him, but once you've confirmed his identity, I'm pretty sure the police will want to take over.'

'The police are here?'

She nodded. 'In the ward. There's two of them.'

'Plain clothes or uniform?'

'They're both uniformed PCs.'

'When did they arrive?'

'About fifteen minutes after Cal was brought in.'

'Is that normal? I mean, do the police usually visit the ICU ward to check up on an unidentified assault victim?'

'It's not *un*usual . . . but, to tell you the truth, I *was* a bit surprised at how quickly they arrived.' She looked at me. 'Is something going on here?'

'Possibly.'

'Is Cal in trouble with the police?'

'It depends who they're working for.'

She shook her head. 'I don't understand.'

'It's kind of complicated,' I said, playing for time while I tried to decide if I could trust her or not. There was no real reason why I should. Just because she *seemed* like a good person, a kind person, a decent person . . . that didn't necessarily mean that I should trust her. But it was all I had to go on. And I quickly decided that it was enough for me. 'It's possible,' I told her, lowering my voice, 'that the people who beat up Cal were either corrupt police officers or thugs who were working for a corrupt police officer. And that officer would like to get his hands on me too. Now, I don't *know* if the two PCs in the ICU ward are working for this particular officer, but if they are . . . well, let's just say that I might need to get out of here in a hurry.'

Lisa looked at me. 'Are you asking me to help you?'

'Yes.'

'How do I know you're not lying?'

'You don't.'

She carried on looking at me for a while, not saying anything, then – seemingly satisfied – she said, 'All right, let's go.'

Cal was in a small private room at the far end of the intensive care ward. The lights in the ward were sterile and bright, and the air was filled with the background hum of machinery. The ward was quietly busy with the efficient bustle of doctors, nurses, and porters. The two PCs – both of them big bruisers in fluorescent yellow jackets – were standing in the corridor outside Cal's room, and when I approached the door, with Lisa behind me, one of them stepped in front of me, blocking my way, and the other one – the bigger of the two – moved between Lisa and me.

'Mr Craine?' he said. 'We'd like a word, if you don't mind.'

'Yeah, fine,' I told him. 'But I think the doctors need me to identify my nephew first.'

The bigger PC looked at his colleague. His colleague shrugged, looking confused. The bigger PC turned back to me. 'All right,' he said grudgingly. 'But as soon as you've finished –'

'No problem,' I said.

I waited for the other PC to step out of my way, then I opened the door and went into the room. As Lisa followed me in and closed the door, I looked over at Cal. He was almost unrecognisable. Lying in the hospital bed, surrounded by monitors and hospital machinery, breathing through an oxygen mask, his right leg and left arm in plaster, his head swathed in bandages . . .

'Jesus Christ,' I whispered.

His face was a swollen mass of cuts and bruises – his lips split and puffy, his nose broken, his jaw discoloured and bent out of shape – and as I approached the bed, I noticed a familiar-looking small indentation in a mess of broken skin on his forehead: the outline of a ring-sized skull . . .

This was Les Gillard's work. He must have been following us, I realised. Or maybe Ray Bishop had called his brother once he'd realised that he was being followed, and Mick had called Gillard, and then somehow Ray Bishop must have lured Cal into a trap at the industrial estate down by the river . . .

I stopped thinking about it.

It didn't matter how it had happened.

It had happened.

'Cal?' I said quietly.

His eyes were so blackened and swollen that I couldn't tell if they were open or not.

I turned to Lisa. 'Can he hear me?'

She nodded. 'He's heavily sedated, but he's awake. He won't be able to talk though.'

I knelt down beside the bed. 'Hey, Cal,' I said softly. 'It's me, John . . .' His eyes opened slightly, fixing on mine, and he gave a faint groan. I looked at him, tears tingling at the back of my eyes, and I took his hand in mine. I wanted to say something comforting to him, something that would make him feel better . . . I wanted to hold him in my arms and take away all his fear and pain. But, most of all, I wanted this never to have happened.

'I'm sorry, Cal,' I whispered. 'I'm *so* sorry . . .'

'John?' I heard Lisa say. 'He needs to rest.'

I leaned in closer to Cal. 'I have to go now . . . you get some sleep, OK? I'll let Barbarella know you're here. And I'll see you later.'

He blinked painfully.

I gave his hand a gentle squeeze, then got to my feet and turned to Lisa.

'It's definitely Cal then?' she said.

I nodded.

She stepped closer to me and lowered her voice. 'And what about the policemen outside? What do you want me to do about them?'

'Nothing. I just need to get out of here without them knowing, that's all. Is that going to be possible?'

She nodded. 'Leave it to me.'

'Thanks.' I glanced over at Cal, then back at Lisa. 'Could you keep an eye on him for me?'

'Of course.'

I passed her one of my business cards. 'You can call me any time. If anything happens, anything at all . . .'

'Don't worry,' she said, taking the card. 'I'm sure he's going to be all right.'

The door opened then, and the big PC leaned in and said, 'Are you ready, Mr Craine?'

'Just coming,' I told him.

Lisa went out first, and as I followed her through the door, she said to the big PC, 'I just need Mr Craine to sign a consent form in case of further surgery. Is that OK?'

Big PC shrugged. 'I suppose so.'

Lisa turned to me. 'The forms are in the admin office, Mr

362

Craine. If you'd like to come with me.'

I followed her down the ward to a small administration office tucked away in a quiet corner. Inside the office, she took my arm and led me over to an adjoining door in the far wall.

'There's a lift along there,' she said, opening the door and pointing down a narrow corridor. 'It's staff only, but it's very rarely used, so you should be OK. Go to the ground floor, and it'll bring you out just to the side of the main entrance.' She looked at me. 'All right?'

I nodded. 'What will you tell the policemen?'

'I don't know . . . I'll think of something.'

I smiled at her. 'Thank you.'

She nodded. 'You'd better go.'

As I headed down the corridor towards the lift, I heard her call out 'Good luck,' and as I turned and waved goodbye to her, I had a feeling I was going to need it.

29

Bridget had the radio on when I got back to the car, and as I opened the door and got in, I recognised the quiet sadness of an old Nat King Cole song.

Since you went away the days grow long,
and soon I'll hear old winter's song.
But I miss you most of all my darling,
when autumn leaves start to fall.

'Nice,' I said.

Bridget smiled. 'Radio Two . . . I must be getting old.' She leaned down and turned off the radio. 'How's Cal?'

'Not too good.'

'Did he tell you anything about what happened?'

I shook my head. 'He's barely conscious.'

She looked at me. 'Any trouble in there?'

'Not really,' I said, glancing through the window, checking the main entrance. 'But I think we'd better get going.'

She started the car. 'Where to?'

'Let's just get out of here first.'

We drove in silence for a while – away from the hospital, back towards town – and although I kept a close eye on the road behind us, trying to make sure we weren't being followed, I didn't have much faith in my abilities any more. I'd got Cal mixed up in all this, and I hadn't managed to look after him, and now – because of me – Bridget was involved. And if I couldn't make sure that *Cal* didn't get hurt . . .

'What's on your mind, John?' Bridget asked quietly.

I looked at her. 'I think we need to stay in a hotel tonight.'

'What about Walter? Hotels don't take dogs, do they?'

'Oh, yeah . . .' I turned round and patted Walter. 'Sorry, Walt,' I told him. 'I forgot about you.'

He wagged his tail.

I turned back to Bridget. 'Can you stay at Sarah's?'

She nodded. 'She'd be happy to put all of us up. She's got plenty of room –'

I shook my head. 'I'm not putting anyone else at risk. I'll find a hotel, you and Walter go to Sarah's –'

'No,' she said firmly. 'I'm staying with you, John.'

I looked at her. 'Bishop and his brother are looking for me . . . maybe not together, but they're both after me. And if they find me with you . . . well, the least *Mick* Bishop's going to do is cause you all kinds of shit. But *Ray* Bishop . . .' I shook my head. 'I can't let him get anywhere near you, Bridget.'

'All right, but *you* can't just keep running away from him either, can you? You have to do something about him, tell someone what he's done. He needs locking up.'

'I know,' I said. 'And I'm working on it. I just need to think things through a bit more. And right now I'm too tired to think clearly.'

'Why don't we all go back to the flat over the shop?' Bridget suggested. 'It should be safe enough there, shouldn't it?'

'Yeah, maybe . . .' I said, thinking about it. 'Mick Bishop knows that we know each other, but I'd be surprised if he's actually in contact with his brother at the moment –'

'So Ray Bishop won't know about the shop.'

'Probably not, but Mick will. He'll have had you checked out as soon as he saw you at the house. He'll know what you do, where you work, how much money the shop makes –'

'Yeah, but he won't know there's a flat above it, because the flat's not officially part of the shop.'

'Isn't it?'

She shook her head. 'Sarah set it up like that for tax purposes . . . I've never really understood it. All I know is that, legally, the flat has nothing to do with the shop. So, if you want, we could go back there, get something to eat, get some rest . . . and you'd have as much time as you need to think things through.' She smiled at me. 'What do you think?'

I looked at her. 'I think that sounds pretty good.'

I told Bridget that I needed to stop off at my office on the way back, so she headed for the old market square and parked the van there.

'I won't be long,' I said to her, unbuckling my seat belt. 'I just need to pick something up.'

She looked at me. 'Are you sure this is a good idea? I mean, if Bishop *is* after you, he's bound to have someone watching your office, isn't he?'

'Yeah, probably . . .'

'Do you *really* need whatever it is you're picking up?'

I nodded. 'It's all right, I know what I'm doing. But if I'm not back in fifteen minutes –'

'Yeah, I know. I'll call Leon Mercer.'

'And –'

'Keep the doors locked,' she said, smiling at me. 'And, yes, I'll call you if I need you.'

I didn't see anyone as I walked up Wyre Street towards my office. The street was deserted, the air cold and damp, and the only sound I could hear was the dull slap of my footsteps echoing into the night. But just because I didn't see anyone, that didn't mean that I was alone. There were plenty of hiding places along the street – shop doorways, shadowed alleys, piles of rubbish bags, extra-large wheelie bins. For all I knew, there could be dozens of Bishop's men watching me.

It was an unnerving experience, and as I approached the office building and opened the front door, I kept expecting someone to jump out at me or something . . . but nothing happened. I went inside, closed the door behind me, took out my penlight, and went upstairs.

The office door was locked. I opened it up, paused for a moment, then went through into the office. I paused again, sweeping the beam of the penlight around the darkened room and listening out for any signs of life . . . but I neither saw nor heard anything that shouldn't be there. I crossed over to my private office, opened the door, and made straight for the wall safe. It only took a moment to open it up. I removed the 9mm pistol, checked there was a round in the chamber, clicked off the safety, and put the gun in my pocket.

I saw the two men across the street as soon as I left the building. They were standing in the shadows of a shop doorway, their faces obscured by the darkness, so I couldn't tell who they were at first. But as I closed the door and stepped down onto the pavement, they both moved out of the shadows and began crossing the street towards me, and as they passed under the sodium-orange glow of a streetlight, I could see their faces quite clearly. The man on the right was about the same age as me. Stocky, dark, wearing a black knitted cap . . . I'd never seen him before. But I recognised the other one. I remembered his hard-bitten face from the grainy video that Leon Mercer had shown me, and when I glanced down at his hand and saw the silver skull ring on his index finger, I knew I wasn't mistaken. It was Les Gillard. The man who'd beaten me up, the man who'd beaten Cal to within an inch of his life . . .

I put my hand in my pocket and took hold of the pistol.

Gillard and the other man had almost reached me now. The other man was looking around as they walked, glancing up and down the street, checking to make sure there were no witnesses, but Gillard was keeping his eyes fixed firmly on me. There was no sense of bravado about him. He wasn't trying to look hard or scary or threatening, he was simply intent on doing what he was about to do. But whatever his intention was – to arrest me, to hurt me, to kill me – I had no intention of letting it happen.

I waited until both men were about three paces away from me, then I pulled the gun from my pocket, aimed it at Gillard's left knee, and pulled the trigger.

The sharp crack of the gunshot echoed dully around the empty streets, and I saw Gillard's leg jerk backwards. He lurched to one side with a strange hopping motion, let out a low pained breath, and fell to the ground clutching his shattered knee.

As he lay there moaning and cursing, the other man stayed where he was, frozen to the spot, his eyes darting frantically between Gillard and me.

'Hey,' I said, looking at him.

He stared wide-eyed at me.

'Go on,' I said. 'Fuck off.'

He hesitated for a moment, glancing down at Gillard again, and then he took off, running as fast as he could up the street.

I waited until he was out of sight, then I put the pistol back in my pocket, stepped around Gillard, and headed back to the van.

30

It was close to midnight when we got to the pet shop. We'd parked the van in a side street, walked round in circles for a while, and by the time we'd cut through a narrow cobbled lane that brought us out onto Market Street, I was fairly sure that we weren't being followed.

Market Street was quiet.

There was no one around.

As Bridget unlocked the pet-shop door, I kept looking up and down the street, but there was no sign of life anywhere. Away in the distance, I could hear the wail of an ambulance siren. It was getting closer, coming this way, and I guessed it was heading for Wyre Street.

'All right?' Bridget said to me.

I looked at her. She'd unlocked the door and was about to go in.

'Hold on,' I said. 'Let Walter in first.'

She opened the door and let Walter in. We waited a few moments, but Walter didn't make any noise, and when he padded back to the doorway, picked up a copy of the *Gazette* from the floor, and stood there with it hanging from his mouth, wagging his tail at us, I reckoned it was safe to go in.

Bridget took the newspaper from his mouth and we went

inside. It was dark, but there was enough light coming in from the streetlights outside to see that everything seemed normal – the fish tanks bubbling softly, hamsters scurrying around, mice nibbling quietly on cardboard tubes.

'Is there a back door?' I asked Bridget as she locked the door behind us.

'Yeah, but we never use it. It's all bolted up.'

'I'd better check it anyway.'

'It's round the back of the storeroom,' she said. 'Down that little hallway, on your left.'

I clicked on my penlight and went out through the storeroom into the hallway. The back door was a solid old thing, locked and bolted at the top and bottom, and I could tell from its covering of dusty cobwebs that it hadn't been opened in years. I went back down the hallway and met Bridget coming into the storeroom.

'Look at this,' she said, passing me the *Gazette*.

A photograph on the front page showed me cracking my elbow into the photographer's face. Just behind me – in the background, but clearly visible – was Bridget. The headline read *STACY'S HUSBAND LASHES OUT*, and beneath that, in smaller writing, *INJURED PHOTOGRAPHER DROPS CHARGES*.

'Shit,' I said, beginning to read the story.

'Is it all right if I put the lights on now?' Bridget asked.

'Yeah, I don't see why not.'

As she put the light on and started climbing the stairs to the flat, Walter trotted past her and lolloped up to the landing. 'Come on, John,' Bridget said. 'You can read that later. It's all just newspaper shit anyway.'

She was right, most of the story seemed to be just the same old rehashed rubbish, but that didn't stop me reading it as I followed her up the stairs. When I got to the third paragraph and saw that the reporter had included both Bridget's full name *and* where she worked, I didn't realise what it meant at first. I wasted precious seconds by stopping on the stairs to read through the paragraph again, angrily shaking my head and cursing under my breath, and only then did it occur to me that if Ray Bishop had read this, he'd not only know about Bridget and me, he'd also know about the pet shop . . .

I looked up and saw that Bridget had reached the landing and was just about to open the sitting-room door.

'*Bridget!*' I called out. '*Hold on! Don't go in . . .*'

But I was too late. She'd already begun opening the door. She paused at the sound of my voice, turning round to look at me, but Walter had already slipped through the gap in the doorway, and even as I called out again – '*Don't go into the sitting room!*' – we both heard a startled bark, followed almost immediately by a muffled thump and a short pitiful yelp. Bridget didn't hesitate, she just barged open the door and went rushing in, and I knew there was nothing I could do to stop her.

'Bridget!' I yelled, pulling the pistol from my pocket as I bounded up the stairs. '*Bridget!*'

I heard another dull thump from inside the room, and then a heavier sound, the sound of a body hitting the floor. And I should have stopped then . . . I should have stopped running, stopped shouting, stopped raging. I should have stopped to think. But I couldn't. My mind had gone back in time, to a hot summer's day seventeen years ago, and I was running up the stairs again, and my heart was pounding, and I was shouting at the top of my voice, 'Stacy! STACY! STACY!', and the whole world was humming inside my head as I crossed the landing and crashed through the open door, and there she was . . .

Bridget.

Not Stacy.

Bridget.

She was lying on the floor, just to the right of the doorway. Her eyes were closed and she was bleeding from the corner of her mouth. A few feet beyond her, Walter was splayed out on his side against the wall. The top of his skull was split open, a bone-white furrow showing through the bloodied fur, and his staring eyes were dull and lifeless.

I saw all this in a timeless moment.

Just before my head exploded.

And then there was nothing.

31

All I could see when I first opened my eyes was a haze of blood-red mist. I wondered for a moment if the blow I'd taken to the back of my head had blinded me, but after a few seconds the mist in my eyes began to clear, and all I could see then was the disarming serenity of Ray Bishop's face. He was sitting in an armchair in front of me – his legs crossed, his hands joined together in his lap – and I got the feeling that he'd been sitting there for some time, watching me, examining me, studying me. There was no emotion in his slate-grey eyes, just a vague sense of detached curiosity, like a scientist studying a bug.

My vision momentarily blurred again, and when I shook my head to clear the fog, a stabbing pain ripped through the base of my skull. I groaned, squeezing my eyes shut, and when I instinctively reached up to soothe the pain . . . I realised that I couldn't move my hand. I opened my eyes and looked down at myself and saw that I was sitting in a straight-backed wooden chair with my arms tied behind my back and my feet bound tightly to the legs of the chair.

I struggled uselessly for a second or two, trying to free my hands and feet, but all that did was send another bolt of pain through my head, making me cry out like a baby.

'Fuck,' I whispered, closing my eyes again. 'Fucking *hell* . . .'

'It's just a mechanism, John,' I heard Bishop say.

I forced myself to open my eyes and look at him. 'What?'

'Pain,' he said, smiling. 'It's just a warning mechanism, an evolutionary development that serves to protect the vessel. Pain lets you know when the vessel has been damaged, or is in danger of being damaged. And then, if necessary, the vessel can shut itself down – or shut down the relevant parts – in order for repairs to be made.' He shrugged. 'Personally, I think a system of warning lights would be a lot more efficient. A lot less fun, of course. But who the fuck am I to argue with the evolutionary process?'

I didn't say anything.

I didn't know what he was talking about.

And, more to the point, the red mist had finally cleared from my eyes now, and I was too busy staring at Bridget to listen to what Bishop was saying. She was sitting on the floor behind him, her hands tied to a heavy brass radiator against the wall. Her jaw was reddened and swollen, her face white with shock, and she was crying – the tears streaming silently down her face. I glanced over at Walter, dead on the floor. The blood on his split-open head was already drying, darkening in the matted fur.

'Bridget?' I said, looking over at her. 'Listen to me . . . Bridget?'

'There's no point,' Bishop said.

I looked at him. 'What?'

'She can't answer you.'

'Why not?'

He looked over his shoulder at Bridget. 'We have an agreement, don't we, dear?'

Bridget glared back at him, her eyes burning with hatred and fear.

Bishop smiled at her, then turned back to me. 'As long as she doesn't make a sound, I don't go over there and cut out her tongue. That's our agreement.' He reached down and picked up a carving knife from a coffee table next to the armchair. 'And so far it seems to be working very nicely.'

I stared at him, knowing full well that he meant what he said – if Bridget spoke, he *would* go over there and cut out her tongue. And it wouldn't bother him in the slightest. This man . . . this middle-aged man sitting calmly in front of me – a picture of banality in a green V-neck jumper, cheap shirt and tie, nylon car coat, and beige cotton trousers – this man was a psychopath, a sadist, a stone-cold killer.

'How did you get in here?' I said to him.

'I'm a ghost, John.' He grinned. 'I can float through walls.'

'What do you want?'

'What do I want?' he echoed, shrugging again. 'No more than anyone else . . . pleasure, felicity, the fulfilment of my needs and desires . . . food, water, shelter . . . survival.'

'What do you want with me?' I said.

'You went through my things,' he replied, carefully placing the carving knife back on the coffee table. 'My personal things . . .' He shook his head. 'You shouldn't have done that.'

I noticed now that my pistol was on the coffee table too. And next to it was a short-handled axe, the blade smeared with blood, which I guessed was Walter's. Also on the table were two mobile phones – mine and Bridget's – both of them taken apart, the sim cards removed and snapped in half. I glanced quickly around the room, looking for a landline phone. There was one on the wall to my right, but Bishop had taken care of that too – the cables were ripped out and the phone socket smashed.

'You should have left me alone, John,' Bishop said.

'Look,' I started to say, turning back to him. 'There's no need –'

'You saw what I did to that other whore, didn't you?'

'Anna Gerrish?'

He nodded. 'I liked her, so I went easy on her. If you piss me off, I won't go easy on that one over there.' He jerked his head, indicating Bridget. 'I'll cut the fuck out of her. Do you understand?'

'Yes.'

'Good.' He cocked his head to one side, looking thoughtfully at me. 'You know . . . I've never killed a man before.'

'Just women.'

'I always think of them as *girls*, not women . . . I don't know why. Perhaps it's just the terminology. I mean, *woman* is such an ugly word, isn't it? It brings to mind a sense of age, a sense of dullness and desiccation . . . do you know what I mean?' He smiled. 'A woman just doesn't *taste* the same as a girl –'

'How many have you killed?'

He looked calmly at me. 'I know what you're doing.'

'I'm not –'

'Playing for time, keeping me talking . . . asking me utterly pointless questions. It's only natural, of course . . . trying to eke out a few more minutes, a few more seconds of life.' He looked at me. 'Everyone does it, you know. No one *wants* to die, no matter how much pain they're in or how pitiful their lives are . . . we'll all do anything to live another moment or two.' He scratched the side of his nose. 'How many have I killed? You'll be the twenty-ninth, John. Which means your whore over there will have the honour of being my thirtieth. What do you think about that?'

'Why do you do it?' I said.

'Why does anyone do anything?'

I couldn't think of an answer to that, so I just carried on staring at him. Of course, he was right – I *was* just playing for time. What else could I do? Keep him talking, keep on thinking, keep on believing that there had to be *some*thing I could do to get us both out of this . . .

I glanced over at Bridget. She was still crying, and she still looked stricken with shock . . . but as our eyes met, she edged her arm out from behind her back, letting me see the small lock-knife in her hand. The cords tying her wrist to the radiator had been cut, and as Bridget quickly moved her arm back behind her, I realised that she'd somehow managed to remove her lock-knife from her back pocket and cut herself free.

'I like it,' Bishop said.

I looked at him. 'What?'

'Killing . . . I like it. That's why I do it. Because I like it. Some people like cheese, some people like dancing . . . I like killing.' He looked at me. 'That's really all there is to it. Satisfied?'

'Your brother –'

'Time's up,' he said, shaking his head. 'No more talking.'

'He knows, doesn't he? Your brother knows what you do.'

Bishop ignored me, looking down at the coffee table.

I said, 'He's been looking after you ever since you burned down your house when you were kids, hasn't he? Ever since you first started killing. That's what he does with all his money. He takes care of you, provides for you . . .'

Bishop picked up the pistol from the coffee table.

'The police know all about you,' I said to him. 'I've told them –'

'No, you haven't,' he said confidently, getting to his feet. 'The only person who knows about me is that scrawny piece of shit in the hat, the one we put in hospital. And Micky will take care of him. And, besides, no one's going to find you until the morning anyway, and I'll be long gone by then.' He began moving towards me, the pistol in his hand. 'The house in Long Road will be empty, Joel R Pickton will have disappeared, and John Craine's body will be found, shot dead – apparently by his own hand – in the same room as the mutilated corpse of Bridget Moran.' He stopped in front of me, the pistol at his side. 'And what do you think they'll find when they search through your pockets, John?' He nodded. 'That's right . . . a half-moon silver necklace that belonged to Anna Gerrish.' He raised the pistol and levelled it at my head. 'Imagine, John . . . just imagine what they'll make of that. The man whose wife was raped and murdered . . . the man who just *happened* to discover Anna Gerrish's body . . . the man whose father –'

'Hey, fuck-head,' Bridget said suddenly from across the room. 'Why don't you just shut up and get on with it?'

Bishop froze for a moment, then slowly looked over at her. She hadn't moved yet, she was still sitting on the floor with her hands behind her back, as if she was still tied to the radiator. Only now, unbelievably, she didn't look scared or shocked . . . she just looked utterly disdainful.

'I mean, Christ, all this *talking*,' she said, sneering at him. 'Yack, yack, yack . . . it's just *so* fucking *boring*.'

Bishop's face visibly darkened, as if shadowed by a passing cloud, and as he turned away from me and began heading over to Bridget, I could have sworn that the room got colder. He didn't hurry, he just walked silently across the room, pausing only to pick up the carving knife from the coffee table. Bridget watched him all the way, her eyes never leaving his, and I knew that she had to be scared to death – she *had* to be – but there was no sign of fear in her eyes.

Bishop stopped in front of her – the knife in one hand, the pistol in the other – and for a moment or two he just stood there, glaring down at her, his eyes unblinking, his body unnaturally stiff.

'God,' Bridget sighed, staring back at him and shaking her head. 'You really are *pathetic*, aren't you?'

His lips drew back over his teeth and an awful hissing sound came from the back of his throat, and just for a moment I thought that she'd left it too late, but just as his body tensed and he raised the knife to strike, she whipped out her hand and buried the lock-knife deep into his thigh. As he let out a shriek and staggered backwards, Bridget jumped to her feet and lunged furiously at him again, stabbing the knife into his belly. He groaned and sank to his knees, dropping the gun and the carving knife from his hands, and then – with a scream of rage – Bridget drove her fist into his face.

'*Bastard!*'

And again.

'*Fucking BASTARD!*'

And as he toppled over, collapsing to the floor and covering his head with his hands, she just went berserk – kicking him, stomping on his head, punching him, slashing him with the knife . . . all the time screaming at him like a banshee. '*YOU! DIRTY! FUCKING! DIRTY! FUCKING! BASTARD! . . .*'

She was killing him.

He'd killed her dog.

She was going to kill him.

And I knew exactly how she felt. He deserved to die, he needed to die . . . he would die. Just like Anton Viner. But I also knew what killing Bishop would do to her, how it would take something away from her, how it would leave her – like me – with a ruined soul . . . and she didn't deserve that.

'Bridget!' I called out.

She stamped on Bishop's head.

'*Bridget!*'

She kicked him viciously in the balls.

'*BRIDGET!!*'

She paused, momentarily confused, and looked over at

me. Her teeth were bared, her hands covered in blood. Her eyes were white and wild.

'It's all right,' I said softly. 'You can stop now.'

She shook her head. 'He killed Walter.'

'I know, but –'

'He killed Walter.'

'Yes, I know. But right now I need you to help me.'

She looked down at Bishop. He was curled up on the floor at her feet, beaten and bloodied, not moving . . . it was hard to tell if he was alive or not.

'Bridget?' I said gently.

She looked back at me, her eyes unfocused.

'Can you come over here and cut me free?' I said.

She nodded, but didn't move.

I smiled at her. 'Please?'

She started walking towards me, stumbling slightly on the way.

'It's OK,' I said to her. 'Just take it easy . . .'

'I'm all right,' she muttered, crying now.

'I know.'

'I just . . . he killed . . .'

'It's OK,' I said. 'It's over now . . . it's over. I just need you to cut me free, all right? Can you do that?'

She stopped in front of me and looked down at the lockknife in her hand. She seemed puzzled, as if she couldn't understand why she was holding it, or why it was covered in blood.

'Come on, Bridget,' I said. 'Please . . .'

She looked at me, blinking slowly. 'Yeah, sorry . . . sorry . . .'

As she moved round the back of the chair and began cutting the cords from my wrists, I looked over at Bishop. He hadn't moved. He was still just lying on the floor, a bloodied mess, but I could see now that he was breathing. He was still alive.

I could feel Bridget sawing away at the cords on my wrists.

'How's it going?' I asked her, wincing slightly as the knife nicked my hand.

'Yeah . . .' she muttered. 'Sorry . . .'

'It's all right. Just keep going.'

I felt one of the cords snap, and then another . . . and then, at last, my hands were free. As I brought them round in front of me and began rubbing them together, trying to get the blood flowing again, Bridget came round from the back of the chair, crouched down at my feet, and started cutting at the cords round my ankles. There was an unsettling obsession to her movements, a traumatised concentration in her eyes . . . and I knew she was suffering badly.

I reached out and gently placed my hand on her shoulder. She flinched.

'Hey,' I said quietly. 'It's all right. It's me . . .'

She hesitated for a moment, then looked up at me. Her face was streaked with blood and tears. 'He killed Walter, John,' she said, her voice a broken whisper. 'He killed Walter . . .'

I sensed rather than heard the sudden rapid movement behind her, but even as I looked up and saw Bishop lunging towards us, I already knew I was too late. Before I could do anything to stop him, he'd grabbed Bridget by the hair, yanked her away from me, and was dragging her violently across the room. He looked monstrous – soaked in blood, beaten and battered, totally insane – and as he manhandled her across the floor, he was snarling at her like an animal.

'Fucking *bitch* . . . *cunt* . . . fucking *whore* . . .'

I went after him, throwing myself across the room, but my feet were still tied to the chair and I crashed down heavily to the floor. I quickly scrambled to my knees and reached back to my feet, yanking desperately at the half-cut cords, but they wouldn't give. I looked across the room and saw that Bishop had stopped by the far wall. He still had hold of Bridget's hair, and as I started crawling towards them, pulling myself along with my arms, dragging the chair behind me, I saw him lean down and spit in her face.

'Open your mouth, *cunt*,' he hissed at her.

'Fuck you,' she said, spitting back at him.

He stared insanely at her for a second, and then – with a savage grunt – he swung her head back and slammed it hard against the wall. The impact was sickening, a shuddering crack of bone on brick, and I watched helplessly as Bridget dropped to the floor in a lifeless heap.

I was still only about halfway across the room, and as Bishop turned away from Bridget and began looking around, I thought he was looking for me. I stopped crawling and stared at him, expecting him to come after me, but when I saw him look my way, his eyes passed over me as if I wasn't even there. And then I got it. He wasn't looking for me – he didn't give a shit about me – he was looking for the carving knife. He wanted to finish off

Bridget with the knife. And as his eyes widened and he set off across the room – hunched over, clutching his belly, limping heavily – I knew that he'd found it. I could see the knife too – half hidden behind the settee – and I knew I couldn't crawl fast enough to stop him getting to it . . . or to stop him getting back to Bridget with it.

I had to free my legs.

If I didn't . . .

I sat up and started pulling frantically at the cords, yanking at the knots . . . but the cord was made of nylon, the knots too tight . . . I glanced over my shoulder and saw Bishop bending stiffly to pick up the carving knife. He paused for a moment, stepped behind the settee, and leaned down again to pick up something else. When he straightened up and turned back towards Bridget, I saw that he had the carving knife in one hand and the pistol in the other.

I looked over at Bridget, and just for an instant my mind flashed back to Stacy again . . . ripped open, butchered, bled white, dead . . .

And then . . . I don't really know what happened. Something inside me just snapped. A howl of rage screamed out of me, erupting from deep down inside, and I put my hands together, raised them above my head, and brought them crashing down on the chair. Wood snapped, and I felt a bone break in my hand, and when I stood up and kicked out at the remains of the broken chair, my feet were suddenly free.

I turned and ran at Bishop.

He'd almost reached Bridget now. He was about two steps away from her, walking awkwardly but deliberately, dragging his wounded leg, and I could see his lips moving as he whispered to himself under his breath. He still seemed oblivious to my presence, but as he started to lean down towards Bridget, moving the knife towards her face, I let out another deafening scream that stopped him in his tracks. He froze for a moment, frowning almost casually, and then – as he turned to look at me – I kicked the knife from his hand and threw myself at him. We both crashed to the floor, and before he had a chance to fight back, I drove my head into his face, breaking his nose, and made a grab for the gun. He tried to wrench his hand away, but he was too weak to put up much of a struggle, and after I'd smashed his hand into the floor a couple of times, he let go of the pistol.

I snatched it up, jammed the barrel into his neck, and manoeuvred myself so that I was sitting on his chest with his arms pinned under my knees.

And now I had him.

He couldn't move.

He was mine.

I glanced over my shoulder at Bridget. She hadn't moved since Bishop had smashed her head against the wall – she was still just lying in a crumpled heap on the floor.

'Bridget?' I said. 'Bridget . . . are you all right?'

She didn't answer.

'Bridget? Can you hear me?'

Still no answer.

'I think she's fucked,' Bishop muttered.

I turned back to him and aimed the gun at his head. He looked up weakly at me, blood bubbling from his broken nose, and tried to smile. 'You're not going to kill me, John,' he said. 'You haven't got what it takes.'

I stared at him, letting him see the hole in my soul, and when he saw it, recognising it for what it was, he suddenly began to panic.

'No!' he spluttered, struggling and squirming. 'Please don't –'

'Time's up,' I heard myself say, my finger tightening on the trigger. 'No more talking.'

And then the sitting-room door crashed open.

32

Mick Bishop came striding into the room like the police officer he was – cautious but confident, ready for anything – and it only took him a second or two to take everything in. He saw me sitting on his brother's chest with the pistol held to his head; he saw Bridget lying unconscious on the floor; he saw Walter's dead body, the broken chair, the cords, the blood . . . and then his eyes fixed on mine and he began moving towards me.

'All right, John,' he said calmly. 'Just put the gun down –'

'Stay there,' I told him, pressing the barrel of the gun into Ray's head. 'If you come any closer, I'll kill him.'

He slowed to a stop and held up both hands, palms out. 'All right, all right . . . take it easy –'

'Hello, Micky,' I heard Ray say. 'What took you so long?'

'Ray,' Bishop said. 'Are you all right?'

'Do I *look* all right? I mean, shit, look what that fucking cunt's done –'

He shut up suddenly as I cracked the pistol into his broken nose and then jammed the barrel into his mouth.

'John,' I heard Mick say. 'Please, don't . . .'

I pushed down harder on the gun, shoving it into Ray's throat . . . and I knew that I'd gone somewhere else now. I'd gone to a place where killing him was no longer enough; I

wanted to hurt him too. Hurt him, then kill him . . . just like
he'd done to Anna . . .

'John!'

And all the other girls . . .

'*John!*'

Make him suffer . . .

'For Christ's sake, you're *killing* him!'

Just like Stacy had suffered . . .

'He can't *breathe*!'

And Bridget . . .

'*JOHN!*'

Bridget.

I pulled the gun out of Ray's mouth. He coughed and
moaned, spitting up blood and bits of teeth.

'Fuck!' he spluttered. 'You fucking –'

I cracked the gun into his head. He grunted, then
groaned, his eyes flickering and rolling. I hit him again and
he went limp. I turned back to Mick and saw that he'd
moved a lot closer to me. He was sweating now, pale and
rigid. He didn't look quite so calm and confident any more.

I pointed the gun at him. 'Go over there and check on
Bridget.'

He glanced down briefly at his brother, then moved over
to where Bridget was lying on the floor.

'Make sure she's still breathing,' I told him.

He crouched down beside her and began looking for a
pulse. I watched him, surprised at how gently he moved –
placing two fingers on her neck, concentrating quietly for a
while, then carefully lifting her eyelids and looking into her
eyes.

'Did Ray do this to her?' he asked, studying her battered face.

'What do *you* think?'

He nodded, still looking at Bridget. 'I don't think there's any serious damage . . . nothing broken.' He eased her over onto her side and carefully tilted her head back. 'It's just a heavy concussion. She'll live.'

'Call an ambulance.'

He looked at me. 'I can't do that.'

'She needs treatment. Call an ambulance.'

He got to his feet, shaking his head. 'It's not going to happen, John.'

I jammed the gun into Ray's senseless head. 'Your brother's dead if it doesn't.'

Mick stared at me in silence for a while, glanced down at Ray again, then went over and sat down on the settee. 'If I call an ambulance,' he said wearily, 'the police will automatically be informed. And when they get here . . . well, that'll be it. Everything'll be fucked then . . . *every*-thing.' He shook his head again. 'I won't be able to talk my way out of it. There'll be too many people involved. They'll find out about Ray and me, the Gerrish girl –'

'And all the others he's killed.'

He looked at me. 'You know?'

'Yeah, I know. I know everything.'

He sighed. 'Ray can't help it –'

'Oh, fuck off,' I spat. 'Don't give me that shit. He's killed nearly thirty women, for God's sake. *Thirty*. He's tortured them, stabbed them, mutilated them . . . and you're trying to tell me that he can't *help* it?'

'He *can't* . . . it's just . . .'

'Just *what*?'

Bishop looked at Ray for a moment, studying his brother in much the same emotionless way that Ray had studied me. 'It's just what he *is*. He's *wrong*. Wrong in the head, the heart . . . whatever. He's got something missing. He was *born* like it . . . he was born broken.'

'And that makes it all right, does it? That makes it all right for him to spend his life killing people?'

'No . . .'

'So why do you cover up for him?'

'Because he's my brother. He's all I've got. He's all I've ever had.'

I didn't know what to say to that. As Bishop sat there, staring silently at the floor, I could see the years of pain and sadness in his eyes, and I knew that it was only *his* pain, *his* suffering, and I knew that what he'd done, what he'd allowed his brother to do, had caused so much more destruction and despair to so many innocent people . . .

'It just happened,' I heard him say. 'I didn't mean it to end up like this . . .' His voice was detached and distant, almost as if he was talking to himself. 'Ray never *meant* to kill Mum and Dad, he just wanted to get back at them for being such bastards. But after he'd burned the house down, and then Pin Hall . . . well, I knew then that he'd got a taste for killing, and that he was going to carry on doing it, and that there was nothing I could do to stop him. So I just thought it'd be best if he moved away . . .'

'Why, for God's sake?' I said. 'What good did you think *that* would do?'

He shrugged. 'If he'd stayed here . . . if he stayed *any*where for too long, he'd get caught. But if he kept moving around . . .'

'It'd be easier for him to get away with it.'

Bishop nodded.

I shook my head. 'And moving around costs money, which you supplied. Money, false ID, cars, homes . . . you funded him. All the drugs you stole, all the bribes you took, all the lives you fucked up – including my father's – you did all that just to make sure that your fucking brother could go round the country brutalising and killing people without getting caught –'

'They were whores.'

'*What?*'

'He only killed whores. Most of them would probably have been dead within a year or so anyway.'

I shook my head, more in annoyance with myself than anything else. I couldn't believe that I was actually *conversing* with this man, treating him like a human being, or that just a few minutes ago I'd almost been tempted into feeling sorry for him.

'You're no better than your brother, are you?' I said to him. 'The only difference is that he's a bit more honest than you.'

Bishop shrugged. 'Well, that's as maybe . . . but none of us gets to choose who we are, do we? Or what we do. You, of all people, should know that, John.'

'What do you mean?'

He smiled. 'Anton Viner . . .?'

I shook my head. 'Viner's –'

'Dead ... yes, I know. It took me a while to figure it out, but once I started thinking about it ... well, it was the only thing that made sense.'

'I don't understand –'

He laughed. 'It's all right, John. You don't have to keep pretending any more. I know you killed him. I don't know *how* you did it, but I know you did.'

'That's ridiculous –'

'John ... John,' he said gently, almost intimately. 'It's all right ... I don't have a problem with it. He killed your wife, you killed him. If I'd been in your shoes, I would have done exactly the same. My only concern is that I didn't know you'd killed him until *after* I'd planted Viner's DNA on Anna Gerrish's body.'

'So you *knew* your brother had killed her?'

He sighed, looking at Ray. 'I told him not to come back. I fucking *told* him ... but he just ...'

'What?'

Mick looked at me. 'He just wanted to see me, that's all. We hadn't seen each other for years ... he said he was lonely. I didn't think he'd do anything while he was here.'

'But he did.'

Mick nodded. 'I guessed he'd killed Anna as soon as I found out that she worked the streets. He always went after whores.' He shook his head. 'They make it so fucking *easy*. I mean, all you've got to do is ...' He sighed, shaking his head again. 'Anyway, I went to see Ray, and he denied it at first, but I knew he was lying. And he couldn't keep it up for long, not with me. He never could. So I got it all out of him – where he'd picked her up, what he'd done with the body – and I *thought* it'd be all right. I thought I'd have enough time to get him out of Hey and sort everything out before the body was found . . .' He looked at me. 'But then you got involved. Not that I was worried at first, because I didn't think you'd stick with it, but once I realised you weren't going to give up, I knew I had to do something. It was too risky to move the body, so all I could do was try to make sure that if it *was* found, there was no way it could be connected to Ray.'

'But why did you use *Viner's* DNA?' I said. 'What was the point?'

'That first day you came to see me, when I told you I'd been going through your wife's case file? I wasn't lying. I *had* been going through it.'

'Why?'

He shrugged. 'I always like to know as much as possible about the people I'm meeting before I actually meet them, so I had somebody bring me all the paperwork on your wife's murder. Paperwork, photographs, evidence . . . I had it all in my office. And later on, when I decided I had to plant some evidence on Anna's body, it was all still there. Nice and convenient. And then, of course, I realised that if the body *was* discovered, and we released the fact that Viner's DNA had been found under Anna's fingernails, everyone's attention would be drawn to you and Viner and the whole serial-killer thing, and while all that was going on, Ray could just quietly disappear. But now . . .' He glanced down at Ray again, then back at me. 'Well, that's out of the question now, isn't it?'

I nodded. 'It's over . . . for both of you.'

Bishop smiled. 'I wouldn't say that.'

'Give me your phone,' I said.

'I don't think so.'

Without taking my eyes off him, or the gun from Ray's head, I reached back and felt through Ray's trouser pockets, looking for a mobile. The front pockets were empty, so I leaned over and dug into his back pocket, but that was empty too.

'You're wasting your time, John,' Mick said to me. 'He doesn't carry a mobile when he's . . .'

'When he's what? Killing people?'

Mick shrugged.

'Give me your phone,' I said to him again. 'Or I'll kill your brother.'

He sighed. 'I'll tell you what, John. You give me the gun, and then we can talk things over. How about that?'

I shook my head. 'I'd rather just kill him.'

'Like you killed Viner?'

'Exactly.'

'But this is different, John.'

'Why's that?'

'Because if you kill Ray, you'll have to kill me too.'

'And why *wouldn't* I want to do that?'

He smiled. 'Because I'm a DCI, I'm a serving police officer. And no matter how dirty I am, no matter how much I'm loathed and despised . . . I'm still a serving police officer. And that means that if you kill me, you *will* go down. Guaranteed. You'll be locked up for the rest of your life.'

'You know what?' I said, suddenly feeling incredibly

tired. 'I really don't care any more. I don't care what happens to me, and I don't care whether you believe me or not.' I looked down at Ray. He was starting to come round now – moaning softly, his semi-conscious eyes gazing up at me. I stared back at him, seeing nothing but a half-dead sack of bones and blood, a heartless thing with a broken head. And in the dulled grey mirror of his eyes, I saw myself holding the gun to my own head . . . and I heard a voice that might have been mine, or it might have been my father's:

It won't feel like anything, John.

It won't feel like anything at all.

And I knew then that all I had to do was pull the trigger.

'What about Bridget?'

I looked up slowly at Bishop. 'What?'

'*You* might not care about yourself,' he said. 'But what about Bridget?'

I sighed. 'What about her?'

'Well, knowing Ray, I'm guessing that she's been through a hell of a lot in the last hour or so. And I'd imagine that when all of this is over, however things turn out, she's going to need somebody to look after her, somebody who understands what she's been through. And I'm sure you don't need me to tell you how it feels when you lose someone you really care for, John, someone who really understands you. Of course, I don't *know* how close the two of you are –'

'You're sick,' I said wearily. 'You know that, don't you? You're genuinely fucking sick.'

He smiled. 'I'm only trying to help you see the bigger picture, John. That's all I'm doing. I'm just trying to remind you –'

'I know what you're doing.'

He looked at me for a few moments, thoughtfully nodding his head, then – very slowly – he got to his feet and began walking towards me. 'So how about it, John?' he said calmly. 'You give me the gun, we sit down and work things out, and that'll be it – end of story.'

'End of story?' I said incredulously.

He nodded. 'Trust me – I can fix this. By tomorrow morning, Ray will be gone, Bridget will be in hospital, and you'll be wherever you want to be.' He stopped in front of me and held out his hand. 'All you have to do is give me the gun.'

I looked up at him, and if it hadn't been for the overbearing weight of tiredness inside me, I might have actually laughed out loud at the idea of trusting him . . . but I was so exhausted now, so lost and black and full of nothing, that I could barely even think. I was deep down in the black place, draped in the darkness, and I'd been there for ever and I'd be there for ever . . .

I couldn't do anything.

Didn't want anything.

What was the point?

The temptation to just end it all was almost irresistible. All I had to do was move my finger . . . I could do that. Move my finger, pull the trigger . . .

Once . . . and Ray Bishop would be gone.

Twice . . . his brother.

And a third time . . .

Nothing.

John?

Fuck everything, just do it.

Listen to me, John.

'Stacy?'

Bishop's right . . . Bridget needs you.

'He's just saying that, Stace . . . he's just using her –'

I know he is. But she still needs you. And you need her.

'I don't –'

Yes, you do.

'I want to be with *you*, Stace.'

I'm in your heart, John . . . always. No matter what.

'I love you.'

I know.

'John . . . ?'

I looked at Bishop. He'd crouched down beside me and was staring into my eyes.

'It's OK, John,' he said quietly. 'Everything's all right . . . just give me the gun . . .'

I looked down at his outstretched hand – seeing the shape of it, the colour, the texture of the skin . . . the lines and the whorls and the pores – and all of a sudden I knew that I didn't have to think any more. All I had to do was place the pistol in Bishop's hand, and that would be it. No more decisions, nothing to think about. Whatever happened would happen. If I lived, I lived. If I died, I died.

The future doesn't exist.

I moved my finger off the trigger, slowly lifted the gun, and placed it carefully in Bishop's hand.

'Thank you,' he said. He studied the pistol for a moment, frowning slightly, then he looked down at his brother.

'Micky?' Ray muttered quietly. 'Are we –?'

'Goodbye, Ray,' Mick said.

He put the gun to his brother's head and calmly pulled the trigger.

33

I probably only sat there for a minute or so, perched in stunned silence on Ray Bishop's dead body, but it seemed like a long, long time. His brother remained where he was too, and when I finally managed to turn my head and look at him, I saw that he was crying. There was still no emotion in his face, and he wasn't making any sound; he was just crouched down on the floor, staring at his brother, the tears streaming silently from his eyes.

I didn't say anything.

I didn't know what to say.

Eventually, Mick took a deep breath and let it out slowly, and without taking his eyes off Ray, he said to me, 'It was the only way. There was nothing left for him. It had to end.'

I remained quiet.

Bishop looked at me. 'He was my brother. I looked after him. I gave him his life . . . *I* had to give him his death. No one else . . . not you. I couldn't let you do it. He was my brother.'

I nodded. 'So what happens now?'

He blew out his cheeks and stood up. 'Like I said, I fix it.'

He held his hand out to me. I reached up and took it, and he helped me to my feet. I looked over at Bridget. She was still out cold.

Bishop pulled a mobile phone from his pocket. 'I'll call an ambulance for her as soon as I've got everything cleaned up in here. I need to make some calls, make some arrangements. It'll take a while, but that's how it's got to be.' He looked at me. 'Are you all right with that?'

I glanced at the pistol in his hand. 'I don't have much choice, do I?'

'No.'

While Bishop got busy on the phone, I went over and sat down beside Bridget. I put a cushion under her head, cleaned some blood from her face, stroked her hair . . . I told her, very quietly, that she was going to be OK. And then I think I probably cried for a while. And then I went into the bedroom and found the bottle of whisky that Bridget had told me about. As I poured myself a dusty glassful, I pictured us lying in bed together, and I could remember almost everything about it – the feelings, the sounds, the scents . . . I could *see* myself in the bed, rolling over and reaching down for my jacket, patting the pockets until I found my cigarettes. I could hear myself asking Bridget if she minded if I smoked, and her saying, 'There's a bottle of whisky somewhere. Sarah's always liked a drop of good malt . . . I think it's in the cupboard over there. Just help yourself if you want.'

And I'd said, 'I'm all right, thanks.'

I remembered all that. But as to *when* it had happened . . . I simply had no idea at all. Today? Yesterday? This week? Last week?

My head was blank.

I just couldn't remember.

I went back into the sitting room, sat down beside Bridget, and lit a cigarette.

It took Bishop about forty minutes – and at least ten separate phone calls – to make all the arrangements, but eventually he put the mobile back in his pocket and sat down on the settee.

'All right,' he said to me, glancing at his watch. 'It's all done. There'll be some people coming round in a while to take the body away and clean everything up. They won't have time to make the place forensically clean – and it'd be too risky ripping out carpets at this time of night anyway – but they'll make sure there's no visible evidence left.' He looked at his watch again. 'I'll get Ray's house sorted out tomorrow, and the rest of it . . . well, you don't need to know about that, do you?'

'What about me?'

He shrugged. 'What *about* you?'

'What's going to happen –?'

'Nothing's going to happen.'

'Your brother was a serial killer –'

'And now he's dead.'

'You *helped* him kill all those people –'

'What would you have done, John? If someone *you* loved, if the only person you'd ever cared about . . .' He sighed, rubbing his eyes. 'I mean, imagine if Stacy had killed people, and you'd found out about it. What would you have done?'

'She didn't –'

'But if she did. Would you have given her up? Would you have had her locked away in Broadmoor for the rest of her life? *Would* you?'

I shook my head. 'I don't know ...'

'I did what I had to do, John. I traded a few dozen worthless lives for the life of my brother. Right or wrong, that's all I did. You can judge me if you want –'

'It's not up to me to judge you. It's up to a court.'

He sniffed. 'If I go to court, so do you, for killing Anton Viner. That's why nothing's going to happen to either of us. You know what Ray did, you know what I did – and what I've just done – and I know what you did. We're all in the same boat, John. We can either sink in it together, or we can survive together. And the way I see it, if we both go down ... well, what purpose will it serve? What good will it do anyone?'

'What good will it do if we both survive? What good will *that* do to anyone?'

He smiled. 'You're a cheerful fucker, aren't you?'

I didn't smile back. 'What about Cal?'

'Cal Franks?' Bishop shrugged. 'He does the same as us – keeps his mouth shut about everything.'

'And if he doesn't?'

'I'll just make a couple of phone calls to some very spooky people who don't take kindly to cyber-terrorists. By the time they've finished with him, he'll be lucky if he knows what a computer is, let alone how to use one.' Bishop smiled at me again. 'Any more concerns?'

'What are you going to do about the Anna Gerrish investigation?'

'Nothing . . . I'll keep it alive for a while, go through the motions of looking for Viner, and then gradually wind it down. No one's going to care. It's just another murder . . . the media will soon forget about it.'

'You've got it all worked out, haven't you?'

He nodded. 'It's what I do.'

'Do you enjoy it?'

He just shrugged again. 'It's what I do.'

I looked at him, sick of talking now. I just wanted this to be over. I wanted to be alone. I wanted to be at home, sitting in my armchair beneath the high window, drinking whisky in the darkness, listening to the whisper of ghosts . . .

A bell sounded downstairs.

'That'll be them,' Bishop said, getting to his feet and heading for the door.

'I want the gun back,' I told him.

He stopped. 'The gun?'

'I want it back.'

'Why?'

'Does it matter?'

He took the pistol from his pocket, studied it for a moment, then looked at me. 'It was your father's, wasn't it? It was the gun he used to kill himself.'

'How do you know that?'

He carried on looking at me for a second or two, then he took the magazine out of the pistol, emptied the bullets into his hand, put the magazine back, and passed the gun to me.

'How do you know it was my father's?' I asked him again.

He dropped the bullets into his pocket, turned round, and left the room without saying anything.

Bridget was finally beginning to come round as I went over and sat down beside her. Her eyelids were twitching, her lips were fluttering, and she was making faint little whimpering sounds.

I took hold of her hand.

It was cold.

'It's OK, Bridget,' I said softly. 'You're going to be fine now. Everything's going to be all right . . .'

But I knew I was probably lying.

THE POWER OF READING

Visit the Random House website and get connected with information on all our books and authors

EXTRACTS from our recently
published books and selected

READING GROUPS Reading